Shattered

Also by K.C. Harper

Shadowed Moonlight

SHATTERED MOONLIGHT

K. C. HARPER

HODDERSCAPE

First published in Great Britain in 2025 by Hodder & Stoughton Limited
An Hachette UK company

The authorised representative in the EEA is Hachette Ireland, 8 Castlecourt Centre, Dublin 15, D15 XTP3, Ireland (email: info@hbgi.ie)

1

Copyright © K.C. Harper 2025

The right of K.C. Harper to be identified as the Author of the Work has been asserted by her in accordance with the Copyright, Designs and Patents Act 1988.

All rights reserved. No part of this publication may be reproduced, stored in a retrieval system, or transmitted, in any form or by any means without the prior written permission of the publisher, nor be otherwise circulated in any form of binding or cover other than that in which it is published and without a similar condition being imposed on the subsequent purchaser.

All characters in this publication are fictitious and any resemblance to real persons, living or dead, is purely coincidental.

A CIP catalogue record for this title is available from the British Library

Paperback ISBN 9781399726719
ebook ISBN 9781399726726

Typeset in Plantin Light by Manipal Technologies Limited

Printed and bound in Great Britain by Clays Ltd, Elcograf S.p.A.

Hodder & Stoughton policy is to use papers that are natural, renewable and recyclable products and made from wood grown in sustainable forests. The logging and manufacturing processes are expected to conform to the environmental regulations of the country of origin.

Hodder & Stoughton Limited
Carmelite House
50 Victoria Embankment
London EC4Y 0DZ

www.hodderscape.co.uk

To those who cherish kindness, and wield it wildly to create the world they dream to live in.

Trigger warnings

Sexual content, cursing, violence, gore, discussion of sexual assault, discussion of child loss and emotional abuse.

Cambrian Conclave
(Preternatural Hierarchy)

North Cambrian Werewolf Pack

Alpha: ~~Ronin Miller~~
Kane Slade

Beta: Joaquin Cruz

South Cambrian Werewolf Pack

Alpha: Victor Davis

Beta: ~~Mila Gonzalez~~
Replacement Pending

North Cambrian Shadow Walker Clan

Dowager: Cassandra Ryton

Second: ~~Anthony Bruno~~
Replacement Pending

South Cambrian Shadow Walker Clan

Dowager: Danika Trevino

Second: Curran Stoll

North Cambrian Magi Coven

Coven Leader: ~~Sierra Harris~~
Mason Beckett

Coven Second: Briar Stone

South Cambrian Magi Coven

Coven Leader: Alistair Jones

Coven Second: Evelyn Whitlock

Chapter One

I sashayed across the tattoo shop, Lucas's massive cake in hand.

The place hummed with weres from Kane's Pack, finishing the last-minute setup for my brother's birthday. The scent of the teal paint we'd coated the walls in four days before still clung to the air while stacks of dark-stained hardwood flooring sat shoved to the back corner, waiting to be laid. The black trim around the windows, doors, and crown molding, red leather seats and hydraulic chairs still needed to be finished, but it was coming.

Lisa Xing, my bestest friend and human owner of No Man's Land, the tavern I *used* to work in, tapped my ass as I passed. "Looking good, chickie."

"Ow," I squeaked, batting my eyelashes her way as I shimmied my ass.

"It's gonna be sharp when it's done," she said, arranging a cacophony of chemically enhanced potions—chemically enhanced because for the weres, shadow walkers, and magi, human liquor didn't affect shit. "When's the official opening?"

I brushed my long, mahogany-colored hair from my shoulders, better exposing my dark brown corset top and flowing ivory skirt. "A month." I peered out the front window of the shop and worried my lip, 'cause after everything that happened with my stepfather, Isaac, and Jared, being separated from Kane made me twitchy. And I'd been twitchy a *lot* lately. Between getting the shop ready to open and stuff with his Pack dragging him away, we'd just been two ships passing in the night.

Tables lined the walls on either side, scarlet tablecloths covering them. Food and drinks overflowed their tops, because, well, the wolves were hungry beasties who liked to eat. Bronze balloons clustered along the high ceiling and framed the entrance—an entrance I kept staring out of, 'cause patient I was not.

Immortal Inc was twice the size of its predecessor with sample sketches lining the back wall. It was a primo location, smack in the Canal District at the unorthodox, neutral grounds center of Cambria, our relinquished city. Well, relinquished after the humans figured out our 'subspecies' existed, to which, Cambria became the solution, separating us. Save where the Talisian Sea bordered the weres' territory in the south, the Cortez Mountain range circled the city like a natural barrier, cutting our kind off from Ithica.

Real estate in said neutral grounds didn't come available often, so when it'd popped up for sale two weeks before, Kane and I pounced at the chance. And with my wolfy lover's seat at the Conclave and associated, virtually bottomless bank account, he'd outbid every other potential buyer and gotten a ridiculously fast closing date to boot.

We'd kept the name in honor of his mother, who'd been killed trying to break him from his former Alpha, Ronin's command—the outfall of my stepfather Isaac's schemes. Another one, anyway.

"That's so fast," Lis said, tucking a strand of her sleek midnight hair behind her ear. Well, kinda sleek. It was less perfect than usual, with multiple strands sticking off in random directions, its shine dulled slightly. Not that she hadn't brushed it, more like it was haphazard. Not as much care, which was way out of character, 'cause Lisa *always* cared.

She'd gotten worse and worse since my stepfather'd waltzed into her tavern and compelled her under his control, just like he'd done with me, and Theo, Mason, Lucas, and mom. A pang of guilt had my stomach twisting, because if not for my connection to Isaac, he'd never have come into Lisa's life.

I removed the glass cake cover and set the miniature sparkler-looking sticks into the icing. Flicking their ends, the spell engaged, those sticks shooting small, celebratory, multi-colored fireworks a foot high. A magi illusion.

Lisa set a stack of plates off to the side. "When's Sierra's dirge?"

Swallowing hard, I straightened. Every magi was offered a dirge, their ceremonial passage after death. Ceremonial because the wraith had already taken their soul to the Iron Hells, the dead's resting place. I'd never been to one, not even my own father's, seeing they were only for active Coven members and I'd been entirely too young.

My heart dropped, lungs seizing when an image of my former Coven Leader ripped across my mind. Her lifeless gaze and the empty, gaping hole in her chest put there by the Phantom . . . by Jared. The memory of him felt . . . strange and weirdly unclear. The harder I concentrated on it, the more it shifted, like trying to see the forest through the trees.

He'd been a regular for my readings at No Man's Land. A fellow magi whose only care was ensuring his wife didn't catch his skeezy ass with one of many side-pieces. A fact that made his role in those murders feel like a leap, but if there was another explanation, I wasn't seeing it.

I rubbed a hand along the back of my neck. "Tuesday, with the full moon." Always with the moon, because the wolves weren't the only ones who followed its cycles.

She leaned a hip against the plastic-covered counter. "Have you seen Mason lately?"

I hadn't actually been around my ex since the day of the fire that almost scorched our asses. The fire that'd been set by Isaac to hide his lab before he vanished. Dead. Maybe. 'Cause Jared's body had been the only one found, but my stepfather hadn't reared his scheming head since, so I could only hope.

"Yeah. I, uh," I cleared my throat, "took the position as Second."

Lisa's angular umber eyes widened when they found me. "And what'd your wolf say?"

Kane's Beta, Joaquin, sauntered closer, and the laugh he let loose as he stepped up beside me was dry.

I frowned. "He said a lot."

My Alpha'd been less than impressed to know I'd be working alongside my ex—an ex I'd ended things with *for* Kane. But seeing my wolfy lover had not one clue said ex was also under Isaac's thrall, Mason was lucky his innards hadn't become outards.

In the three weeks since, I'd tried every way possible to tell Kane the truth, but Isaac's compulsion made my tongue a dead weight, immovable and useless.

Lisa's hand found her hip. "Do you even *want* to be Second?"

Grabbing a stack of cutlery, I organized it beside the cake.

I'd told Isaac I'd accept the position as a ploy to keep my ass alive, and while every spiteful bone in my body had me wanting to revolt, I just... couldn't. After what'd gone down with Mason and Ronin, the havoc they'd been forced to wreak, I wanted a hand in the Coven. Wanted some way to help. To protect. And see if maybe there was some path outta this compulsion mess for all of us.

I shrugged. "I wanna do more."

"Not what she asked, banshee," the Beta said.

I pursed my lips and huffed. The trouble with pushy friends was all the damn pushing. "I never wanted this kind of responsibility but having access to the Conclave means I have a voice. After everything, I don't want to be on the outside."

Lisa flicked me with the tip of her finger. "You're the Northern Alpha's claimed mate, chickie. You're never on the outside."

Joaquin cocked his brows and tipped his head her way in a "what she said" gesture.

There was that, but still... "That doesn't help me with the Coven."

Being Second gave me access to the Recovery Center, the health facility at the heart of Cambria. The source of the

Conclave's endless income. "Unity for a common cause," that offered preternatural treatments and cures . . . as long as you were uber wealthy and human. A sickening notion.

Cassian, one of Kane's Pack, crossed in, trays of food in hand. Lis headed his way to help.

Biting the quick of my nails, I bobbed right and left, peering out past the nearby oak trees and down the road. "Where *are* they?"

Getting the memories Isaac had stolen back—memories of the child he'd had stripped from my womb. Memories of him using Ronin to force Kane away, to make me think my wolf abandoned me. To fray the threads of my tattered heart so I'd give up on him. And I had. But he'd never given up on me.

After the chaos Isaac'd unleashed, I hadn't exactly coped, especially when my Alpha and I were apart—which had been more than I'd preferred of late.

Joaquin batted my hand from my mouth. "Take it easy." Light from the black chandelier overhead struck his hazel eyes, making their color strikingly vivid. "Kane's got Lucas. They're on their way."

I scoffed and set a palm over my heart. "Forgive me if recent events have me twitchy."

He inclined his head because he'd been there, helping my Alpha hunt Jared before they dragged me and Mason from the fire.

Sage, there was so much I needed to say, so much that was tearing me up inside. The truth about Isaac, my mother, our child. It clawed at my heart. Begged for release.

My gaze flicked to Joaquin's, then away, then back, then away again.

He sighed, soul-weary and deep. "You've got an idea I already don't like."

I plunked my hands on my waist and offered him my best scowl. "I haven't even said anything yet."

Kane's cousin Theo thumped closer, his dirty-blond hair wet, like he'd come there straight from the shower. He dropped his elbow onto my shoulder, the weight of it dipping me sideways. "It's your face."

My scoff game was on point. "What's wrong with my *face*?"

A mischievous spark lit Theo's expression. He flicked his hand in my general direction. "What isn't?"

Gone was the hollow that'd taken root beneath his sable eyes, put there by Isaac's compulsion. A power he shouldn't have had, but seeing he'd used his smarts as a chemist to strip shadow walker venom of its genetic markers—of *Ivy's* genetic markers—he most certainly did. And like the snake he was, he'd used that concoction to take us over. Control us. Get his blood-stained fingers into the upper echelons of Cambrian power, then wreak his revenge.

The Beta sighed, staring at the ceiling like he prayed for strength. "Out with it, banshee."

I swatted Theo like the pest he was, then answered, "I wanna learn to defend myself . . . or something useful like that."

Theo's brow arched, his expression screaming *You can throw a punch*.

Considering I'd launched one straight at his face when I'd thought he worked *with* Isaac . . . Yeah, I could call on my power if I needed, but when it came to actually fighting, I didn't know what the Iron Hells I was doing.

"Not the time for this conversation," Joaquin said before his eyes went unfocused, the same way they did anytime he and my Alpha were having their secret, wolfy chit-chats.

I stabbed my finger into his chest. "Do *not* tell him about this, Joaquin!"

He blinked, and his eyes returned to normal. His expression was impassive as his stare dropped to that finger, watching it like a bug he itched to swat. "He needs to know."

"Joaquin—"

"He'll discuss it when he gets here," he said, annunciating each word.

Squaring myself to him, I pursed my lips.

He made a show of eyeing the Pack, then canted closer and said through his teeth, "Pri-vate-ly."

My gaze narrowed, annoyed at whatever political preternatural minefield I'd clearly stumbled into, but I clamped my mouth shut because the last thing I, or any of us, needed was more trouble.

Lisa sauntered back, balancing a massive tray of pizza dogs in her hold. Theo grinned and reached for them.

I smacked his hand away. "You touch those before my brother gets here, and I will neuter you!"

Every wolfish gaze in the room turned my way.

"Careful, chickie," Lisa said, setting the tray down. "This crowd looks hungry."

Snickering, I grabbed a potion, lifted it in cheers, and downed it. It tasted like piss, but it burned on the way down, doing the trick. Better than the magi-spelled Tonic I'd previously been hooked on . . . one I'd used to slow the tidal wave of emotions that tried to drown me in the years Kane and I'd been torn apart.

The sound of a truck's familiar engine rumbled in the distance. My lungs shuddered while I took an easy breath.

Headlights cut across the parking lot, then tracked through the windows and over every face in the room. The robin's-egg blue, 1952 Chevy pickup truck, parked. Its doors popped open. Kane stepped out and rose to his towering height as the surrounding lights hit his profile. His navy, long sleeved shirt stretched across his broad shoulders, showing every ridge and sinewed line of muscle beneath when he prowled toward the entrance.

My mouth watered as I eyed my right wrist and the small heart tattoo there. One Kane had given me. His first ever.

When he crossed in, those silver topaz eyes locked on me, their color rolling like liquid metal. My heart settled, because iron fires, I'd missed him.

Across the shop, stares dropped.

His Pack cleared a path 'cause, neutral ground or no, ticking off the North Cambrian Alpha was the biggest of bad ideas. Not that he'd expect them to cow, but actively blocking him was a challenge. And challenging Kane Slade was a good way to separate your head from your body.

I trailed my fingers over the claiming mark along the side of my neck, the one that declared me his. The one I'd wanted—*needed*—because it tethered us and meant sharing his extended life. Living together. Dying together. Because it meant never being without him. It was the same mark he'd used to track me to that burning warehouse. And I'd thanked the wraith and all things holy my stepfather'd had not one sweet clue what it could do, otherwise he'd have left me and—by default—Kane, the permanent kind of dead.

My Alpha's stare dropped to that mark, and the corner of his mouth arced up. Warmth pooled low in my stomach, stoking a fire that never extinguished. I pressed my thighs together. Shadow and sage, he was badass, beast, and brawn rolled into one sex-charged package. And he was mine.

"Someone's hungry," Lisa said, gaze crinkling at the corner.

I stroked my palm up my arm. "The wolves always are."

She jabbed my rib with a finger. "I wasn't talking about him."

My face heated a thousand degrees before Kane stepped into my path. His stride was even when he stalked closer, the gait of a man who knew what he offered—the threat he oozed. My fingers itched to run through his hair, that mix of gunmetal gray, light smoke, and white, enticing. Like the predator he was, he hunted me.

My head craned up to better see him.

His deep, commanding voice rumbled through me. "You're staring, Bry."

That was a rule, wasn't it? Don't hold their wolfy eyes lest you wished for trouble . . . good or bad.

I bit my lip, my lady bits doing the happiest of dances as I purred, "Mmhmm." Power of obsidian, the things he did to me.

He grunted, gruff and promising, then nipped the corner of my jaw.

Sage, we'd been apart for so long, shattered pieces until he'd fought his way back to me. Until he'd ripped and clawed and tore his way through Ronin's Pack to take the Alpha seat. Until he'd ended the command that had stolen him from me.

"I brought someone for you," he said, tipping his head behind him.

I ducked my gaze past him as Lucas crossed inside. A cheer went up around the room and a smile lit my face as I happy-clapped and squealed. The Pack closed in on him and he loosed my favorite mule-like laugh. And iron fires, I'd missed that sound. It'd been stolen for so long. Too long. All our lives had.

Kane stepped aside as I scurried forward, wiggling through the wolves until I latched my arms around Lucas's gangly neck. "*Happy birthday!*"

He patted me on the back before wriggling from my grasp. "Thanks," he said, a deep red blush staining his cheeks.

My heart did a pathetic somersault in my chest.

Theo edged in and clapped my brother on the shoulder with a wicked smirk. "You've aged, boss."

Yeah, Lucas might've only been sixteen, but for everything he'd endured, he could've been the oldest one there.

I mashed a hand in Theo's face to shut that saucy mouth. "Ignore this mongrel, Lucas." Darting in, I pecked his cheek again. "How are you?"

He lifted a shoulder. "Good."

"You look good," I agreed. And he did. Healthy. His violet eyes were clear, no signs of the psychotropic V drug that'd consumed him before. The one he'd taken to cope with the mayhem his father had unleashed on his life—*our* lives. V was dangerously addictive and outlawed for a good goddamn reason. I'd come so close to losing him when its poison accumulated in his bloodstream, until my Alpha'd come along and saved him.

"Alright, enough," he said, batting me away before he retreated, putting distance between us.

I frowned at the dismissal.

Him being clean eased some of the pressure that'd crushed my lungs and made it impossible to breathe. But I couldn't shake the fear that he'd slip. And I'd kept his leash tight . . . when he was with me, anyway. Lethal addiction aside, being high had put him at risk of losing control and shifting. A big ass problem seeing changelings like him were hated. Feared. Not a shock since the originals, like Isaac, were escaped torturers from the Deep of the Iron Hells, known for chaos, they were instigators with a history of wreaking havoc. Their ability to take the shape of anyone just by touching a skin cell, made their power more dangerous than any preternatural in the damn city, hence the "kill on sight" bounty on their heads, and Isaac's "I'm totally a human" cover story.

A girl around Lucas's age lingered behind him, hands fidgeting with her sleeves. She stood several inches shorter, her sepia-toned skin rich. The smile she wore was bright when she found me.

"Hannah." Lucas cleared his throat. "This is my sister, Briar." He gestured around. "That's Lisa, Theo, and Joaquin."

The Beta shook her hand before Theo scooped her up in a bear hug. "Welcome to the club."

She went rigid, until my brother laughed and pried her free.

My eyes widened as I stood there, slack jawed, Lisa's expression the mirror of my own, because Lucas had brought a . . . *girl*?

Hannah—the name was vaguely familiar. A name he'd mentioned to Kane the day my Alpha'd brought him Renew, the ridiculously expensive pill with chemically filtered healing properties that'd cleared his drug-addled system. The day Lucas's life had turned around.

Kane extended a hand and closed my gaping mouth.

The smile in Lucas's eyes was bright, not a pup anymore, but not quite a man. And the way he looked at her . . . it reminded me of how Kane looked at me, and it warmed my heart, but still, after everything we'd been through, my trust issues ran deep. My brother was *finally* finding his feet. The last thing I wanted was someone rocking his emotional boat and knocking them out from under him. Which meant I needed to know her. Figure out where she stood. What kind of risk she might pose.

I blinked several times before my brain kickstarted. "Hannah!" I offered a nod and a tentative smile. "It's nice to meet you."

Lucas frowned like he'd expected more.

"You, too." Her voice was soft, kind—just like her chestnut eyes. But Isaac's eyes had lied. Eyes couldn't be trusted—new ones, anyway.

"Lucas has told me so much about you," I said, throwing an obnoxious wink his way.

He dragged a hand through his hair, and mumbled, "Oh, sage."

Hannah chuckled, then reached for that hand, threading her fingers through his. My brother's narrow chest inflated.

Theo's brow arched high. His stare tracked to mine before he sniffed and wiped away a fake tear with a proud 'Our boy's growing up' expression.

He most certainly was and I was trying super hard to figure out exactly how to feel about it.

Some music kicked on, upbeat with a heavy base. Whoops and cheers went up around the room. Setting her chin on my shoulder, Lisa said, "I can't stick around. Gotta get back to the bar."

I patted her hair. "Thanks for helping."

She pecked me on the cheek. "Come see me soon."

"I will."

With that, she gave my brother a birthday hug, and left.

Joaquin pulled back a chair at the head table and set himself down. The rest of our group moved to follow. My brother took his place beside Hannah while my Alpha lowered himself into a seat, completely commanding it like the king he was. Those molten eyes found me. He patted his thigh, then waited.

I aimed for the chair beside him, and bit my cheek to stifle my snicker, because irritating Kane Slade was the fuel that fed my fire.

His head cocked, and that molten stare flashed. Gripping my flowy skirt at the waist, he jerked me to him. My heart fluttered like a fledgling's wings—erratic and clumsy. I went airborne as he lifted, maneuvering me onto his lap, using the cover of the table to slide a hand between my thighs.

I sucked in a sharp breath. He didn't touch anything, but iron fires, he was close. He offered me a brash smirk, because he and I were cut from the same damn cloth.

But sage, I'd missed him. Missed his arms around me. Wished we could just stay that way; me glued to his side like the clingy, desperate mate I was.

"Make room, witchy," Theo taunted as he nudged my side and thunked himself down.

Witchy? I rolled up my very short mental sleeves because them was fightin' words. "Wait, am I getting a hint of . . . " I made a show of sniffing the air and his still damp persona, "wet dog"?

For the second time that day, every set of preternatural eyes swiveled my way and poor Hannah turned ashen. I might've tried to console her, but really, the wolves' bite was *wayyy* worse than their bark.

"It's fine," Lucas loud-whispered to her. "Briar's gonna get herself eaten someday. We've all accepted it."

My Alpha barked a laugh.

I gasped and stabbed a finger at Theo. "That sassitude is your fault!"

He batted my accusation aside, then turned to Kane and chucked a thumb my way. "You just had to pick this one."

Kane's broad hand flexed possessively over my hip while he bared a canine at his cousin.

Grabbing one of the pizza dogs, Theo met my stare when he bit into it. Slowly. Crumbs sloughed over his shirt, and he wiped his greasy fingers on his pant leg.

That saucy little mutt! Threading my fingers together, I settled them over the table. "Where's the better half of your DNA, Theo?"

"She's right here," his sister Naomi proclaimed, fluffing her hair with a dramatic flair as she sauntered toward us, her claimed partner, Autumn, bringing up the rear behind her. Naomi shoved her brother's shoulder. "Stop being a pest, pup."

I grinned and set a palm to my chest. "Ah, Naomi. Your presence always warms the cockles of my heart."

Theo grumbled under his breath.

My brother edged closer to Hannah, their shoulders touching. Lucas smiled before he straightened in his seat and made the introductions.

Naomi waggled her brows. "Happy birthday, big guy."

"Thanks," he said as he reddened again.

Theo eyed the cake like the starving mongrel he was. "You gonna cut that, Boss?"

Lucas grinned, then grabbed the nearby knife and got to work. He and Hannah doled pieces out while the group fell into conversation.

Kane's arms locked around my waist, and he crushed me to his chest. He and my brother exchanged a glance.

"What's up, Big Bad?" I said inside his mind, using our touch-necessary, wolfy connection.

He huffed a laugh. *"Luke wants a tattoo."*

Oh, hells no! *"He's only sixteen, Kane."*

An easy incline of his head. *"That's what I told him."*

My gaze narrowed. *"Why does it feel like there's a 'but' coming?"*

"I think he needs something that's his." His thumb grazed a slow line across my stomach. *"I wanna offer him a job. Let him apprentice with whichever wolf we hire. Give him something to work toward."*

And keep him outta trouble.

"The kid's been through a lot. He needs a direction. Some goal or an endgame."

Dragging my finger over my Alpha's cake, I raked the icing off the side. His lip arced up at the corner, and that stare flashed.

Naomi rapid-blinked. "Did you just . . . take his food?"

I snickered, 'cause I'd taken his food before. A *lot*. There was scarce a meal between us where I didn't steal off his plate. "What's his is mine."

Kane's chest rumbled. *"And is what's yours mine?"*

"Yes . . . unless it's on my plate. Touch that, and I will cut you."

Angling forward, he tugged my hair to the side, set his teeth to my throat and raked them across it. Predatory, but easy.

Sage, I loved him. He filled every part of me, from the far reaches of my sad little soul, to the chambers of my clumsily beating heart. I was his. We'd walked through fire to find each other again, and I was never giving him up.

I shimmied against him, getting closer.

His cock twitched, and his hands cinched over my hips. "*Easy*, Bry." Then inside my mind, "*Don't make me bend you over this table and ruin your brother's birthday.*"

I shimmied again.

He growled.

My gaze drifted my brother's way. Hannah leaned into him, whispering something in his ear—something that'd *never* be private around the dangerously sensitive hearing of the nosey ass weres present. Lucas loosed that goofy laugh.

I sighed. My wolf was right, my brother *did* deserve a win—a leg up. Something that was his. He'd had enough taken from him. I set my head back on Kane's shoulder and grumbled, "*Fine. Lucas can apprentice.*"

He popped his hip up then reached into his back pocket and pulled out a card, addressed *To Luke*. His chest pressed into me when he leaned forward and chucked it my brother's way. "That's for you."

Lucas's grin was wide. Too wide. The kinda wide that said he'd known what was coming. He tore it open. That grin stretched so far across his face, it touched my soul.

Kane chucked his chin Lucas's way. "If you want it, you're scheduled for the opening."

Scheduled? Pump the brakes! Had they just . . . tag teamed me? Oh, that sneaky pack of mutts! I eyed my wolfy lover askance.

The wink he offered was devastating. My mouth watered.

Lucas angled the card Hannah's way.

She bounced in place, celebrating for him. "How's it work, anyway?" she asked. "The tattoos?"

Theo pointed toward a stack of vials lining the shelf behind the main counter, each filled with an off-white, ground up powder. "Moon dust."

Kane dipped his head to hide his smirk, while I bit my lip to do the same, because it'd been the same lie Theo'd told my brother years before.

"Don't believe him," Lucas told Hannah before he aimed a light punch at Theo's side. "He's just being an idiot."

Theo yipped and dodged, shoulders shaking as he laughed.

My brother's arm fell across the back of Hannah's seat when he explained, "Preternaturals heal too fast for human tattoos to work, but were claws scar us all, so they mix it with the ink to make it permanent under the skin."

Her eyes went wide. "So, that stuff's what, powdered claws?"

"Technically bone." He nodded. "But, yeah."

"That's so cool!" she said, voice high and sincere.

Heads snapped toward the entrance when it cracked open, and my mother stepped in.

My Alpha's body stiffened, forearms flexing as he rolled his hands into fists. "*The shadowed moon's Lana doing here?*"

I swallowed hard. Sage, I wished I could tell him the woman he knew wasn't the woman she was. That everything she'd done, all the cruel things and crueler words, had been Isaac's compulsion. Isaac's bidding. I wanted to tell him everything, to get us out. Find a way. Something. Anything. I trailed a nail along the hem of his sleeve. "*I, um, asked her to come.*"

His stare narrowed on me. Hard. "*She treated you and Luke like shit for years, then came crawling back after Isaac ditched.*" He rolled his shoulders. "*You don't owe her anything, Bry.*"

Ditched. Not *exactly* the reason for my stepfather's absence but seeing Kane had not one clue about Isaac's role in anything, that'd been his take on things. If only he knew the half of it.

Ducking my chin, I shrugged. "*I'm trying something different.*" I rolled my hair around a finger and slid from his lap. "*I'll be alright, Big Bad.*"

His exhale was gruff and grated through his throat. His molten stare trailed me as I left, but he didn't fight me.

Aiming mom's way, I twisted the wide, titanium band of the obsidian ring on my index finger until it faced my palm, and I clasped it. The heat of its energy rolled through me, channeling from my heart where my power lived. I drew on it, then threw a cocoon over our conversation to shield it.

Lowering my arms, I gripped my opposite wrist. "Thanks for coming."

"Of course." Her cobalt gaze, the match of my own, flicked around. "Thanks for inviting me."

"How are you?"

She tucked her wiry, salt and pepper hair back from her face. "Good. Glad I can finally talk to you."

Glad because Isaac'd wielded her love for me like a weapon, forcing her cruelty. It was still there, his power over her, but him being gone meant he wasn't there to use it.

He'd driven a wedge between us, one I wanted desperately to remove. Inhaling deep, I braced against my next question. "Have you heard from him?"

She shook her head. "No. Nothing."

The tension in my body ebbed. Not completely. But every day without him was a goddamn gift. My mind drifted, a face searing across my memory. One I couldn't get out of my head. One I wanted desperately to free. To send home. "Any idea where Ivy could be?"

"I don't." She swallowed hard. "I'm sorry, Briar."

"No, don't apologize." Not for him.

Eyes were on us, their weight heavy. One silver topaz pair in particular.

Mom shrank in on herself, gaze downcast. "I don't think . . . I should probably go."

My face fell. "You just got here." I wanted time with her, to talk, but with Isaac's command still locking our tongues, there was naught we could do on that front.

"I'm not wanted."

Not wrong. The weight of the tension was so thick on the air, it was a wonder I could breathe. Still— "You don't have to."

"No, I do," she said, selfless, like the mom I remembered. The mom from before. "This is about Lucas. I don't want to take away from that."

My brother glanced our way.

Mom offered a small wave. She found me again, her smile tight. "I want to hug you."

"Then hug me."

"I shouldn't. I've been down this road, sweetheart. Your Alpha will have too many questions you won't be able to answer. This will be easier for you if we do it slowly."

My heart squeezed. No doubt, she was right, but that didn't stop the sting, 'cause I wanted her there. Wanted the time that'd been taken. To learn who she was. To love her like I used to, before everything. Before Isaac.

"I'll call you soon," I told her.

Inclining her head, she turned on her heel and walked out.

Aiming for the table again, I settled back with my Alpha.

"*You good?*" he asked across that connection.

"*I'm good.*" A truth, one he'd know seeing weres could scent a lie. Well, not a lie exactly. More your panic *when* you lied.

He grunted but said no more.

"How's school?" Naomi asked Lucas, pulling my attention.

"Alright." He tipped his head Hannah's way. "She's helping me get my grades up."

That was news. Good news. And I'd take as much of that as I could get when it came to him. That earlier worry resurfaced, and I pinched my chin as an idea blossomed.

Kane's thumb stroked along my jaw. "*What's going on in that head of yours, Bry?*"

"*Nothing,*" I replied, too fast, too breezy.

"*You're plotting.*"

True or not, I crossed my arms over my chest, indignant on my own behalf. "*I would never!*"

He nudged his face into the hollow of my neck. "*Liar.*"

I hmphed. "*Fine. I wanna get to know her. Lucas looks happy, but he's still in a dangerous place.*"

He inclined his head. "*What were you thinking?*"

Angling to the side, I nudged Hannah's arm and blurted, "We should do a double date."

Lucas and Hannah eyed me in unison. She smiled, bright and genuine. "I'd love that."

"How's Monday?" I asked.

Kane's stare creased at the corner. "I've got the hearing."

Right . . . the one where his wolves got to make requests. As Alpha, the entirety of that Northern territory was his, and everything in it. His people could own land or modify it, but major change required approval. His, to be exact. He'd put things off to focus on me when he'd first taken the Pack. But those responsibilities had snuck up and bit us on the ass. That and a weird shift of power bids. Lower level, but still an issue.

I fought the pout that tried to force my lip out. I got it, I did, but, iron fires, I just wanted some time. Taking a slow inhale, I told Hannah. "We'll figure out another time."

Leaning back, I gave my Alpha my weight, then peered over my shoulder at him. "Are you at least free to go furniture shopping Saturday?" Furniture we needed for the house . . . and shop.

Kane winced, guilt lining his eyes before he and his Beta exchanged a glance. Some silent conversation passed between them.

"I can take you, banshee," Joaquin said.

My pulse quickened, pounding in my head when I silently scolded my Alpha, "*Please tell me you didn't just order Joaquin to Beta-sit me?*"

There wasn't an ounce of apology in the level tone of his reply. "*I did.*" He stretched his neck. "*A lotta shit's happened, Bry. I won't fucking lose you again.*"

Lovely sentiment, except . . . "*The point was spending time with* you."

He tensed beneath me.

I blew out a heavy exhale that sent my hair flying. Wolves!

The music changed to a softer tempo. Hannah peered at Lucas through her long lashes. I read the words on her lips when she asked, "*Wanna dance?*"

He scratched his cheek, neck turning scarlet. His chair scraped across the floor when he stood. She moved in behind him as the two aimed for the makeshift dance floor.

Naomi's gaze met mine, brow lifting in a "so stinking cute" kinda way.

Kane rose, taking me with him as he carried me out there too. Settling my feet down, he crushed me to his chest and started swaying to the music.

I looped my arms around his neck and sighed. Tucking my head into the hollow of his throat, I breathed in that musk and wilderness scent while I twisted my fingers through his hair.

"*I'm trying, Bry.*" Trying to do the right thing. Trying to be there.

"*I know,*" I silently murmured, because he was. And I loved him for it. Swallowing hard, I pivoted the conversation. "*Why can't I talk about training, Kane?*"

His arms banded tighter. "*Because it implies you don't think I can't protect you.*"

Hold up. "*From the Pack?*"

Even inside the recesses of my mind, his voice pitched low. "*From anyone.*"

I blinked in rapid succession. It was the dumbest of dumb reasons, but the last thing he needed were issues because of my misstep. And having the Conclave or anyone else think that . . . to make Kane vulnerable in that way . . . "*That's not what it means.*"

He inclined his head. "*I know.*" His hand flexed over my waist, kneading the flesh there. "*You should learn,*" he agreed. "*We just gotta keep it quiet.*"

I could handle that. "*I want you to teach me.*" I raked my tongue along his throat, taunting when I said, "*Unless you'd prefer someone else—*"

He growled, deep and resonant. "*Finish that sentence and you'll regret it.*"

I smiled, all proud and teeth because a punishment from Kane Slade was the super kind of fun.

"*I've got a few hours in the morning.*"

I hated resorting to schedules, begging for any scrap of time with him, but that wolf was my life. He was it for me, so if that's what he had, then I'd take it. Pressing up onto my toes, I peered at him through my lashes and let my pout free. He nipped my bottom lip then arched a lone brow, his heated palms grazing down to my hips.

A soft little mewling sound escaped me.

"Cool it, you two!" Theo snickered when he strode past, walking backwards as he headed for the food table. "There are children present."

I jabbed a finger toward the corner. "And we set the kiddie table up just for you!"

Kane choked a laugh. "Fuck me, I've missed this mouth, Bry."

Wiggling my ass, I shimmied closer, 'cause there were many more wonderful things my mouth could do for him.

My phone pinged with an incoming text. I tugged it from my handy-dandy skirt pocket and checked the screen.

Mason:
You up for going over a few things at the RC tomorrow afternoon?

As Second in the Coven, I was on the hook for handling administrative stuff; collecting dues, and earnings portions. Or in the case of the Recovery Center, distributing the permits required for Purge and Tonic and other magi-made products when and where required. I hadn't gotten to that part yet, so, like it or not, it was definitely time.

Kane's brow ticked high, because he knew me. Knew every expression and sound. Read every reaction. Every*thing*. "What's up, Bry?"

Seeing my Alpha had not one clue Mason was under my stepfather's thrall and wasn't, in fact, the slimebag he thought him to be, there was not one doubt in my mind how things were about to go. Bracing, I showed him my phone. "I start tomorrow."

His eyes sparked while his jaw ground.

Lovely. Looked like my career was off to a killer start.

Chapter Two

Wind whipped across the yard the next morning as I trained. It rustled the trees and rippled the lake. The fire-kissed colors that tinged the sky waning as the sun climbed.

Kane's wilderness and musk scent carried strong on the air as he crouched low—a predator eyeing prey. His movements were rigid. Had been since that text from Mason the night before. And I hated that the little time we had was tainted by it.

"Aim for the right," he instructed.

My grip on my obsidian tightened while I drew on my power.

"We're just working accuracy, Bry, not power." He chucked his chin toward my hand. "Release the ring."

I shook my head. "It's my only advantage, Kane."

"For force, yes. But a strong punch is useless if it doesn't land." He raised his arms, palms out when he repeated, "Release it."

Grumbling under my breath, I did as he said. He pushed a big, square knuckled right hand forward—my target. I swung, grazing his pinky, the hit going wide.

I frowned and stared at my fists like I didn't know them. "How the Iron Hells did I miss something that big?"

He was stiff as he maneuvered behind me, those thick, corded arms grazing over mine, his body encompassing me as he took my wrists. Lifting, he positioned my hands where he wanted them.

"The elbow's the hinge," he said, voice level as he went there next, then demonstrated while he spoke. "If they're too high, your flanks are exposed. Too low, you can't protect your head."

He positioned me smack in between. From there, he moved to my hips, those hands so big, they wrapped to my ass. "You're too angled."

His heat enveloped me, and I peered up at him over my shoulder.

He cleared his throat. "I'm trying to help you, Bry."

I pressed back into him and dragged my lip between my teeth. "Same, Big Bad."

His stare dipped there and flashed, but he made no move.

My shoulders fell. "I miss you, Kane."

Some of that tension eased. His exhale rattled through the recessed chambers of his chest before he nuzzled into the hollow of my throat and raked his canines over my claiming mark.

My mouth ran dry.

Taking my waist, he turned me to face him. The hard planes of his torso pressed into the soft curves of my chest. His calloused hand stroked my upper arm as it climbed, sending a warm shiver down my spine. Hooking a finger under my jaw, he angled my face to his before that low voice thundered through me. "I fucking miss you too."

"Tell me what's wrong, Kane. Talk to me," I uttered.

"You know what's wrong, Bry."

My own exhale was equal parts resignation and bracing 'cause I was definitely about to poke the bear—or wolf, as it were. "What if Mason's changed?"

He went rigid, then pulled back. "You're *defending* him?"

I scoured the dusty corners of my mind for a way to *actually* answer that question but at every turn, Isaac's leash pulled tight. Twisting the string of his hoodie, I looked away. "He saved me, Kane." And he had, 'cause had it not been for Mason, I'd have burned in that fire Isaac'd set to hide his lab.

His grip flexed against me as he angled closer. "He did a fuck of a lot more than that."

"If it wasn't for him, I'd be dead."

His large, rough hand took my face, completely engulfing it before he brought me back to him. "I'm grateful, Bry. So damn grateful. But you don't owe him anything. And if he thinks that gets him a pass for the rest of the shit he pulled, he's fucking wrong."

Wraith take me, I wanted to share that truth so he'd understand. Not that they'd suddenly be besties or anything, but it might've dulled his murderous edge. If I couldn't be honest, I'd need to use the next best thing—logic. "He's my Coven Leader, Kane. Conclave. Gutting him is not an option. You'll need to work with him too. Do something to him and we've got problems."

His stare flashed voltaic, charged with a current of rage. A low growl tore from the dredges of his throat.

"I'm Second now. You need to accept that."

His mouth drew up in a snarl, but he had the decency to keep it shut.

"I'm not asking you to like Mason," I said. "You just have to trust me."

He leaned in, words rough along my temple. "I trust you, Bry. Don't ever doubt that. But he's not you. I can accept his role. I can accept yours. But no one fucking hurts you, so don't expect me to forgive him." He shifted until that molten stare speared mine. "Because I don't forget."

I huffed a resigned breath. Without being able to talk, I supposed it was the best I could ask for. "Alright, Big Bad." I looped my arms around his neck and gave him a gentle kiss.

"Good." He nipped at my cheek. "'cause I'm taking you to the dirge."

I tapped a finger against his chest. "You can't. It's only for magi."

"Then I'll sit in the truck and wait. Jared got himself dead before we could question him. We don't know if he worked alone."

My brows shot high. Shadow and sage, he was so close to sniffing out that trail.

"Told you already, I won't take chances. Not with my mate." He nudged my jaw, the barely-there stubble along his own making a *tsh* sound when it grazed my skin. "But if Mason says anything, or tries anything, or breathes wrong, there will be no goddamn mercy."

Canting my head, I questioned, "Mercy?"

His lip pulled back, baring his canines when he repeated on a snarl, "*Mercy*."

Not sure I'd call Kane's approach merciful, but then he was a were. A mated Alpha, to boot. His willingness to accept threat on any front hovered well below zero. My face twisted. Maybe mercy *was* the word.

His mouth found my temple. "I'm sorry I'm gone a lot, Bry. Things shouldn't always be like this."

Shouldn't? My nod was small as I traced a nail over my heart tattoo.

"Let me do something. Make it up to you. Take you to dinner tomorrow night. Just the two of us."

My stomach fluttered. "Is Kane Slade asking me on a date?"

"Do I need to ask?"

"You probably should." I checked my nails. "I'll need to consider your offer—"

His hand landed on my ass, and I squeaked.

"Down, boy." I hid my smirk and pushed at his chest before I scurried back. "You're gonna have to earn me."

He crouched low, a lupine grin taking his lips. "That so?"

I backpedaled more, heart thumping in anticipation, because playful Kane was my favorite Kane, outside of take control Kane . . . or sexy-time Kane.

Advancing a step, he angled his head down, eyeing me through his brow. "There's nowhere you can go that I won't follow. You can't run from me, Bry."

Ha! Wanna bet? I bolted, squealing as I fled. His fast-pounding steps closed in while I barreled across the yard, totally aware I'd only made it that far because he'd *let* me. But when it came to me, my Alpha enjoyed the chase.

He lunged and a lone arm latched around my waist, bringing me up short until I went airborne. He flipped me to face him, then jerked me to his chest. I wrapped my legs around his hips. Gripping the ruffles of my skirt, he hitched it high, hands sliding to my ass. He carried me to the house, then backed me against the façade, and crushed himself closer.

I trailed my tongue along my teeth.

His torrid gaze dipped to my breasts and lingered. Those eyes hooded. "I'm hungry, Bry."

The rigid length of his cock pressed into the apex of my thighs, and I rolled my hips, grating over it. He grunted a primal and promising sound as he pressed in harder. Sliding his thigh forward, he gave it my weight. His touch raked my sides as a liquid heat pooled in my core.

"When are you gonna learn?" He cocked a taunting brow. "Don't pick fights you can't win."

Oh, but rankling Kane Slade was my life's purpose, so picking fights wasn't just a passion, it was an obligation. I trailed a finger down my cleavage and offered him a temptress's smile. "I wasn't aware we were fighting."

A low thunder rumbled through his chest before he drew his fingers into his mouth and laved them with his tongue. Gliding them up my thigh, he hunted my wet and ready core. "I fucking love these skirts."

"You just love easy access." My smile turned sheer vixen. "Why do you think I wear them?"

He growled and shifted my thong aside, thumb seeking that wanton bundle of nerves at my center. The gasp that broke from me when he found them was a hunger that matched his own. He worked me in an easy rhythm. Controlling. Dominant. Patient. The exact opposite of me when I tore at his belt to free him.

"I'm gonna fuck you now." His fingers sank deep. "Hard."

I rocked my hips, enjoying his calloused touch inside me while I hissed, "Yes."

Withdrawing entirely too soon, he ripped his shirt over his head and whipped it aside, putting the deep ridges of his chest and stomach on full display. His thumbs hooked into my thong, snapping the lacy material before he tossed it aside. Tugging the tie of my corset, he loosened the top, baring me to him. He palmed my breasts, stroking their peaks and my head fell back as I moaned.

"Shadowed moon, you're beautiful," he said, tone gruff as he braced himself with a hand against the wall. And, sage, he looked good.

My heart thrummed wildly and the smile that took me scorched. I clutched his back as my mind homed in on a thought. A dream. One that'd been ripped from us before. One I wanted so much I could taste it.

Pressure built in my chest, crushing my lungs until I could barely breathe before I blurted, "I wanna try again, Kane."

His hold dug into my flesh, kneading deep. "Try what?"

I bit my lip, gaze lifting to his. "For a family."

His eyes flared, their blaze lighting the world like a second sun as a wildfire of emotion ignited there. Desperation. Hope. Need. His palm tracked to my collarbones and along my neck before it engulfed my jaw. He canted closer, mouth brushing mine once. Twice. He sealed that finite distance between us with a snap. Arching forward, he molded himself to me, kissing me with his entire body until I was breathless and lost in him. That tongue delved deep, and my hands plunged into his hair, knotting in its strands. He pressed closer, his breaths ragged when he took and tasted, sating his need.

I drew back, flushing as my shoulders heaved and I draped my arms around his neck.

"I want this, Bry. I do. But an Alpha's baby could be hard."

I nodded. The genetic hierarchy of preternaturals meant our child *would* be a were, and if that little pup had even a fraction of Kane's strength, I was gonna be one exhausted momma. But nor did I care. "Is that a yes, Big Bad?"

His arm bracketed my waist, a possessive, wolfish smile cresting his lips. "That's a fuck yes."

I trailed a finger along his temple, and over his mouth. "If I don't take today's pill, my magic will burn through what's in my system fast. I can be ready tonight. After that, all bets are off. If this works, you'll be stuck with me."

His stare speared mine, his voice a gruff rasp when he said, "The hells d'you think I claimed you for?"

I beamed. Slipping a hand between us, I unclasped his jeans before I drew down his zipper. Slow. Steady. Taking his rigid cock in my grasp, I stroked. He bucked and I opened for him, guiding him to my slit. His hips rocked and he groaned, making a gradual advance before he sank deep and grazed every desperate nerve in my core.

He thrust again and again, sheathing himself to the hilt. I moaned, arching against him, my body a ravenous riot of sensation, eagerly taking every damn inch.

Growling, he tore me from the wall and took me to the ground. "I want everything you've got, Bry. *Everything*." His hips arced, sharp and hard when his mouth crushed mine, the kiss bruisingly deep.

My body climbed, high and fast. "Oh, sage." The orgasm hit and my head threw back, his name on my lips.

He kept pace, hips slamming forward as pounded into me. Over and over and over, he seated himself. His body went rigid, and he grunted as he came hard, flooding me with his heat. He kept rocking, riding our waves until he slowed, then stopped altogether.

His hooded gaze found mine, a sated smirk taking that mouth. I moaned a happy sound, and his grip plunged into the hair at the base of my neck. I started to roll again, ready for another round.

His stare went unfocused, and he looked off into nothing before he cursed. "Iron Hells." Pulling back, he sat up, stare creased when it found me. "I'm sorry, Bry."

My heart plummeted. Sorry the moment was over. Sorry our fun was done. Sorry, 'cause once again, the Pack called.

***

Kane pulled us up to the Recovery Center's manicured staff lot in my shiny new black sports car. It was all leather seats, carbon fiber pieces, fancy screens, and a million buttons I'd never understand. But I loved going everywhere with him in that classic truck. Loved that old ass bench seat that prohibited personal space. Still, with both of us having the adultiest of responsibilities, especially ones that were bound to overlap, another vehicle had been a must.

My Alpha'd insisted on taking me, which, petty or not, was logical, considering whatever pesky Pack troubles he needed to face were there too.

We climbed out and headed up the white stone walkway toward the even whiter river-stone-covered building before us. The windows were trimmed in gold, the place all smooth edges and clean. The path was lined with impeccably trimmed hedges that looked entirely out of place in our overgrown city.

The sunproof glass doors to the RC slid wide before we crossed inside. The place was the definition of sterile with white walls, glossy slate floors, silver and chrome polished accents. The only pops of color were the orange lounger style chairs in the waiting room and the cross logo that stood backlit behind the front desk, each end of said cross representing a group: magi, shadow walkers, wolves, and humans.

Joaquin stood waiting to our left, hands clasped before him.

I swallowed hard, suddenly feeling entirely out of my depth. I was an Aura. Read people's timelines like a clock. I didn't know the first thing about Coven ledgers and affairs and—

"You good?" my Alpha asked, voice a low rumble when his heated palm settled against the small of my back, fingers flexing deep.

His touch steadied me, brought my heart to an appropriately wild rhythm. I inhaled deep.

"*You don't need to do this, Bry,*" he said across our bond.

Cassandra Ryton, Dowager of the Northern shadow walker Clan floated toward us. Her gold, lace and satin vintage gown flitted on the air, the look a fashion forward for her previously Victorian era tastes. Her gaze glided my way, the hauntingly crimson shade something the nearby human's sight wasn't acute enough to catch.

Her white-blonde hair slid forward as she bowed her head. "Briar Stone, it is good to see you."

Shadow walkers didn't freak me out—much—but Cassandra was of the older-than-dirt-and-dangerously-seductive variety. We'd forged a bizarre respect through Isaac's chaos, one I wasn't exactly sure I understood, but as long as she wasn't eyeing my neck like a meal, we were golden.

"I'm surprised to see you here . . . in the daylight," I replied as a cluster of whispering humans veered around us, heading inside.

"We have tunnels to shield us so we may walk in shadow."

That was reasonable, and disturbing. "But, like, isn't it past your bedtime?"

The Beta rolled his eyes.

Cassandra's lip twitched. "The wicked do not rest, Briar Stone." Finding Kane, she said, "I am told the Atrium's repairs have been completed." Her chin angled up. "My people say you have left quite the mark in there."

My brow furrowed, attention darting between her and my Alpha. "Mark?"

A savage smile stretched the Dowager's face, one that reached her eyes. And one that looked very close to amused. "Your scents are everywhere."

Scent*s*? Plural.

Joaquin rubbed his temples. "They'll never get them out."

My hand latched around Kane's wrist when I hissed in his mind, "*Our sex stained the Conclave?*"

He smirked, all wolfish and proud.

Power of obsidian. A scorching heat seared my flesh, concentrating in my face. I was on fire, I had to be, because my skin freaking hurt. I stared at the ceiling, praying for escape. Maybe if I was lucky, it'd implode, offer me a quick death instead of the slow one they doled out.

"I must take my leave, Briar Stone. The hours have been long this day. I am in need of rest and my coffin awaits," Cassandra said.

Wait, had she just made a joke?

"I should like to see you again soon," she added. Offering Kane and Joaquin a goodbye, she took her leave.

I didn't know what Cassandra and I were, exactly. Not exactly friends, but not, *not* friends.

Joaquin's stare tracked her as she moved. "That was . . . interesting."

I opened my mouth to reply but looked up when Kane stiffened. His head angled to the right where a lighter ebony skinned woman emerged from a back office. She stopped several feet away, her RC lab coat crisp where it settled at her sides. She tapped at a tablet she held, the obsidian ring glinting on her index finger marking her as magi. One of Alistair's, seeing she looked not one ounce of familiar to me.

Something in my stomach stirred. "Who's that?"

Kane cleared his throat.

My head drew back. Wait. Was he . . . nervous?

The woman's gaze lifted, and I guessed she was closer to my twenty-three years. Her russet-colored eyes locked on my Alpha and widened. "Kane?"

His stare slid to me, then back. He inclined his head. "Whitney."

Sooooo, he knew her, and if the tense set of his shoulders said anything, it was that he didn't like knowing her in my presence.

His hand flattened over my spine. "*We used to date.*"

I went rigid, body turning to stone while a bitter tang coated my tongue. Jealousy, raw and wild, seared through my veins.

He must've read that reaction on my face, 'cause his next words came quick. "*It was before I ever met you, Bry.*"

My heart pounded in my ears while a stinging pain gripped the back of my throat. How had we been together as long as we had and that was the first I'd ever heard of it. "*You conveniently left that out.*"

"'*Cause nothing else mattered after you.*"

I hated that it ached so damn much, but the idea of him with anyone else, willingly. It'd been different with Amber, when Ronin's command forced Kane to obey, in hopes I'd hear and move on. But with Whitney . . .

Kane had been my first *everything*, and here he'd gone and had a life before me. Touched and kissed and wanted another woman—the utterly gorgeous one sashaying our way.

A gruff grunt broke from his throat.

Whitney's gaze landed on him.

She stood several inches taller than me, mostly because of her black stiletto heels. Ones she moved flawlessly in, rivaling any shadow walker for grace. The angle of her jaw was soft, curves prominent. She was stunning by any standard.

Because of *course*, she was.

She stopped before my Alpha and smiled, then leaned in for a hug. Kane was stiff, stare flicking my way when he gave her a lone pat on the back.

My heart twisted and so did my fist with the possessive rage that overtook me.

Righting himself, Kane's hold cinched against me. "Whitney, this is my mate, Briar Stone."

Whitney's gaze narrowed like my name was familiar. If she was from Alistair's Coven, she'd doubtless heard my mother's reputation. Known Lana Stone had been ousted from his Coven for funneling drugs to human patients at the RC—for Isaac's benefit.

Dealing to humans should've landed my mother one of two punishments at the hands of the Conclave; death or banishment to the Talisian Sea. But Isaac's control over Ronin, Anthony, and Victor meant the Conclave left her to Alistair's devices.

Kane stretched his neck. "I thought you weren't here Mondays."

She tucked that tablet against her chest and brushed her long, fine braids back from her shoulder. "One of the girls needed a personal day, so we swapped shifts."

Wow. Alright. I huffed a sardonic laugh. "*You know her schedule?*"

"*We've run into each other a few times.*"

"Didn't think that was worth mentioning?"

A low growl thundered through him.

Joaquin's brow arched high.

Whitney's gaze darted between us. "I've, um, heard a lot about you, Briar."

From Kane? Or just in general? My smile was tight.

She raised her free hand, palm out. "Good things, I swear."

Ugh. She was utterly sweet, and it pissed me off. Not that Kane would've been with anyone cruel or unkind. But a snarky bitch who I was justified to hate would've been nice.

Kane's hold slid to my waist when he pivoted my way, eclipsing me and consuming my sight. *"You're upset."*

I had a million questions I needed to ask if I wanted the ache in my chest to subside, but the moment before us was unequivocally not the time.

"Bry," he pushed.

Mason rounded the corner, shoving his black-rimmed glasses further up his nose—a nose with a pink and still-healing scar over the bridge. One my Alpha'd gifted him after the last Conclave meeting fell to shit.

His copper-colored stare drifted my way before he rubbed the back of his neck. When he spotted Kane, his stride hitched, and he tugged the high collar of his lab coat. His attention dropped to where we touched. I swore he winced, but it was there and gone so fast, I wasn't sure I'd seen it at all. "Briar." He cleared his throat, voice tight when he inclined his head. "Kane."

My Alpha grunted in response, which, everything considered, was better than the alternative. At the very least, it trumped a gutting.

Gripping his opposite elbow, Mason found me. "Are you ready?"

"Yeah," I said, still deciding if it was true.

My Alpha's hold on me locked tight.

I couldn't gauge if his reaction was related to my ex or his, nor did I have the strength to parse it out. My gaze slid from him, to Whitney, then back again. "*Have fun catching up,*" I silently hissed, then I pulled from his touch and stepped away.

His hand latched over my wrist, jaw working while those voltaic eyes bore deep into mine.

Sage, I was so pissy. But Kane Slade bled loyalty. He wanted me. Loved me. Had done everything for *me*. Still, having his beautiful past stare me straight in the face was clearly more than I could take.

Mason, Whitney and Joaquin looked everywhere but at us.

Sighing, I murmured across the bond, "*We'll talk later.*"

His silvered gaze tracked between my own, thumb grazing my tattoo. He gave a slow incline of his head. "*Later.*"

I slipped free, then moved to Mason's side and left, sighing as I vanished around the corner. The RC was shaped like its logo with the lobby at its heart. The place was broken into wings; were labs to the north, shadow walkers to the south, the human treatment center to the west. We aimed east to the magi wing.

My stomach churned, and every possessive impulse in my body begged to run back to my Alpha, climb him like a tree and mark my territory. I shook myself. Sweet sage, if that's how *I* felt, what had it been like for him, watching me with Mason all that time?

Mason fidgeted at my side, then ran a hand through his dirty blond hair like he had no clue what else to do. "Everything alright?"

My heart twisted when we passed a dark-stained wooden door with 'Sierra Harris' embossed on its front.

"Yeah," I breathed. "It's fine."

His mouth tugged to the side. "It doesn't look it."

My stare narrowed. Empath or not, using his power to peruse my emotions was a hard intrusion, never mind that Coven mandate named it a clear-cut no-no. "Please don't read me, Mason."

He raised his hands. "I'm not, I swear. You just look upset, is all." His voice gentled as he faced down the hall and said, "You *can* talk to me, you know, if you want."

I swung my foot, scuffing the floor, then peered his way. "Can I?"

He shoved his hands in those lab coat pockets and hiked his shoulders. "You made what you want clear, Briar. You love *him*." He tipped his head toward my claiming mark. "You belong to him. But that doesn't mean I don't care. I'm just trying to help."

I pulled in a steadying breath and forced myself to relax . . . kind of. "I'm sorry. There's just been a lot and I'm not sure I've processed it all."

The singular nod he offered was solemn. "Yeah. I get that."

There was a pain in those words that had my stomach clenching, because if anyone understood what I'd been through, having his life and love stripped away, it was him. But if I planned to move forward, really make an effort at the position as Second and be around him—trust him again—I needed to clear the air. I needed answers.

We closed in on the secure labs, a chrome sign above the entrance reading *Magi Observation and Assessment Facility*.

Pursing my lips, I peered his way. "How much of it was you?"

His brows furrowed in question when he brandished two keycards, handed one to me, then set the other over the small box with flashing blue lights on the wall. A high *beep* sounded out, followed by a click when the secure latch released.

I folded my arms over my chest. "How much of what happened was real and how much was Isaac?"

Grabbing the door's vertical metal handle, he cracked it open, then crossed inside. "I did things to keep you, Briar. Things I'm not proud of." His stare dropped. "I should've helped more with Lucas. Never should've given you that Tonic. Never should've agreed to Sierra's deal." He shook his head. "Those are on me. But everything after; blackmailing you, threatening to go to the Conclave and involve Ithica, the proposal . . . that was Isaac."

The room was lined with silver and frosted glass, sit-stand desks that held state of the art computers. Each had multiple screens, wireless keyboards and sleek, ergonomic chairs. A series of tablets sat docked on the far table, while windows lined the walls to my left showing a series of labs where several other magi worked.

I wanted to believe Mason, but— "You had a ring."

He exhaled good and slow before he aimed for one of those desks, set himself into its black leather seat, and gave it his weight. Dropping his elbows on his knees, he inclined his head.

My heart twisted in my chest, hands flying to my mouth when that truth hit like a shovel. Wraith take me, he'd had a *ring*! "Oh, sage, Mason."

The smile he offered was sad. "I had it for a while." He scrubbed a hand over his hair. "Couldn't find the right time."

Not a shock, considering my life had been one Lucas-based emergency after the next. But still, I'd called it quits while he'd been ready to *propose*.

I closed in and settled my touch over his forearm. "I'm so sorry."

He glanced away. "I guess a piece of me always knew you weren't all in. I think it's why I fought so hard to hold on. I don't know. Maybe I thought I could sway you. Still, as much as it stings," he straightened and met my gaze before he offered a weak smile, "it's better like this."

Any lingering confusion or anger toward him vanished like dust on the wind, 'cause it turned out I wasn't the only one who'd had their foundation shaken.

My attention lit on a pair of Caster Stones that sat on either side of the entrance. They were polished black and reminded me a crap ton of the ones outside No Man's Land.

Mason followed my line of sight. "Sierra put them in last year to keep anyone from sharing their research."

"Pump the brakes. She spelled them to shut her own people up?"

He inclined his head.

What the hells? That felt awfully paranoid . . . and limiting. "So, what? We can't talk about anything we do here outside this room?"

"We can." Taking up a small box on the desk, he extended it my way, then gestured to the other magi. "But they can't."

I popped that box open. A newer, darker, and decidedly larger obsidian ring sat nestled inside the indigo velvet casing. "Thanks?"

A half-smile crested his expression. "It's taken from the inner rings, closer to the concentrated core of our Motherstone. It'll give you a stronger pull and has a counter-cast so the stones won't work on you. Perk of being Second."

Innnnnteresting. But magi had a process. For obsidians to connect to you, your blood had to be given over . . . "Don't I need a ceremony or something so I can tether with it first?"

"You did that when you joined."

Right, because each obsidian Motherstone was unique to its Coven. When you bonded with it, you bonded with its power and the others connected to it. As long as that new ring was from the same stone, the connection stood.

So a power upgrade without the pomp and circumstance? I'd take it. Plucking the ring out, I swapped it with my old one. Its marquise shape looked sleek along my finger, the facets clean and precision cut.

"It's beautiful."

"I'm glad you took the job," he said as he swallowed hard, then swallowed again. "I need someone I can trust."

I twisted the sleeve of my coat, 'cause nothing about that sounded good. "Trust with what?"

He scratched his chin as he peered around. "Sierra was up to some stuff."

I propped a hip against the shelf to my right. "Yeah, that human industrialist from Ithica she had dealings with." Dealings to shore up her allegiances and financial status by selling them potions behind the Conclave's back. Not the bestest of plans, but . . .

He nodded. "Turns out, they ended up expanding their arrangement." Gliding the drawer to his right open, he took out a stack of papers and dropped them down before me.

My gaze narrowed on them. It was in a familiar scrawl, one that matched the open-ended Binding Vow my Alpha'd been given for his participation in Sierra's get-the-Conclave-working-together-so-Ithica-doesn't-bomb-us-into-oblivion plan. A vow that necessitated his request to *any Coven* must be granted, lest the one who'd rejected it be killed.

"These are Sierra's," I said.

Mason's nod was tight. "Her private notes."

With the tips of my fingers, I spread them apart and started reading. And reading. And *reading*. Ingredient lists. Magi extractions. Human volunteers. Experiments; failed and successful. Serums upon serums. The further I went, the more my expression twisted. "What is all this?"

"Modifiers."

The furrow of my brow was deep. "Gonna need a bit more on that one."

He indicated the note before me. "There's more I'm still trying to sort, but if I'm reading this stuff right, Sierra built a serum that offers humans magi powers."

My spine locked straight. Shadow and fucking sage. Give them *our powers*? What the hells had been wrong with her? Just what we needed—Ithica armed with their iron fleet *and* our abilities. Bad. Super bad.

"We can't let this get out, Mason." We needed to destroy it, burn those pages, and never speak of it again.

He exhaled long and slow, the strain in his expression deepening to pained. "That's kind of the problem."

The hairs on the back of my neck stood on end, pulse thrashing wildly in my ears when I asked, "What do you mean?"

His stare pinned mine, words dropping low when he said, "I mean the serums are missing."

Chapter Three

The air in the restaurant was warm. Candles lit the room, flickering over every table. My gaze drifted around while small fireflies winked and blinked above me. A magi-forged illusion. They flitted below the dark blue ceiling, creating a night-sky effect that reflected off the faceted and mirrored walls. The place was otherworldly and utterly stunning.

My Alpha hadn't just made a reservation for *us*, he'd reserved the entire damn restaurant. Which meant it was empty as hells and twice as lonely when he didn't show.

I'd barely seen him since the RC, 'cause of course, he'd been called away *again*. Between the Pack, and whatever problem had gone down at Immortal Inc earlier that day, we'd not gotten a chance to talk. And we desperately needed to.

I couldn't get those missing serums out of my head, or Whitney. Couple that with Sierra's dirge the next day, and I'd needed my Alpha's comfort. His warmth. Just . . . him.

The maître d', Marisol, an older magi from my Coven, stuck her head out from the back room, checking on me . . . again. Each time, her crinkled wince grew deeper, and my face burned.

A nagging sense had pricked my spine as I'd waited at the house for Kane to get me, until he'd sent a text asking me to meet him there. When I'd arrived, the second text came through saying he'd be late. Followed minutes later by another.

Fuck. Shit's going down. I'm stuck, Bry. I'm not gonna make it.
I hadn't responded. Just stared at that heart tattoo while I called mom with a change of plans.

An embarrassing and lonely while later, she, Lucas and Hannah stepped inside, and Marisol led them my way.

Lucas reached for Hannah's hand as she untucked it from her sleeve and smiled before her gaze skimmed the room, then that ceiling. Her eyes widened.

My brother was spiffy and the teenage version of "dressed to impress" with his hair brushed back, clean, fitted jeans, and a black, polo-style shirt on.

"You look so pretty, Briar," Hannah said, then smiled. "Thanks so much for inviting us."

Us. Like her and Lucas were already a package. Another check in her sweetheart box. "Thank the RC and Kane's bottomless bank account."

She covered her mouth to hide her laugh.

Lucas's brow furrowed. "Where *is* Kane?"

"Pack emergency," I said, waving a hand to brush off his concern. But it didn't work for my own. "Order whatever you want, the menu is your oyster."

Lucas nudged my shoulder with his fist. "Thanks, sis."

My brows lifted. Sis. Better than bro, I supposed. Had I just been upgraded? I swept my arm wide. "Sit wherever you like."

They aimed for a two-seater booth on the other side of the room and sat down across from each other.

Mom lowered herself opposite me, then reached over the table and set her hand on top of mine. "You're upset."

Her touch was still . . . foreign. But sage, it was wanted. *Needed.* I'd longed for it. And in that desolate moment, it felt good. "Just some stuff with Kane."

She brushed her thumb over my wrist. "I understand there's a lot we need to figure out between us, and a lot of ground to make up, but I want you to know, you can always talk to me, Briar."

Inhaling deep, I inclined my head. I desperately wanted to bridge the cavern Isaac had cleaved between us, and there was only one way to do that. Besides, I needed the ear. "It's just . . . he's always gone with the Pack lately. I know he's Alpha, but it feels excessive."

Her head dipped as she considered. "Do you think there's something else pulling him away?"

Something else, as in did I suspect he was lying. That nagging sense from earlier trickled back in. Frowning, I shoved it aside. "No."

She dipped her chin in a nod. "Good. Because he loves you, Briar."

My shoulders fell. "He tells me that, it's just hard to *feel* it when he's never there, you know?"

"I do." Her gaze turned wistful. "When you were younger, your father and I had the same problem. He was so career focused."

It was the first time she'd spoken about dad without disdain or bitterness. I wanted to ask if that was an Isaac thing but hated to interrupt or sour the mood . . . more.

"At first, I thought he was avoiding me. That our family'd become too much, and he was quietly moving on. But in the end, he just wanted to provide. Give us the best life he could."

Difference was, simply *being* the Alpha got Kane that juicy Conclave cheque, so providing wasn't an issue. Still, Kane Slade wasn't a man to half-ass anything. It was whole ass or nothing.

Mom offered me a soft smile. "You don't see what I see. What *everyone* sees. The way he moves when you're there. The way he watches your every expression. You're the force he's pulled to, the one he revolves around." Her eyes misted and she dabbed a tear. "I love that man for you, Briar. And every time he pulled you away from us," she loosed a small laugh, "or told me where to stick it, I loved him more, because he did what I couldn't. He protected you. You're his mate. To him, it's his job. One he takes very, very seriously."

But the Pack was his job too.

I took up the midnight blue napkin beside my plate and folded it over, then folded it again. Was I just being greedy? Wanting him all to myself?

Hannah set her elbows on the table and giggled. And Lucas's violet eyes lit up, sparking like fireworks. They were like something straight outta some cheesy romance movie, and it was damn near the cutest thing I'd ever seen.

I hadn't needed cute when I'd found my Alpha. I'd needed smart, and strong, and unyieldingly loyal. I'd needed a possessive passion as Kane kissed me on a dancefloor, or the intense and fiery hunger while he took me in the bed of his truck.

But Lucas's life had been rough, when it came to love, he needed somewhere soft to fall. He needed sweet, and kind, and cute. He needed Hannah. It was written in the way he settled when her fingers brushed his. The way his gaze always sought hers. And the way his smile touched his eyes.

Lucas had lost his innocence at his father's hands, but with Hannah, it was like he got it back. Not all of it. Some things just couldn't be recovered. But the silly, life-shouldn't-be-that-hard bits, she gave him those. Showed him a gentler way. And like my mother with Kane, I already loved her for it.

My brother leaned across the table and pressed a kiss to Hannah's lips before he pushed up and aimed for the washroom.

I bit my lip and Mom laughed. "Go," she said. "I know you want to."

"I'll be back in a sec," I said, and scampered Hannah's way, my bare legs sticking to the leather as I stole my brother's seat.

Swiping my hair from my face, I said sweetly, "I hope you're having fun."

She sat straighter and lowered her arms to her lap. "Very much. It's nice to be included in family stuff."

My head canted. "Has Lucas met your family yet?"

"My parents died when I was a baby."

I winced. "I'm so sorry. I didn't mean to pry." I totally did but hadn't meant to open a potentially painful wound in the process.

"It's okay. I was a baby when it happened. My grandparents raised me. Gram passed two years ago, so it's just me and Grampa now. He's pretty easy." She laughed. "Tells me he's too old to deal with drama."

"Well, he should know he's done a beautiful job with you."

A shy blush stained her cheeks.

"What are your plans when you're done school?"

Her gaze dropped. "I'm, um, still trying to figure it out. I guess I'll have to see what I present as after I get my obsidian, but I think I'd like to own my own business someday."

"Briar," Lucas grumbled from my side, forehead furrowing deep.

"Sorry." I said, scooching out of the booth as I raised my hands in placation. "I'm a tad protective."

"No, I get it." Hannah replied, smiling at my brother as he retook his seat. Clasping one of his fingers, she twirled her own around it. "Lucas told me about the V and how bad things got."

My brows climbed to my hairline. Not that his addiction had been much of a secret, but I was proud of him for that openness. For not hiding behind manipulation and lies like his father.

She smoothed her napkin. "I'm just happy he's got someone watching out for him."

I gave his shoulder a light shove. "I know my big sister stuff is driving him batty right now, so I'll leave you to it." I offered them a wink. "You two have fun."

Lucas rolled his eyes while Hannah giggled as I turned and sauntered away.

My phone buzzed with another text, one I scowled down at as it soured my mood.

Joaquin: Kane's hands are tied.

Me: I'm painfully aware, Joaquin.

Joaquin: No, you're not. He can't leave, banshee.

I pursed my lips and was halfway through turning the device off when another text came.

Joaquin: Naomi challenged another Omega.

My brain screeched to a halt, and so did I. *Naomi?* What the Iron goddamn Hells?

An Omega. Someone lower in the Pack. Why? It just . . . didn't fit with the woman I knew. And it pissed me the fuck off.

My teeth gnashed when I punched her number. It rang and rang, before her answering machine beeped.

"You better call me back before I hunt you down and de-claw your ass, Naomi Slade!" I said before I jabbed the end call button. I called her again. Beep. Voicemail. "I fucking mean it!" Snarling, I shoved the device away.

My rage was a fire that burned for a million damn reasons, but top on that list because her pissy ass challenging another were from the Pack had put her and Autumn at risk. Had cost me my date. Time with my Alpha. Time for my heart to feel a little less sad.

Breathing deep, I headed back to mom and my table. But with each step, that ache in my chest deepened, because mad or not, I just missed Kane. Wanted him there. And no matter what way I cut it, at the end of the night, I'd be going home alone.

***

I sat on the dock, late afternoon sun beating down while my feet skimmed through the tepid water. The waves rolled, growing wider and smaller as they vanished into the distance.

Naomi'd won her fight but had returned not one of my calls. By the time my Alpha'd rolled through the door the night before, I'd long since gone to bed. In favor of sleep, I'd stared at the ceiling while knot after knot tied my stomach, because the notion of Whitney and Kane just wouldn't quit. The notion of him touching her. Looking at her like she mattered. Like she was the only thing in this world. Like he looked at me.

Kane'd been as exhausted as I'd felt when he apologized with his body, taking me long and hard. It'd been nice, until life crept back in.

I had a few hours until the dirge, hours I'd hoped to spend with him, and each second the clock ticked down was an iron weight crushing my chest. I'd read Mason's instructions. Understood my role and how it was supposed to go. But I didn't *want* to say goodbye to Sierra, to think about what'd happened or the mess she'd left in her wake. I just . . . didn't want to go. I wanted to stay with Kane, at our home, away from the world where

I could keep him to myself, if only he were there. Not that he was far, seeing he was just inside with a horde of the Pack, dealing with wraith only knew what this time.

The sound of car engines carried before the back door popped open. My Alpha stepped out. His head angled my way, those silver topaz eyes on me. His expression was tight. Weary.

I looked away.

The thump of his feet closed in. "Bry?"

Flicking my toes through the water, I tried to control the frenzied beat of my heart. "Yeah?"

"You alright?" he asked, tone pitched low like he was tentative.

I lifted a shoulder.

He stopped so close behind me, his heat pulsed over my skin. "Look at me."

My mouth ran dry. I didn't move.

"Please," he said, the words strained.

Sighing, I swallowed around the lump in my throat, and angled my gaze to his.

Slowly, he crouched at my side. "Say what you need."

In that moment, I needed so, so many things. Too many. But above them all, one hunted my thoughts. It gnawed at my chest and squeezed my lungs until it was harder and harder to breathe. My gaze fell to my feet again. "How long were you and Whitney together?"

The crease around his eyes was deep. He rested a square knuckled fist against the dock and gave it his weight. "A year."

A *year*? A whole goddamn year? Jealousy, bitter and cold cut through my veins. "And you didn't think I should know?"

"My life started with you. Nothing before then mattered."

My heart did a flip inside my chest. A little one.

But still, she had to hold some meaning to him, and sage, it made my heart sick. Yes, he'd chosen me—*claimed* me—but the idea that his calloused hands, that mouth and body had once been hers . . .

Did she remember what it felt like to be in those arms? Kiss him? Have him inside her? My lungs collapsed, shoulders heaving while I tried to suck in air. My hands balled into fists while

I fought the sudden and uncontrollable urge to claw her pretty eyes out. To know more. Know *everything*.

My throat stung when I pushed, "How did you two meet?"

His body grew taut, muscles cording before he banded an arm around my waist, and crushed my back against his chest, voice rumbling through me when he said, "Don't torture yourself."

Pfft. That ship had long since sailed and sunk into the depths of my tumultuous emotional sea. "How, Kane?"

The exhale he let loose was ragged frustration. Or resignation. Probably both, because if my Alpha knew anything about me, it was my sheer relentlessness. "She came in for a tattoo."

My breath hitched. "You told me my tattoo was your first."

"It was," he vowed. "I was just apprenticing at the time." Still, there was something in the way he answered, a hesitation that had my lungs seize, because Kane Slade was not a man to hesitate. There was only one question I could think of that'd worry him enough for that. If I was smart, I wouldn't ask it. But I'd never been accused of that before.

I steadied myself when I half-turned to see him. "Where'd she get that tattoo, Kane?"

He shook his head. "No."

Wraith take me. Bile kissed the back of my throat as my hand latched over my abdomen. "Tell me—"

"*No.*" His grip locked down around me. "She and I were a thing a long goddamn time ago, Bry. A fucking lifetime ago. I didn't even know who I was until I met you."

Sure, but seeing I'd *just* discovered their past, for me, it was fresh and raw and ugly. A wide and bleeding wound.

Power of obsidian! I gripped my hair at the temples. I could barely think around it.

His thick finger hooked my chin and forced my gaze to his. Lines of tension creased his expression, rooted deep like they touched his soul. "Things between me and Whitney ended for a reason."

Sure, but had that reason been his? Or had it been hers?

Taking my waist, he turned me to face him, then drew me flush against him. "I claimed *you*." He set his forehead to mine. "Once you showed up, I was fucking lost." The rough, five o'clock shadow along his jaw grazed my claiming mark and a warm shiver tracked down my spine. "You're the only thing I could see. *Do* see. Whitney's my past, and you're my goddamn everything."

My nod was gentle against him and some of that pressure cinching my heart eased. He loved me. I knew he did. He'd proven that fact again and again . . . but I was greedy for him, and the idea of anyone else holding space in his heart squeezed my chest so tight, it made it hard to breathe.

That stare flashed liquid silver. Angling down, his mouth found the delicate curve of my ear when he growled, "It's you, Bry. Only you. You're it for me."

My fingers twisted into his hoodie, and I let those words settle against my soul. Kane was bound to me. He was mine. Not hers. Not anyone else's.

Mine.

Iron fires, the way he loved me was unparalleled. He loved my broken and bent pieces, the missing ones. *All* of me, unconditionally. Forever. And I loved him.

My stomach soured, and my face fell. What was wrong with me? Laying the guilt at his feet for something he hadn't done wrong. He'd fought his way free of Ronin's command to get to me. *For* me. Why was I being such an ass?

Tears stung the backs of my eyes. "I'm sorry, Kane."

His thick, calloused fingers flexed against me as he shook his head. "I get it, Bry. Believe me, I fucking get it."

Considering my connection to Mason, he most certainly did. I'd met Whitney all of once. *Once.* If that's how I felt over a woman he'd dated before he'd even known I existed, how did he feel about Mason? How much worse was it for him? Sage, the restraint he showed . . .

My exhale was ragged while I sagged against him, giving him my weight as I brushed my lips over his. My gaze trailed the hard angles of his jaw, and up to those silver topaz eyes.

The tension in his honed muscles eased before a rough, thundering growl rose from his chest. "Keep looking at me like that and I'm gonna do something about it."

My heart fluttered and a small smile crept across my face.

He arched a lone brow. "Fight? Or fuck, Bry?"

I snuggled deeper. Closer. I could never be close enough.

He stiffened, body turning to stone, stare distant as he talked to the Pack. His hand clenched, knuckles going white while the tendons there corded under his skin like they tried to tear free. He cursed, and that stare refocused.

His body was stone when he stood, taking me with him as he rose to his looming height as he settled me on my feet.

My expression pinched. "What's going on?"

He took a step back. "More shit with the Pack."

I tried, *really* tried to keep the irritation from my voice when I said, "Again?"

"Again." His chest sank on an exhale when he pivoted, then strode for the house, his gait stiff.

My head drew back. "Kane?"

"It's fine, Bry." He popped the back door open. "We should get ready." He crossed inside.

I stared after him for several long moments before my face twisted, 'cause like hells *that* was gonna fly. Scampering across the yard, I barreled through the kitchen. The hiss sound of the shower had me aiming upstairs where I burst into the master bath.

His clothes lay pooled on the floor as he stepped under the water, shoulders hung like the burden they carried dragged them down. He angled his head to the side, not enough to see me, but enough for the pulsing of his jaw and the storm on his horizon to come clear.

My mouth ran dry as I stripped everything off. Stepping in with him, I settled my palms over his back and uttered, "Talk to me, Kane."

A jagged breath rattled through his chest. He pivoted to face me, those molten eyes wild.

Silence.

"*Kane?*"

"I can't yet, Bry."

There was a shadow in his gaze where his wolf stalked him, fighting to break free. Whatever bothered him weighed heavy.

My pulse kicked up. "What can I do?"

He rolled his shoulders. "Distract me."

I stilled because what the hells had happened? I'd find out, but until then, there was one thing—one tool in my arsenal I could use. One that'd always worked before.

Biting my lip, I edged away until my back pressed against the far wall. My hand settled over my lower abdomen, then skimmed down, down, down, until it dipped inside my folds. A soft pant broke from me, heat pooling between my thighs as I found that sensitive center and worked it.

Kane's voltaic gaze watched that hand with the hunger of a starved beast. His chest heaved as he advanced. One step. Two. He loomed over me, angling forward while his hard length pressed into my stomach.

I moaned.

His palms crashed against the tile by my head, caging me in. His breath was forced through his clenched teeth. Restless. Intent.

Working myself harder, I breathed, "I want you inside of me, Kane."

The sinewed fibers of his forearms flicked and pulsed when his hands flexed. "I won't be gentle."

Sage, he was . . . not mad, but almost . . . lost. Like he couldn't make sense of something.

The smile I offered was pure vixen as I made a show of stroking myself. "Then I guess it's a good thing I want it rough."

He stretched his neck before an arm dropped and he palmed my breast, fingers latching over my nipple. I sucked in a soft hiss.

"You like that?" he rasped.

My attention locked on the lust-fueled fire that burned in his eyes. "Yes." Taking his wrist, I slowly replaced my fingers with his own. "But I like this more."

The snarl that broke from him was a feral need that fed my own. Reaching between us, I curled my touch around his thick, ready cock, and stroked. His free hand dropped to my hip, hold digging deep.

That animalistic bite of pain had my thighs clenching and I worked him faster when I ordered, "Kiss me, Kane."

Water tracked over his face in lazy rivulets while his grip slid over my throat until it latched around my jaw. He angled me up, forcing my eyes to his before he canted forward, his need palpable when his mouth descended on mine. Our tongues met, and I teased him with my own. Tasting. His touched skimmed back, locking over my ass. His hips rocked, thrusting into my hand.

A desperate urgency seized my core. Sage, I needed him.

I broke from the kiss, breathless as I flattened my palm over his chest, and guided him back. My gaze locked with his and held as I lowered myself to my knees.

His expression turned rabid, and the heat that pooled between my legs almost scorched. I trailed my tongue across my lip, craving him. I wasn't just hungry, I was goddamn ravenous. His hand encased the base of my skull before it torqued and he gathered my hair, a ponytail in his grasp.

I sucked in a soft gasp while the muscles along his neck and forearms strained. His cock surged. My tongue trailed the back of my teeth before I set it to his tip. His shaft twitched, and I wrapped my mouth around him, then took him deep.

"Fuck," he snarled through his tightly clenched jaw, an eager, wolfish sound. He set a palm against the wall, giving it his weight, stare angling down to watch me.

Wraith below, he was sexy. The long lines of his torso, the way he commanded power, and the way he always looked at me, like he was an addict, and I was his drug . . . like he'd never get enough.

I rocked back and forth, then sucked deeper still. His hold on my head cinched tight. I set a rhythm, grazing my tongue over his end before he guided me forward and his cock kissed the back of my throat.

My gaze collided with his. His lip arced up and I purred inside.

Big Bad liked it deep.

I set a ruthless pace, stroking with my hand as I retreated, before taking him again and again. His breaths ripped from his throat, guttural and heated. He was close, and I was wild with the need to please. But not yet.

Drawing back, I smiled. "I want you to taste me, Kane." I stared up at him through my lashes. "Now."

He growled and jerked me to my feet. Lifting me from the ground, he tossed me over his shoulder and exploded from the shower, and out to our room. Stopping at the foot of the bed, he threw me onto my back. I gave the mattress my weight, arms ranging languidly above my head. Dropping onto all fours, he hooked my legs over his shoulders. His grin was a brash promise when he lowered himself down and set his mouth to my clit.

I mewled, head throwing back as my hand plunged into his hair. He worked me, stroking that riotous cluster of nerves while his fingers slid inside me, curling forward to hit my g-spot. I arched off the mattress, heels digging into his spine.

"Oh, sage. Just like that."

He groaned, the eager sound of it driving me wild. I arced my pelvis, grinding against him while I took everything he gave. My orgasm crested fast, searing through me like wildfire. I cried out, body writhing against him while that pleasure sparked across every nerve. But I needed more. I needed *him*.

"Fuck me," I begged. "Fuck me hard."

Withdrawing, he rose then prowled over me, his dense, thickly muscled torso eclipsing mine. "Open for me, Bry."

My walls constricted. He wasn't even inside me yet and I was ready to implode . . . again. A warm shiver trickled down my spine. My thighs parted.

He gripped his cock and set it against my slit. "So fucking wet for me," he said as he pinned me with his stare, then drove inside.

A throaty gasp broke from me as I bucked under him. Taking my ankles, he enveloped them with one calloused hand and anchored them against his chest. The position added the perfect kind of friction that had every corner of my body screaming for more.

"Don't stop," I said, voice a honeyed, staccato pant. *Please, sage, don't ever stop.*

Twisting, I angled my ass slightly to the side, giving him access. "Do it."

He kneaded that flesh as a rogue smirk touched his eyes. His hand drew back, then came down on it hard. *Smack.*

I sucked in a sharp, wanton breath. His shaft sank deeper, surging into me over and over. The bed groaned as it slammed into the wall. His chest and abs were strained, veins and muscles there taut. His jaw ground when he filled me, every line of him touching every sensitized corner of me.

I draped my arms around his neck, letting him give and take whatever he needed. My body was his to use. His to fight. His to fuck.

"Do you like me wrapped around your cock like this, Big Bad?"

"Shadowed moon." He drove himself faster. "You look so goddamn good, Bry."

The primal sound he loosed rumbled through me as he withdrew, then reared forward. My head angled back, mouth opening on a wordless scream. My body was a tempest of sensation, restless and indecent and greedy. I rocked my hips, taking every damn inch.

Sweet sage, I loved him. He was a salve that licked the wounds along my heart—just like I did for his.

Kane threw my legs apart and hovered above me. His arm latched across my back and over my shoulder, locking me in place when he sank into me. I tugged his face to my throat as I coiled myself around him, nails raking his flesh.

His hips pumped, giving me everything while he filled me to completion. Arcing into him, I met his thrusts. Hot thrills chased through my core as another orgasm barreled to the forefront. Wild. Insatiable.

"Come for me, Kane," I begged.

He didn't disappoint.

He grunted, muscles of his torso working while I shattered around him. His mouth crashed against mine, catching my cries. A gruff rumble tore from his throat as he drove deep. I whimpered, body sealing around him. His savage growls grew louder. He bucked and bucked and bucked until he spilled himself inside of me. We rode the last waves of our climaxes together before he slowed more and more, then stopped altogether.

I broke from the kiss, hands twisting in his hair as we caught our breath, and he collapsed on top of me. The sheets and blankets beneath us were soaked from wicking our moisture, but I didn't care. It was worth it. *He* was worth it.

The longer we lay there, the more his tension slithered back in.

"It's later, Kane." Angling to better see him, I uttered, "Tell me what happened."

He cursed as he pressed his forehead into my throat, along my claiming mark. "I won't be waiting outside the dirge for you tonight."

My stare narrowed, because there were very few things that could keep him away—not one of them good. My voice was weak, barely audible. "Why?"

His gaze met mine and a clamp latched around my chest, crushing so hard it forced the air from my lungs when he said, "Because my position as Alpha's been challenged."

Chapter Four

I stared out the windshield of the truck while the hum of the tires droned in the background. I sat on the bench seat beside my Alpha, so tight to his side, his arm slung across my chest just to work the shifter. I may have been upset, but I still needed to touch him. Know he was there. Feel his warmth, the rise and fall of his chest. Just . . . *him*.

Challenge. Fight. Danger. Kane. The thoughts ricocheted off the hollows of my skull like an iron bullet.

I flicked the stitching along the hem of my black cocktail dress, trying to control the frenetic pulse in my ears. The sun died on the horizon, and strands of its dusty orange light broke through the rain clouds that rolled in. Scattered drops of water fell, speckling the glass while the distinct scent of ozone filled the air.

Two vehicles followed. Wolves Kane ordered to guard the dirge—or more specifically, me.

I dragged a hand through my hair. "I should be there, Kane." There with him, not leaving his side. Sierra deserved every accolade, but she was gone. He wasn't.

"No." His tone was level. Final. It wasn't a command, but it wasn't far off.

We'd been having the same argument since he'd told me, running the same circle. But I kept nipping at his heels like the feral mate I was.

My breaths were short and shallow, heart beating like a snare drum. "I don't wanna leave you."

His grip on the wheel was so hard, it groaned beneath his hold. Those square knuckles were white, tendons taut under the strain. "You can't be there, Bry."

I shoved his shoulder. "You'd come if it was me!"

"I don't wanna kill anyone, but if you're there, I will, 'cause the wolf will fix on protecting you. I need my mind in the fight. If it's not—" He shook his head. "I won't take that chance."

"What *chance*, Kane? Say it." My voice hitched. "That something could go wrong? *That* goddamn chance?" I shoved him again. "Just say it!"

His expression pinched and he let loose a rough exhale. "Don't be pissed, Bry. Not now. Please."

The desperation in those words clawed at my soul because it wasn't *his* fault some power hungry, fragile fucking were was after him.

I wasn't really mad, not even close. No. I was goddamn *terrified*. Tears seared the backs of my eyes, but I couldn't cry—wouldn't. Not in front of him. He was right. He needed to focus, and me crumbling to pathetic little pieces wasn't about to help. He was strong—so unendingly strong. He'd be fine. I couldn't handle anything else.

I set my head on his shoulder with a thump.

Wolves were always testier during the full moon. It wasn't like they'd sprout fur or anything, but they were called by it. Affected. From a logic level, I got it, but my anarchic emotions weren't on page. "Who is it?"

He cleared his throat. "Someone mid-level."

"Who?"

"Would you even know them?"

Chances were close to nil seeing his Pack was several thousand strong. I hmphed. "I don't get it. I thought they needed to climb the hierarchy to challenge?"

He shook his head. "They should, but they don't have to."

"So, what," I flailed my hands, "if they're strong enough, they can just . . . leapfrog everyone?"

He shifted the truck down a gear, then rested his hand over my thigh. "Strong or determined enough, yeah."

Kane was a good Alpha. Theo had said it himself; the Pack was better since he'd taken over. So, none of it made sense. "Did something happen between you and this jackass?"

He veered us into the full-to-brimming lot of the Grand Hall, a former human opera house that served as Cambria's site for funerals of note. The place was six levels of intricately laid, off-white mosaic tile in a herringbone pattern that was practically leached of color. Morning glory vines climbed the strategically placed trellises along the entrance and lower-level windows, their trumpet shaped azure, fuchsia, and indigo flowers sitting closed under the moonlight.

Rolling his shoulders, he said, "Not that I know of. But it is what it is."

Because a challenge issued had to be met, lest it be viewed as a weakness. And weakness among wolves was a problem with a capital P.

He downshifted again. "We'll be alright, Bry."

We because our lives were tethered. My foot bounced like a sullen teenager. I couldn't care less about myself. Not that I didn't value my life, but without him— No, I couldn't go there. "You'd better be. Because if anything happens to you, I'll hunt you down in the Iron Hells and kill you again myself."

He huffed a laugh, but it was rough, and the smile that took him didn't touch his eyes.

The tires crunched against stone as he pulled to a stop and put the truck in park. He stretched his neck, stare scanning the area.

"Don't worry about me, Kane." It wasn't like *I* was walking into a fight.

He grunted. "I'm not leaving till I check this place."

A grumble that could've warred any Alpha for potency tore up my throat. Scooching away, I reached for my door. His hand latched onto my dress, and he dragged me across the seat toward him, then maneuvered himself out. The vehicle groaned and lifted in his absence.

I flailed my arms, gesturing to the cacophony of cars around us. "The entire Coven's here, Big Bad. Li-ter-al-ly!"

Those eyes blazed when they speared mine. He edged forward until he stood between my legs. "There'll only be five wolves guarding the outside. The rest of the Pack's gonna be there for the challenge. Let me look, Bry. I need this."

He needed to do *something*, and if that was what it took to keep his focus, I'd give it. I set a palm against his chest, the beat of his heart steady, just like him. I softened my smile. "Alright."

His hand took mine, completely enveloping it. Slipping from the truck, he held tight as we scaled the Hall's half-moon shaped stairs. He drew open the gilded door, then filled the frame and stopped. Every magi turned my Alpha's way, falling still as his stare tracked the lobby. Several heartbeats passed before he crossed inside and brought me with him.

The crowd parted as we advanced across the honey-toned marble lobby. The stuff decorated everything; the floors, walls, towering pillars that climbed and climbed and climbed their way to the ridiculously high glass ceiling.

Kane aimed us for the auditorium, then maneuvered over the threshold.

Red velvet seats lined the tiered floor while level after level of gold trimmed balconies overlooked it all. The stage stood at the head of the room, a casket wreathed in black flame at its center—not *real* flame, but forged by an Illusionist, like Jared had been.

I swallowed hard and looked toward Mason, who stood stage right speaking with several of our people. He tensed when he found my Alpha. Pushing up his black-rimmed glasses, he offered us a tight nod.

Kane's eyes were voltaic as his power tore from him, rocking me back a step. He openly scented, stalking through the place like he owned it, because really, it wasn't like anyone there could contend. It wasn't an outright threat, more like a caution to anyone the seven shades of dumb enough to try anything.

"It's clear." He turned my way and rolled up his sleeves. "I should go." He took my waist. "If you need anything, my people are right outside." An instruction, not a request.

My stomach contorted. *Challenge. Fight.* Iron fires take me, I didn't want him to go.

Gripping the base of my neck, he angled my face to his and edged closer. His jaw brushed my cheek once. Twice. His mouth crushed against mine, tongue diving deep. The kiss was bruising, and steady, like he tried to reassure me and a soft, desperate moan broke from me as I clung to his shirt. But entirely too soon, he pulled back.

My shoulders were high, legs weak when I promised, "You're it for me, Kane. Only you. Always."

His eyes flashed like he worked hard to leash his wolf. "I know."

"I'll call you when I'm done, and you *will* be here to get me." I couldn't consider anything less. Wouldn't.

The grumble he let loose was primal when his mouth met mine again. It was brief, and warm, and not nearly enough. He drew away, the muscles along his forearms tensing and flicking as he clenched his fists. His words were low and hoarse when he vowed, "Later." Pivoting, he left, taking my heart and everything I was with him.

Some nagging sense deep in my chest told me to give chase. To wrap myself around him and refuse to let go. Beg and scream and plead if I had to, because I suddenly couldn't shake the feeling that something wasn't right, but whether that was fear or intuition, I had no clue.

No one approached. Not that I'd ever been popular with the Coven. Or that I'd even tried considering my mother's reputation. After Mason—at Isaac's behest—superseded the typical vote and *appointed* himself Leader, he hadn't made any friends. And me being by his side meant I hadn't either.

Straightening my spine, I drew back my shoulders, forcing a confident air I unequivocally didn't feel as I descended the tiered stairs toward him. Steps away, a newly familiar voice cut through the din.

"Briar?"

My lungs seized when Whitney sauntered toward me wearing a black dress that hugged her jealousy-inducing curves like a heated kiss. She offered me a beautiful, soft smile, her black stiletto heels tapping over the Persian rug-styled floor as she sashayed closer. Her movements were flawless, and I swallowed back the bitter tang that seared my tongue.

"It's so good to see you again," she said.

My stare narrowed, voice flat when I asked, "What are you doing here?"

She brushed her long, fine braids back from her shoulder. "Sierra was my aunt."

Well, shit. The resemblance was definitely there in the angles of her face and those russet-colored eyes. I worried my cheek between my teeth. "I'm so sorry for your loss." And I meant it because, my wildly erratic emotions toward her aside, I wasn't a complete ass . . . all the time.

"Thanks." She adjusted the bronze chain strap of her purse. "She was the only family I had left."

I winced.

"It's fine." She gave a wave of her hand. "We weren't particularly close. No falling out. Just lived separate lives."

I nodded. "She was a good Leader." Stepped over the line and had some secret shady deals in the works with Ithica, but her intentions *were* to help the Coven, so, overall, good. And I was glad someone connected to her would be there.

"Thank you." Her stare dropped to my throat and my claiming mark before she tipped her head toward the door. "I ran into your wolf outside."

There was that bitter tang again. Sage, why was it so hard to control that possessive rage? "I hope he was nice."

"Of course," she smiled, "he always is." She adjusted that purse strap again. "I swung by Immortal Inc yesterday and Kane showed me around. You've done a spectacular job with the place. Seriously. It's beautiful."

The words seemed sincere but—Wait. *What?* A sharp piercing pain stabbed my heart. He'd told me he'd gone to the shop but mentioned not a damn thing about her being there too. Power of obsidian, *why*?

The tightening of my throat stung. "Oh," I said, trying to hide the tremor taking my voice. Maybe it was innocent. I was still pissed and hurt and any number of other things, but there was a simple explanation. Wraith take me, there'd better be! "Are you looking to get a tattoo or something?" Another one in some other private place she wanted my Alpha to see?

She shook her head. "No, not yet. I was just helping Kane with something."

My hands fisted, nails digging painfully into my palms. I opened my mouth to ask her what the iron fires that something was when Mason appeared at my side.

"Hey," he said. Sweat slicked his hairline and tracked over his temples. His glasses glided down, and he pushed them back up. He tipped his chin. "Are you ready?"

No. I wanted to harass Whitney with questions until I figured out what the shit was going on. I didn't wanna say that final goodbye to Sierra. To take my place before the Coven. But ready or not, time was up.

I rubbed my trembling hands over the front of my thighs and lied, "I'm ready."

Whitney gave us a nod, excused herself, and headed for her seat in the front row. Mason pivoted, aiming for the stage, and I fell in beside him. Tugging one of my cap-style sleeves, a wave of dizziness took me, and I stumbled.

He took my elbow, steadying me. "Hey, you okay?"

"I'm fine," I said, low.

His stare tracked over me, but his eyes stayed focused, so at least he didn't read me. Guiding me up the stairs, he added, "You're pale, Briar."

Not a shock, considering.

"If this is too much, you don't have to do it."

But I did. I'd accepted the position as Second, which meant I had responsibilities. And Sierra's dirge was certainly not the place to start shirking them. I'd deal with my own crap, but that was a later problem.

My nod was small. "I can do it." And I could, because the Coven needed it. Needed that stability only Mason and I could provide. The assurance that things were in hand. They unquestionably weren't, seeing I had not one clue what I was doing, but there was no other choice.

My gaze locked on the casket, the ache in my heart familiar—one I'd felt before, for my father. His dirge was smaller, not nearly so grand—according to mom, anyway. My ass hadn't been Coven yet, so I wasn't permitted to attend. And it stung to not have that send off. That closure.

Mason released me and strode to center stage. I closed in, then, unsure what to do with my hands, linked them before me while I stared out into that sea of solemn faces.

Adjusting his suit's lapels, he stepped up to the microphone at stage left. "Thank you all for coming. Briar and I are grateful for your presence." I offered a tight smile.

"Sierra guided the Northern Coven for ten years. Some of the most prosperous it's ever seen. Many of us earned our obsidians under her rule, but all of us grew with her. Revered her. Loved her."

His voice hitched. He glanced my way, eyes bloodshot and glassy.

My chest constricted. He'd been Sierra's Second. Worked close and learned from her. In the midst of my own chaos, I'd completely overlooked his.

Taking a deep breath, I gave him the minute he needed when I steadied myself, and projected my voice, "She devoted her life to us," I cleared my throat, "and her death. She's in the wraith's arms now, but they need our light to find their way, because the Iron Hells await."

Mason sniffed, smoothed the length of his tie, offered me an appreciative nod, then resumed. "Let's guide her home."

The wraith had taken Sierra's soul the night she'd died, which meant the Rite was ceremonial. It offered an end. A finality. A goodbye.

Shuffling sounded when every arm was raised, and hands sealed over their rings. I turned inward, pulling on my strength.

A low wave of heat simmered around the room, followed by a soft emerald-colored light. It started small as each magi's power unfurled, moving like thin wisps of smoke while they coalesced. That light grew deeper, vaster, so immense, it cloaked the room before it climbed, climbed, climbed.

My gaze landed on Whitney, whose arms stayed by her sides, seeing she wasn't one of ours, wasn't linked to our Coven's strength. But just the sight of her had my bitterness rolling in again.

The power that surged around me—*through* me—was so overwhelming, I fought to hold my feet. We were separate and one. Small streams flowing to a limitless ocean.

It was hot and cold, push and pull, give and take. It filled my soul and stole my breath. It was nothing and everything. It was like never I'd ever felt. It welled inside of me, and welled, and welled.

The massive crystal chandeliers overhead shook and clanked. Dust fell from the ceiling and walls. My obsidian seared my skin. *Sage, was it supposed to hurt?*

A loud thunder boomed through the room, knocking everyone back. Gasps and cries pierced the chaos as we collapsed in unison, the sounds reverberating against the walls.

My shoulders heaved as steam rose from my ring—and no one else's. I didn't know what the hells it meant, but the last thing I wanted was any kind of attention.

I lowered my arm.

Everyone peered around, brows furrowed.

Mason blinked hard before he rose and turned my way. "You okay?"

I inclined my head. Didn't know if it was true, but at least it was an answer. He offered me a hand and I awkwardly took it with my *non*-smoldering one.

"I take it that's not normal?" I asked, words tremulous. And I thanked the wraith herself it wasn't even close to out of place in that moment.

"No, it's not." He swallowed, Adam's apple dipping low when he faced the room again. His mouth opened to speak.

The clunk of the auditorium doors opening echoed through the space, followed by a silence so absolute, my ears rang. Every gaze was fixed on the entrance.

Low mutters of conversation rippled through the room as Jared's wife, Piper, shuffled inside, and the sight of her made every hair on the back of my neck stand on end.

Her gaze darted around like she didn't know if she was welcome. And honestly, I was trying to figure that out myself. She *was* Coven, so there was no issue on that front, but considering what her husband had done, that he'd taken Mason and I, tried to kill us…

Images flashed through my head. Isaac. Jared. Sierra's body. The fire. Some were clear, others hazy. The harder I tried latching onto them, the more they slipped away. Why couldn't I remember? Get a clear picture?

My blood ran cold, because there was only one answer to that.

Isaac.

Piper's eyes met mine before she shuffled deeper in, her stride uneven. She whirled a strand of her purple hair about a finger when she settled into an open seat about halfway down.

Mason cleared his throat. "If, uh— If everyone's alright, we'll resume."

A cascade of muted and out of sync yeses filled the room.

He straightened his tie again then gestured to that coffin and instructed, "Please, say what you must as you touch the fire of her life one last time."

The staccato pound of feet carried when, row by row, the Coven approached. Mason and I led, followed by Whitney and the rest. The line created a serpentine trail around the space, winding about the distant rows to make room while hand after hand passed through that black flame as each magi spoke their words.

Mason fell into conversation with Whitney, while I moved off to the side. Away. 'Cause the last thing I wanted—

"Briar," a meek voice said from my right.

I peered that way, my brain stutter-stepping when I found Piper standing less than three feet away. My throat seized and I fought not to amble back.

"Can—" She worried the bow on the cuff of her dress. "Can we talk?"

She's not Jared. She's not Jared. I repeated it like a damn mantra because I needed something to steady the erratic thump of my heart. "*So* not an appropriate time, Piper."

"Please." She clasped her hands before her, eyes wide and desperate. "It's important."

I folded my arms over my chest. "What's this about?"

She dug the toe of her shoe into the floor, gaze flicking around before she pitched her voice low. "I wondered if you could do a reading for me?"

My head jerked back, any trepidation long gone, replaced by a glower of the 'are you freaking kidding me?' variety. "You want a reading *now*?"

"I just—" She dragged her lip through her teeth. "I hate to do this here, but you don't work at No Man's Land anymore and I couldn't find you." She peered around again. "I have something important you should see."

Hard pass. I sliced my hand to the side. "We're done here." I was tired and hurt—Whitney sashayed past—and so unfathomably confused. I needed answers. Needed to call my Alpha so I could make sure he was okay before I bit his ass and got them.

Gripping my wrist, Piper begged. "Please!" At my scowl, she jerked her hand back and her shoulders fell. "I'm sorry." Her eyes turned bloodshot. She sniffed and twisted her obsidian around her finger in a frantic loop. "It's just . . . after Jared, no one trusts me anymore. But I promise, I have something you *really* need to know."

I exhaled good and slow. I was punishing her for her husband's crimes. A man who'd snuck around behind her back so he could screw anything with a pulse—a man *I'd* inadvertently helped do it. He might've been a cheating, murderous piece of trash, and she might've been daft enough to hitch her wagon to his horse, but she wasn't him. And she was every bit his victim.

Shaking out my shoulders, I gentled my voice. "Tell me then."

"I can't. I— I have to *show* you."

"Why?"

"I saw something." She stared down at her feet. "At the Recovery Center."

The hairs on the back of my neck stood on end until realization struck like lightning and my vertebrae locked straight. The missing serums! It was my turn to grab her. "What do you know?"

"It's better if you look."

I worried my tongue between my teeth and gripped my obsidian tight. Was she too afraid to speak the name? Was the person there? "Where should I start?"

"Two hours ago."

A knot twisted my stomach so tight, bile kissed the back of my throat. My hands trembled, and I clenched my fists to control them. Releasing a deep exhale, I drew on my power, let my eyes go unfocused, and homed in on her six o'clock sunset marker.

A chemical scent hit me first, like a sharp and acrid wall. Piper stood in front of a dust-coated mirror and a squeaky squeal pierced the aura as she scrubbed her hand across it.

There was a whimpering sound. A woman.

"Briiiiiiiiaaaaaaarrr."

That voice. I knew that voice. No. It couldn't be.

Piper's face rippled before it melted, fading into the skin. Her eyes morphed, the color chasing away until that violet shade consumed. Her hair shriveled and dulled to a mottled gray.

The Piper before me tugged a piece of her hair, twirling it around a finger. My attention locked on that hand and the scar there—a scar the shape of my teeth. *My* teeth. Not the real Piper. A changeling. *Isaac!*

No. Isaac was supposed to be dead. *He was supposed to be dead!*

Inside the memory, Isaac leaned into the mirror and a malevolent smile that was more animal than man stretched across his face. "I'm so happy to see you again, Briar."

Chapter Five

My adrenaline spiked, heart pounding in my ears. My gaze darted around. I had to warn Mason. Warn everyone! And I needed to run before Isaac said anything else. Before his walls sealed in around me. Before he used the only thing he needed to compel me. His voice.

My feet pressed into the floor, legs tensing as I readied to bolt. "Mason, ru—"

"You will not run or give me away, Briar," memory Isaac said, that stare was fixed on himself in the mirror. On me.

No. *No. No!*

A wave of dizziness swept over me while the walls of his compulsion closed in. I couldn't breathe. I couldn't think past the terror barreling through my soul. I tried to suck in a harsh breath, but no noise followed. My chest moved in an easy, soundless cadence, the complete antithesis of the scream that echoed off the bones of my skull.

Mason's stare snapped my way, brow furrowing while every joint in my body seized, jaw locking tight at the order. The Coven milled about, wiping tears and comforting one another. They needed to know. Needed to run. Needed to call for help so my Alpha could gut Isaac where he stood.

"Briar?" Mason said.

Sweat slicked my spine. *Kane.* I needed him, because whatever Isaac was about to do . . .

Blood thrashed in my ears while tears blurred my vision. Tears that, considering the setting, wouldn't draw attention.

I'd been such an idiot letting myself believe Isaac was dead. I'd been so desperate for it, I'd lulled myself into accepting the lie. There'd been no body, for sage's sake. But Isaac was a rat, slipping through cracks to make his escape.

A soft whimpering sounded in the memory again. Isaac brandished a knife and with great precision, crouched to where Piper lay, her stringy, purple hair fanned out around her.

The room was a cold and utilitarian-style basement. Unfamiliar, because he was hiding. Always hiding.

"I'll be needing your assistance, Briar," Isaac said.

The Piper-Isaac offered my hand a brief squeeze before she released, like she comforted me. Like she cared. My blood ran cold.

Isaac set the iron blade to Piper's chest and her skin hissed and sizzled from the contact. The scent of burnt flesh filled the aura. A tear slipped down her cheek as she stared skyward, eyes fixed, wide, and wild.

"Be still now," he ordered her before his voice brightened, "And be sure to tell your husband I said hello." He drove the dagger deep. Blood spurted from her mouth, poured over her torso. She didn't fight. Didn't move.

My stomach rolled and I fought to hold its contents when they begged to escape.

Piper fell limp. Her eyes were lifeless, a milky cast replacing the pupil. A gaping hole sat open in her chest. Blood stained her skin and clothes. So much blood.

Isaac wiped the knife against his pant leg as he pushed up. "Shield this conversation between you and I, Briar." His stare landed in the mirror as he ran a hand through his hair, raking it back, and tinging the strands red. "You can leave the aura now."

I did as he said, then trembled violently as I drew on every ounce of goddamn power I had to fight against the compulsion, to lunge across the barely-there space between us and scratch his throat out, but just like every time before, it didn't work.

A small hum of sad laughter rippled through the magi as the first began to leave, streaming out of the auditorium, completely oblivious to the danger that breathed.

My pulse pounded like a stampede in my head. "Isaac, please. Don't do this."

The laugh that broke from him via Piper's lips was so dark, it shadowed the room. "You don't even know what I want, yet."

Yet. The word was a ticking bomb that counted down my freedom. My gaze darted to Mason.

Isaac followed my line of sight. "You should invite him to join us. I'll be requiring him for what's to come."

Not an order, so like the hells I'd comply—

"Now, Briar."

My chest heaved. I moved, rigid, when I found Mason and waved him over.

His brow furrowed, attention roving between me and the Piper-faced-Isaac before me, then back. He excused himself from Whitney and strode to my side. I expanded the cocoon around our conversation, hating myself as I pulled him in.

He wicked a bead of sweat from his forehead as his glasses slid further down his nose. Straightening, he pulled back his shoulders, authoritative. "What's going on?"

"I'm so glad you're here, Mason," Isaac said, using his own voice—a wildly terrifying sight paired with Piper's face.

Mason staggered back. "Iron Hells!"

Isaac raised a hand. "Don't bother calling for help, Briar already tried that."

Wraith take me. "Just stop, Isaac. Lucas is good. He's healthy, finally getting his life back. Leave him alone. Let us be. *Please!*"

The shake of his head was slow, his sigh heavy, like some disappointed parent. "I'm his father, Briar. I can't simply abandon him."

"You already did."

"Tsk. Tsk. Just because your father wasn't there, doesn't mean every man leaves his children. Some of us are made of more. Not Kane, of course." He crossed his Piper-shaped arms over his chest. "If only he'd been stronger, he could've protected *your* child. But he's weak, just like you, and your mother, and all the rest. Weak, and pathetic, and mine."

The rustle of bodies moved past, giving us a wide berth.

My body heated when I snarled, "Why don't we tell Kane what you've been up to, then? See just how *weak* he is."

He bared his teeth in a grin. "I'd love to. I suppose it's too bad he's been so busy lately, isn't it?"

The dread that locked down my rib cage made it hard to breathe. "What did you do?"

"Your wolf has made accessing you quite difficult." He flicked Piper's hair over his shoulder. "I needed him out of the way."

"What. Did. You. *Do*?"

"You're asking the wrong question, Briar. It's not what I did that matters. It's what I'm about to do."

Ice cut through my veins. It slowed my heart to a stop when I swallowed around the dryness in my throat.

Mason shook so hard, his hair vibrated around his glasses. "What are you about to do?"

"I thought you'd never ask." Isaac grinned, words light. "Sierra shared some things before I removed her still-beating heart, you see."

I flinched.

He advanced and set a palm over my shoulder like he cared. Like he consoled me. He was close . . . Close enough for me to do violence. Gouge his eyes out, kick him and then kick him again. Keep kicking until he was broken and bleeding—until he stopped moving. But that wasn't possible because *I was frozen*.

"She didn't perform well under torture. Tried to save herself. Divulged everything she'd been up to, but—as you both know—I'm singular in my focus. Her death was useful."

Wait, everything she'd been up to? Power of obsidian, no.

Mason paled beyond the stain of death.

The line of magi to say goodbye to Sierra grew shorter. The hall growing emptier.

Isaac's grip on me locked down, fingers digging painfully deep. "I admire Sierra's ambitions. And I mean to pick up where she left off." When next he spoke, the sharpness in his words cut to my soul's quick. "I want the deal she intended to broker; use her work to tap into that human market."

Oh, sweet sage. Isaac working with the humans, that couldn't happen. He'd bring us to war. Since gutting him wasn't an option, information was my tool. I needed more. Needed everything he had. And if I'd sussed out anything about him since learning his truth, it was that the asshole loved to talk.

My hands clenched into fists, nails cutting into my palms. "What's so special about the human market?"

"Money, and allegiance, dear stepdaughter." He canted his head. "If I'm the one to offer the weapon that levels the playing field between our species, then by default, I should sway them to my loyalty."

"They already have weapons." Big, military grade iron ones pointed straight at our preternatural heads.

"That they do, but the beasts of Cambria are not the only danger in this world."

No, we weren't. The wraiths, demons, fae, and other unknowns beyond the Talisian Sea were there, but still . . . "What's that got to do with anything?"

"You didn't know?" he taunted. "Your Coven Leader suspected Ithica would ultimately cower, since coming for us would only put a target on *their* backs."

My brow slammed down, 'cause the entire damn purpose of her brokering that backdoor deal had been to *stop* Ithica's attack. And she suddenly thought they wouldn't come? No. That wasn't right. She had to believe it on some level. Kane would've scented it otherwise.

My shoulders fell when realization hit like a shovel, because she had believed it. She'd just used us to shield Cambria while she got busy manufacturing serums to corner that secondary human market. Used us to hedge her goddamn bets.

Piper-Isaac's heels clicked when he shifted. "I'll give her credit. She created a perfect binding solution. All I need is the specific mutations for each species, and I can tailor it." He flicked his wrist through the air. "Would they prefer wolf powers? Shadow walker? A specific magi skill? It's quite genius, really."

He'd actually seen them. Worked with them. My stomach dropped. "*You* stole the serums." It'd be easy enough, seeing he could slip into a second skin and just waltz on in.

He set his free hand to his chest. "Of course, I did. I'm a chemist, Briar. How else am I to recreate her work if I haven't first studied it?" His mouth thinned. "I'd never destroy my lab without a plan."

A plan? This was far past a plan. 'Cause if he had the humans in his pocket, he had more than toys to play with, he had a goddamn army. One with our stolen powers.

"For now," he said, "Mason will search for any additional information Sierra might've had on her buyer. And Briar will assist me in this transaction."

My head snapped back. "What?"

"For some asinine reason I will never understand, Sierra spoke highly of you to her associate. She expects you in your former Coven Leader's stead. And when we meet, you will convince her to work with us."

Me? I barked a laugh so bitter, it was a wonder he didn't taste it. "Why are you doing this?"

"Because I dream big, Briar."

Dream big? Dream *big*? He'd destroyed Lucas, took my mother. Kane. Our goddamn child! "You've taken *everything* from me!"

"Oh, no. Not everything." He tapped a finger over his wrist. "Not yet."

My breath broke from me in pants. "Kane will slaughter you."

His laugh was sharp when it scraped over my flesh. "He'll have to find me first. But very soon, I think his focus will be somewhere else." He threaded his fingers, linking his hands before him. "You're integral to what's coming. For this plan to work, I'll need you away from your wolf."

The air left my lungs, and I fought not to collapse. "Don't, Isaac. You can't take him from me." Not again.

He shook his head. "He'll ask too many questions, Briar. And they'll be questions you can't answer. I can't have Kane sniffing around to ruin things." He gripped my wrist as a venomous grin took his lips. "But we both know Kane won't believe things between you are in trouble unless you lay some groundwork first."

My heart raced, beating against my chest. "Groundwork?"

"I've already helped you by constantly pulling him away, as if you aren't his priority," he said like he'd given me some gift. "Now it's your turn. I want you to cause trouble with Kane. Pick a fight, or two, or ten. Whatever it takes for you to convince him."

My legs buckled and I collapsed, landing hard on my knees.

Every remaining eye in the room snapped our way. Hands rose to hearts. People whispered. Doubtless, they thought it grief . . . and on that, they weren't wrong.

Mason advanced and rested a hand over my shoulder. "You don't need her, Isaac. I can broker the deal. Use me."

"That's where you're wrong." He eyed me. "In Sierra's absence, this human *insists* on Briar's presence."

My chest caved.

Isaac stroked his chin, almost assessing when he found Mason. Schemes danced in the depths of that stare. "Since you're so eager to help, you can start by taking Briar home."

Mason's eyes went wide.

Let him take me home? Sage, it'd be like shoving a hot iron in Kane's heart. I couldn't do it. My teeth ground as I forced myself to my feet and squared myself to Isaac. "I won't."

"Oh, yes," he said, gaze spearing mine. "You will."

The power of the compulsion stole my breath when his command pressed in.

No. Please. *No!*

He gave my arm a gentle pat. "I understand this is distressing, but the worst will be over soon." He leaned close and my world crumbled to pieces as he whispered in my ear, "Oh, and, Briar, dear, you might want to brace."

Chapter Six

The auditorium was empty, the Coven and Isaac long since gone. Mason and I left, walking down the marble hallway toward the exit. Our footsteps echoed off the walls as I stared down at the text on my screen.

Kane: I'm on my way.

I hadn't called him like I'd said. Turned out, I hadn't needed to. Tears blurred my sight, searing my skin while they tracked down my cheeks and I struggled to keep my feet.

I shook my head. "I can't do this, Mason."

His breath exploded from him in shallow bursts. Sweat slicked his forehead, beading in the curve of his temple. His glasses fogged as he shoved them up his face once. Twice. "I'm sorry, Briar."

We closed in on those glass doors and every step closer was a countdown. "I can't help Isaac. Not again. With both of us, he's got the Coven. We've gotta figure a way outta this."

Isaac's words consumed me, running like a tickertape on loop through my head. *Make it believable. Make it believable. Make it believable.* But I loved Kane with all I was. That wolf consumed me. Convincing him I didn't want him . . . Sage, there was one thing that might work—one I'd already planned to address, but not like this.

I clutched my chest and forced myself to breathe.

"So, what do we do?" Mason asked, voice shaky, eyes wide as he reached for the door. Not that I blamed him seeing the preternatural bomb we were about to lob.

That countdown ended. The clock chimed. I wanted a plan—*needed* one—but time was up. "Just, let me handle Kane."

He inclined his head and pushed the entrance wide. A knot twisted in my chest that pulled so taut, it made it hard to breathe. I crossed outside.

The rain fell, fast and heavy, fitting for my desolate mood.

An ebony skinned wolf stood to the right under the awning there. Cassian. Outside Joaquin, he was one of Kane's strongest, most trusted. Hence the guard position. He eyed me, Mason behind me, then me again.

My stomach twisted for an entirely different reason. Kane. His challenge. We were still breathing, but that didn't mean he was alright.

"Go get your car," I told Mason, chest tightening as I braced. "I'll be there in a minute."

He inclined his head, feet thumping over the concrete as he beat it outta there.

I swallowed around my dry mouth, and it cut like razor blades in my throat. Dread clamped down, squeezing the air from my lungs when I found Cassian. "Where's Kane?"

He raised his hands. "Almost here. Alpha's good though, and so's Theo."

Kane was alright. Thank sage, he was alright. Wait . . . My head snapped back, eyes narrowing on him so tight, they muddied my sight. What the actual hells? "*Theo?*"

His thick, black brows dropped, the line between them creasing deep.

My heart rate kicked up. Water rolled from my hair and face like a torrent. I blinked hard and understanding struck. Kane had been cagey when I'd asked who'd issued the challenge. Someone mid-Pack. Someone he hadn't wanted to lose control with. Someone he hadn't wanted to hurt.

"*Theo* issued the challenge?" I said, 'cause I needed to hear it. Needed all the truths on the table.

Cassian scratched his neck, glanced over his shoulder, then back to me like he wanted to be anywhere else. He inclined his head.

And Isaac had sent him—Kane's goddamn cousin—to distract my Alpha.

I huffed a broken laugh. Shame, potent and hot at what I was about to do, seared my veins and I looked away. Again, and again and again, Isaac won. And I needed to fucking stop it.

A sharp, white sedan pulled up to the nearby curb, Mason behind the wheel. A second later, another vehicle crested the horizon. A truck. Lights aimed my way—blinding as they stole my ability to see. Its tires crunched against the asphalt when it veered toward the Grand Hall.

I pivoted, agony piercing my heart when I aimed for Mason's car.

"Briar?" Cassian called.

"I'll meet Kane at home," I threw over my shoulder.

Twenty-six agonizing steps later, I threw Mason's passenger door open and scrambled inside. He was pale, his breathing was erratic. His body trembled so wildly, it took three attempts to put his car in gear.

His wipers snapped back and forth at full speed, giving me a clear line of sight when Kane's truck whipped up to the curb, tires shrieking as he slammed to a halt. His voltaic eyes were on me when he exploded out and aimed our way.

"Bry!" he roared, but there was an agony there. A hurt and a confusion. One that broke me.

"Drive," I told Mason, violently tearing my hands through my hair. Loosing an explosive exhale, I screamed, "Just drive. Just drive. *Just fucking drive!*"

A second later, Mason hit the gas.

***

"He's gonna kill me, Briar," Mason said as we closed in on Kane's house—*our* house. But for how much longer, I had no clue.

Sage, the thought had me doubling over. I gripped my chest, trying to catch my breath.

But Mason wasn't wrong. His evisceration certainly was a viable option, because Kane *would* know I was coming, and I had not one doubt he'd be waiting.

The car smelled heavy with the cloying scent of grief . . . and fear. Whether it was mine or Mason's, I couldn't tell.

My watch said we'd been gone an hour, but time had blurred. It moved fast and slow as we took turn after turn, weaving randomly through the streets of the neutral grounds. The hum of the city and buzzing neon lights bombarded my already cluttered brain. But I'd needed the distance to think, while Mason'd just been aiming to extend the clock on his life.

Kane had called again and again. I hadn't answered. Couldn't. Because what the hells was I supposed to say?

I'd tried to gather my torrential thoughts, but it was like catching moonlight. Every time I reached for them, they slipped through my fingers.

"Just drop me at the end of the driveway," I told Mason.

He nodded, because really, the more distance between him and my Alpha, the better. Veering to the side of the road, he slowed, the crunch of his tires over the asphalt growing louder.

Kane sat on the top step of the porch, elbows on his knees, hands hung. His downcast stare lifted then slid from Mason to me. Rolling his shoulders, he rose.

I worried my lip, bracing as I opened my door and climbed free. "Just go," I told Mason, then closed him in and aimed for the house and my fate.

Mason punched the gas, kicking up gravel as he fled.

Kane's jaw ground, the muscles and veins along his neck stark against his skin as he breathed deep, scenting me.

I pulled a ragged breath, bracing as Isaac's order locked my consciousness down. I threw my hand up. "No closer, Kane."

He crushed his eyes closed, then reopened them like he wasn't sure he'd heard me right. He stopped dead, brow sinking low. "The Iron fucking Hells going on?"

Obsidian, he'd faced off against his cousin. I wanted to ask if he was okay. If Theo was. But instead, I methodically treaded the minefield Isaac had lobbed me into, because I couldn't say anything I didn't believe if I didn't want my wolf to scent it.

So, I offered the only truth I had—one that broke my heart and had those tears sliding free again. "You lied to me."

My Alpha inhaled good and slow, fists clenching by his sides as if he tried to calm himself . . . or keep control. "I'm gonna need more than that, Bry." He advanced a step, that molten stare sparked, then ignited, blazing like the moon. He stretched his neck, hands flexing at his sides. "Start talking."

I squared myself to him, voice thick with pain and rage and a thousand other emotions too chaotic to pin down when I hissed, "*Whitney*."

He turned to stone. His throat dipped.

His silence was answer enough. And, sage, it hurt on so many levels because Isaac was in control. Because I didn't want to do this. And because Kane *had* lied.

His next step was measured, cautious, like I was a skittish animal he tried not to scare off. "Bry—"

That compulsion kicked in again, and I veered, stalking past him toward the house. My exhale shuddered through me, my legs tired and unsteady.

He pivoted, tight on my heels, the pound of his heavy footfalls sounding out as he hunted me. "Is this how you deal with shit now? Taking off with your goddamn ex?"

No. That was unequivocally Isaac's, and so was my next response. "That alone time with yours yesterday seemed to do *wonders* for you."

His expression fell.

I stormed ahead, bursting through the front door, then aimed for the stairs.

"Iron Hells, Bry. Fucking talk to me."

I glared at him over my shoulder. "You sure you wouldn't feel better talking to Whitney?"

"Shit! Just wait." He lunged forward and latched onto my wrist, forcing me to face him. His broad, dense body towering over me. Those silver topaz eyes wild.

Jerking from his hold, I stepped back, fully aware it was only because he let me. Hating that Isaac forced this—capitalized on it. And hating that it was real.

Kane's arms fell heavy by his sides. "I should've said something."

"Yeah," I said, the word cold. "You really should have."

"There's nothing between Whitney and me."

"Oh," I set a palm to my chest. "And, what, you expect I should just take your word on that now?"

His head lowered when he stared at me through his brow. "What's that supposed to mean?"

"You said she's your past, and then you, what? Sneak off to meet with her? Shadow and sage, she came to see you yesterday. Says she sees you *often*. You hid that from me, Kane. All of it!"

He cursed, bowed his head and clenched his fists. "There's a reason, Bry. I just . . . shit. I didn't want you to read into it."

"Oh, yes," I threw my arms up, "'cause hiding it from me was an A-plus strategy."

"I know. It was goddamn stupid. I fucked up." He scrubbed the back of his neck, expression desolate. "I'm so fucking sorry."

"You told me you had stuff to do at the shop yesterday." I folded my arms over my chest to control their shake. "Was it her?"

He cursed, but didn't deny it.

My stomach plummeted. The pain that stabbed my chest hit on a level so deep, it stole my breath. "You're making up reasons to get away from me now? To see another fucking woman?" A sob broke from my chest, and I gripped the rail to hold myself steady. "Did she get another tattoo? Huh? Did you put it somewhere *special*?"

His Adam's apple dipped low when he swallowed hard. "It's not what it looks like, Bry. I swear. I'd *never* fucking do that to you."

A desperate, broken sound escaped me. "But you did, Kane." My vision blurred when a new well of tears surfaced. "You knew I was home, waiting for you, begging for your goddamn time while you were off meeting with *her*. A woman you used to fuck!" My voice quavered when I finished, "You knew it would hurt me. It's why you hid it, right? Because you knew how I'd feel. You knew. You knew! *You fucking knew!*" Those tears poured free.

He crushed his eyes closed. Sagging forward, he dragged his hands through his hair, stretching the skin of his forehead. "Bry—"

"It's because you know I can't scent it, right?" I uttered. "A lie."

His eyes snapped open, flaring wide. "No. Shadowed fucking moon, just listen."

Questions. Questions weren't statements. Questions couldn't be lies. It was like the compulsion had a voice of its own when I pushed on, pressing its advantage. "Didn't count on me talking to her, did you?"

His shoulders fell.

"DID YOU?"

"No," he said, voice low.

The answer cut to my quick, hitting a place and pain I hadn't felt since he'd left me four years before. "So you just leveraged that fact?"

He jerked his head back. "Leveraged?"

"Yeah, leveraged! It's why you didn't tell me about Theo, isn't it? Just someone mid-level in the Pack? That's what you said, wasn't it? That's who you are now?"

He cursed, then cursed again. "I'm so goddamn sorry, Bry. I didn't tell you because I didn't want you to worry."

I advanced and shoved at his chest. "Worry about you fighting Theo? Worry about you losing control and killing him?" I shoved him again. "Or worry about you *fucking your ex*?"

His eyes flashed, going feral. "Just listen. I'd never—"

"You talk out both sides of your mouth, Kane. Don't tell me I matter then hide *everything* from me."

He reached for me, calloused hands sealing around my arms. "Iron fires, please, let me explain."

I wanted him to. Wraith take me, I wanted to know what'd driven him to that. Why he'd been with her. What'd happened between them. *Needed* a reason that didn't claw my heart to shreds. Something that fit with the wolf I knew—the wolf I loved. The mated were who'd given me his life in every way when he claimed me. Because without those answers, I was drowning in a sea of agony.

But the compulsion couldn't give him that chance. Couldn't let him offer a reason that made sense. Its power welled in my chest, and in the scheme of Isaac's order, Kane was exactly where I needed him.

Unbidden, I swung my blow. "Why? So, you can betray me *again*? Tell me what I wanna hear?" I hiccupped another sob. "You tricked me, Kane. Used my weakness to your advantage so you could see her. *Another woman*." My heart shattered and I wrapped my arms around myself to hold those pieces together. "You think I want your excuses? How can I trust them? Shadow and sage, what else are you hiding?"

"Nothing, Bry. I swear it," he said, chest heaving on his brutal breaths.

"I deserve better." I shook my head and edged back. "I can't talk to you right now." A truth from the compulsion. I gripped that railing tighter, because my legs were weak, and wraith knew I needed the support. "I'll take my old room."

"Iron Hells, Bry. No." His stare tracked around like he looked for answers. A solution. Something. "Don't leave. We gotta fucking sort this."

"You had your chance to do that, Kane, but, instead, you lied." I swayed, hating that this was real. And hating that I couldn't stop it. "Just . . . leave me alone." Giving him my back, I dragged myself up the stairs, and down the hall until I sealed myself in that desolate and soul-breaking spare room. Staggering forward, I collapsed onto the bed, rolled to my side, and crushed my knees to my chest.

My heart plummeted and my face fell slack. Tears streamed. Hard and fast and so filled with anguish, they were heavy against my skin. They slipped from my cheeks and onto the bed, staining the pillow. My body sagged and the sob that burst from me ripped at my soul.

This couldn't be my life. I wouldn't allow it. I couldn't sit by. Had to do something. Had to act before the quicksand Isaac tossed me in swallowed me whole.

As soon as I could see, I'd text Theo and Lisa and Mason . . . we'd figure this out. We had to. There was no other choice. But in the meantime, I tucked my chin to my chest, and forced myself to breathe as the agony took me.

Chapter Seven

Lisa and I weaved past a cluster of hacking humans as we closed in on the Recovery Center. The grass lining the RC's perimeter was freshly mowed, the scent carrying on the air—along with the odd green blade that fumbled across the concrete. The only place in Cambria that was manicured, where nature was controlled. And I hated it.

"Kane might've been talking to Whitney, and, yeah, it looks all kinds of shady, but it doesn't fit, chickie. Not with the way that wolf looks at you." She shook her head. "There's no one else."

Once some of the previous night's emotional-filled fog had cleared, I'd come to the same conclusion. But Lis was a straight shooter . . . like the "right through your tattered heart with the painful truth" kinda straight. So hearing it from her was the backup I needed.

I hooked my key ring over my index finger and stared down at the stone-carved wolf there. When I'd shown it to my Alpha weeks ago, he loosed an appreciative growl, then bent me over the hood of his truck to show me just how much he liked it.

Lisa adjusted her polka-dot dress shirt and combed her fingers through her frazzled hair. "How's he doing?"

"He was waiting for me when I got up," I said, fighting back the tears that just wouldn't goddamn stop. "I don't think he slept." Not that I had, at all. I'd spent the night crying and raging and crying some more, torn between my writhing hatred of Isaac, and my complete and utter confusion over Kane.

Eventually, I'd come to reason, at least on my Alpha's front. He was a good man—the best. He had a purpose for what he'd done with Whitney. He had to. I couldn't handle anything else.

Lisa winced. "What'd he say?"

"That he loves me. He gets why I'm mad. Knows he hurt me and he's sorry, that he'll talk as soon as I'm ready." And I was ready. So damn ready, but Isaac's leash pulled taut around my neck, doing its job when it dragged me outta the house. Away from Kane, just like Isaac wanted. A sob escaped me. "I couldn't even answer. Just walked out."

The sight of him as I left, shoulders hung, expression caved, looking utterly gutted . . . it gutted *me*.

She set her head on my shoulder, then wrapped an arm around me and squeezed tight like she tried to hold me together. "I'm so sorry, chickie."

I sniffed and hiccupped, swiping at the moisture that stained my cheeks. "Sage, he was just so empty."

A clunk sounded to my left. The hairs on the back of my neck stood on end. Victor Davis, the South Cambrian Alpha and Isaac's well-trained mutt, strolled down the path toward us. His dress shoes clicked against the polished concrete. His maroon suit had a crossed, light pink plaid pattern over its entirety and was paired with a matching fedora. It was veneer he failed to execute. Like he wanted it to look expensive but couldn't quite manage. A tacky knockoff. He was strong, hadn't climbed the Pack hierarchy by accident. But he wasn't Kane strong. He had power, still, power had layers, and his were fragile. Lacking.

His stare locked with mine before he peered down his broad nose at me.

There was something in that expression. An awareness. As if he was in on some secret—and there was only one secret we shared.

Isaac.

I rolled up my very short mental sleeves. "You knew."

His stare flashed.

The warm breeze stole strands of my hair, dancing them across my face.

Was barking at him my smartest move? No. Was it the dumbest thing I'd ever done? Also no. But for some reason I didn't comprehend, I couldn't stop myself. That new obsidian burned against my finger again while a foreign rage settled inside me. It forced my spine to straighten and my nonexistent hackles to rise. It summoned my lips from teeth and begged for violence.

His brow lowered and he blinked before he angled his hat down, shading his eyes.

Pump the brakes, had he just . . . hidden? Not one to quit while I was ahead, I pushed for an answer I'd wanted since I'd realized something was up.

"Why didn't you tell Isaac that Kane could track me through the claiming mark?"

He rolled his shoulders. "It wasn't for your benefit."

Oh, I had unequivocally no delusions on that front. Victor helped Victor. Full stop. Which meant only one thing. "So you're protecting someone." And it couldn't be just anyone. No. This was someone who mattered to *him*.

His nostrils flared.

"We can help each other, Victor."

His shoe clopped as he shifted position. "Who says I need help?"

"You did," my smile was deep, and bizarrely confident, "the second you hid something from your puppet master."

Lisa tensed.

He advanced a menacing step, and my ring burned hotter as I held my ground. Power of obsidian, what the Iron Hells was wrong with me . . . and my survival instincts?

"I help myself," he snarled. "Now leave it the fuck alone." With that, he side-stepped me and stalked away.

I loosed a ragged exhale.

Lisa's eyes were wide on me, which, fair. She blinked in rapid succession. "What the shit, chickie?"

My mouth thinned and I twisted my face in answer, 'cause fucked if I knew. My gaze dropped to my obsidian, and I twisted it around my finger as we crossed inside. First it was my weird power surge at the dirge, then this. It was the new ring. It had to be.

Suddenly starved, I wove her through the magi wing, and she took the place in, a critical eye that bordered on judgmental. Not that I blamed her, seeing the level of wealth there was well past obnoxious.

"What time did Theo say?" she asked.

I checked my watch. "Should be here any second."

"And Mason?"

I shook my head. "Crickets." Not that I blamed him, seeing distance from me *was* the safest strategy for his survival.

Stepping up to Sierra's old office, I brandished my keycard. The machine beeped, green light flashing before I pushed the door open.

"What exactly are we looking for here?" Lisa asked as she scanned the ebony-stained, intricately carved bookcase on the far wall. Skulls with jaws wide and impossibly long incisors dotted the corners. Clawed wolf hands formed the shelves, while large chunks of obsidian acted as the dividers.

A massive black and rusted cauldron made from some non-iron related metal sat in the corner, ash from sage only knew how many years of incense burnings filled its hollows. The air was thick with a smoky vanilla scent.

The place was a gothic dream.

Aiming for the desk at the head of the room, I said, "Anything connected to this deal or her research."

She tucked several strands of hair behind her ears. "You think she'd keep it here?"

"She and Mason were the only two with access to this place." I shrugged. "Doesn't hurt to check."

Her brow furrowed. "He didn't already look?"

I dragged the top drawer open. "Yeah, but it was before he knew about the stolen serums."

Plucking a book from the shelf, she flipped through its pages. "So he might've overlooked it."

A knock thumped at the door.

Lisa closed in and popped it open.

"Hey," Theo said as he stalked in, Naomi nipping tight at his heels. Her head was down, shoulders caved. Her eyes didn't lift. Not good for any preternatural, least of all a wolf.

My gaze locked on Theo's in a "*What the hells is she doing here?*" glare.

The dark circles under his eyes were so black, they were practically bruises. He looked tired, the soul-deep, heart sick kind. His smile was forced and tight. "She's one of us."

I sucked in a sharp breath. "Sweet fucking sage," I said, stomach sinking when I found her. "No, Nay. Not you too."

She plunked herself onto the teal velvet, high-backed couch. Grabbing one of the matching throw pillows, she hugged it to her chest and sank deeper into the seat. Her nod was somber. "Yep."

Theo ran his palm over the scarlet damask wallpaper, head moving in an arc as he took in the room. "This place doesn't really fit with the rest of the RC's . . . style."

"No, it doesn't."

Dropping his arm, he set himself down beside his sister.

I moved to the next drawer down and tipped my chin Theo's way. "So, you're alive."

The laugh that tore from his throat was sardonic. "Barely."

My chest constricted. "What happened?" I'd wanted those details from Kane, but, well . . . Isaac.

He cursed, the whites of his eyes going bloodshot before he swallowed hard. "The Pack was calling for me to concede but I couldn't." He dragged his thumb and forefinger over his brows. "Didn't end until he knocked me out." He slumped forward, elbows on his knees, head in his hands. "Any wolf other than Kane and I'd be dead."

Because Kane hadn't climbed the Pack by accident. He was strong in every damn way. Especially his restraint.

"You should've seen Kane's face." Nay shook her head. "He was so gutted."

I had no doubt, considering everyone in his life was turning on him. First Nay, then Theo, and me. Not that Kane hadn't hurt me, because wraith knew, he had. But ditching wasn't how I wanted to handle things.

My tattered heart ached for my Alpha.

Theo stared at the black-stained hardwood and huffed a ragged breath.

I cursed. I hated seeing them like that, a jaded, busted version of themselves. Ironic since it was like looking in a mirror. But focusing on them was easier, 'cause I couldn't look too closely at my own reflection.

What they'd been through, all to distract Kane. Get him away from me so Isaac could sink his hooks in.

Power of obsidian. There was dismal, and then there was us. I flicked the hourglass at the edge of the desk with my nail, the contact making a loud *tink*. "How're you holding up?"

He ticked a finger my way. "I should be asking you that."

"You should," I lifted a shoulder in an attempt at brevity, "but you're kind of a dick, so . . ."

His lip tugged at the corner. "Remind me again why I put up with you?"

I shuffled the ridiculously random contents of the drawer. My brow lowered, gaze fixing on something long and phallic, and battery operated. I shuddered, then returned my attention to Theo. "You're loitering at *my* work. I'm putting up with you, ya smarmy ass."

He set a hand over his chest. "Oh, Theo. You're the kindest, most amazingist friend that ever friended. Thank you for coming to keep my lonely butt company."

Naomi's huffed, the first sign of life I'd seen since she'd arrived.

"Company?" I flicked a hand, gesturing around us. "You're the one whining, Puppy McPupperson. You're keeping me distracted."

"Wow," he deadpanned before annunciating every syllable when he finished, "I'm so glad I came after you *invited* me!"

I forced a grin while Lis grabbed a leather-bound notebook.

"Seriously, though," Naomi asked me, raking a nail along the couch's arm. "How are you?"

My face fell. "Utter shit." I plucked a day planner from the drawer. "You?"

"Shit." She chucked her chin her brother's way. "You?"

Theo gave a thumbs up. "Shit!"

"How's the Pack?" I asked.

"We're, um…" Theo scratched his head. "Kinda on the outs right now."

I propped a hip against the desk and cracked the planner open. "What do you mean?"

Nay set her chin on her knees. "The two of us challenging days apart has them talking. Paints it like we're making some kind of power move or something."

Oof. "How're things with Autumn?"

She shook her head. "She looks at me like I've lost my mind. Doesn't understand why I'd do it, 'specially when it risks both of us."

I mean . . . fair.

"I just don't get it," she said. "Theo could've made that challenge. Why me?"

Not wrong. Isaac definitely didn't need her for that. I stared down at the miniature door decorating a mushroom shaped lamp on the desk's corner and rubbed my temples. "Who better than you two to fuck with Kane." Because Isaac wasn't just strategic, the jackass got his kicks out of the torture. The agony.

"I don't understand why he hasn't gone for Kane directly. Don't get me wrong, I don't want him to. But he's already got you. He *could* get to him."

Lisa's gaze lowered when she leaned a shoulder against the bookcase. "Because he's scared."

Theo's face twisted, his stare incredulous. "You think Isaac's scared?"

"No," I murmured. "He's terrified."

Inclining her head, Lisa flipped a page on that book. "He wouldn't seek this control, wouldn't do any of it, if there wasn't an outcome he feared."

Theo's shoulders rose on a heavy inhale. "Back in that barn, he said he wanted vengeance."

I worried my lip. "Yeah, but I think it's more. I think he's afraid to die." It made sense. He wouldn't be aiming for a genetically modified human army unless he wanted a shield. And he'd only want a shield if he thought there was something to be shielded from.

He picked a piece of lint from his sleeve. "Everyone's afraid to die."

Lisa shook her head. "But he's not everyone."

No, he certainly wasn't.

Naomi's voice grew distant when she caught our train. "Because he's a changeling who escaped the Deep."

"And what does he think's waiting for him in the Iron Hells when he goes back?" Lisa said.

Nay settled her feet on the floor. "He'll go back one way or another someday."

Theo's chin dipped. "I'd say he's aiming for later."

"*Much* later," Lis agreed before her gaze met mine. "And he thinks facing your wolf is his fastest ticket back."

Because my Alpha was. Isaac hadn't gone for Kane years ago. He'd used Ronin to do it. And, still, Kane fought his way through. Ended his former Alpha, and with him, his command. He'd broken loose.

Kane had always been strong. He'd taken Lucas then. Seen Isaac for the coward he was. And Isaac knew that Kane knew what he was. What he *really* was, on every level. Changeling. Pathetic. Weak.

My Alpha was too strong for Isaac to sic his lackeys on. And too smart to hold. If Kane ever suspected what Isaac had done to Lucas—to *me*—there'd be nothing left for the Iron Hells to take.

"What, uh—" Theo dragged a hand over the back of his neck, peered his sister's way, then back to me. "What happened with you and Kane?"

Shadow and sage, the wolves couldn't keep their damn muzzles shut. I sighed. "What'd you hear?"

He shook his head. "Nothing. The whole Pack felt it, though."

My gaze narrowed. "What exactly did you feel?"

"Torment." He hiked his shoulders high in a shrug. "You're the only thing that'd affect him like that."

I clutched my chest. "Isaac happened."

God-fucking-damnit! I wanted to hurt him. To smash something iron over his head and let his wounds bleed out. Slowly. My fist slammed onto the desk, and it shook from the contact.

We were just players on his messed-up chessboard—pieces to be used at his whim. But every game had rules, and in that realm, even pawns had power.

No one would ever fight for me the way my Alpha did. That man was my life. My heart beat for him. He'd already sacrificed everything, suffered and clawed and fought his way back to me. *For* me. He had the scars to prove it.

And it was my turn to fight for him.

At the end of the day, there was only one thing that mattered. My life with Kane. Always him. Always *us*. That wolf was it for me. He, Lucas, and the Pack, *they* were my family. I wouldn't lose them.

My hands rolled into fists. "I can't let Isaac do this." I shook my head and swiped a tear. "I won't."

Theo straightened his spine, head up. Ready. "What do we do?"

"We can't overcome the compulsion," a feral smile split my lips, "so we find a way around it." My spine locked straight when a conversation lurched to the forefront of my mind. One between Kane and I after I'd learned the truth, that he'd been under Ronin's command.

"You cheated the system," I said.

"No, Bry. I worked the system."

Then another conversation, one with his Beta.

"You gotta know the lines so you can dance around them."

Know the lines. The limits. The holes. The weaknesses. *Isaac's* weaknesses. Sage! It was right there. I might not be able to shirk the compulsion, so straight up outing Isaac wasn't on the table, but I wasn't out of options. Me, Theo, Naomi . . . all of us could sure as shit shoot off some flares and pray someone noticed.

My heart rate kicked up, adrenaline pulsing through my veins. It wasn't hope. Hope set expectations. Hope whispered promises. And hope was more than I could bear. No, it was a dark and twisted promise to myself, one eager for vengeance.

Kane had scaled the Pack's hierarchy. One fight at a time, he'd climbed to make his way back to me. My way out wasn't clear. There was no straight path forward. Mine was a labyrinth of commands to navigate.

Isaac always skirted the edge of trouble, hidden in the shadows. I could only hope it was a mistake that ran him headlong into an iron spike. Didn't even need to be *my* iron spike. I wasn't greedy. Hostile and vengeance-filled, sure, but *never* greedy. I'd be more than happy to share in gutting him. It was only fair everyone got their turn.

Lisa's phone rang and she narrowed her eyes. "I'm sorry, chickie," she said as she pulled it out. "I left Harriet in charge at the bar and—"

I waved her off. "It's fine. Answer it."

I needed to think anyway. Come up with a plan. Needed to figure out what each of us offered. Our strengths and Isaac's weaknesses. Figure out how to undermine him. 'Cause I desperately needed to go home and see a were about a wolf.

Lisa crossed the room, then clicked her device. "Hey." Her gaze went wide, face paling while her body froze.

My brow furrowed. "Lis?"

Slowly, her head swiveled my way. "She's here," she said to whoever was on the other end. A pause. "No."

The strain in those words was thick, like she struggled against them, and it set my teeth on edge. Alarm bells blared like a fire brigade.

Lisa ambled closer as if she was pulled by some invisible force and grabbed my elbow. "I'm so sorry, chickie."

My lungs seized when realization struck, and I jolted. Isaac. Shadow and sage, *it was Isaac.*

Theo shoved to his feet, whites of his eyes showing when he mouthed, "*Run!*"

Lisa's gaze went bloodshot and glassy. "I don't have a choice. I'm sorry. *I'm so sorry.*"

I couldn't let him talk. Let him say anything that bound me tighter. Couldn't let him sink me more.

Things flew from the desk, crashing to the floor as I scrambled wildly for the door. Lisa pulled her phone from her ear. I reached for the handle. Close. I was close. I could make it.

She pressed for the speaker.

An invisible vise gripped my spine, and that chain around my neck cinched taut.

"Briiiiiiiiiiiar," Isaac crooned.

Bile climbed the back of my throat as I threw the entrance wide. No. Please! We were just coming up with a fucking plan! PLEASE!

Naomi lunged for the phone, teeth bared like she'd smash it.

Isaac's voice was almost melodic and sweet when he ordered, "Stay put until we're done, and do not hang up on me."

My breath rasped through my lungs when the compulsion took hold and I froze, and seeing he hadn't attached a name to that command, so did everyone else in the room. Sweet sage, no.

His tone darkened. "Tsk, tsk, Briar. You should know better by now."

Sweat slicked Theo's forehead and he glared at that phone like sheer will alone could destroy it.

My teeth gnashed and I whimpered before forcing a feeble scream through them. So damn feeble.

"Enough of that," Isaac said like dealing with me was a chore. The clank of something glass sounded in the background. "I suspect you've sufficiently laid the groundwork with Kane?"

My vision blurred when tears welled to their surface. Don't answer. Don't answer. *Don't answer!* "Yes."

"Excellent!" he replied. "You're going to come to Mason's now. And you're not going to tell anyone about it."

An invisible knife plunged into my heart, and I doubled over. No. I couldn't. Kane. He'd sense where I was. What kind of message would that send?

Isaac was a fake. A fraud. His strength forged on the backs of real power. He wasn't a predator. Predators didn't hide. No. Isaac was prey that mimicked. He hid behind faces and lies to shield himself. Isaac was dangerous, but not Kane dangerous. Isaac needed weapons to make himself strong. But Kane *was* the weapon.

Question was, could I use it? I needed to stop my stepfather. Give him pause. Lob a threat. *Something.* I couldn't tell him Kane would track me through my mark, give away that intel. But seeing my Alpha was a were, there was another way he could find me.

"Kane will scent me, Isaac. He'll follow my trail. He'll come for me."

There was a smile in Isaac's voice that twisted his knife so deep, the damage was irreparable. "Oh, but, Briar dear, I'm counting on it."

***

The drive to Mason's was a clock that ticked a countdown to the end—*my* end. Because once Kane felt where I was through the claiming mark . . .

Tears blurred my sight.

I trembled wildly as I crossed through Mason's gated property inside Northern Coven territory and his house came into view. The place was massive; a three-story, one-way, glass-fronted monstrosity shaped like a box. A series of pristine, off-white concrete slabs comprised the driveway, lined with impeccably kept red and white flowers. The yard was wide, the grass cut where it butted against the forest, secluding him.

Like the RC, it looked modern and sleek and entirely out of place in our overgrown city. And it could've been the Iron Hells themselves for what lurked inside.

The black metal front door swept open. Isaac skulked in the entrance, a bitter, impatient smile twisting his face. "It's good to see you, Briar."

Good to see me leashed and brought to heel.

He waved me to him. "Come quickly, now. The fun is about to begin, and I doubt we'll have much time before trouble arrives."

My heart careened against my ribs when I exited my car and advanced against my will, each step heavy as I shuffled toward the house, then crossed that threshold.

The interior was a monochromatic series of blacks, grays and whites. It was all polished stone, muted furniture and completely, utterly lifeless.

A loud trill filled the room, echoing around that desolate space. My phone. I jerked it free. Kane's name flashed across the screen. A sharp pain lanced my chest, and I clutched it.

"Don't answer that, Briar," Isaac said, sealing the door with a click. Crooking a finger, he aimed for the basement, smile broad—an eager child at show and tell. "Follow me. We have other business to attend."

The metal stairs shrieked when we descended, bowing slightly under our weight.

An iron cage occupied the far corner. My gut clenched at the sight of Ivy huddled against the cement wall at its back. Her semi-translucent flesh was riddled with elongated burns—from the bars, no doubt. She hissed, her crimson gaze wild. Cold. Animal. She was a shadow, but barely a walker. The pieces were there, just not together. Scattered.

My stomach twisted at the sight of Mason slumped against the opposite wall, his head hung. His gaze lifted, his creased eyes filled with an apology. One he didn't owe, because this chaos lay at my stepfather's feet.

There was a shuffle inside the cage as Ivy shifted side to side, limbs on the ground, crouched low. Scuttling like a spider, her intense crimson eyes were on me. But if there was a thought behind them, I couldn't discern it.

To my right sat a chrome shelf filled with row after row of serums—the missing ones from the RC. And wolfsbane. So much damn wolfsbane.

Isaac followed my line of sight. "Ah, yes. I'm wearing it now. But not Mason, of course. I'll be needing his scent nice and fresh."

Of course, 'cause no way Isaac'd risk Kane landing there and scenting *him*.

Pump the brakes. I tensed and my blood ran cold as my venomous glare tracked to my stepfather. "What the hells does that mean, Isaac?"

A smile spread across his face that pulled back from his teeth while he withdrew a syringe filled with something red. "It's time for phase two of this plan, Briar."

An iron dread seared my veins, and my gaze flicked to the door. "What are you doing?"

He laughed. "This is my insurance."

I retreated a step. My hand twitched, begging to wipe the expression from his face. "I'm already compelled, Isaac."

He frowned like I was simple, then displayed the syringe, rolling it in his grasp. "This isn't compulsion, Briar. This," his smile was a venom so potent, it burned, "is sweet Mason's blood."

My eyes flew wide, and I scrambled back, crashing into a stack of boxes behind me. They tumbled to the floor with a hollow thwack. Mason's blood! Sweet sage, it'd obliterate Kane's scent. Replace it completely. My Alpha would think the worst. He'd be broken. Shattered moonlight that would never be healed. There'd be nothing left. Nothing to salvage.

I needed to beg. Plead. *Anything!*

Air exploded from my lungs as I hyperventilated. "You don't need to do this," I said. "I'll do anything, please, just don't." Don't take Kane from me. Don't rip my heart from my chest. "*Please!*"

"It doesn't need to go that far, Isaac," Mason snarled.

"Enough, both of you." Isaac's spine straightened as he squared his shoulders and dusted his hands. "Don't fight me now, Briar."

My breaths heaved as he closed in, setting the needle's sharp tip to my arm, and emptying its contents.

He patted my arm. "Now. Down to business! I've got some ground rules for our little game. First, you're going tell Kane the two of you are finished, and that you're returning to Mason. I suggest this will give things some . . . " He rolled a wrist. "Finality. You will not touch your wolf, or cry in front of him. You will not tell him, or anyone outside my circle of control, how you feel about him."

A cry ripped from the hollows of my throat and sliced through my world. "No," I whimpered, the sound sad and pathetic like the shuddered beats of my heart. I grew dizzy. Couldn't think of anything but my Alpha. *Kane*. It'd break him. He couldn't take it. We wouldn't survive.

My chest caved when the heat of that blood flooded my system and the devastation sealed in.

"I'll be needing a few more bodies for my research, so you'll continue diverting the Conclave for me," Isaac added. "You will answer anytime I call. And finally, you will share nothing of my plans unless it is to me, or someone you *know* to be one of my people."

Each word was a shovel in the ground, digging my grave. A sob built in my chest. "Kane will know something's wrong. He won't buy it." He would. He had to because if he didn't, I was alone. So painfully alone.

He leaned close, nostrils flaring when he made a show of sniffing the air. "You're going to make him believe otherwise." He tossed the syringe aside with a clank. "I know this feels like the bottom, but I promise you, it *can* get worse."

The swell of adrenaline that coursed through my veins moved like liquid flame. My teeth ground, body coiling. "You'll die for this."

"No," he said without a shred of doubt. "I won't." He canted his head, eyeing me like an insect. "You're pathetic, Briar. Just like your mother. You're not Kane's little bitch anymore." His arm dropped and he grinned, all malevolence tainted poison. "Because I own you now."

I wanted to tell him to shove his smug proclamations up his changeling ass, but the wall he'd built around me was too high to scale. So I'd have to find a way through it.

He dusted his hands. "I must take my leave." His smile was all poison and tainted promises when he turned it on Mason. "Be sure to help her if she needs it."

Mason's head shot up, eyes wide. "Kane'll slaughter me, Isaac."

And he would. Rip him apart until he was nothing but itty-bitty Mason bits. And after that, the Covens would call for Kane's head.

Isaac's foot landed on the bottom step, hand waving dismissively. "I require Mason, Briar. Do make sure that doesn't happen."

Power of obsidian. The order fell over me, and I swallowed around the lump in my throat. My body grew heavy, hollow stare fixed forward. I focused on breathing, because if I thought about what was to come, I'd never survive.

Chapter Eight

I sat on Mason's couch, lungs blazing with the need for air while I waited.

I stared at my phone and the four missed calls from Kane. It'd been twenty excruciating minutes since Isaac had left, and each one that passed had my vision tunneling more. My pulse thrashed in my ears as I tried to work the problem, figure out something. *Anything*.

Mason paced the living room, his feet pounding a chaotic beat that echoed through the empty house. He shook wildly, shirt thumping with the frenetic drum of his heart. I didn't need to scent his fear because it pulsed off him in waves. And so did mine.

The rev of a vehicle engine roared as it drew closer. Closer.

Sage, Kane, just turn around. Don't come. Don't come. Don't come!

That engine grew louder. Almost there. Adrenaline shot through my veins.

Tires shrieked just outside as an all too familiar truck careened into the driveway.

Time was up.

Rising on unsteady legs, I moved on autopilot, controlled by Isaac's will as I headed for the door. I found Mason over my shoulder, voice quavering when I instructed, "Stay inside."

He swallowed hard. "That's not gonna stop him, Briar."

My gaze pinched at the corners. Order from Isaac or no, the chances of Mason's survival were less than nil.

A roar boomed from the driveway, one that shook the house. Shook my bones. Rattled my soul.

My obsidian clanked violently against the door's handle when I took it in my tremoring grasp and twisted. My knees were weak, barely holding me as I stepped outside. I moved like a robot, stiff and programmed. I had no control, only response. But I felt *everything*; the scorch of the sun against my skin, the splinter of my heart as it shattered to pieces, and the ragged pain that filled the air. Kane's pain, and mine.

Dirt drifted my way, coating my skin and throat when it turned my already burning eyes to sandpaper. Kane surged from the truck, his silver topaz stare savage. His corded neck strained while his shoulders heaved. The sight of him like that, completely untethered, ravaged me.

The Beta dropped from the passenger side, head angled low and fixed on me.

My Alpha advanced, and time moved in slow motion the instant he scented the air. The instant that thought hit.

He stopped dead. His chest caved and those silver topaz eyes creased before the light in them guttered. He staggered back, crushed his eyes closed, then forced them open. He shook himself like he tried to reset. As if what he'd just found didn't make sense.

"Bry?" he rasped, like he pleaded for it not to be real. For an explanation he could fathom. Anything but what it was.

The shearing of my soul was absolute.

He raked his hands over his face, breaths coming in harsh bursts. "What are you doing, Bry?"

My throat stung like razor blades sliced it with every exhale. I couldn't answer that question . . . not directly, which meant I had to deflect. And, sage, the cruelty of it. "What do you think?"

My Alpha edged forward, spine straightening until he reached his towering height—a wall of preternatural brutality. He shifted his stance, feet shoulder-width apart, arms out from his sides. When he finally spoke, his voice was hoarse. "You came here for him?"

No, Kane. Never. I love you! You*!*

I tested the answer in my mind. Isaac's order meant saying yes wasn't on the table, Kane *would* scent the lie. Words escaped me, so I let that silence stand. Trees rustled. A branch cracked.

Kane's breath hitched.

Slowly, his attention tracked to the house, that molten stare charged with violence. The roar that tore from his throat was menace drowned in agony. It was the most excruciating, heart-rending and terrifying thing I'd ever heard.

He flew past me, and a loud boom filled the world when the metal front door buckled and bent as he exploded through it.

My heart lurched, and I gave chase. "Kane, no!"

When I burst inside, his torso was mid-arc as his fist flew, catching Mason square on the nose. Blood burst out, painting them both and misting the air with the scent of copper. Mason careened back, crashing through the glass table there. It shattered beneath him, its cubed shards flying in every direction. He grunted, legs dangling limp over the frame while his eyes rolled in and out of focus.

I sucked in a sharp inhale. Shadow and sage! Another hit like that and he'd be dead.

"Kane, stop!" I screamed.

My Alpha dropped to a knee, grip latching around Mason's throat. He lifted, skin peeling back from his square knuckles as those boned claws extended.

My frantic and pleading gaze snapped to Joaquin. The shake of his head was infinitesimal, his silent message clear. *No.*

No. He wouldn't help. No. He wouldn't intercede. No. No. No!

I threw myself forward, thrusting myself between my Alpha and Mason's dangerously limp body.

Kane reared back before he snarled, "Move!"

"No."

"FUCKING MOVE, BRY!"

"NO!"

His head snapped back, and his stare dropped to the claiming mark on my neck like it'd tripped a switch. That focus slid to Mason, a new fire igniting.

I shook my head. "Either stop or go through me."

"JOAQUIN!" Kane roared.

The Beta approached.

"Do *not* sic him on me, Kane!" Iron fires. I was gonna have to hurt him—no, not hurt, *gut*. Rip him apart. Shred every vestige of what we had. He wouldn't stop otherwise. And I had an order to follow. I steeled myself because what I was about to do would cut deeper than any knife—the infected kind with a gaping wound that'd fester and never heal.

His arm drew back.

The compulsion played with my words, choosing delicate truths. Misdirecting statements that wouldn't throw alarms. Not ones I wanted, but truths, nonetheless. And Iron Hells take me, I didn't know how I'd survive. "You and I are done, Kane!"

He froze, fist hovering in mid-air. His throat dipped. His hand shook. He swayed, that hold on Mason faltering, before it released. Mason collapsed to the floor in a pale and bloody heap.

"What?" Kane said, stumbling back before he fell to the ground.

I love you. It's Isaac. IT'S FUCKING ISAAC! "You heard me."

His gaze muted, and he moved like he was lost. His voice was so rough, it was barely more than a rasp when he said, "What the fuck is this?"

Beyond him, Joaquin's stare narrowed, head canting slightly, as if what he'd just heard didn't make sense, or he didn't believe it. But judging the collapse of Kane's chest, *he* did.

With every ounce of strength I had, I straightened. "We're done."

He pushed to his knees, and the sight of my Alpha like that had my lungs seize. "Talk to me, Bry. Fucking talk to me." The words were guttural. Animal. Not his own.

His attention was on me, and I needed to keep it that way.

I rose and took several steps aside. Away. "You know what you did." I shook my head. Tears seared the backs of my eyes, begging to fall. To show him that truth . . . that I didn't want this. "There's nothing to say."

"Like fuck there's not." He barreled to his feet and advanced. Scampering back, I collided with the wall, and he closed in tight, his torso less than an inch from mine, arms coming up as he penned me in. "You fucked him?"

Wraith take me. Those words. His pain. Still, it was a question. A pause. Because with the wolves, it was different. They touched and tasted, their scent lingering everywhere on their mates. But Mason wasn't a wolf. And while I smelled like him, no doubt, it was off. Would Kane think I'd washed? Rinsed those traces away? That Mason and I had fucked in the shower?

My hands fisted at my compliance when I deflected, "And what about you and Whitney?"

"Shadowed moon! Nothing happened with me and Whitney. Fucking nothing, Bry."

I believed him. Sage, I believed him with everything I had. But none of that mattered. "Your actions imply otherwise."

The creases around his eyes deepened. Regret. So much regret.

"You hurt me." Truth, but not honesty.

He cursed and tore his hands through his hair so hard, his forehead pulled taut. "I'm sorry, I'm so goddamn sorry." His head hung. "Iron Hells, I just asked her for help. We already lost one baby. I thought," he looked around, eyes wild. "Thought maybe it was my fault. Was fucking terrified me being an Alpha would be an issue. Be harder on *you*. I asked her to look into it. See what she could find. I should've said something, but I didn't wanna put that on you. Didn't want you carrying it. Just needed to know what I could do."

The relief that careened through me was chased by an anguish so hot, it burned. He'd done it for us. For *me*. That was the Kane I knew. The man who'd fought for our second chance.

Who'd yearned for our child. I wanted to thank him, throw my arms around him. Anything but what came next. "Why would I ever believe you?"

He winced. "Because I love you, Bry. Please."

The pain that lanced through my heart nearly stopped it from beating. But he wasn't listening. My gaze flicked to Mason and back. The amount of blood ringing his head was the concerning kind of bad. I steadied myself, then lobbed my next blow. "There's no more talking, Kane." I cut my hand through the air. "We're. Done."

Joaquin's brow dropped.

Kane's stare hardened when it speared me through. "I don't believe you."

I loved him. He was it for me. But none of that mattered when I launched my killing blow. "Liar," I hissed. "You can scent a truth, Kane."

He looked away like he was lost or wounded, then staggered back. His eyes pinched at the corners, thoughts spinning inside them. His attention flicked to Mason, then to me. "Did he hurt you?"

The words wrecked me. No, not Mason, *Isaac*. Isaac *hurt me*! I wanted Kane to ask something I couldn't answer. Corner me with his words until I was *forced* to lie—forced to give him doubt. Something that'd compel him to stop me. Instead, I shook my head.

His fingers flexed, rolling into fists so tight, veins stood out against his skin. "Say it out loud, Bry."

Seven Iron Hells, I didn't want to. I wanted to reach out, touch him, be near him as long as I could, because once he walked away . . . I couldn't go there. Isaac may have sunk my ship, but I'd spend the rest of my life swimming if it meant reaching my Alpha again.

I crossed my arms over my chest to hold myself together.

"FUCKING SAY IT!" he roared.

A truth I could offer. One he could scent. One that was about to send all kinds of the wrong message, but the only one that would work. The only one that would heed Isaac's command and make Kane question my loyalty. Question *me*. I swallowed around the lump in my throat before I broke the foundation of his world, and mine. "No. Mason didn't hurt me."

His body drew so taut, muscles strained under his skin, looking ready to tear from the bone. "So, what? You screwed him for *spite*?" He shook his head. "You're temperamental as the hells and twice as brazen, but you're not vindictive."

"Does it really matter anymore?"

"Yes. It matters," he seethed. "*Everything* with you fucking matters." He violently rubbed the back of his neck before his hollow gaze locked with mine and held, and held, and held, like he waited for me to take it back. Like it didn't make sense. "First, you're friends with Lana, and now . . . *this*? What the hells is going on with you, Bry?" He cursed then cursed again. "Is he *making* you do this?"

Kane trusted me. Wouldn't be struggling with what stood before him otherwise. He didn't want to believe it. He was right there, on the edge of that truth, but still so damn far.

I shook my head. "No."

His throat dipped as he swallowed hard. A tortured, broken laugh that held not one ounce of humor ripped from his chest. His arms fell to his sides, heavy, like they weighed him down. His eyes reddened, a sheen of moisture glossing their surface. His chest hitched when a lone tear slipped free.

Inside my mind, I screamed, and clawed, digging my nails into the tattered remnants of hope that slithered from me like blood. *I'll fix this, Kane. I'll find a way. I'll fucking fix this.*

The sight of him breaking broke me. I didn't want him to go, 'cause wraith only knew if I'd see him again, but the sheer torture in his eyes was too much to bear. "Leave, Kane."

"This isn't you," he said, then staggered back, retreating one step. Another. Each one a void between us. "This isn't fucking you." His chest heaved, and that molten stare snuffed out. Dull. Vacant. Dead. "Make it make sense, Bry. Just make it make *fucking sense*!"

I'd never forget the sight of him that way. The agony of it seared my memory and I tried to reach for him, to no avail.

The silence that fell severed us.

He looked at me, then away, to my hand, then away. His gaze was unfocused. Lost. As if he didn't know where he was or how he'd gotten there.

"I need you to leave," I repeated, because if I wanted to help Mason, I most certainly did.

"Need," he said as Mason's blood dripped from his chin, landing on his shirt. He watched me for one agonizing heartbeat. Two. Turning, he gave me his back and stalked away. The thump of his feet on the floor was uneven as he crossed outside, and I followed through the window when he reached his truck, then stopped.

Look at me, Kane. I love you. I FUCKING LOVE YOU!

He climbed in and closed the door.

The Beta lingered, attention tracking from me to Mason's moaning form, and back. It was gradual, methodical. Several torturous seconds later, he left, then took his place in the passenger's side. The engine rumbled when Kane reversed out the driveway, put the truck in gear, then left. His taillights faded, eaten by the distance.

Kane. The man I loved, my Alpha, the reason my heart beat. My *mate*. He was gone. *He was fucking gone!*

I stared after him, muscles begging, pleading, *fighting* to give chase. To nip at his heels until he stopped. To tell him the truth— to tell him everything. But my chain cinched tight. Confined by a lock only Isaac held the key to.

My breath exploded from me followed by a howl of pain— one I barely recognized as my own. I dropped, knees colliding with the ground. Tears seared my sight as I crawled to Mason.

He groaned, chest shuddering on a breath. His eyes opened as he sucked in a sharp hiss. "Briar?"

A broken sob tore from me. I couldn't speak, so I just nodded.

He rolled to his side and, slowly, sat up. Rubbing the back of his head, he peered at me. I didn't know what expression painted my face, but with the way his tensed, I gathered, of the two of us, I looked worse.

Reaching out, he pulled me to his chest. "I'm so sorry."

If I'd thought I'd known agony before, I'd been painfully wrong. Isaac had promised to destroy Kane and me. Looked like he'd succeeded.

Chapter Nine

I cried as I cleaned Mason's face, and that shattered, cubed glass that'd filled every piece of his living room.

There wasn't a corner of my body that didn't hurt; neck, back, hips, lungs, heart. Everything. My sobs were endless. My tears ran dry.

Eventually, I shuffled my way to Mason's couch and sank onto the cold, black leather—fitting for my desolate emotions. The thing was new, and stiff, and far past uncomfortable.

Time passed in a blur while I lay there, staring at the white stucco ceiling as the light faded. Night turned to day, and that day grew long, but I didn't know if I'd slept.

Taking up my phone, I eyed at the screen, trailing a finger over a picture of Kane. A smirk crested his mouth, the just-for-me kind he wore when he was the vulgar sort of hungry.

The light padding of feet had my head canting to the side. Mason ambled into the room, a fresh bag of ice held over his cheek. His face was a macabre collection of deep blood bruises that ringed his eyes. The swelling over his nose set his glasses askew, torquing them to the right.

His stare found mine when he set himself into the white velvet chair across from me. "You alright?"

My gaze dropped to that image of Kane. "I'm breathing." Sitting up, I tucked my knees to my chest. "How're you feeling?"

The laugh that broke from him was dry. "Like I look." He rubbed his forehead and sucked in a sharp breath. "Feel like I'm getting pretty good at this now. Probably shouldn't complain. Guess it could've been worse."

Oh, it could've been much, much worse. The "time-for-Mason's-dirge" kinda worse.

He peered away and scratched the back of his neck. "I can, uh, get the spare room ready for you."

"It's fine." I waved him off. "I'll keep the couch."

He inclined his head, body sagging like simply being conscious drained him.

I ticked my chin up, feigning confidence, 'cause maybe if I faked it enough, I'd make it through. "I can't just give up, Mason." We couldn't let Isaac link with the humans. Forge that Ithican army he was so keen to get.

I couldn't trust my mother. Not that she didn't love me, but she'd long since given up. I didn't think she understood the concept of trying anymore. And I'd never include Lucas.

He inclined his head. "There is something . . ."

"What do you mean?"

"Well, maybe something. I'm still looking into it."

My brows climbed and I sniffed as I leaned forward. "Gonna need more than that, Mason."

His mouth tugged up at the corner. He winced, and shifted that ice pack across his face, cubes clinking as he shuffled the bag. "Turns out, the serums Isaac got weren't the only ones."

My spine snapped straight. "There were more?"

"Yeah." His stare flicked to the basement door where Ivy lurked below. Gripping his obsidian, he threw a barrier around our conversation. "These ones specifically for magi."

Hope sparked in my chest. "What do they do?"

"I'm still figuring it out. But from what I can tell, I think they're enhancers, or something."

My heart fluttered, voice desperate when I asked, "What do you mean?"

"I don't know." He adjusted those glasses and gave the chair his weight. "I need to test them more."

"Test them how?"

"On myself, I guess." He lifted a shoulder. "Only way to do it accurately is one at a time, so it's slow going."

My nod was sharp, and I squirmed, wriggling to the edge of my seat and throwing my hand up like an eager kid. "I wanna help."

"I won't ask you to do that."

"You're not asking. I totally volunteer." That arm dropped. "I've gotta do something, Mason. Me, Theo, Naomi and Lisa . . . we wanna try. I need to feel like I'm moving forward." Bridging that gap to my Alpha. I couldn't be stagnant.

His expression creased, which, considering the swelling there, was impressive. "We don't know what this stuff is."

Fair point. "But we did know Sierra." I grabbed the white decorative pillow to my right and hugged it to my chest. "She was power hungry."

"I wouldn't say that—"

I cocked my head, my expression of the "bitch, please" variety. "She brokered a deal with the humans behind the Conclave's back."

He tried to straighten those glasses again. "Okay, accurate."

"Exactly. So, if we hold with the Sierra-had-a-shady-ass-plan-and-wanted-an-advantage theory, then the chances were, she was manufacturing something useful."

His eyes narrowed. "You think she intended to safeguard the magi?"

"It fits." At least she hadn't thrown us fully under the bus. I took a steadying breath. "I know things with you and I went sideways, and you've got no reason to help—"

"I'm in, Briar. Just tell me what to do."

The line of conversation struck an idea, one that'd piss Isaac off to no end, but if I wanted to interrupt him at all, it needed to be done. I worried my lip. The thought of seeing Kane again . . . sage, I wanted to, desperately. Still, my heart twisted so tight, it could hardly beat. What would I see in those silver topaz eyes? Desolation? Or hate?

Swallowing hard, I said, "Call a Conclave meeting."

He tensed. "For when?"

"As soon as they can make it."

"What's it about?"

My phone rang. I picked it up and stared at the screen. I didn't want to talk, but if she called, there was a reason. Probably a bad one.

"Crap. Gimme a sec," I told Mason, then answered. "Cassandra?"

Mason's brows lifted.

"Briar Stone," she replied. That lyrical lilt was weaker, as if she were tired—unnerving for a preternatural that never slept.

I blinked hard against the pounding headache that moved in. "What's wrong?"

"I have a body."

Fucking Isaac. I fought against the nausea that teased the back of my throat. Setting my elbow on my knee, I lowered my head in my hand. My heart hurt for Cassandra. For the loss of another of her people.

An idea bloomed in my mind, and that hope Mason had stoked burned brighter. 'Cause Isaac wasn't the only one who could make plans. "Tell me where."

***

The North Cambrian Dowager's "den" could've better been described as luxury living on steroids. A series of massive, thirty-floor high-rises with blacked out windows edged the pale brick road.

White stone lined the façade, while silver and black accents made up the balconies along the corners of the buildings. Etched glass climbed above the entrance to the super distant top bearing the sigil of Cassandra's Clan—a waning moon overlaid by a string of smaller stars, the symbol of night.

No guards hovered out front. Not that it mattered considering the venom line meant you couldn't cross without an invite. That was the story anyway. Hard to confirm without evidence seeing I'd never seen the inside of a shadow walker's home.

The sun died on the horizon as it sank beneath the edifice. It splashed the sky in a deluge of pinks that drew elongated shadows over the earth. I parked in the visitor lot under a canopy of weeping willows out front and exhaled a breath, praying it wasn't dinner time.

Oh, sage. I must've had a death wish going in there alone.

Leaning a shoulder against the car door, I popped it open and climbed free. It swung silently when it closed, cutting me off from Kane's faint wilderness scent. I squinted against the dim toward the bright, ethereal, blood red figure that haunted in the entrance.

Cassandra.

Fitting, really. Terrifying, but fitting.

My footsteps padded over the ground as I aimed her way, looking like I'd just rolled out of a laundry hamper in yesterday's clothes. The air was cool and damp against my skin. It seeped deep, sending a chill straight to my bones.

I peered around. If Kane knew where I was, he'd straight up murder me—

My hand flew to my chest, shoulders caving as I brought up short, struggling against the buckle of my knees. Kane *would* know where I was, but he wouldn't come. Wouldn't bark at me for strolling straight into a shadow walker's den of bitey death. Isaac had made sure of that.

Cassandra's crimson gaze hovered inside the entrance. She didn't blink or waver as she glided toward me, protected by the waning shadows, her vintage, off the shoulder dress billowing around her.

I righted and swallowed hard.

She stopped at safety's edge beyond the sun's rays. So close, if one of those semi-translucent toes of hers so much as wiggled, they'd be barbecue. Her nostrils flared as her attention raked me up and down, taking me in. "Briar Stone," she greeted. "You look—"

"Like shit?" I said through a thick, forced laugh while I smoothed the unsmoothable wrinkles in my top.

She scented me . . . my change. I had no doubt about it. I waited for her to say it. To ask. Push. Something.

Instead, her head canted, the movement owl-like and awkward, as if she tried to mimic a human but didn't quite know how. "Broken."

Oh, how right she was. I ran a hand through my bedraggled hair. My brain must've punched its clock, 'cause it refused to work. Was I supposed to hold her gaze? I bit my lip and shrugged.

That thirsty stare homed in on my mouth before she glanced away. "Come." Her scarlet dress wisped and fluttered on the air as she spun on her very pointy heel. "The body is this way."

I scampered to her side. "Are you alright?"

"Frances Trevino and I were not what you may call close, but the circumstance is . . . unsettling." Crossing inside, she held the tinted glass door wide.

Something about the name twigged, but I couldn't place it before my gaze skimmed a small line trailing the perimeter of the door while I lifted a hand and reached forward. It pressed against something hard, immovable. And completely, utterly invisible. Okay, kinda cool.

Cassandra watched me like a cat with a bug. "Please, come in, Briar Stone."

The invitation was necessary for me to cross, but formal. Bizarrely so.

I stepped over that threshold, and a prickle tracked along my skin. The hairs on my arms rose. Not in warning, more like some odd power. It was cool against my flesh and felt old. The Cassandra Ryton kind of old.

Weird.

Inside, the foyer rose high, climbing to the absolute top. Interior balconies on each floor covered the right and left. Flower boxes lined their rails, giving the place a sweet, floral scent. Elevators sat at the back, while at the front, a soft waterfall cascaded down the glass, pooling in a river that flowed into a koi-filled pond at the center, its drip and trickle carrying through the vast space.

Power of obsidian. There was affluence, and then there was incomprehensible wealth.

"Wait." I peered at her from the side of my gaze. "No coffins?"

Her lips tugged at the corners. "Is this not what you expected?"

Wild, opulent, stylish. "It's kind of exactly what I expected."

She guided us to the elevator bank, and the door dinged open. The walls and floor were glass, and I held my breath when she pressed for the twelfth floor, and we ascended.

"So . . ." I rocked on my heels. "You, uh, get many visitors?"

"You are the first."

My face twisted. "Like, the first in a while?"

The soft waves of her white-blonde hair slipped over her shoulder as she shook her head. "Ever."

Oh. Lovely. What the sweet sage was I supposed to take from that? I forced a laugh, an erratic, staccato sound that rivaled Cassandra for inhuman awkwardness. Considering time meant something different to the shadow walkers, "ever" rang heavy from her mouth.

A massive elevator to our left rode down, some fancy-ass car in its center. My mouth opened. Closed. Opened. Then closed again.

A ding rang loud when we reached our level. Stepping out, I squinted into the dark. So damn dark. Stumbling over . . . something, I tugged the hem of my shirt. "How do you even see in this place?"

"We are built for the night, Briar Stone."

Ah, yes. That. I blinked, letting my eyes adjust. Several seconds later, her silhouette came clear.

She veered to the right.

"Why a . . ." I flicked my wrist through the air, "communal setting?"

"Some of my people are old. If one is not careful, solitude and age can make us . . . less human."

I choked down a laugh.

"Our lives are long. The world dies around us, but we persist. We keep our clan close so we do not become recluse and lose sight of what matters."

My nod was slow, 'cause the sentiment was kind of beautiful.

Her arm swept out, indicating the first in a line of doors that stretched far into the distance. "These were Frances Trevino's personal quarters."

Again, with that name . . . I followed after her and the intense copper scent of blood that hit had my heart stutter-stepping.

The sheer arrogance of Isaac to sneak into the heart of a shadow walker's den and slaughter one of their own. I had no words—and I had a lotta words. Not many of them useful, but, still, a lot of them.

Isaac wasn't an idiot. So, what the shadow and sage would drive him to take that kind of risk? Unmitigated hubris? Desperation? Or something else?

The place was open concept and spacious. A sectional couch hugged the back corner while a record player with a wall full of vinyl filled the neighboring shelves. A white dining table with four chairs sat opposite the living room. But otherwise, it was very minimalist.

"I offer a generous monthly stipend to my people, but she was clearly a walker of simple tastes," Cassandra noted. Drawing back her shoulders as if to steady herself, she flicked a finger toward the kitchen to our left.

The hairs on the back of my neck pricked as I paced deeper and rounded the marble countertop. My hand flew to my throat. Frances's body lay face down in a puddle of blood. Her head sat at an awkward angle, arced back at the neck. The telltale scent of ether hung heavy in the air. The ephemeral and translucent wraith would be there to collect the Iron Hells due soon.

But her hair, there was something about it . . . that same shock of red I'd seen before.

I turned to Cassandra. "Is she—"

She inclined her head. "She is Danika Trevino's sister."

Trevino! Hence why Frances's name had been familiar. First Ivy, then Frances. Two sisters Danika had lost. I winced and took a knee. Frances's body was loose when I rolled her so she was face up. Jerking back, I sucked in a sharp gasp. My head snapped Cassandra's way.

"It is different," she said.

Understatement of the century. Blinking hard, I forced my attention back to Frances. Her mouth hung slack while two jagged and gouged holes sat where her eyes should've been. Blood seeped down her cheeks, and temples, soaking her vibrant hair.

Bile kissed the back of my throat again. Swallowing hard, I half-turned to Cassandra. "When was the last time she was seen alive?"

"Shortly after eleven o'clock."

I gave a sharp nod, then gripped my obsidian. Drawing its power, I let my gaze fall unfocused and clenched my hands into fists, bracing as I sought the time marker, and dove in.

Frances was seated in an opulent common room that mimicked an old-time theatre. Red velvet seats lined the place while curtains with gold tassels were drawn back from the screen. A sea of crimson eyes surrounded her, fixed on a movie whose credits rolled.

Shadow walker movie hour. Weirdly . . . normal.

"Hello, Briar," a woman's voice said. It was higher with a nasal quality, and wholly unfamiliar.

I jolted and fell back onto my ass, heart beating like a kickdrum in my chest because *what*—and I could not stress this enough—*the actual fuck was that?*

"Briar Stone?" Cassandra said.

"Sorry." I shook myself as my gaze dropped to that new obsidian, then back to Frances's body. "Just getting used to my new ring."

"Do not fear, Briar. It is Frances to whom you speak."

I froze. I was losing it. Absolutely goddamn losing it. 'Cause I was pretty sure the dead vamp had just—

"You are perfectly sane. But we are short on time. Once the wraith arrives, I will be lost to you. Please. We must make haste."

What the shit? The corpse was talking to me. I gripped my thighs to hide the tremble of my hands because *the corpse was talking to me!*

"No, not my corpse. You commune with my soul."

Somehow, not much better. I shook out my shoulders, trying to steady myself. It didn't work. How was she even hearing me?

"I hear your mind," she answered. *"You need not watch what happens. Just ask your questions and I shall answer."*

Oh, thank sage, 'cause the idea of watching what would come, of smelling it and feeling her emotions, had not been on my "want to do" list.

The Dowager's crimson gaze narrowed on me. It was subtle, but it was there.

Did I tell her? *Should* I tell her? I didn't know. Needed to figure it out first, weigh the pros and cons, which I most certainly didn't have the brain capacity for in that moment. So, I kept my mouth good and shut.

"Quickly, now, Briar."

Right. Uh . . . what the hells did I ask? *"Um. Was it Isaac?"*

"It was."

My gaze flicked around. If he meant to use the serums he'd stolen to offer the humans our powers, I had no doubt he'd come for Frances to get whatever shadow walker portion he'd needed.

Iron fires. What the actual fuck was wrong with him? *"How'd he get in?"*

"He compelled me to invite him."

Not a shocker but then . . . *"Why do it here? Why the heart of Cassandra's home?"*

"To undermine our Dowager by painting her defenses as weak."

To show Cassandra couldn't protect her own. Protect Danika's kin. To pit the Southern Dowager against her. He'd already started the havoc with Kane.

Her voice wavered. Fading. *"He aims to sow dissension, Briar. To create chaos amongst the Conclave."*

My chest tightened. *"Why?"*

"So, they are no longer united when the time comes."

That answer gave me several things. First, if Isaac tried to undermine Cassandra, then she unequivocally wasn't on his team roster. Second, he feared her just as much as he feared Kane, third, Cassandra trusted me a lot. Like, a lot, a lot. And fourth, we had a shitstorm of trouble headed our way.

Unmitigated piece of changeling garbage!

"The wraith comes now."

No! Not, yet! That scent of ether grew, and, sage, I'd never smelled it so strong. It burned my airways, and I coughed to clear them. *"I'm so sorry, Frances."*

"You must stop him, Briar."

"I will," I vowed, praying to all things holy it was a vow I could keep.

Wind gusts from the wraith's wings snapped my hair back as she came, and Frances's aura vanished.

My body sagged. I released my ring. "She's gone."

Cassandra drifted closer. "Did you see anything of consequence, Briar Stone?"

"I didn't see who it was." A misdirection, but not a lie. I wouldn't protect Isaac by choice. But I needed a method, a path forward. It didn't matter that I knew the truth, what mattered was leading Cassandra—or *anyone* else—to it. Or trying to, anyway.

My shoulders drew back as I took in the space again. Time to work that system.

"You don't have visitors, so who *is* allowed in here?"

"Only our human feeders and the shadow walkers I have made may cross."

I shuddered. Annnnd, moving on.

Linking my next question to Isaac wasn't doable, but I could sure as heck make it general. "Is it possible to be forced?"

"Forced?"

"Forced to allow someone in?"

Her crimson gaze narrowed, in thought or something else, I had no clue. Her chin drifted low in a nod. "It is possible, yes." Her head canted. "Is this what you believe, Briar Stone?"

"I can't say." A truth. I needed a way to slip Ivy in. Link them somehow, and have Cassandra do the same. I shifted against that cool, tile floor. "Why were Ivy and Frances here? In your Clan? Why not with Danika?"

"Danika Trevino could not bring herself to turn her sisters, and so, I did it for her."

I scrubbed a hand over my leg. "Did either of them have enemies?"

Her preternatural stillness was predatory, and only interrupted by the slight sway of her skirts. "You suspect they are linked?"

Oh, I more than suspected. "I'm just looking for similarities."

Those crimson eyes considered. "They were ambitious. It is possible."

A direction to follow, a rope to grab onto. But there'd been something in the way she'd said it, something that twigged my interest. "You think Ivy's gone?"

"I think she has been missing too long to believe otherwise."

Shittiest of shits. I wanted her to know, to find a way through those iron bars that penned Ivy in, but how I'd lead her there, I had no damn clue.

Worrying my lip, I veered down another track. Exactly how long had the sisters been under Isaac's control? I rose. "Had they been acting strange before?"

Cassandra straightened to her full, airy height. "Strange how, Briar Stone?"

The flash of a memory.

I skidded to a stop beside Anthony and Kane. A loud tsh carried through the room when I set the barrel to Anthony's temple. "Why do you want me dead, asshole?"

A single tear slithered down the side of his face. "I need you dead."

I wasn't seeing a difference, but his emphasis implied one existed. And it turned out it had, seeing Isaac had owned him the same way he owned me.

"For her." He panted. "For her!" His head swiveled like a crack when he attacked, his mouth opening wide, teeth extending toward me.

I pulled the trigger.

Shaking my head, I broke from the searing images. They left traces of blood and bone across my mind. Everything red. Dead.

Cassandra's eerie, unblinking gaze was on me.

I rubbed the tightness at the center of my sternum. Clearing my throat, I lifted a shoulder in a half shrug. "Strange like . . ." Isaac's compulsion meant I choked on the name, so I improvised, "anyone else you knew?"

"You refer to Anthony Bruno?" A question, yet not. Her expression was impassive, but there was something deep in the recesses of those crimson eyes. Something akin to regret. "I do not know. I will seek these answers."

Her sorrow dripped from those semi-translucent pores, so thick and heavy on the air, I swore I could scent its bitter spice. My heart twisted, because I'd added to that pain.

My words were soft when I uttered, "You didn't hate me after."

That delicate brow lowered. "Briar Stone?"

"After I killed him." My gaze locked with hers. "He was your Second, but still, you didn't hate me."

She shifted, balletically resting one palm over the other. "I do not know what drove him to the Madness, and when the moment came, I regret I could not bring myself to end his suffering. But I will not fault you for saving yourself from it."

I'd opened a box. One full of puzzle pieces I could lob at her feet. "How's Olive?" Anthony's wife. His widow. The one he'd been protecting from the version of him Isaac had created. My stepfather's doing, and mine.

Her brow ticked up, intrigued. "The human still grieves." She threaded her fingers together. "I was not aware you knew her."

My pulse pounded, beating against my veins. I nudged that thought. Isaac didn't know about Olive, nor she about him. She wasn't a threat or something I needed to shield. Time to lob a breadcrumb. "She came into No Man's Land a while back for a reading."

The tilt of Cassandra's head was sudden and sharp. Inhuman. "About Anthony Bruno?" she replied, *totally* fishing.

I chomped that bait like a rabid, adrenaline-laced fishy. "She thought Anthony'd cheated. Thought he'd compelled her to forget what he was up to."

Her head righted, voice going level. "She has said nothing of this."

"That's because she can't." I crossed my arms over my chest. "The Caster Stones outside the tavern are spelled to keep humans quiet about what goes on in there after they leave."

"Fascinating," she said, that luring lilt rolling the word around her tongue. She glided to the couch and something creaked when she settled herself down. Whether it was her or the furniture, I didn't know.

"I take it you haven't been in a while?"

"I have never been, Briar Stone."

My palm settled on my chest. "Not even in your youth?"

The ghost of a smile. Or possibly a warning. With her, I was fairly confident the two were interchangeable.

"And had he?" she questioned.

"Had who what?"

"Had Anthony Bruno compelled her?"

Curious *that* was the detail she'd twigged on. "Yes. He had."

Her chin lifted, that crimson gaze narrowed. "Interesting."

I furrowed my brow and waited . . . and waited. "You're not the least bit curious if he cheated?"

"That is not necessary. I entrusted Anthony Bruno with my life and my Clan. I did not select him as Second by accident. He was a walker of principle. He held my respect. If his wife thought he cheated, it is not because it was true, but because he preferred it to the alternative that tortured him."

Shadow and sage, she'd hit the nail on the head so hard, the *ping* it made rang in my ears. I needed to keep pushing. Hard. "You think something was torturing him?"

Her otherworldly gaze pierced mine. "I have not wandered this world with my eyes closed, Briar Stone."

I scrubbed the back of my neck because our trajectory had opened a door to an answer I so desperately needed. One I suspected, but with the way preternaturals gripped their power cards so close to their chests, didn't know for sure. And if I wanted out of the mess I was in, I *needed* to know. "Has Olive gotten those memories back?"

"Why do you ask this?" There was an edge to the question. Not anger but . . . something.

I paused, considering my best tact. A truth, a shielded one, but a truth, nonetheless. "My aura reading's a skill, but my real strength is knowledge. The more I know, the more I can interpret what I see. The more I can understand. The more I can help." I prayed.

She studied me with that crimson gaze. "Any power the compulsion held dies with its master. Olive Bruno's memories would have returned upon her husband's death."

Dies with its master! So it *was* the same as the weres. Theirs were linked to the Alpha, but still, kill Isaac and I'd kill the compulsion. Hope exploded in my chest.

"Do you suspect these things are related?" Cassandra asked, jerking me back to the conversation.

Crap! How did I answer that without throwing a wrench into things? Lead, but don't reveal, my new goddamn motto when I used my same words from before. "I can't say."

Her attention pressed on me. Unwavering. It closed around my throat and constricted my airway.

I scrubbed a hand over the back of my neck. "How common is the scent of blood around here?"

She straightened her spine like she'd shoved an iron rod down it. "Very."

I frowned.

"When the humans are here and the thirst takes us, things can get . . ." she rolled her thin wrist and fanned her long-fingered hand, "messy."

My gaze widened.

"You are surprised at this answer?"

I tugged my skirt's hem. "I'm surprised at the honesty."

"Is this not what we do, Briar Stone? Share our truths to assist one another?"

My mouth opened. *Was* that what we did? I supposed it was.

"When Frances Trevino was killed, I was elsewhere engaged." At the arch of my brow, she added, "I was lost to the Hunt."

Lost to the Hunt? Nausea crested like a tidal wave, 'cause that definitely sounded like something I didn't wanna know, but there were a bunch of those things in my head already. "What's that mean?"

"When the hunger strikes, we are overtaken by the need. It is too powerful and primal to overcome. We must satiate that mania, otherwise we cannot be controlled, or reasoned with."

Oh, how lovely. I scratched my cheek. "Wouldn't Frances's blood stand out? One of your own?"

"The blood in our systems is *not* our own. It is the remnant from our feedings." She shifted, crossing her legs with the rigid grace of a mannequin. The movement looking less about discomfort and more "it's what non-walkers would do". Her smile was stiff, a practiced move that hadn't been perfected. "You are an attentive woman."

I flicked a nail over the hem of my shirt. Even to my own ears, my laugh was pitiful. "When you're the weakest one in the room, you learn to pay attention."

Next she spoke, her tone was even. Level. "You are many things, Briar Stone, but weak is not one of them."

My face heated as I scratched my chin. The words were so resolute, it was hard not to believe them. I wasn't about to dismiss her. Dismissal was tantamount to disrespect and disrespecting the Dowager under her own roof was a thousand shades of stupid.

She rose. "Come. Let us leave here." Gliding with that ghostly grace, she led us out. "Can I offer you a beverage?"

My face twisted. "You keep *beverages* on hand?"

A smile that touched her blood-tinted eyes drew across her face. "We do."

Why in the obsidian she'd need bev— My face contorted. Oh, hells no! "Cassandra! Do *not* tell me you marinate your food first?"

The sound that broke from her was high and bright, like the tinkle of a bell. It only chimed once, but it was unmistakable. And dangerously hypnotic.

Had I just made the vamp queen . . . laugh? I might've patted myself on the back if it wouldn't have drawn said vamp queen's attention.

"Our meals are prepared during the Hunt, Briar Stone."

Iron fires take me, but *why* did I need to know? "Prepared how?"

Her incisors lengthened. "The human's fear spikes their adrenaline, and adrenaline is like ambrosia in their hot veins."

Wonderful. *So* glad I asked. The nervous titter that bubbled up my throat was sheer self-preservation.

"Do not fret, Briar Stone. You are safe with me."

Under the circumstances, "safe" felt like a relative term. "Says the woman who's offering me beverages!"

She set a palm to her chest. "Social etiquette decrees it is frowned upon to feed on one's friends."

"Ah, yes. Well, etiquette *is* important." Wait, had she just called me a *friend*?

Her shoes clacked as she steered us back to that elevator. "Do not fear. The humans take their pleasure of the venom. Lest they would not volunteer." Another walker moved further down the hall. "You have your codes, as do we. Any participants must be willing. We are not crude. It is a Hunt, not a kill. Satisfying though it may be, it is not necessary to bleed the humans dry."

I supposed there was that.

She offered an austere bow of her head. "I greatly appreciate your assistance. You have given me much to consider."

A bitter tang coated my mouth because I had the answers she wanted. Needed. Had Ivy's location, everything at the tip of my tongue, and regardless of whether the betrayal was intentional, the guilt swept in.

"I received word your Leader requests a Conclave meeting." She angled my way. "Will you notify the wolves of your findings before then?"

My heart plummeted. If only I could. But there was something there in her question. Like it was baited. Leading. As if the words had been strategically picked. "I'm surprised you want me to."

"Secrets have not served us before. I mean to learn from my mistakes." She canted her head, then repeated, "Will you tell them?"

Why did I get the feeling she already knew the answer? "If there's something you want to know, you can just ask."

She rolled her wrist. "Indeed, but subtlety is paramount in such times."

I snorted. "Cassandra, you're about as subtle as a freight train in a library." But truth be told, I appreciated it because on some level, it meant she cared. Or maybe it was just morbid curiosity. Were those mutually exclusive for her? Either way, she was paying attention, and attention was what I needed.

If it wouldn't put her fangs so close to my neck, I might've hugged her.

"I simply seek to understand," she said.

My smile was faker than Isaac's existence when I replied, "Understand what?"

"Why you smell like sadness."

My eyes flew wide, and I threw my hands up, palms out. "Pump the brakes. You can scent emotion?"

A long, pale finger tapped beneath her eye. "I scent your tears. I have difficulty with the troubling rumors of you and your mate." A question but not.

Word spread *fast* through the Cambrian gossip lines.

I hated knowing I carried another man's scent. And more than that, I hated that she knew it too. But Cassandra was playing poker, and I didn't have a hand, so I forced her to show her cards. "You can smell more than my tears, Cassandra."

Those elevator doors dinged open, her gaze trailed down my torso, then back. "That I can."

"Then I think you have your answer."

"No, Briar Stone. I have only more questions." She canted closer. "You and the wolf are mated. Your pieces match. But this," she dragged her nail through the air, pointing it at my body, "does not fit." Her lip tugged up at the corner like she tried to soften her expression. "I do not believe it." She rested a hand on my shoulder. She was stiff as a corpse and twice as cold when that lip climbed higher. "Because I sense you do not believe it."

Chapter Ten

"You can talk to *dead people*?" Theo balked the next morning as he raised his fists and strode toward me. His eyes were wide, caught somewhere between excitement, panic and fear. All were valid. All were reasonable.

That bright morning sun cut rigid beams across the hardwood floors of No Man's Land, making me squint when it hit my peripheral vision. The place wasn't set to open for a couple of hours, and as it turned out, the medium-sized dance floor made an A-plus training ground.

Naomi and Lisa sat on the golden marble bar top, legs dangling down its front while they watched. The former's gaze was dismal as she stared into her drink. Yeah, it was early, but it wasn't like I'd tell her to stop, 'cause our situation was pretty dismal.

Popping a shoulder, I said, "Looks like it."

I adjusted my clothes . . . well, Lisa's clothes—ones I'd borrowed until my pay cheques as Coven's Second started rolling in. The pant-waist cut into my stomach almost painfully seeing the things were entirely too small for my curvy ass.

Theo lunged, fast and powerful. Pushing off with my left foot, I side-stepped. The flat of his palm caught my shoulder, spinning me in a sharp arc, for the six-thousandth time.

He danced back, then shifted into a crouched position, arms wide, stance ready. "What else can that fancy new ring do?"

Finding my feet, I rubbed said shoulder and moved in a wide circle around him. "No clue. It's more of an 'on the job training' exercise."

"So, what's our next move?" Naomi asked.

Clearing my throat, I shuffled left, away from Theo. "Figuring out Isaac's strengths, and ours."

Theo smirked, then chucked his chin my way. "You hoping to punch your way outta this?"

I offered him a decidedly rude finger.

Lisa's hands curled over the edge of the bar when her gaze lifted to mine. "Isaac's ability to plan." She paused. "That's his strength."

"And he's good with his words," Nay added.

My nod was sharp. "Exactly. So, on both counts, we've gotta be better."

"You? Good with the wordies?" Theo taunted.

There went that rude finger again. "No. We're careful with our language. We use it to *our* fucking advantage. Not his."

Nay's eyes flashed as she leaned forward. "How?"

My smile was dark. "Make people think there's something wrong." Striding around the bar, I reached under the shelves and grabbed a bottle of Tonic.

Lisa's eyes hardened. "If you take one sip of that, I will—"

"Trust me, Lis. I've got this." I shoved it into my purse. "We just gotta get people asking questions. Draw attention to ourselves."

Her nod was slow before her gaze fell to her feet. "No one in Cambria's looking at me, chickie."

My lungs hurt at the hollowness in her eyes, and the lonely, desolate expression she wore. I closed in, stepping before her and taking her hands in mine. "I'm looking."

Theo coughed, then mumbled under his breath, "Not helpful."

I raised my smacky hand at him in warning, then returned to Lis. "You've got something else we need." I arched an expectant brow. "Access to the Southern wolves."

A small knowing smile tugged her lips when she picked up what I put down. "Victor."

I winked.

Naomi glanced between us and frowned. "Care to fill the rest of the class in?"

Stepping back, I moved into position with Theo again. "She uses Victor's Pack to figure out what the hells he's hiding."

"Oooooh," Theo said. "Well played." Darting in, he swept his foot out and knocked mine from beneath me. I fell onto my ass and stared skyward at the ceiling's wooden beams.

Gritting my teeth, I clambered up and growled. "I keep losing my stupid balance." We'd been going like that for an hour already and I'd barely managed to dodge him once.

"Widen your feet and bend your knees more," he said.

"Hands up and ready," Nay called. "You're not strong, so you gotta be fast."

My arms flailed, gesturing at myself. "This *is* my fast!" My fastest, which, in comparison to a were, was pathetic at best.

She frowned.

The bottles behind the bar started clanking as the train clacked by, carrying humans on their way into the neutral grounds. It rumbled louder and louder until I couldn't hear myself think, then faded into the distance as it passed.

Theo cocked an eager brow. "Maybe that fancy ass ring can help."

Hmm. Could it? I'd used my old one for power before. Not my Alpha's kind of power, but enough to break Amber's pretty nose after she'd come to stir trouble not long ago. I sighed wistfully. The crack that nose had made under my fist satisfied me down to my withered soul.

But speed was a different beast. Gripping the ring hard, I drew on that power, then flicked a finger at Theo. "Let's go, pup."

He grinned. Faster than I could track, he advanced. His hand shot out. I shifted to the side, but not before said hand collided with the center of my chest. I grunted as I lifted from my feet, and crashed to the ground.

Theo closed in and stared down at me. "I'mma say that's a no."

I groaned and took his extended hand. "What an astute observation." My heart sank. That new ring had worked before, done its thing at Sierra's dirge, and when I'd barked at Victor outside the RC.

Lisa kicked a heel off and it clopped to the floor. "What about Kane?"

I canted my head. "What d'you mean?"

"Your obsidian lets you draw the power inside you, right." She tugged her cheek with her teeth. "Why can't you draw from him?"

Dragging the back of my hand across my forehead, I wicked the sweat away.

Her gaze narrowed, expression expectant. When I didn't answer, she added, "He's inside you, chickie."

Nay and Theo watched, excitedly volleying between us.

Scampering up again, I said, "It doesn't work that way."

Naomi set her drink down with a clack and sat up straighter. Her eyes widened, the first spark of anything close to life I'd seen in days. "How do you know?"

I didn't. Not really. Regardless, there was one fact I couldn't overlook. "Magi and wolves have paired before."

"Yeah," Theo cut in, "but you've got that new fan-dangled ring . . . and Kane's an Alpha."

"A fucking powerful one too," Naomi said, rolling her fingers around the rim of her glass.

Theo's stare was narrowed, thoughts churning deep inside. "I've never heard of an *Alpha* claiming a magi before."

Neither had I, but still . . .

"Exactly," Lisa said, then lifted a shoulder. "So, why not?"

My mouth opened, then closed, then opened again. There *was* a connection between Kane and I. Something tangible that bound our lives. He wouldn't be able to track me anywhere if there weren't. Seeing he could share his life and healing with me, actually *give* me things, that bond wasn't just one way. And if I could take that . . .

I worried my lip, considering, because what *if*?

I huffed a breath. "I wouldn't have the first clue how to access it."

Naomi lithely dropped to the floor. "Look for him."

Look for him the same way I looked for my own power. Shadow and sage, it was worth a try. Shaking out my shoulders, I held tight to my ring, prayed to the Iron Hells themselves, and closed my eyes.

Diving deep, I aimed for my heart where my strength lingered. I waded through as it lapped around me, pushing and pulling like an indecisive, slow-moving tide. Nothing stood out.

I eyed Naomi. "What's Autumn feel like for you?"

"I don't know how to explain it. She's a part of me. Like my shadow. Separate from me, but inseparable too. She's everywhere. I guess she feels like . . . home."

Home. I looked again, but this time, I pulled back, taking a birds-eye-view instead of the close-up from seconds ago . . . and there. Something shimmered. Something silver and decidedly powerful. Had that been there before?

I reached for it, closing in.

A knock came at the door, and all heads whipped that way.

"Iron fires take me," I breathed. My chest caved and I released my obsidian, clutching my arms around myself to hide their shake.

Theo and Naomi went rigid.

"What do we do?" Lisa asked.

What the Seven Iron Hells was *he* doing there? Swallowing around the lump forming in my throat, I said, "We let him in." Slowly, I headed for the entrance, unlocking it before I swung it wide.

A cool breeze whipped through when Joaquin crossed over. The Beta's hands were loose at his sides, stare on me.

My gaze darted past him, seeking another face—one with silver topaz eyes that could see through to my soul. One that I missed so much, it goddamn well hurt. One that wasn't there. I glanced around as if the answer to what the obsidian Joaquin was doing there would reveal itself. Unshockingly, it did not.

"Hey," I said, 'cause it was as good an opener as any.

Had Kane sent him for the car? Unlikely, seeing he was by himself and his own sat out in the lot, but then sage only knew what else he could want. Hopefully not to gut me.

He inclined his head and strode deeper in, his gait steady. His moss green, light knit sweater was crisp and fit him like it was custom. His attention tracked to Naomi, then hardened when it speared Theo.

Joaquin wasn't a beast of a man like Kane, but in that moment, the power and menace rolling off him was damn near palpable, and I fought not to retreat. Still, my heart twisted, wringing tight deep in the hollows of my chest, because I'd missed him too. A lot. I'd missed his dry tone. Missed his head shakes and eye rolls. Missed the family he'd become and hated what he thought I was capable of.

Naomi ducked her gaze and slinked to the side. "I should go." She turned to her brother. "Theo?"

Theo peered my way, his silent question clear, "*Need me to stay?*"

If the Beta'd wanted them, he had his wolfy methods to reach them, which meant whatever his purpose, it was all about me. Wonderful. The shake of my head was subtle. "Reschedule?"

"Yeah. I'll text you later." Theo grabbed his jacket off the back of the chair to his left, then tapped his palm over the table there. "Take it easy, Briar." A soul-deep sadness creased his eyes—a mirror of my own—when he dipped his chin and followed Nay out.

Joaquin's glare flashed, tracking them with every step until they crossed outside. Pivoting, he closed in on the stools, and dragged one back, its feet scraping across that hardwood floor before he set himself down. His expression was flat. Indecipherable. And trained on me.

Lisa wiggled her ass off the bar and slipped gracefully to the floor. "I'm just gonna . . ," She peered Joaquin's way. "Go anywhere else." Grabbing her downed shoe, she beat feet outta there.

Facing the Beta, my voice went high to the point of squeaky when I said, "'Sup?"

His attention lowered to the clothes I wore, then returned. He flicked a hand toward the room in general. "What was that?"

"They've, uh," I scratched the length of my throat, "taken over my training." The silence that fell was so dense, I swore tumbleweeds rolled by. I worried my cheek between my teeth and rocked back on my heels, trying to gauge him. "So, whatcha doin' here?"

"We had plans." His voice was level. Unreadable.

Plans? My brow furrowed so low, I could scarce see him. Wait, did he mean— "You're here to go *shopping*?"

The incline of his head was slow.

My mouth opened, then closed, then opened again. My furniture shopping expedition. The one the Beta'd agreed to tag along for. Kane's idea. To guard me. I cleared my throat, then fought the tears that pricked the backs of my eyes. "After what happened, I just assumed . . ."

"You didn't cancel."

I kinda figured the cancellation was implied. And it wasn't like I needed said furniture anymore. But he was there. He'd come. After everything, he'd still come. I bit my lip while a spark of something, not quite hope, but a breadcrumb that could lead to it, settled in my chest. Not that I complained. I desperately wanted him around, it just . . . didn't make sense. "Why?"

"Do I need a reason?"

He probably wouldn't go wolfy on me, but I *had* lobbed a bomb into his Pack, and as Kane's Beta, his allegiance was beyond question, so who could say for sure? I lifted a shoulder. "Kinda, yeah."

His weight shifted from one hip to the other. "Like I said, we made plans."

I stared down at my feet. "I just figured you'd hate me."

He flexed his hands and leaned his elbows onto his knees. "I don't get you, or any of this shit, banshee, but I don't hate you." He flicked a finger at the outfit of Lisa's I wore—the one that was practically a second skin with how tight it was. "Besides, pretty sure you left everything at Kane's. You need supplies."

Whether it was him upholding an obligation or some other reason I couldn't decipher, I didn't care. Nor was I about to push him on it because I *wanted* this. To grip my old life with my grubby fingers and never let it go. Joaquin was a friend. An ornery one who rivaled Lisa for honesty. One who'd slowly grown on me . . . like a fungus. And he was a connection to Kane—a tether. If I had Joaquin, I still felt like I was Pack.

Regardless, it was another chance to light some fires and pray to the wraith herself he saw the smoke. And, yeah, he was right. I did need everything.

I narrowed my gaze on him. "You get why this is weird though, right?"

His head canted my way. "That's not the only thing."

Heat flooded my face, and I rubbed the back of my neck. "Just let me grab my purse." I scuttled around the bar, gathered my things, and called goodbye to Lis.

Joaquin led as we left, heading outside. The sun backlit the surrounding buildings that painted the ground in long shadows. Spanish moss hung from the nearby trees, swaying in the slight breeze. The warm air kissed my skin as we closed in on his vehicle. A new one. Some sleek, black Mercedes SUV looking thing that said G 550 on the back. Whatever that meant.

My fingers flexed over the passenger handle. He'd known where I was, and, short of him super stalking me, there was only one way he could've known that. "How's the Pack?"

He popped the driver's side open. "You really wanna know?"

Yes. So much goddamn yes. I bit my lip and looked away as I slipped into my seat.

The vehicle rocked when he climbed inside. Shoving his key into the ignition, he turned it over and a low rumble sounded out. The thing was all leather seats, fancy buttons and even fancier screens. It suited him.

"Things are shit. Kane's . . ." He dropped it into gear, lifted a shoulder and hit the gas.

My throat tightened. "He's what?"

"Walled off."

The twisting in my chest was like a vise that locked over my ribs, breaking them one by one. Walled off. Isolated. Alone. Because of me. Because of what I'd said. What *I'd* done. Because of Isaac. "He's not talking?"

"Barely. Only to me, but even that's limited." He side-eyed me hard, his silent message clear. *I'm surprised you'd wanna know.*

I fought not to flinch. "I never wanted to hurt him, Joaquin." Not for one damn second.

He inclined his head, then veered us toward the road. "Is Lucas still gonna work at the shop?"

I didn't want him to change the subject. But with things between Kane and I finished and Isaac back on the scene, I needed to touch base with my brother. See he was okay.

I pulled out my phone and punched a text.

Hey. Just checking in. You still up for apprenticing?

Crickets.

A familiar fear gripped the base of my spine. Holding my breath, I typed again.

You around?

Again, nothing. Not out of the norm for a teenage boy, but with his past, it wasn't what I'd call reassuring. My shoulders drew up as I tensed. "Crap."

Joaquin peered my way. "What's wrong?"

I worried my lip between my teeth. "He isn't answering."

"Could just be busy," the Beta said, sounding less than convinced.

Shaking my head, I dragged a hand through my hair. I took a steady inhale, then lowered my shoulders and forced my panic aside. Did I just . . . need to trust him? 'Cause, obsidian, that was a hard ask. Like, the super kind of hard. Things had been bad so long, switching that paranoia off was a job of its own. But he'd gotten clean with Isaac around before. I prayed to the wraith and the Seven Iron Hells themselves that still held.

Hedging my bets, I texted mom.

Is Lucas alright? He's not texting me back.

Mom: He's okay. He's just out somewhere.

I frowned. Not exactly an answer, so not optimal. But better than the alternative.

Mom: I was actually about to text you. Isaac's asking for Purge.

My mouth thinned into a sharp line, and I punched my next message so hard, my nails clicked against the screen.

The hells does he need that for?

Mom: He's moving V again for cash until this other deal goes through.

I huffed a sardonic laugh. "Of course," I grumbled, gaze flicking to Joaquin.

He cocked a brow in question.

I'd have shown him the phone, but, well, compulsion and all. "Purge," I said, because really, need I say more?

Silence reigned for several long seconds, then, "Need to go back and get it?"

I shook my head. "I'll grab it when you drop me back here for the car later." Either way, I still needed to lay eyes on my brother. See for myself he was good. Besides, I could use it, take the chance to throw up a flare or two. I texted mom back.

Meet me at the Atrium tomorrow night at seven. Bring Lucas with you.

I shoved my phone away as Joaquin aimed us east. My brows furrowed low. "I thought we were going to buy stuff?"

"We are."

I stabbed a hand to my right. "The shopping center's that way."

"It is."

I waited for him to elaborate. And waited. And waited. "Care to fill me in, Joaquin."

"We're not going to the shopping center."

My words were dry when I replied, "Sorta pieced that much together already." I folded my arms over my chest. "So, pray tell, where *are* we going?"

Cutting the wheel, he took us through the hotel district where the non-preternaturally married humans were permitted to overnight. Their clustered skyscrapers were mirror-windowed and covered in clematis, the indigo-colored flowers wide as they hunted the sun.

"The Canal District," he said.

I might've been the Coven's Second, but that didn't make me Conclave. My forthcoming salary would be good, still, it wasn't the super deep-pockets kinda good. "The Canal District's a tad lavish, Joaquin."

He flicked his hand, dismissing me.

Scoffing, I set an elbow on the lip of my door and plunked my head into my hand. "Fine, prepare to have your time wasted."

Before long, the Beta pulled us up to the affluent shops that lined River Street—just down from Immortal Inc. My heart pounded in my ears, drowning out all sound and thought, save one. Kane. His name rolled through my veins, and across my soul. The ghost of his touch kissed my memory, and sage, the pain that filled that void had me fighting not to clutch my chest.

This was a bad idea. The baddest. But I'd take being close to my Alpha any way I could, even if it tore me apart.

Joaquin angled toward me. "He's not there."

Oh. I slumped and turned away. Popping my door open, I climbed out.

The Beta let me lead and I aimed down the cobblestoned sidewalk through the buzzing crowds and organized chaos to a high-end catchall store. The bat-shaped bell over the door jangled as we passed in. The place was dimly lit by well-worn black candles, their wax dripping in long rivulets down their sides. The shelves lining the walls were carved out of gray stone into some scaled serpent, the racks in the center formed from its inverted clawed legs, and the counter to pay, its wide open, jagged-toothed maw.

I weaved us through, eyeing the hyper-stylish, and bizarrely practical clothes. Taking a circuitous path, I pulled piece by meticulous piece—choices entirely unusual and wholly intentional. I grabbed jeans, dress pants, and a few pretty, but comfortable looking tops. In the end, it didn't matter what they looked like, only the message they conveyed. I'd have preferred unflattering, bland and ill-fitting, but if I was waving a white flag, it was key Isaac didn't spot it. It needed to be subtle enough to escape the wrong notice and peculiar enough to catch the right. A fine, dangerous line to tread.

Joaquin's brow tracked high, a perfect arch when he noted, "No skirts?"

No. Skirts were for Kane. For his ease of access to my body. A fact my Alpha well knew. One I prayed to the wraith he remembered.

I shook my head and fumbled as I tried to drape the clothes over my arm. My heart rate kicked up a handful of frenetic notches while I let the stark weirdness of my non-reply stand.

He snatched everything from me, grabbed a handy dandy cart, all domestic and entirely un-wolfy, then tossed my stuff inside. "Why?"

Worrying my lip between my teeth, I thumbed through another array of pants and worked an answer. "I don't need them anymore."

His nod was slow and singular. "You ready for the Conclave meeting tomorrow?"

Yes. And a thousand times, no. "What do you think?"

"I think it'll be interesting." He leaned his forearms against the cart's handle. "Heard you helped Cassandra yesterday."

There was only one place—one Dowagery shadow walker—that information could've originated from. Curious. I pulled out a pair of low waisted denims, checked the size, tossed them into the cart and offered him a side eye. "Keeping tabs on me, Beta?"

"Something like that." He gestured toward the makeup aisle. "You need any of that stuff?"

I needed all of that stuff. My head bobbed and I veered that way.

He tapped a finger over the side of the cart. "You doing alright?"

I lifted a shoulder in a half-shrug. "I'm doing." Short. Sweet. And a complete non-answer. Just the useful kind I needed.

His brow tugged down. "Anything you wanna talk about?"

Oh, if he only knew. "Like what?"

"I think you know, banshee."

"I think you're right, but I'm still gonna make you say it." First, because I couldn't afford assumptions, and second, rankling him brought my magi soul a sad sliver of delight.

He rolled his eyes and pivoted toward the blushes. "How 'bout what happened the other night."

My heart slammed to a stop and my mouth ran dry. "You were there, Joaquin."

"Mhmm." He propped a hip against the wall there, then folded his arms over his chest. "And I still don't get it."

"Not sure I can enlighten you anymore." Considering my mouth was sewn shut with an iron thread.

He grumbled under his breath. "Fine. Why Mason?"

I stiffened. Shitty. Shit. *Shit!* What the hells was I supposed to say to that? "I already gave that answer."

"No. You said you were done with Kane, not why you picked your ex." His stare held mine. "Didn't make sense then. Doesn't make sense now."

At least there was that. My words were decidedly even when I replied, "I don't know what else to say."

His gaze narrowed. "You still want Kane."

Yes. Sweet sage, *yes*. I grabbed a blush pallet in a series of soft coral tones. "Is that a question or a conclusion?"

The weight of his attention was heavy and un-goddamn-yielding. "You tell me."

My adrenaline kicked me into hyperdrive, and I flicked a hanger with the tip of my nail. "I can't talk about him with you."

His brassy laugh was more interest than humor. "A truth."

My gaze glided to his in the tester mirror. There were several ways my comment could be taken and seeing I had not one clue which one he'd picked, my face twisted in response.

His stare went unfocused in that wolfish way, like he was somewhere else, with someone else. It stayed that way for one breath. Two. Three. He blinked and he was back.

I wanted him to keep asking questions. Because being around him made my heart hurt a little less, and I'd take every second of reprieve I could get.

Instead, he cleared his throat. "I'm interviewing the new artist for Immortal Inc Thursday. You free?"

I cocked my head. "Me?"

"You're co-owner, banshee. You get a say."

Pursing my lips, I grabbed some brown eyeliner, and ultra black mascara. "It just . . . feels wrong to take that kind of control."

He lifted a shoulder. "Maybe. But if Lucas is gonna apprentice, whoever it is will have access to him."

Well, shit. When he put it that way. "What time?"

"One."

I didn't know what the Beta's ultimate motive was, if he even had one, but I'd take it. "I'll be there."

Snatching up the rest of the supplies on my "desperately needed" list, I plunked them in with everything else. "There. Done." I dusted my hands. "Happy?"

He exhaled an exasperated breath and stared at the ceiling like it might offer patience.

I pointed us toward the checkout and lay everything onto the counter while the clerk started scanning. The Beta edged in beside me, pulled a black credit card from his wallet and handed it to the girl—the same credit card he'd used last time we'd shopped together. The one from the Pack. Kane.

My head snapped his way. "What are you doing, Joaquin?"

He scowled good and deep, offering me a "*What's it look like?*" expression.

The shake of my head was vehement. "No. It's not right, like, at all." I'd taken enough from my Alpha—from the whole damn Pack—I couldn't take anymore.

"Listen, this . . ." He waved a flippant hand, "*thing* with Mason aside, you're still Kane's claimed."

I angled away, gaze down and words low when I uttered, "We're not together, Joaquin."

"Doesn't matter if you're together. It's his job to protect you."

Job. Like it was a burden. Not that I had any right to be upset. Well, I did, seeing none of what happened had been my choice, but in Kane's eyes . . .

My voice softened. Gentled. "I can afford this stuff." Barely. But I could.

"Not what I meant, banshee." He advanced a step. "It's his responsibility."

Responsibility. That word had any number of meanings, but in Pack politics, stripping Kane of it meant undermining him, something I'd *never* do willingly.

The cashier's gaze darted between us, card held high like she didn't know how to proceed. I gave her a resigned nod and she ran it through. The Beta looped the bags over his arms, and we left. Piling them in the back of his SUV, we climbed inside, and he steered us out of the Canal District.

I dropped my forehead against my window, gaze holding on Immortal Inc as we passed. "What now?"

"We've got one more stop."

"I've got everything I need."

"Not everything."

The way he said it had my ears pricking. I sat up straighter. "Where are we going, Joaquin?"

He flicked his signal light, the tick, tick, tick sounding out before he said, "Your place."

My brows furrowed low. "I don't have a place."

"You do now."

My jaw dropped. "Say what?"

We crossed the border of the Northern Pack's territory. *Kane's* territory.

Joaquin parked us in front of a high-rise condo building and my attention angled up as we climbed out and he grabbed my things.

The place was burnt clay brick covered in thirty-foot creeping stems, each filled with blooms of white roses. They wrapped up and around the lower balconies, dusting the air with a rich, floral scent. Large Caster Stones carved into the shape of gray wolves guarded either side of the main entrance. A bronzed placard above the front entrance read: 'Let any who enter keep peace and let those who do not await the justice they've earned.'

Not ominous, at *all*. Even still . . . My attention tracked Joaquin's way. "Since when are there magi Caster Stones anywhere in wolfy territory?"

He adjusted the bags so he held them in one hand. "Since the Alpha's claimed moved in." He arched a lone brow like he waited for me to challenge him, but I'd need to get my sputtering brain cells back online for that. Not that I *wanted* to challenge him. Things between Mason and I were better, but want to live with him, I did *not*.

Joaquin reached into his pocket, then handed me a gold keycard. I set it over the high-tech pad beside the etched glass entrance. The door swung open, and I stepped through. A female were in a security uniform stood behind a desk to the right. The Beta offered her a tight nod.

The lobby was all polished onyx marble with three chrome-doored elevators. I stopped, having unequivocally no clue where to go.

He indicated the furthest to the left. "That one."

"Something wrong with the other two?"

"You get your own." At the utterly confused twisting of my expression, he added, "It's for the penthouse."

My head snapped back. The penthouse? As in, an entire floor? Kane got me an *entire floor*? I wanted to read into it, wraith take me, I was desperate to. But Joaquin was right, I was Kane's responsibility. Abandoning me left my ass vulnerable—open to attack, which left Kane open too, seeing we were a package deal. Well, our lives were, anyway. And in every way possible, I'd turned myself into his biggest liability. Maybe it was just his permanent solution—a message that we were over. The thought made my stomach roll while bile seared the back of my throat.

Using my card again, I selected the eighteenth floor, and we climbed, and climbed, and climbed until we reached the summit. The doors dinged, then ground open to an ivory marble lobby with a plush shag rug in the same shade. My heart stuttered as I stepped inside.

The place was open concept with a sunken living room and a clear line of sight over Cambria's neutral grounds. The soft brown leather couches had that faint, new, chemical sorta smell, like the protective plastic packaging they'd been shipped in had just been stripped away. The kitchen was off-white cupboards, and state of the art, stainless steel appliances. A wide balcony rimmed the southern half, while to the north, the bedrooms.

Swallowing hard, I headed that way.

The bed was king-sized with an olive-green upholstered headboard, a thick, heavy looking cream toned duvet, and a linen-colored plush carpet. It was soft, and lavish but still . . . comfortable.

A dark-stained wicker egg chair sat in the corner. It faced the floor-to-ceiling window with a line of sight to the entirety of my Alpha's territory. Tossed haphazardly on its plush taupe cushions was a black hoodie I'd recognize anywhere.

Kane's.

My finger twitched, itching to reach for it, to throw it over my shoulders, wrap it around me and pretend it was him. I inhaled deep, my Alpha's musk and wilderness scent subtle on the air.

The Beta set my bags down beside the walk-in closet. From the corner of my vision, his stare was heavy on me, but obsidian only knew what he saw.

"This is yours too." He chucked that black credit card onto the dresser. "If you need anything else, let me know."

My throat tightened, tears of guilt pricking the backs of my eyes. My nod was singular and small. "Thank you, Joaquin. For today," I clarified. Power of obsidian, for everything.

He watched me for several unfathomable seconds before he tipped his head. "You're welcome."

I eyed that hoodie again and breathed deep, clinging to Kane and that life with everything I had. I couldn't let go. Couldn't let it slip through my fingers. Because if it did, I didn't think I'd survive.

Chapter Eleven

My car's tires crunched over the bone-dry ground as I pulled into the Atrium, the abandoned human mine that comprised the Conclave's meeting place. The moon broke through a tuft of clouds, beating on my windshield in wide beams.

I'd spent the night in my condo curled up in Kane's hoodie. I'd wanted to wear it there, never take it off, but seeing that fell into the "don't let Big Bad know how you feel" category, my compulsion had another idea.

Wrapper crinkling, I shoved the rest of my hamburger in my mouth, practically swallowing it whole, because sage knew I was gonna need the strength.

I slowed to a stop beside my mother's car where it stood off to the left, butting against the back edge of the lot. Her bedraggled hair stuck off in all directions, hands locked on the wheel, gaze aimed at her lap.

I adjusted my black dress pants, and form-fitting, full-coverage top, attention tracking to Lucas. He sat slumped in on himself in the passenger seat, those violet eyes were clear, but desolate.

My stomach plummeted and I climbed out. Popping Lucas's door open, I crouched by his side. "Hey."

He stared straight ahead, voice muted when he replied, "Hey."

"What's wrong?"

The answering laugh he let loose was so acidic, it was a wonder it didn't burn.

My attention tracked to my mother.

Her expression creased. "Isaac thought Hannah was in the way."

I crushed my eyes closed while my hands curled into fists. In the way? *In the goddamn way?* I got why he hated me, but Iron fucking Hells, he couldn't just let his son be? Let him have *one* thing? No, of course, he couldn't. He'd seen that pattern before. Seen me fall so madly for Kane, everything I was shifted. What mattered, and who. I became a problem—a threat. So he'd headed my brother off at the pass.

Think, Briar. Think. Opening my eyes, I straightened my spine. Language. It was all about language. "Tell me what he said, Lucas. Word for word."

His head thumped when it landed against the seat's rest. "He took my phone and told me to end things with Hannah."

My brows furrowed. A one-time order, not permanent. "That's it?"

"Yeah," he said, nod tight.

"Then take mine and call her."

"No."

I dragged a hand across the back of my neck. "Please, Lucas. Don't you dare let her go. Not for *him*."

The shake of his head snapped his hair around his forehead. "She deserves better."

Better. As if he wasn't worth it. The depth of my agony knew no bounds. "Lucas—"

"No," he said, the word hard. Final. "It was different before when I thought he was gone. When he came back, I hoped he'd just leave me alone, but he won't. He never will. I'm not gonna do that to her."

Iron fires. Hannah'd made him smile. Pulled him from his shell. Made him fucking happy.

"He's never gonna stop with me," he said. "Not until I'm like him."

My mother sniffed and wiped a tear.

Taking his face between my hands, I promised, "You're not him, Lucas. You could *never* be him because you care about more than yourself."

His nod was stiff and barely there.

I hated that he'd let Hannah go, but I loved him for that selflessness. Sage, every day he was more and more a man. And there was only one influence for that—one wolf who'd shown him what it was to exist with substance.

"Why can't he just die?" he said, then swallowed hard.

He needed hope. A light at the end of the goddamn tunnel. Something to get him through. I loved mom, but she wasn't strong enough to work against Isaac. She'd had her chance—had a thousand of them. But Lucas ...

I wrapped my arms around him and held tight. Leaning close, I pitched my voice low for only him to hear. "I'm working on it."

His head snapped my way, eyes wide.

Pulling back, the incline of my head was slow, and I held his violet stare so he'd see every ounce of "*I fucking promise*" I could muster.

My mother's brows furrowed.

The wind rustled through the Japanese lilacs that dotted the lot, carrying that overly sweet, floral scent. Arrant leaves skittered across the ground and skimmed my shoes before they flitted on. The rumble of an engine approached as its lights cut through the night. It grew louder. That familiar truck advanced, its large tires grinding over the ground.

Kane sat behind the wheel, those silver topaz eyes molten when they locked on me.

I froze. Couldn't breathe. Sage, why couldn't I breathe? I thought I'd braced, knew what to expect, but the sight of him had my heart pulsing in my head, *screaming* ... until I spotted the woman in the passenger seat. I blinked hard and looked away, then did a double take.

Was that—my eyes narrowed to slits—*Whitney*?

My world dropped out from under me, axis tilting. My face flushed and I grew dizzy. I grabbed mom's car to steady myself.

He'd brought *her*? His goddamn ex?

He parked, turned to her and said something, then climbed out. Stalking to her side, his shoulders straining against the material of his navy hoodie when he popped her door open.

She slipped free with that graceful ease, landing delicately on the ground. There was still a good foot between them, but they were close. Too close.

What the iron fires was she doing there? What was it? Some messed up fucking date? My chest caved, lungs refusing to work. He'd said she was nothing. His past. That I was his everything. That things between them ended for a reason.

I'd only been gone for days. *Days!* And he'd brought her?

I was fighting for him—for us—and he'd just . . . moved on? He knew it'd hurt me. Sage, I'd practically gone feral after I'd met her at the RC. And everything in me begged to again, because *I* was his claimed. *I* was his fucking mate!

Whitney's gaze met mine, the whites of her eyes exposed as she turned ashen. She brushed those fine braids over her shoulder, scratched the side of her cheek, and glanced away.

Had she made the move? Or had it been him? Was she just some rebound? His own revenge? 'Cause he'd brought her there—to the Conclave—where he *knew* I'd be. It was a message. Had to be. Why else do it? It wasn't like the place was a hotspot for dates. Had he *wanted* me to see? To know I'd been replaced? It didn't sound like him, but then I hadn't just ended things between us, I'd obliterated them.

Nothing else made sense.

Wraith take me, they even looked good together. Whitney was beautiful. That elegant poise a perfect contrast to his sex and brawn and brutality. They fit. Made sense.

If I'd thought I'd hated Isaac before, it was nothing compared to the fire-fueled loathing that scorched my soul then. My breath ripped from my throat in rapid pants, hand sealing over my obsidian. The metal seared my skin. I staggered again, stumbling to the side.

Lucas followed my line of sight and turned to stone. "Who the hells is that?"

My mother winced.

I peered around, lost. No concept of who or where I was. It just didn't make *sense*. No, that wasn't true. Kane was who he was.

Someone else wanting him—him finding another woman—wasn't a surprise. Not really. I'd just refused to consider the prospect because there were only so many pieces of myself I could lose before there was nothing left. A shattered shell. A husk.

The knife through my heart sank deep. It twisted, and cut wide, bleeding me out. Slowly. It hurt. Shadow and sage, it goddamn hurt!

My chest burned as spots flashed in my vision. Kane was mine. My love. My heart. My soul. My mate. My fingers trailed my claiming mark. *Mine!* I balled my hands into fists, nails digging into my flesh—nails I wanted to claw Whitney's stupid, pretty eyes out with.

Lucas's tone hardened. Protective. Pissed. "Who *is* that, Briar?"

Tears seared my sight as I shook my head. "It doesn't matter."

He unlatched his seatbelt.

Oh, shit! The unequivocal last thing I needed was my brother going head-to-head with Kane, because that wasn't about to go well for anyone. My hand shot out. "No, Lucas." My gaze found his, my silent message clear. *Let me handle this.*

He hesitated, veins pulsing in his neck while his eyes hardened, but his head dipped in a bow, so I'd take it.

I righted and closed his door. Grabbing the Purge from my car, I sauntered to mom's side, face burning like a flame was lit beneath it when I passed it over. "You should go."

Her words were quiet, and quavering when she whispered, "Are you alright?"

The question was general—not specific to Isaac, which meant shielding my answer wasn't required. Time to shoot up some flares. The desolation of my voice was thick, and pained and so goddamn real when I answered, "Does it matter?"

Her lower lip trembled as she gave a delicate nod.

Leaning into the car, I wrapped her in a hug, held tight for one breath. Two. Three. I released and pulled back. Easing forward, she drove away. Dust kicked up, filling the air before it coated my lungs.

From the corner of my gaze, Kane watched . . . them, or me, I didn't know.

I wanted not to feel. Just for a while. To give my heart a second to beat without that all-consuming agony. I just needed to breathe. But more than that, I needed to get my head together. Needed to think because this wasn't just about me. Lucas, mom, Theo, Nay, and Lis . . . they all needed help. I wouldn't abandon them.

Whitney might've been there with my Alpha, but Kane was a good man, and his presence offered an opportunity.

I shook out my shoulders and steadied myself. Clutching my purse, I plucked out the Tonic and the clump of tissues I'd stashed there. I raised that bottle high for my Alpha to see, then sloshed it around, and unstoppered it.

Taking a mouthful, I leaned into the car, pretending to look for something, and spat it into that handy dandy tissue, because like the Iron Hells I'd ever use that stuff again. Besides, if I wanted to work my plan, I needed myself clean. My head clear.

I straightened and those silver eyes flashed. Kane's jaw flexed, the muscles of his neck cording. Boy, he was mad. Whether it was the Tonic or my existence that set it off, I didn't know. And it hurt, hurting him. I wanted to know if he was alright. Wanted to feel his arms around me. Sink into him. Needed it. But that wasn't about to happen without—

I froze when an idea struck. Because there *was* another way.

My tongue prodded my cheek. It was such an intrusion, went against Coven rule, and was a shit ton of problematic. But I *could* use it. Poke that wolf to get his attention. 'Cause my hope hinged on him. He was my North Star. My guiding light. If he'd moved on . . .

He ripped his stare away and turned it on Whitney. Taking my obsidian, I gripped it tight. Sage, forgive me.

I exhaled, then searched Kane's sunset markers, deciding where to go. My chest tightened. My hand trembled. I scanned, fast forwarding like a movie, quick flashes of images flickered by with no sound.

I fought not to hyperventilate as I screamed in the prison of my mind, clawing at the walls to break free. I needed a something to cling to—a life preserver. A memory that wouldn't shatter me. One that reminded me what it was to be loved by him.

Veering back, I aimed for a time I knew. One that'd give me what I needed. To feel how much he cared. To hear him say my name the way he used to. Warm. Hot. Craving.

I dove in.

Kane unloaded the last of the lumber to frame the flower garden and set it to the side of the house. His stare landed on me as I bent over, skirt tracking higher while my fingers tapped each board to count them. His attention fell on my ass before it snaked down my legs, then back up. He inhaled long and deep.

It was bizarre, watching things through his eyes. Watching me.

The earthy scents of soil, wood and sawdust coated his aura, every note of cedar filling my senses. Yeah, I'd read other wolves before, but it'd never been so . . . overwhelming. Was it him? His power as an Alpha? Iron fires, it was strong.

I straightened and angled my head back, peering over my shoulder as I offered him a salacious grin. "Like what you see, Big Bad?"

He crossed his arms over his chest and leaned a hip against the truck. "Mm-hmm." His emotions hit like a freight train; content, confidence, pride, excitement, amusement, and love. Sage, so much love.

The force of it was so staggering, I stumbled.

I sashayed his way, lips parting before my tongue trailed over my bottom teeth. A trace of vanilla tinged the air, growing stronger the closer I came.

Pump the brakes! Was that what I smelled like to him? It was so . . . good. No wonder he'd been obsessed.

The low rumble in his chest was a primal hunger. He reached for me, and his fingers dug deep into the flesh of my hips as he lifted. I squeaked when he twisted and set me on the tailgate. He edged forward, knee nudging my legs apart as he stepped between them.

His mouth descended, crashing against mine. Those arms banded around me as our tongues met and he took and tasted.

I moaned and a feral want ripped from him. So damn powerful. It screamed, ravenous. Content. More.

My body heated, and I trailed a finger over my heart tattoo.

A pair of silver lights flashed through the aura. No. Not lights. Eyes. Kane. The Kane in the present. I sucked in a sharp gasp and released my obsidian with a snap.

He rolled his shoulders, brows sinking low while his molten stare speared me and he stormed my way.

Caught.

Ooooooh, shit! My plan had worked, and I was about to get myself maimed because of it. Genius, Briar. Absolute *genius*! Running was a *bad* idea, but I was plum outta good ones, so before I could think better of it, I beat feet for the Atrium.

Bursting inside, I whipped past the dual, iron knife packing, black-clad guards. I careened down the hall, under the massive, hand-carved salt chandeliers and into the main room, then sealed myself inside. As if that would help.

The pound of heavy footfalls closed in, and I lunged away an instant before the door exploded open and Kane filled the entrance.

I back-pedaled, slamming into the garnet encrusted wall. He stalked forward until he stopped less than an inch away. His heat pulsed over me, that musk and wilderness scent surrounding me. His broad, dominating form edged closer and his hands crashed against the wall. Chest grazing mine, his knee drove between my thighs, pinning me in place. I gasped as he loomed over me, a deep thunder tearing from the recesses of his throat.

Iron Hells, but the feel of him against me was so damn—

Wait, he could . . . touch me? And Isaac's compulsion hadn't balked? Realization struck like a brick to the face. Because he'd ordered me not to touch Kane, not to keep Kane from touching me. A loophole. One I praised all things holy for, because regardless of his rage, having him close was a salve to my soul.

He scented the air—scented me. My *weakened* scent, well, the Mason part of it anyway considering my powers would've burned it off.

Hope. So much more hope. I needed it. Wanted more. Was so damn greedy for it.

Those eyes blazed igneous, and full of some incomprehensible emotion when he growled, "The shadowed fucking moon were you doing?"

I couldn't think—couldn't breathe. My mouth opened to respond but nothing came out. My fingers dug into the stone at my back. I drew my lip between my teeth, fighting with everything I had to reach out, run my fingers through that hair and tell him I loved him. Tell him the truth. Beg him to take me back, then help me rip Isaac to pieces so small, he'd be less than dust.

But my stepfather's chain pulled tight.

Kane was sinew, power and sex fused into one dangerous beast of a man. My stomach clenched and my mouth watered. I trailed my tongue along the back of my teeth. *Touch me more, Kane. Please, just touch me more.*

He rolled his neck when he pushed through his clenched jaw, "What were you looking for in my aura?"

Um. Yeah . . . that. I swallowed hard. At least I'd gotten his attention—his majorly pissed, dangerous, Alpha wolf attention. But I clearly hadn't thought things through, because what the obsidian was I supposed to do from there?

"You're staring, Briar."

Not Bry. *Briar.* It was a subtle, but preternaturally hard gut punch, and I fought not to double over. It sounded so wrong, so detached. Kane Slade was nothing if not intentional, so doubtless, he'd used it by design.

I looked away.

His warm hand locked around my chin, completely engulfing my face. He forced my gaze back to his. The growl he let loose was harsh, and primal, and absolute restraint. "The hells is with you and Lana?"

I blinked. Thank the wraith, he'd noticed. But of course, he had. This was Kane, an Alpha through and through. He kept his eye on threats, and from where he stood, I was most definitely one of those.

"She's, uh," my fingers flexed against the wall, "going through some stuff."

He glared through his brow. And not having one sweet ass clue what to say, I lifted a shoulder.

The curse that tore from him echoed through the room before that anger was thrown my way. "You're using again."

I turned away. Or at least, tried to, but his grip locked down, touch hot, and unyielding. It dug into my flesh but there wasn't any pain. Obsidian, it felt good. I wanted more. Wanted his hands everywhere—to never let go.

"*Why?*"

Because I want you to look, see something's wrong. Hear me scream for help. But that truth was beyond me to offer, so, short on words, I shook my head.

He huffed a dark laugh, and pressed tighter, body crushing mine. "Luke deserves better than this shit."

The shudder of my heart was so loud, I was shocked he didn't hear it. "Yes." I glanced down to his mouth, and back again, then tested my next words against the compulsion and got no resistance. "What's Whitney doing here?" A question, not an admission. A technicality. With an answer I desperately feared.

His calloused thumb tracked higher, rasping along my jaw. His tone was an even, low rumble when he used my words from outside. The ones with my mother he'd very clearly heard. "Does it matter?"

Yes. Wraith take me, it mattered so goddamn much. "You're here with her." A statement, but very much not.

His hand fell and my skin turned cold at the absence of that touch. "Yeah." That palm landed against the wall again, the tendons of his forearm rolling under his strain. "I am."

No apologies, not that he owed me any—not that he owed me *anything*.

Agony seared my soul, "Why?" I demanded, as if I had any right.

His head canted to the side and his voice rolled through me like thunder when he repeated, "Does it matter?" My throat locked around an answer, and when I didn't give it, he angled closer, staring at me through his brow. "Why are you with *Mason*?"

Mason. That name from Kane was poison on my skin. What he thought stung. Because of Isaac. Because I was trapped. Because I was still fighting my way out.

Show him something, Briar. Anything!

My breath quickened as I tugged my out-of-character pant leg. His attention flicked there and held.

Push, Kane. Please, just push harder. I needed him to ask another question—the *right* question. Not that he'd know what that was, but maybe if I just willed it hard enough . . .

There was a knock at the door. It slid open. Kane's neck corded as he peered toward it and Whitney stepped in.

Chapter Twelve

"Kane?" Whitney said, tone sheepish as she advanced. "Is everything alright?"

He cleared his throat, arms dropping to his sides before he took a step back. "Yeah."

I wanted to scream, tell her to fly her witchy ass off. That what happened between us was none of her goddamn business. Kane was mine. MINE!

But that was the thing, he wasn't. He'd come to the Conclave with *her*. Another woman. Someone else. Not me.

Not mine.

My limbs weakened and I gave the wall my weight.

Alistair stepped in, the Southern Coven Leader's attention shifting between the most awkwardest of standoffs between Whitney, me and Kane. I braced for him to offer that ochre-colored hand in one of his crushing shakes—no doubt a habit of rubbing shoulders with the preternatural elite. Instead, he gave me a nod and beelined for his seat.

Two long, live-edge tables sat across from one another, newly replaced since their predecessors had been obliterated after Anthony lost himself at the last meeting. A circular, stone-carved map of Cambria occupied the floor in the middle, covered by thick, impeccably kept Plexiglass. The divides were like a poorly cut pie with the were territories to the east, magi in the middle, and shadow walkers to the west. Dead center of it all sat the neutral grounds of the Atrium, Recovery Center, Canal District and No Man's Land, among other things.

Victor crossed over next, plum suit fitted over his frame with that wannabe gangster-style fedora angling down. Not shielding his eyes but shadowing them. Amber was tight on his heels. Her skin-tight leather pants creaked as she moved, eyeing Kane like a meal while she over-eagerly swayed her ample hips.

Kane's stare pinned mine, an exhale rattling through his chest like he had a shit ton more to say. And, sage, I wanted him to say it.

The door swung wide, and Mason appeared, face still swollen. The bruising was less, like a mud and blood-stained lake. He spotted us and sank in on himself as he pushed his black-rimmed glasses up his nose.

My Alpha's torrid glare tracked Mason's way and held for several terrifyingly long seconds before he edged away from me. Tipping his head to Whitney, he gave me his back and stalked to his seat, his lithe frame tensing with every powerful stride.

My chest hitched while spots danced in my vision, and it took all my will to keep my legs from buckling. *No. Come back. Please, don't leave me. COME BACK!*

Mason advanced several tentative steps my way. His wide eyes flicked between me and my Alpha. No, not my Alpha. Not. Mine.

"You okay?" he asked, stroking his fingers down my arm.

What the actual hells? We might've been forced to fake our relationship, but that hadn't opened the door for him to get handsy. I latched onto my obsidian, whipped a cocoon over our conversation and snarled through my teeth, "What are you doing, Mason?"

"Calm down, now, Briar," Isaac's voice said from Mason's lips—Mason's *skin*. "We wouldn't want anyone getting the wrong idea about us." He brushed several strands of hair back from my shoulder. "Be a dear and act like you care for poor, sweet Mason."

I tensed. My gaze flicked to that scar on his hand. He was a thousand shades of death wish and dumb showing up there, but if he knew what I was up to, why I'd asked Mason to call that meeting . . . Shit. Shit. Shit! I needed my plan to come through. Needed a failsafe with the humans. Something to slow his charge—or stop it.

He peered Kane's way. "What was that show about?"

My laugh was sardonic, and I couldn't contain the hiss in my tone when I answered, "Shockingly, he's still a tad pissed about what happened."

He laughed, sharp and cutting. A caution, or more likely a promise. "I'm pleased to hear it."

Exhaling slow, I tried to calm the rapid-fire beat of my heart. "What are you doing here?"

"Staying in the loop, Briar, dear," he said through a counterfeit smile.

My gaze lingered on Kane as he lowered into his seat. It groaned when he sank down, claiming it like a throne. He leaned back, giving the thing his weight. His shoulders extended beyond its rest, the ridges of his dense muscles on display through his shirt. Whitney stood slightly back and to his right. She didn't belong there. She belonged with her Coven Leader. Across the room. Away.

Isaac's stare drifted to her. "Who knew you were so easily replaced."

My breath hitched when that ugly truth cut deep.

"Oh, and, Briar," he said. "Do find me at Mason's tomorrow."

A pit formed in my stomach, taking root and burrowing deep. "Why?"

He winked. "Our Ithican friend is ready to meet."

My blood ran cold.

His lecherous hand settled on the small of my back. "Now, release the conversation for me," he ordered, then guided me toward Mason's seat—the one *immediately next to Kane*.

Isaac's spine was rigidly straight when he took his place. I positioned myself behind him and eyed Kane. And what I wouldn't have given to know what he thought. What he felt. He was so close. Just within grasp, yet totally out of reach. If I could just touch him, bridge that wolfy link to talk to him. Lob more answerless answers his way. Make him question.

Pain stung the back of my chest, and I turned away, gnawing the quick of my nail.

Joaquin stepped to my side, flanking his Alpha when he set his position between Whitney and me. A barrier I welcomed. He tipped his head. "Hungry, banshee?"

A small, pathetic smile took me, and I nudged him with my shoulder.

Amber fluttered her lashes as she watched Kane, lip rolling between her teeth like she was caught in some memory. I cleared my throat. Her gaze flicked to me and the glare I threw her way was so sharp, it could've cut. She trailed a finger down her cheek, mimicking a tear.

My hand twitched, itching for an ultra-stabby weapon to plunge through her neck. Visualization was key to success, after all. Maybe I'd make a vision board—one shaped like a bullseye with her face at the center.

"What's she even doing here?" I seethed.

Joaquin's chin angled up. "She took over Mila's role."

Sage, give me strength because my thirst for blood in that moment would've rivaled any shadow walker. Amber was Victor's new goddamn *Beta*? Amber, who'd helped Ronin destroy Kane and I. Amber, who'd fucked my Alpha against his will. Amber, who'd relished every brutal second of it.

A snarl built in the back of my throat. She didn't deserve to look at him. Breathe the same air he breathed—or breathe at all.

Rage seared my veins so hot it would only be cooled by vengeance. I gripped my obsidian hard, fingers turning white. My power pulsed, and that metal burned.

Kane stiffened. Rolling his shoulders, his head half-turned my way.

Cassandra glided past, drifting like liquid smoke as she moved. Her hair was pulled up in a loose bun, while her golden, corset-waisted dress shimmered, flitting on the air. "Briar Stone," she greeted. "It is pleasant to see you again."

"You, as well," I replied.

Danika, the Southern Clan Dowager crossed over next. Her fire-kissed hair was unkempt, sticking off in every direction, that crimson gaze cast in shadow and trained straight ahead. It darkened her soul—if she had one of those. There was a hollowness there, obvious from the black circles under her eyes. Could shadow walkers . . . cry?

The vamps didn't unnerve me like they used to—mostly—but the agony that coated the air was palpable and it set my teeth on edge. Danika was wounded, and wounded predators were nothing if not dangerous.

I inhaled deep and leaned Cassandra's way. "Is she alright?"

She shook her head. "No, Briar Stone. She is not." Her expression was impassive when she turned it on that Mason version of Isaac, raking him up and down before she glided down beside him.

"This should be interesting," Joaquin deadpanned.

"If everyone would like to take their places," Alistair called to the room, taking a page from Sierra's book. Requests worked. Commands didn't. Commanding apex predators was only advised if you sought the deadliest of trouble.

The scrape of chairs and rustling of bodies carried as everyone settled in. Silence descended.

In the periphery of my sight, Whitney watched me, and the weight of that attention irritated like sandpaper grating my skin.

Cassandra drifted to her feet. "I wish to discuss the death of one of my people."

Alistair bowed his head. "The Southern Coven is sorry for the loss of another shadow walker—"

"Her name was *Frances*," Danika cut in, words shrill as they sliced through the room. Her hands curled against the wood, those black painted, talon-shaped nails gouging deep.

The hair on my arms stood on end.

Kane angled forward, setting his elbows on the edge of the table. It widened his shoulders and tugged his shirt, outlining the dense brawn beneath.

"Frances," Alistair noted. Not an admission of a wrong. Admissions were backpedaling. Backpedaling meant imbalance. Imbalance inside the Conclave was the *super* sort of bad. More like a course correction to steer down a less lethal path.

Cassandra swept her arm, gesturing my way. "At my behest, Briar Stone did a reading for me. She did not see who it was."

Danika's gaze hollowed. "What else do we know?"

I adjusted my full-coverage top, feeling decidedly exposed. My pulse thrummed in my neck, calling the walkers like a dinner bell.

"There wasn't a trail when I scented Cassandra's area." Kane shook his head. "Wolfsbane."

Wait . . . he'd been there?

"So, it's like before?" Alistair said.

Danika glared at me—through me—her expression contorting. "You said *Jared* was behind everything." She slammed a fist onto the table. A crack echoed through the room, a split fissuring the wood. It didn't collapse, but a second hit like that and we'd be needing another replacement.

I couldn't tell if it was a comment or an accusation, but Kane didn't move to rip her throat out, so I accepted it as the former.

My neck was stiff when I uttered, "I can no longer say."

Joaquin shifted, linking his hands before him as he said to the room, "We intended to question Jared's wife but she's MIA."

"Wasn't she at the dirge, Briar?" Mason-Isaac asked, voice high and innocent.

Absolute ass! "I saw her face." Her face on Isaac's skin, but her face, nonetheless.

"So, she's hiding?" Danika snarled.

Alistair's eyes creased like he considered. "Did anyone actually *watch* him die? Are we certain he's—"

"He's dead." Kane's jaw flicked when he said through his teeth, "I pulled what was left of him from the ashes myself." A truth they could scent. No questioning it.

I froze. Pump the brakes. He'd done *what*?

Casandra's voice softened to that dangerous lilt. "Do we suspect an accomplice?"

"One that was missed," Amber agreed, words bright when her eyes landed on mine.

The Southern Dowager's glare raked my way. Again.

My hands clenched when I visualized punching Amber's stupid, perfect face.

The corner of Victor's mouth tugged down.

"What do you think, Briar? Would you say they're connected?" Alistair asked.

I cleared my throat and repeated, "I can no longer say."

Mason-Isaac shoved his glasses up his crooked nose while he glared at me. Kane found me over his shoulder, that stare flashing while his Beta bombastic side-eyed me.

Victor angled forward, elbows thunking on the table when he asked, "Is there anything *can* you say?"

My brow dropped low. Was he trying to corner me? Or trying to help? 'Cause his wording warred my own for meticulous. Either way, he'd opened the door for my plan—the reason I'd wanted that meeting in the first place. "Yes. I *can* say that we need to consider Ithica."

Mason-faced Isaac turned my way, his expression impassive, but those eyes . . . those eyes were fueled with hate, but he had enough power as it was, so he could kiss my ass if he thought I'd be stopping.

"We know they have an arsenal. We barely beat their clock last time. I'd say this time, we head them off at the pass."

Alistair tugged the sleeve of his shirt. "Our intel says that Ithica has removed the General who led their army. I suspect that must mean something."

Good to know, but still . . . "And replaced them with whom? Someone better? Worse?"

Cassandra's head cocked, that owl-like curiosity piquing. "What is it you are proposing, Briar Stone?"

"I think we should loop them in, form a treaty. Give them an Embassy or something. A presence in Cambria so we keep the lines of communication open." It might not stop my stepfather, but an allegiance with their government could throw a preternatural sized wrench into his plans. I hoped.

"Briar," Isaac said, "we should discuss this later."

Inwardly, I smiled. 'Cause if he wanted to order me, he needed his *own* voice to do it, not Mason's. Was I playing with fire defying him like that? Yeah. But he'd said it himself—with Sierra's contact requiring my presence, he needed me to help broker his fancy-ass deal, so it was a chance I was willing to take. "We don't have time. Once Ithica catches wind of this murder, no doubt, that clock to war'll start ticking again. This heads it off at the pass."

"But that gives them eyes inside our walls."

If he'd thought that play was gonna work . . . "They need them." I shrugged. "They don't trust us. To them, we're dangerous in every way. The weapons are their countermeasure. Give them a foot in the door. Let them see behind the curtain. Show them they can work *with* us."

"And how would we influence their choice of representative?" Alistair questioned.

My head cut to the side. "We don't. Any pushback from us'll look sketchy. So, they pick who they want."

Mason-Isaac glowered. "That makes us vulnerable."

I gnashed my teeth. "It's not about *us*. It's about Cambria. The point isn't control. The point is progress."

Amber's lips thinned to a white slash. "And what do you get out of it?" Turning to the room, she jumped up on that invisible soapbox. "She's power hungry and opportunistic. I don't think we should trust her or whatever this plan is."

My glower was strong. What was this? A smear campaign? A move to discredit and undermine me? To plant distrust with the Conclave? Or just with Kane? Either way, she'd thrown down the motherfucking gauntlet.

Kane flattened his palm against the table. His eyes blazed a molten fire that reflected off the sheen of its surface.

Cassandra's stare lingered on Amber so intently, it looked personal. "That is not your decision to make."

Amber scoffed and folded her arms over her ample chest. "What? She was with Mason until Kane took Alpha. Then the second Mason became Coven Leader and offered her a shiny new position, she jumped right back to his dick. She gets around more than a carnival ride."

An agitated rumble grated up Kane's throat, rough, like sandpaper over stone. His head angled down and the glare he pinned Amber with would've had me running. "Muzzle your fucking Beta, Victor." A wave of his raw power surged through the space and rocked me back. "Or I will."

My ring grew hot as Joaquin edged in, flanking my side.

Every beastie across the room sat stiller than death, either ready to riot or retreat. Isaac turned to stone. A coward unfamiliar and unmatched against the biggest of boys.

To say Whitney was ashen would've been an understatement. Her gaze darted toward the door like she wanted to flee. Sound choice. Run that pretty little ass right outta—

Victor tugged that fedora low, hooding his eyes when they flashed. A barrier. Something to hide behind. A weakness. Veins throbbed in his neck while the muscles there corded, and he crossed his arms over his chest. "You read my mind, Slade." He peered toward his Beta, and when next he spoke, the command surged through the space. "Shut it."

Amber's nose twitched and the glare she offered me might've brought a smarter person to heel, but that person wasn't me.

My gaze fell on Kane and my body grew light, heart fluttering in my chest. The last thing I wanted was him standing in the gap between me and Isaac's minions, but the fact that he was willing to had to mean something.

Kane's calloused hand creaked when it balled into a fist. His square knuckles turned white, the tendons straining over the bones. "Any offense to Briar is an offense to me and I will fucking handle it."

Right. Not about me. About politics. He was there with another woman, for obsidian's sake. How much did he hate himself? How much did he regret hitching his life to me?

Danika flicked a finger Amber's way. "My distaste for the Beta aside, her point is valid. Briar's history muddies her motives."

"Sweet fucking sage. It's not about trusting *me*," I snarled. "It's about protecting more than our goddamn egos. About making the smart choice. Ithica *will* learn what's happened if they haven't already. They're not gonna risk the panic again. How many times do we play chicken before they call our bluff? They'll only let this go so far before they're on our doorstep."

Cassandra inclined her head while Joaquin's elbow thumped my ribs, and he lobbed a "*Cool it, banshee*" glare my way.

The Southern Dowager's voice rose when she found her counterpart. "You abide this?"

"I abide Briar Stone's right to command respect from those gathered here, heedless of their station."

"You come to her defense, yet leave my sisters for dead? Under your own roof?"

My chest tightened. Bracing against the accusation.

The crimson in Cassandra's gaze deepened, her long fingers flexing, but she made no reply.

Isaac shifted in his seat, a toddler proud of the mess he'd made. Of the chaos he'd wreaked. Of the seeds of chaos he'd sowed.

Alistair sighed, good and long as he ran a hand over his hair. "Briar makes a valid point."

Silence fell.

"I suggest we call a vote," Cassandra said. "I am fond of Briar Stone's idea. And so, I say yes."

"Same," Alistair added.

Mason-Isaac scratched his cheek, then scratched it again. "I'm just . . . not sure."

Cassandra glided to face him, body so inhumanely rigid I was surprised she didn't creak. Her crimson eyes darkened, a carnivorous anger simmering there. "You do not agree with your Second?"

He swallowed hard, that Adam's apple dipping low. "I just think we should consider it more."

Kane shifted, that glare flashing when it angled his way. "We're considering it now."

Iron fires, if I could've kissed him, it would've been the most indecent of thank yous.

Mason-faced Isaac looked away. He coughed into his hand, then coughed again and mumbled, "Yes."

Kane inclined his head, his lone word flat. Unequivocal. "Yes."

"What say you, Victor?" I prompted, trying to get him talking . . . or something.

He linked his hands over his abdomen, then inhaled a slow, ragged breath. His movements rivaled Cassandra for stiffness when he gave a single incline of his head.

My gaze narrowed on him, considering. He'd been quiet. Decidedly so. I'd always taken that silence for cowardice, but suddenly, it looked a shit ton more like avoidance. Of not helping. Had I read him right? *Was* he a mutt like Amber? Or was he just good at playing both sides to the middle? Getting what he needed while he toed Isaac's line?

Danika's lip ticked up again and again as if she fought against baring her teeth. "If we think it might save someone *else's* kin," she flicked her wrist, "then yesss."

Alistair adjusted his collar. "I'll see word is sent to Ithica immediately."

Rolling her neck, Danika's taloned nails clicked against the table as she raked attention across the room. "Two sisters I've lost. Two sisters *dead*." Her skin creaked like a dry leather hide when her hands clenched into fists. "When we find who did this, I will bleed them slowly. I will drain the life from their eyes. They will suffer." That crimson stare locked on Cassandra. "And so will those who helped them." Pushing her chair back achingly slow, she rose. "Are we done here?"

Nods of assent rolled around the room.

Her glare shifted to me and held as she left.

I swallowed hard.

Isaac rose, then leaned in and set his mouth to my cheek in a stomach-churning kiss. He pulled back and smiled. "See you later."

Bile climbed my throat, burning my tongue.

Beyond him, Kane's attention weighed heavy for one heartbeat. Two. His jaw flicked and pulsed when he clenched it, pushed up, and stalked to the door. He held it wide for Whitney, who practically fled before he pivoted on his heel, and left.

Joaquin faced me, voice flat when he said, "That was one way to do things." He rubbed his temples between his thumb and forefinger. "Do me a favor and try not to piss anyone else off and get yourself killed."

"No promises," I said with a wilted smirk.

He stared at the ceiling for patience as he aimed for the exit.

"Fingers crossed, I'll see you Thursday," I called after him.

The room emptied while Cassandra lingered, hands clasped before her as she watched me. She headed for the door, moving slow, like she waited for me to follow, so I did.

"That was interesting, Briar Stone."

Oh, interesting didn't begin to describe what'd just happened.

Her hand flitted in my direction. "You seemed a bit . . ."

Antagonistic? Problematic? Driven by a madness induced by the piece of shit changeling I was dying to gut?

She tapped her chin. "Out of character."

I scuffed my shoe over the floor and loosed a sigh. "I'm not really feeling myself lately."

"This much is clear."

Worrying my lip, I considered. She'd said we were friends, and while I had no clue exactly what that meant to an indeterminately old shadow walker, I knew what it meant to me. And friends didn't hold back or walk ridiculous, preternatural political lines. They said what should be said, and I owed her, so screw the power imbalances. "Thanks for the help back there."

"No thanks are necessary. I find exposing Amber's weaknesses rather enjoyable."

"Ha!" I snickered. "You're such a predator."

That incisored smile stretched across her lips, and for once, it didn't unnerve me. "That I am."

I stuffed my hands into my pockets. "I'm surprised you let Danika get away with that."

"Danika grieves. I allow her room to do so." The *"to a point"* was silent. Those crimson eyes grew distant. "In truth, Briar Stone, I understand Danika's pain. I feel it deeply." At the narrowing of my gaze, she added, "When I was but a girl, I saw my father slaughtered."

My chest twisted. Even though it'd been, like, a long ass time ago, there were some wounds that just never fully healed. "I'm so sorry, Cassandra."

She bowed her head. "It is why I became a shadow walker. To give myself time so I may hunt the changeling who did it. For my father, and for vengeance."

I went rigid. A changeling. Seven Iron Hells. My mouth ran dry, and I swallowed hard around it. Guilt stung my chest. "Did—" I cleared my throat. "Did you find them?"

Something akin to a smile crested those lips. "Yes. It took many, many years, but when the day came, I watched his end in the light."

There was something in the wording, something off . . .

That smile vanished. "I worry for you, Briar Stone. Are you happy?"

The conversation pivot was so sharp, I had to fight the whiplash. I tested an answer in my mind, then cocked a lone brow. "Decidedly not."

She faced me, giving me the full weight of her unwavering attention. "May I speak freely?"

After what she'd done . . . "Always."

The crimson in her gaze lightened. "I do not like him for you."

Him. Mason. Pfft! Get in line. "Why?"

"I created my people. I love them. It is my mantle to shield them. This is the way of things. But he does not intercede. He lets you stand alone against the conflict." She moved with that balletic grace as she rested an icy palm over my wrist. "And he does not shield you."

An ugly truth if ever I'd heard one. I worried my cheek between my teeth, because she was smart. Vigilant. And entirely more human than I'd ever given her credit for.

"Though, I must say, your scent has much improved."

I smirked. "Improved?"

"Indeed, Briar Stone. You no longer smell of tears." She angled closer, those fingers flexing over me. "And you now barely reek of *him*."

Chapter Thirteen

My stomach snarled as I scampered around in Mason's kitchen, foraging for food. The place was all gray cupboards, sparkly black marble, and white slate floors. He'd super committed to that crisp and colorless theme.

Sage, I was hungry. I tugged my slightly loose pants up and grabbed one of those individual yogurts. Tearing open the lid, I scooped my fingers in, then licked them dry.

Mason sauntered in and smirked, those glasses sitting askew over his collection of fading bruises. "I have spoons, you know."

I shook my head. "No time." Finishing it off, I checked my watch and worried my cheek between my teeth, a heavy weight settling around my shoulders. Ominous.

Isaac would be there soon.

My brain had been running thoughts of this meeting on loop. What would Isaac do? What would he say? What would the *human* say? And what would be next?

At least I'd affected some change with the Conclave's votes. Gained some traction. Maybe convinced a few people something was off—or that I was an idiot. But I needed more. Help. Information. *Something*.

My gaze locked on the basement door. There *was* someone who'd been around since Isaac's compulsion began. One shadow walker in particular who might know what could make that difference.

And time was short.

Mason's brow dropped. "What are you thinking?"

"Who says I'm thinking anything?"

He brushed his intentionally disheveled blond hair back from his forehead. "Your face."

"Okay, fine." I discarded my empty container and dusted my hands. "I wanna talk to Ivy."

His grimace was deep. "She's not all there, Briar."

"I know, but she's been with him a long time. Probably knows him better than anyone." I lifted a shoulder. "It's worth a shot."

He rubbed the back of his neck. "If Isaac figures out what we're up to—"

I rapid-snapped my fingers. "Hence why we must make haste."

His mouth pulled at the corner, and he gestured toward the door. "Lead the way."

Compliant Mason was a personal fave.

Inhaling long and slow, I braced as I filled my lungs to the brim and aimed for the basement. Ivy was a shell. Unpredictable. Going in meek could flip her predatory switch and shut what remained of her logic down. Sure, there was an iron cage between us, but I needed *her*, not the starved and deranged vamp she'd become.

Straightening to my full height, I padded down those squeaky metal stairs, Mason nipping my heels. I eyed Isaac's serum stores, hand twitching at my side, begging to destroy it all. Light it up and burn it down.

A shuffling pulled my attention, and I glanced toward it. Ivy lurked at the edge of her prison, set back from the iron bars. Her crimson gaze was wide. Wild. Her lip ticked like she fought from baring an incisor.

How far had she retreated on herself? Was there any awareness left? Any humanity? I rolled up my mental sleeves and steadied my thrashing heart, because there was only one way to find out.

Taking a seat on the bottom step, I channeled my inner Kane when I kept my eyes forward, and my shoulders wide. "Hey."

She blinked and edged back a foot, her straw-like fire-kissed hair immovable and matted to her head. Mason set his hip against the rail and her eyes snapped to him.

I raised my hands, palms out. "We're not gonna hurt you."

Her voice was hoarse, unused when she said, "You couldn't, magi girl."

Of course not. I'd never match her preternatural power or violence. But that wasn't the point. "I hoped to ask you some questions," I said. "If that's alright."

That crimson gaze sparked. She inclined her head.

I internally fist-pumped the air. "How long's Isaac had you?"

Her head pitched like a raven, cocking from one side to the next, her lone word throaty when she said, "Long."

"I'm sorry."

Scuttling to the side, she came closer, stare narrowed when she inspected me. Intrigued. Like I was a spectacle. Which, considering her only other entertainment was the odd bug tittering by, seemed fair. "Not your fault."

A headache ebbed in, and I rubbed my temples between the heel of my hands. "Has he caged you the entire time?"

Her nod was singular and sharp. "He requires the venom."

Mason folded his arms over his chest and clarified, "You mean yours?"

"Yes," she hissed.

"How does he get it?"

"I am compelled."

I'd assumed as much, seeing she could rip Isaac's throat out with just one of those filthy, tattered nails. The difference in strength between them was so marked, it was incalculable. Which begged my next question, one I was fairly certain I already knew the answer to. "Whose venom did he use?"

She flattened a palm to the floor. "My own."

My head fell. What was it Isaac had once said about his compulsion recipe?

"When you remove the shadow walker's genetic markers and break it down to its singular, effective component, anyone can use it."

So he'd just stripped *her* from it. Weaponized that power against her. But was there something there? Some hole in his plan? Something useful to stop him?

I shuddered, shifted to better face her, then flicked my hand toward her cage. "Why the iron? If he's controlling you, why does he need it? Couldn't he just order you to keep quiet like the rest of us?"

She hovered a hand over the bars. Her flesh sizzled. She held. And held. She pulled back. "Because I near the Madness."

That sounded the opposite of good. But then, that word. It was the same one Cassandra'd used to describe Anthony at the end. I tipped my chin her way. "What is it? The Madness?"

She skittered sideways, legs moving in segments like a spider, eyes trained on me. "Walkers are not built to be caged. Our minds do not suffer the isolation well."

"Isaac's had you a long time, a lot longer than Anthony. Why'd he break so fast?"

"The age, it quickens such things."

So, Anthony was old. My gut twisted, guilt stinging my throat while I braced for my next question. "Can it be reversed? If I got you out?" Bracing for that answer had my pulse thrashing faster, 'cause if it could be and I'd put that iron bullet through Anthony's head—

"No, magi girl. Once the mind darkens, we are beyond saving."

My shoulders sagged. "Is there anything you can tell us about Isaac? About changelings? Something that can help?"

She shifted to the side. "He must be killed. Returned to the Deep."

I inwardly face-palmed myself because that answer was the literal definition of *not helpful*!

Her head stayed facing me while her eyes darted across the room. "He comes now." She retreated to the back of her cage, fading into those shadows. "Our time is up."

The hum of a car engine closed in, the crunch of tires following when it veered into the driveway. Isaac.

Shit. I gripped the rail tight before I pivoted, following Mason back up the stairs.

Mason's face corkscrewed as he closed the basement door. "Was that . . . useful?"

"Hells if I know. But we need answers. Whatever we can get about changelings."

He shrugged. "The Recovery Center's got a library. Researchers use it for histories and viability. I can check it, see if they've got anything."

Grabbing his hand, I squeezed hard. "When can we go?"

"It's a restricted area. Each group has limited access. If both of us go in there, it'll draw the wrong attention."

The wrong attention. Victor.

Through the living room window, Isaac climbed from his vehicle.

I inclined my head and aimed for the door. "Bring me what you find. Two eyes are better than one."

***

Isaac sat in the passenger seat of my car, his expression dark. The sight of it had every hackle in my body rising and set my teeth on edge.

I'd plugged the coordinates he'd given into the vehicle's GPS, and the more we followed, the deeper my frown grew. Especially after it led us onto a dirt road between large swaths of farmland, with nothing in the distance.

Rubbing my chin, I side-eyed him. "Where the hells is this taking us?"

"Where they wanted to meet," he replied, tone flat.

They wanted to meet in a decidedly uninhabited region at the base of the Cortez mountain range along the northern edge of Coven territory? Why? So, they could murder us where no one would hear our screams? "There's no border crossing here, Isaac."

"I'd suggest that's the point."

Wonderful. The red flags just kept getting redder.

He shifted in his seat. Restless. "I see what you're doing, Briar." His stare found mine. "Trying to sabotage my plans."

Pfft. Of course, I was. Like obsidian I'd just let him run his game plan unimpeded. "You can't have free rein, Isaac."

His shoulder lifted. "Haven't you learned by now, stepdaughter? I can have whatever I want."

A cold shiver slithered down my spine. "You have no idea the shit you're stirring here."

That malevolent lip arced at the corner. "Don't I?"

I clutched the wheel harder. "If I'm such a problem for you, why not just take my face?" Sure, Sierra'd convinced this human I mattered somehow, and I didn't *wanna* give Isaac ideas, but there was a reason. Had to be.

"Because I can't," he spat.

My face twisted in a "You're shitting me, right?" expression.

"I can take your face, but replicating your *mouth* is beyond my scope."

A backhanded compliment if ever I'd had one. At least I was one of a kind. "What do I need to know?"

"I'll do the talking."

Ha! That was a recipe for disaster. I needed an in to block him . . . or at the very least, stall. "You said Sierra told whoever this is to deal with *me*."

"Yes, but you're a problem I don't wish to attend to today."

Maybe not, but still . . . "It's gonna look kinda suspicious if I roll up knowing not one damn thing about this product, Isaac." Sage, just tell me what we're dealing with.

His jaw clenched, nostrils flaring. "I've already informed her about the product." He shifted. "This meeting is to decide if she'll work with us."

Decide if she'd trust us, more like. I could work with that.

The end of the road loomed ahead, melting into a twenty-foot wide, grassy path that cut through a hilly, indiscriminate farm field. I eyed the map again and frowned. Pulling to a stop, we climbed free.

Isaac took the lead, aiming down said path before he threw over his shoulder, "You *will* help today."

The compulsion kicked in and I looked away to fight my smirk, 'cause he was sure as shit gonna regret that wording.

My phone rang. I sent it to voicemail. Several seconds passed before it buzzed with a text. My brows dipped as I eyed the screen.

Joaquin: What the shadowed goddamn moon are you doing at the border, banshee?

I hadn't exactly broadcast that information, which meant there was only one place—one wolf—he could've learned that from. My stomach fluttered, limbs tingling before reality hit. Kane cared, but just like the Conclave meeting, it was about preservation.

My shoulders drooped as I dodged some kind of thorny bush, then I punched my response:

Keeping tabs again, Beta?

Joaquin: Something like that. What's going on? You in trouble?

Yes!!! Sweet sage, I pulled on my ring, trying to force my fingers to work, to answer those questions, but Isaac's stupid order had other plans. So, I gave another one of those non-answer answers I'd gotten the super kind of good at:

I'm not running off.

A pause where I could practically see him glowering at his phone.

Joaquin: Not what I asked.

Obsidian, how I wanted that. But him busting onto the scene would throw up alarms for Isaac, 'cause I'd need a viable reason for the Beta to find me . . . a reason I didn't have. Which was exactly why I sent back:

You care about me or something?

His indisputable answer came fast.

Joaquin: Yes.

I stared down at that lone word while the stark honesty of it had tears prick the backs of my eyes.

Joaquin: Now, quit dodging or I'm coming to find you.

Shittiest of shits. I typed a quick reply.

It's business stuff. I don't have time to talk, but I'll see you tomorrow.

Joaquin: Your ass better be there when I come get you.

I swiped my eyes and fought my smile.

I'll be there, nosey. Promise.

We crested the small hill and Isaac peered my way. Sniffing, I shoved my device away.

A woman stood in the distance, her hair not actually her own. A gray wig covered her head, the style a short pixie cut that spiked off in strategic directions. She looked somewhere in her forties, her dark shades shielding her eyes. Tugging the lapels of her crisp, white pantsuit, she approached.

There was an air about her, the way her chin angled just a tad too high, spine a bit too straight. She walked like she owned the place. Like she'd never faced a problem her authority couldn't fix. Like she'd never heard the word no.

She held her phone at eye level, examining the screen. Her gaze snapped back and forth between us and whatever she looked at, then tucked it away.

Mason-faced Isaac smiled. "I'm—"

"Mason Beckett and Briar Stone," she said.

Well, alright then. I extended my hand.

She took it. "Zahara Abbott."

While her grip aimed for hard, I ran with wolves, so it hit somewhere just above firm. "I've heard much about you, Briar."

I grimaced. "Not really sure why."

Her mouth curved high like I'd just answered some question. "How'd you and Sierra even meet?"

Zahara smiled. "A chance encounter in the neutral grounds."

I scoffed. Chance encounter, my ass! "You mean you scoped her out."

Her laugh was telling. "After some research, I thought she'd be the most . . . amenable to my proposal."

The cock of my brow was sharp. *Her* proposal? "So the serums were your idea?"

"The outcome was my idea. The implementation, hers."

My head dipped in a nod. Interesting. But I needed more, because if I could understand *her* motives, maybe I could figure a way to sway them *anywhere else*. "Why do you want this?"

A cool wind cut down from the mountains, sending a chill across my skin and ruffling Zahara's hair.

"Because I don't like being weak," she said.

I rubbed my temples. "You're anything but, Zahara. Ithica *has* weapons."

Her expression darkened. "That they do." She angled closer. "But I'd much prefer to *be* one."

My head spun, limbs going weak. Wraith take me.

She tugged her shades free, those onyx colored-eyes sharp. "You think our government is strong, but they fear you as much as you fear our iron. And what happens to us if our stores deplete, and the bullets run out?"

I raised my hands. "Okay, but what if—and hear me out on this—we just didn't fucking fight?"

Isaac set a hand over my elbow, fingers digging deep when he squeezed.

She smiled, but nothing about it was pleasant. "You're born predators, Briar. And I no longer want to be prey."

Sweet sage.

The shake of her head was slow. "For the time being, this is merely a . . . precaution."

"Excellent plan," Isaac said, nostrils flaring as he offered me a warning glare. "Precautions are always necessary."

Zahara's stare raked him like she'd forgotten he was there— or that he was the dirt on her very expensive looking shoes. She gestured to me. "Why is it you *don't* want this?"

I internally rubbed my palms, because boyyyyyy had Isaac picked the wrong order.

Not about to lie, I lifted a shoulder in answer. "I think handing our power over for you to weaponize is a crap idea. You've got no clue about the arena you'd be stepping into. You don't know how to control it. And, if I'm pegging you right, you don't give a single shit how bad things can get. You just want control."

"*Briar*," Mason-Isaac said through his tightly gnashed teeth.

"What?" I scoffed, seeing my opening. "You said help." I smiled. "I'm helping." Maybe not helping him, but in the scope of his sloppy order, helping Cambria still counted.

Zahara's gaze narrowed. Scrutinizing. She flicked a finger my way. "I can see why Sierra was so fond of you."

Fond of me? I wasn't really connecting those dots, 'cause Sierra throwing a crap ton of garbage at my feet didn't overly feel like fondness.

"You're the counter." At my deeply furrowed brow, Zahara explained, "Anyone seeking success needs at least one person who'll be honest with them. To counter their ideas and point out the flaws in their plan. They need this because it tells them what requires work. Where the chink in their chain might fall. Where to focus their efforts." Her expression was soft and the opposite of her words when she said, "Your reticence to this deal only drives my interest further, because it tells me what you have *is* dangerous, and I'm about to get my money's worth."

Well, mother-fucking shit!

Mason-Isaac's shoulders drew back, eyes going bright.

Zahara's fingers threaded together as she faced him. "I want it tested before an exchange is to be made."

"I can collect humans to—"

"No. Ithica monitors human border passage into Cambria. If any of our people go missing on your side, there will be questions. If they go missing on mine . . ." She paused to let that sink in. "I'll gather my own subjects and we'll set up an exchange. I'll bring them to you here. Tomorrow."

Isaac cleared his throat. "What would you have me do with them when I'm done?"

Zahara waved a dismissive hand. "Whatever you will." Her eyes locked with mine and she smiled. "I thank you for your input, Briar. I do look forward to working with you again."

Chapter Fourteen

My room was warm, steam clinging to the air from my ridiculously long shower. I sat wrapped in Kane's hoodie while I stuffed my face with a sandwich and rocked in my egg chair, staring out the floor-to-ceiling window to my Alpha's territory while I killed time until that interview with Joaquin.

I'd messed up with Zahara. Bad. I'd barely slept the night before. Tossing and turning and hating myself for playing it all wrong. For opening my mouth at all.

My phone buzzed and I pulled it free. The lobby security camera displayed a shot of Theo's face . . . I thought, anyway, seeing said face was mooshed against the screen. I shook my head and pressed the code to enter. Less than three minutes later, Theo sauntered outta the elevator, Naomi at his back.

"Move," he said, shoving me aside before he darted into the condo like a wound-up pup. Eyes wide, he scurried from room to room. "This place is killer."

"Indeed," I said, doing my best Joaquin air. Tugging my navy yoga pants higher, I aimed for the sunken living room. "I'm especially fond of the dying-alone lifestyle I've cultivated here."

He barked a laugh from somewhere down the hall. "You know what I mean!"

"Yeah," Nay cut in, heading my way. She set a hand over the arm of the leather couch before dropping herself onto it. "Kane's got good taste."

I set my phone on the coffee table. He did. It was gorgeous, and so damn lonely, my chest hurt. I tugged my pants higher again, frowning down at them. They were brand new, for sage's sake. Why were they suddenly loose?

Her gaze tracked to the window and the neutral grounds below. "He's taking care of you, Briar."

If by that she meant "offering his claimed a secure place to sleep so no one ripped my vulnerable throat out in my sleep", then sure. "He's with Whitney."

Naomi winced, but she couldn't have heard anything to the contrary, seeing she didn't counter it.

Theo's head poked around the corner, followed a second later by the rest of him. His mouth thinned; brows low. "I don't get that. It's all kinds of fucked up."

I dragged a hand through my hair and glanced away, 'cause no way I could dwell on that. *That* way lay agony. That way lay a stone wall I had no clue how to scale.

"How've things been going with the Pack?" I asked.

"Well," Theo's brows waggled mockingly, "we managed to get Kane's attention."

Nay snickered and tossed a pillow high before catching it again. "Piss him off, more like."

My attention tracked between them. Waiting.

"We, uh," she tucked that pillow behind her head and scrunched her face, "kind of, started sleeping in Theo's car."

I blinked hard, then blinked again. "Come again?"

"What?" Theo threw his arms in the air. "You said get attention."

I *had* said that . . . And if it worked, I wasn't about to complain. I rolled my wrist. "So, what's the 'piss Kane off' part?"

Theo looked away while Nay scratched her scalp. "We might've, um, set up shop in the Immortal Inc lot."

The image of Kane's "what the literal fuck" face when he found out . . . The laugh I barked was my first real laugh since everything had gone down, and it felt so damn good.

Tapping his chin, Theo mused. "It was probably the flames that triggered the fire alarm."

My spine locked straight. "You built a goddamn *fire*?"

He scoffed and flailed his arms. "How else was I supposed to cook the hotdogs?"

"Sweet sage." I mashed my face into my palm. Peering through my fingers, I asked Nay, "How's Autumn taking this?"

"She doesn't get it, which," she cleared her throat and stared down at her lap, "is the point."

I dropped my hand to my side and dipped my head in a nod. "Why don't you guys move in here? It'll keep your asses from burning down the Canal District and show everyone we're linked somehow. Besides, I've got tons of room."

They eyed each other in unison.

"It's a killer idea," Naomi said.

Theo's grin turned ravenous, head panning as he scanned the condo again. "Wicked."

My shoulders sagged in relief, 'cause the idea of them being here meant ebbing the loneliness . . . some, anyway. I plastered on my pathetic-at-best eager face. "So, what's on the docket?"

Theo's lone clap had my ears ringing. He skip-jumped across the room and shoved the dining table aside, clearing space before he flared his arms wide. "Square up, buttercup."

Blowing out a resigned I'm-about-to-get-my-ass-handed-to-me breath, I stripped Kane's hoodie off, leaving me in my white, also slightly loose, long sleeve top, and made my way there.

"Just like last time," he said. "Try and get away."

Nay cupped her hands around her mouth. "Watch his eyes and hips. They'll telegraph where he's gonna go."

I set my position, crouching low. He slipped forward, quick as a shot. I darted left. He caught me in the shoulder, but only grazed. It wasn't perfect, but it was better than staring at the ceiling from the comfort of my floor.

I smiled.

Theo tipped his head, impressed. "Someone's been practicing."

I had, but still, it wasn't enough. I needed to get better, and I needed it fast. Worrying my lip, I twisted my obsidian.

Naomi leaned forward and rubbed her hands together. "Oh, thinky Briar's always fun."

"No," Theo cut in, "thinky Briar usually means trouble."

My lip tugged up as I gripped my ring tight. "I wanna look for Kane again."

"Case in point," he mumbled under his breath.

Ignoring his smarm, I drew my power, closed my eyes and dove deep, reaching for that tether to Kane. I kept diving until I found that same warmth from before. My essence wrapped around it like fallen mist from the sky, and I stopped. The shape, it was almost like . . . a wolf.

When I brushed that connection, my ring heated, then smoked, followed immediately by a wave of power so strong, I collapsed to my knees. It tore through the room, rocking Theo and Naomi back.

"Holy shit!" Nay said, righting herself.

Theo rapid blinked as he shook himself out.

Naomi shifted to the edge of the couch, voice high when she asked, "Are you alright?"

I swallowed hard and took myself in. "Yeah. I'm good." The stutter step of my heart had me clutching my chest. Tears stung my gaze, and I took a happy, shuddered breath. Obsidian, had Kane felt that?

Theo looked me over. "What the hells did you just do?"

"I found him," I uttered, a tear slipping free. "I found Kane." It'd felt familiar . . . just like the flare of power that'd knocked everyone on their asses at Sierra's dirge.

I grimaced. *Oops.*

Sage, it wasn't the ring . . . it was *him*. Or maybe it was both. Either way, he was my power source, like some Alpha-fueled battery.

"Face off with Theo," Nay said as I rose. "Try it again."

He gave her a thumbs up, tone dry and decidedly less confident when he said, "Great idea."

Crossing the room, I set myself, legs braced as I gripped that power again. Theo raised his fists, cocky grin long gone. His body was stiff as if he braced or regretted his life choices. Both were possible. Both were likely.

He advanced.

Time crawled, everything moving in slow motion. I lunged, my body foreign to me, movements so fast, I could hardly control them. The whites of Theo's eyes flashed a second before my hit landed. My aim was off, so it caught him in the ribs. The punch threw him aside, and the sickening crack that sounded when the bones there shattered made my stomach drop. He flew back, smashing into the wall, then dropped.

My hands shot to my mouth. "Iron Hells!" I ran and took a knee beside him. "*I'msorry, I'msorry, I'msorry.*"

Nay appeared a breath later.

Power of obsidian, is this what Kane felt? Did he even know what he was?

"Uggggggh," Theo moaned, clutching his side. "I'm good. Just give it a sec."

Sweat beaded his brow, and his breaths turned short and shallow while the sickening clunk-crunch of his bones realigning carried through the room.

I cringed, guilt souring my stomach.

Naomi paled.

Theo lay still for several agonizingly long minutes before he grunted and groaned, then slowly sat up, shoulders heaving when his attention tracked to me. "Shadowed fucking moon," he said, voice a croaked taunt. "Whose dumb idea was this again?"

Naomi sagged, then patted the top of his head. "Stop whining, pup."

I bit my lip. "Maybe if you were a better teacher . . ."

His stare narrowed on me, but there wasn't any malice there.

The elevator door dinged and ground open. I jolted, body going rigid as I whipped that way.

Kane strode out, that broad, imposing frame taking up all the space in the room. He scented the place, stare flashing when it tracked to our motley crew's team huddle. He stopped dead.

My pulse kicked into overdrive, blood thrashing in my ears as I traced a finger over my heart tattoo.

A breath later, Whitney crossed in.

My chest caved, lungs refusing to work. I fought super damn hard to control the rage and pain and staccato beat of my heart, because he'd brought her there? To my condo? *My* space? Wraith take me, why?

Pushing unsteadily to my feet, I faced him, fighting the quaver in my voice when I uttered, "You've got a key."

His answer was unequivocal. "Yes."

I glanced away. Back. Away again, then back. "What are you doing here?"

He tipped his head to his cousins, tone a low rumble when he answered, "I came for them." That molten gaze hunted me. "Joaquin's waiting at the shop."

Nay and Theo tensed when they helped each other to their feet.

I peered at my watch, expression contorting. "I thought I wasn't meeting him till two?"

Rolling his shoulders, he stalked deeper and set his hip against the marble counter. "Schedule changed."

I wanted to read into him, but his tone, posture, all of it, was so flat it was a goddamned wall. Still, there was something in the answer, something that twigged my attention. "What's going on, Kane?"

He folded his arms over his chest. "Interview's bumped up." He chucked his chin my way. "I'll lock up when I'm done."

Dismissed from my own condo. I fought not to flinch. "Yeah," I said, tone quiet as I looked away. Pivoting, I grabbed my purse and offered Whitney a seething glare while I aimed for the elevator.

She worried her cheek between her teeth and scurried to Kane's side.

I hated her. *Hated* her! It wasn't fair. Wasn't reasonable. Wasn't anything, except the cold, bitter truth.

Pressing the call button, the doors dinged open. Clearing my throat, I found Theo and Nay. "When you're done, grab your stuff," I gestured down the hall. "And pick a room."

Kane's stare narrowed. I held it for one second. Two. The doors ground closed, cutting me off from him as I left.

Chapter Fifteen

My car hummed when I veered us into Immortal Inc's lot. The day was overcast, drizzle dusting the windshield. Dark clouds threatened in the distance.

My stomach torqued as I stared toward the shop's massive front window, trying to get my mind off the scene in my condo and failing miserably. Kane. Whitney.

The Beta waited on the step until I climbed out, and he closed in.

"So," he cocked a lone brow, "new roommates?"

I rolled my eyes and jabbed his arm. "You wolves gossip worse than teenagers."

"Banshee," he pushed, that brow cocking higher.

Clasping my hands, I rocked on my heels. "They need *somewhere* to live."

"They have places to live. They're choosing to be homeless." He adjusted the lapels of his sweater-vest. "Wanna tell me what the hells Kane just walked in on?"

I shrugged. "I told you before, Theo's training me."

"Why?"

"I doubt Kane's an option anymore."

"Did you ask?"

I worried my cheek, heart tumbling over itself.

The Beta's stare narrowed on something past me.

I followed his line of sight to a utilitarian, three-story building made of silver metal, and one-way glass. The thing was modern with sleek lines cut to military precision with the words "Embassy of Ithica" emblazoned above the door.

A moving truck sat out front. Men and women in crisp suits climbed its ramp, unloading the monstrous thing.

"They didn't waste any time," I said, then grinned at the Beta, eager to shove my foot in that Ithican door. "Let's go introduce ourselves, shall we?" Pivoting on my heel, I cut to the sidewalk, then darted across the street.

"*Banshee!*" Joaquin snarled through his teeth.

I patted the side of my leg. "Come on, boy."

There was that snarl again.

His feet thumped as his long strides caught him up and he flanked my side. His stare pinned mine. My grin grew wider.

A security guard wearing shades and dressed in head-to-toe black swung the main entrance wide, and a lone man looking close to thirty strode out. He was tall, somewhere just over six feet, and unsurprisingly human. He moved like he owned the place, shoulders back, head up, royal blue eyes fixed on us.

He closed in, fastening the button of his sharp, navy designer suit, then extended his hand. "I'm Bower Caddel, Ithican Ambassador."

The Beta gave it a sharp shake. "Joaquin Cruz."

"The North Cambrian Beta," Bower noted, then turned and offered that hand my way.

Swiping the falling mist from my lashes, I stood tall and took it. "I'm Bri—"

"Briar Stone, Second in the Northern magi Coven," he noted, his grip cinching tighter. Not painful or a threat, more surveying. Interest.

Looked like someone had done their homework.

Joaquin's stare fell to that grip, his tone flat when he said, "And the claimed mate of the Northern Pack Alpha."

A sharp gust of wind cut through the street as Bower's chin dipped in a nod. "A mate who resides separate from said Alpha?"

My brows rocketed up my forehead. It wasn't a challenge. Not really. More like an acknowledgment of his awareness. Of *Ithica's* awareness. The real personal kind. Not that my split from

Kane had been a secret, but realizing exactly *who* it'd reached was . . . troubling.

The Beta's lip drew up, exposing a particularly pointy canine that looked ripe for a throat ripping. "That changes nothing."

I couldn't gauge if Bower tested boundaries or tried to set them. Regardless, his balls were either really big or begging to be ripped off. With Isaac's bullshit in full swing, I couldn't afford the latter, so I tugged my arm free and awkward-laughed. "Nice to know my reputation precedes me."

Ithica choosing a guy like Bower—confident with an air of "death wish"—was a strategy. A presence to remind us we weren't the only players on the board. Not prey, but not quite predator either.

Joaquin's stare went unfocused, lost in one of those wolfy conversations.

A wave of . . . something hit me. It burned my chest and bittered my tongue. The world tinged in red. Emotions. Powerful ones I didn't recognize. They were coarse, raw and rough around the edges. They were rage and fear and . . . they weren't my own. Or maybe they were. I couldn't separate them because they were a part of me. All consuming.

I shook myself and cleared my throat. "It's, um, interesting to meet you."

Bower tucked a weather-dampened strand of his white-blond hair back from his forehead, that gaze taking me in again. "I'm happy to be here."

Was he flirting? Or just dumb? Maybe both, 'cause flirting was pretty dumb. Either way, he clearly pushed for a reason, hence why I flailed a waggly-fingered hand his way. "Why do I get the feeling you're sussing us out?"

He bowed his head. "Of course, I am, Miss Stone."

Miss Stone? "Kinda honest, aren't you?"

He eyed Joaquin. "Is lying an option?"

The Beta's lip pulled up at the corner, pure lupine. "No."

Bower smirked, then returned his attention to me. "Ithica's very interested in you, Miss Stone."

"*Me?*" My face twisted. It might've been admiration or a threat. Either way, it was confusing as all get out. "Why?"

"Because you're at the center of everything."

The Beta's attention roved between us.

A car drove past, the tsh of its tires over the damp ground loud as I frowned. "I'm Second in my Coven. Of course, I'm neck deep in this trash heap."

The weight of Joaquin's glare chiseled through my skull like a pickaxe.

Bower's mouth twitched. "You're a magi. Less powerful than the rest but counted as equal among them. Kane, Cassandra, Mason, your Beta here. Even Victor, though, I suspect that respect is born of the threat you pose."

My mouth opened, hung there for an impossibly long second, then closed. "And exactly what threat do I pose?"

He tapped the side of his nose. "A person with powerful friends is a powerful person, indeed. And you have many of those. It's clear you have a way with them, Miss Stone."

I shook my head. "I have a way of pissing them off."

"And, yet," he flared his hands wide, "here you stand."

There was that. But seriously, how the iron fires did this human know so goddamn much? It wasn't the worst-case scenario, seeing I'd hoped for someone to subtly work against Isaac with. Still, I didn't know how to feel.

Joaquin's attention turned assessing.

"I admire your honesty, Miss Stone. To Cambria, the rest of this world is prey. But you, little mouse, you bite back."

Little mouse? The guy was slick, turning what should've been an insult into a confusing compliment. "I'd consider myself more of a feral squirrel with no sense of survival instincts. Not a primo case study. Navigating the Conclave is a 'proceed with caution' venture."

"And there it is." At my furrowed brow, he finished, "Your honesty makes you wildly unpredictable, and conversely, easy to work with. They know it, and so do we." He wicked the rain from his forehead and gestured to the moving truck. "I must go.

There's still much to do." He smiled and tipped his non-existent hat our way. "I look forward to our next . . . encounter."

***

Joaquin side-eyed me when he closed in on the entrance of Immortal Inc, pulled it wide and waited. A lone brow rose. "You just gonna just stand there?"

A small smirk tugged my lips. "Maybe."

He stared at the sky for patience. "Get inside."

I stepped over the threshold and took the place in. The dark-stained hardwood floors were finally done, their finish perfect. Tarps hung over the hydraulic tattoo chairs and shelves while an old steampunk style register sat ready on the counter.

The Beta shoved a rolling stool my way, then took one for himself. "How're ya doing?"

Lowering myself down, I kicked my feet off the floor and spun in a circle. "Alright."

His stare flashed and he peered at me from the corner of his hazel gaze. He set his elbows on his knees. "You don't look it."

I scoffed and spun myself again. "What's that supposed to mean?"

"It means you look like shit."

Wow. I stopped, face twisting into a grimace. Brutal, but okay. "Thanks?"

He rose, the thump of his feet carrying when he aimed for the back office. Several instants later, he returned, a stack of snacks in hand. He chucked them on a small table to my left and aimed a finger at me. "Eat something."

The glower I offered him when I plunked my hands on my hips was feeble at best. "Excuse me?"

"You heard me."

"First of all," I raised a finger, checking off my short but mighty list, "I have been eating. Second, I'm not hungry." My stomach growled.

"Your clothes tell a different story." He stabbed his hand at the food. "Dig in."

My gaze narrowed as I glanced at one of the mirrors leaned against the wall and took myself in. My new clothes *were* looser, cheeks sallower, jawline sharper while dark circles streaked beneath my eyes.

What the hells? I wasn't the smartest, but nor was I daft enough to weaken myself. If I wanted to weave my way through Isaac's compulsion labyrinth, I'd be needing my brain cells functioning at full capacity.

I frowned as I popped open a bag of chips. Grabbing a decidedly unrefined handful, I shoveled them in my mouth. And my frown absolutely turned upside down at the sight of the brownies there.

Joaquin crossed his arms over his chest and leaned a hip against the counter. "Seriously, banshee. You starving yourself or something?"

"Shadow and sage. I told you I've been eating," I said around a mouthful of tasties. "Since when are you so pushy?"

"Since you decided to stop answering questions."

I held my breath. My heart pounded against my ribs. He'd noticed. Thank obsidian, he'd noticed!

"So," he chucked his chin my way, "anything you *can* talk about?"

There was an emphasis in his tone—a distinction in those words.

Sage, I wanted to tell him everything. Sure, he'd noticed something was off, but it wasn't enough. Off could mean anything. He'd had a lifetime of wolfy politics to learn the ropes. To know when to duck or dodge. I was an amateur at amateur hour. Seriously lacking.

My grimace was deep. "No."

His stare sparked. He inclined his head.

Biting the inside of my lip, I grabbed one of those brownies. "Things any better with the Pack?"

His mouth thinned, lines of strain creasing his forehead. "No. They're rough."

Because Kane had been rocked. Because I'd shaken that easy confidence—broken his belief. I winced and my shoulders sank. I swallowed around my stricken throat. "How so?"

"More power bids than usual."

Power bids? "Against *Kane*?"

"Not since Theo." He raked a hand through his hair. "It's mostly lower-level stuff right now. But there's a shift. Everyone can feel it. The Pack's restless. It's only a matter of time before it reaches the top."

Nausea twisted my gut, because the top wasn't just my Alpha. "You think they'd come for you too?"

"I think the Pack's a hierarchy. When stuff's unstable, there's an instinct to stabilize it. They look for that calm, and if they can't find it inside the Pack, then they look for control, which means the challenges start."

I scratched along my arm. "How come you never went for Alpha, Joaquin?"

He glanced down, then rubbed his hands over his pant legs. "I'm good at management. Not authority. I'm strong, but not Alpha strong. Kane was the right one for the job."

Joaquin didn't see what I saw. His command and control—he was absolutely Alpha material.

The ghost of a conversation whispered across my memory. A conversation with Kane about Joaquin and their former Alpha. I worried my cheek between my teeth. "What happened with you and him?"

"Who?"

"You and Ronin."

He ran a hand through that jet-black hair. "What makes you ask?"

The way he went rigid every time his former Alpha's name was mentioned. The way his voice hardened, like he readied for trouble. "That day at the Conclave meeting—the first day we met—you told Kane to come for that challenge."

He took up a clean paint brush from the tray beside him. Flipping the handle through his thumb and index finger, he tapped it on the counter, then flipped it again. Flip, tap. Flip, tap. Flip, tap. "Because Ronin's time was up."

Tugging my ear, I let my gaze fall. "Why?"

He canted his head and lifted a brow. "I'll tell you mine if you tell me yours."

I plucked lint from my pants and rolled it between my thumb and finger. "Tell you my what?"

He squared himself to me. "Your secrets."

An anticipatory kick of adrenaline buzzed through my veins. I flicked that lint away. "What makes you think I've got secrets?"

"Because you're acting secretive."

My snicker was ridiculously tight. "And how exactly does one *act* secretive, Joaquin?"

He pointed that brush toward my face as if that was answer enough. The skin of his throat pinched when he lowered it. "You're not a vault, banshee. You wear your thoughts on your tongue—one you run a lot. And suddenly, you're not running it. Just tell me why." A pause, then, "Please."

Please. He'd said *please*? Joaquin had always barked like the wolf he was. Please had never been in his vocabulary. My chin dropped to my chest, needles pricking the backs of my eyes. 'Cause what did I say to that? What *could* I say? So many Isaac-formed obstacles blocked my path. I didn't wanna steer him away from that track, but I was trapped, which meant confirming it wasn't an option. So, I did the only thing I could. I lifted a shoulder in a shrug.

He inclined his head, stalking me with those eyes like I was a puzzle he tried to piece together. Loosing a harsh exhale, his stare grew distant. "Ronin called a hit on my brother."

The change of subject nearly gave me whiplash, and it took a second for my brain cells to link his words, but when I did . . . Iron fires, take me. I didn't even know he'd had a brother. My chest tightened, voice barely above a breath when I said, "I'm so sorry, Joaquin."

He stared down that brush. "Matias was climbing the Pack quick. I think Ronin knew he couldn't face him, so he had him killed." His hand fisted. "I wanted vengeance, fought my way to Ronin, but the closer I got, the more I realized I wasn't strong enough. Not just to face him, but to run the Pack. And so did he."

Wasn't strong enough for Ronin *then*, but now . . . "If he knew you hated him, why keep you as Beta? Why not come for you too?"

"Because me as Beta did him a favor. Made it look like we were a fucking team." He stared out the window to his left, regret etched in the lines around his expression. "But then Kane came along." He rolled his shoulders. "Ronin tried gutting him too, but Kane was too strong. He knew he was fucked."

"When did it happen? Your brother, I mean."

He cleared his throat. "Five years ago."

Five years. Had it been Ronin fighting to control the Pack? Or Isaac?

There was a small flash in the recesses of Joaquin's eyes. His lip drew up and he bared a canine. "Kane's a good guy. Always has been. Once he started his climb, most of the Pack just backed off, let sleeping wolves lie. But not everyone."

My pulse boomed in my ears, voice weak when I asked, "What happened?"

The laugh he released was so dry, I was surprised he didn't spit dust. "He killed them."

I sucked in a harsh breath and dropped my hands to my knees to steady myself. I'd suspected, but actually hearing those words . . .

"Fights *need* to finish, banshee. If you wanna climb the Pack, there aren't any weapons. It's your own strength or nothing. It's law for us. Someone needs to win. Someone needs to lose. The lines in the Pack have to be drawn. Decisively."

My head spun, growing light. Dizzy. "Can't someone just concede?"

He lifted a shoulder in a half shrug. "Depends. Terms can only be negotiated before the fight. Otherwise, once it starts, that's it. No going back. No rules added. No yielding. Kill or be killed."

My eyes crushed closed. The things Kane had done. The things he'd endured. I'd known his climb to freedom had been brutal, but not like that. He was brash, and protective, and dangerous. But he wasn't cruel. If he'd killed them, it was for a reason. And he'd done it for me—for Joaquin. I fought not to double over.

"He did what he had to. He always will." There was a weight to the words, like there was more to them when he set that brush aside. "If anyone gets between him and his purpose, they're dead." Joaquin gripped the edge of that counter. "I don't know what's going on; whether there's trouble with you and Mason, or something else, but you're not right, banshee."

My heart slammed against my ribs.

He angled closer. "You can talk to—"

The door to the shop popped open and a were crossed in, a sketchbook-style case in hand. His coal black hair was longer, just past his shoulders but clean and bone straight. His angular eyes were chestnut and keen, and overlaid by a pair of thin silver glasses. Tattoos covered his neck, and what I could see of his arms while his white dress shirt was crisp, well fitted, and topped by a form-fitting gray vest.

Joaquin's gaze fixed on our newcomer and flared. The Beta straightened, then ran a hand over his clothes, smoothing them before smoothing them again.

"Hey," the guy said. "I'm Ezra Warren. I'm here for that interview."

Pushing off the counter, Joaquin advanced and extended his hand. Ezra took it, and the appraising look he offered the Beta sent a titter through my chest. Joaquin blushed.

Actually. Fucking. Blushed.

"Nice to meet you," the Beta said. Nervous. It looked good on him.

Ezra's mouth arced at the corner. "You, too." He turned my way.

"Briar," I replied.

He tipped his head in greeting. "Briar." Raising the leather case he carried, he said, "I've got some sketches and pics of my work, if you'd like to see." His confidence was easy. Smooth. No pretentiousness or airs. No wolfy challenge or posturing. An Omega? Either way, I liked him already.

Joaquin cleared space on that counter and nodded. "That'd be great."

Ezra laid his work out, and my eyes widened. There was a bit of everything in there. Simple flowers, intricate portraits. Lettering, shading. His lines were clean and sharp. His work crisp and absolutely flawless.

I rose and edged closer. "This is beautiful."

"Agreed," the Beta added, then cleared his throat like something was stuck in it. "What kind of experience do you have?"

My phone buzzed with an incoming text. Stepping away, I checked the screen.

Hannah: Briar, I think something's wrong with Lucas.

My stomach dropped, thumbs flying across the screen as I typed my response:

What d'you mean?

Hannah: I hate doing this, but . . . I think he might be using again.

I swallowed hard.

Never apologize for caring.

What happened?

Hannah: He texted from your mom's phone. His words are all jumbled. I couldn't make out what he tried to say. I messaged him back, and he's stopped responding. I know it's not much but I'm worried.

A warning at the base of my skull pricked. It felt like a guillotine ready to drop when I replied:

No, thank you for telling me. Any idea where he is?

Hannah: I think he's home.

I punched right back:

Sit tight. I'll figure out what's going on.

Hannah: Thank you.

The energy I kicked off must've been palpable, 'cause Joaquin's stare locked on me. "Banshee?"

"It's Lucas." I shoved my phone away. "I've gotta go. Something's not . . ." I took a deep breath and headed for the door. "Something's not right. I'm gonna head down to mom's and check on him. See what's up."

Lines of strain creased the Beta's forehead as he closed in, body tense while he shifted, stiff and restless. He pitched his voice low when he said, "Let me know if Victor blocks you at the Southern boundary." Not an order, but not a request.

"It's fine, Joaquin. He gave me clearance to cross when I need."

His stare flicked behind him and back. "You aren't with Kane anymore. Shit's changed now."

My stomach caved and I gripped the door—something to steady myself and keep my knees from buckling because his words hit like a sucker punch to the gut. I'd always be linked to Kane, but I wasn't *his* anymore. Wasn't his lover, his mate. Wasn't his anything. He'd moved on.

I had to get outta there before the pieces of my soul peeled apart—pieces held together by a pitiful concoction of chewing gum and wrapping tape. One misstep and it'd all crumble.

"Let me know," he repeated. "And tell Lucas to get his ass up here for a visit."

My gaze met his when I swallowed around the dryness that burned my throat. "I will."

Chapter Sixteen

The rain poured, making the puddles deep and the road slick as I whipped through the neutral grounds and approached Victor's territory. I tore past the human-occupied hotels and the parking lot that stood as a holding place for passage issues, not slowing when I flew across the boundary's red-painted line like a bullet. A line that sat quiet and empty. Ominously so.

I ordered the Bluetooth system to call my mother for the thirtieth time, to no avail.

The forest on Victor's side climbed high, my wipers on blast. I veered left and right, avoiding the deep tire grooves of water to keep from hydroplaning. Weaving through the back roads was a slow torture, but before long, I skidded to a stop in my mother's driveway.

The trees around it loomed, her gray, one-story bungalow a less than pretty parcel containing all my fears.

Scampering from the truck, I barreled up those chipped wooden steps and through the door. The scuffed, Tuscan-yellow walls a stark contrast to the rank stench of the drug den inside.

"Lucas?" I called, ducking my head around the corner to peer into the living room. A handful of men were draped over the couch, passed out, or unconscious. Not that there was a difference. Slurping sounds snapped my attention to the corner. Some guy sat in the lounger, head leaned back, mouth open while a woman knelt between his legs, head bobbing as she sucked him off.

His attention landed on me, and a languid grin stole across his skeezy face. "Wanna turn, baby?"

"Shadow and fucking sage," I said as I veered toward my brother's room.

"Lucas. I need you to swallow this, Lucas," my mother's voice carried from down the hall.

My heart dropped. I bolted, bursting inside.

Lucas laid back on his bed, eyes closed. My mother hovered over him, her gaze wide. The bottle of Purge she held was pressed to his mouth and angled up.

No! I scrambled to his side.

"He's not taking it," she said, the words broken and frenetic. "How long's he been like this?"

She shook her head, voice weak when she said, "I don't know."

"Lucas?" I pleaded. Nothing. "*Lucas!*" My pulse thrashed in my ears, adrenaline pumping through my veins. I shook him. Again, nothing. My breath ripped from my throat, jagged and cutting.

His skin was ashen, almost gray. His chest rose and fell, but it was shallow and slow. Too slow. Wraith take me. "*Lucas!*" I needed to get the Purge into him but that'd never happen if he didn't fucking wake.

My mother sobbed softly in the background as I drew my hand back and slapped my brother hard across the face. My palm made a loud crack against his cheek. His eyes flew open.

Thank sage! I shoved the Purge against his lips. "Drink this, Lucas! Now!"

He groaned and clumsily batted it away.

I thrust it back, then pried his mouth open with my fingers. Tipping the bottle up, I poured the contents into his throat and pinched his nose shut. He coughed and spit and gagged, misting bits of the liquid in the air, but got most of it down.

His lone word was slurred when he said, "Stop."

My phone rang. I snatched it up, hand shaking wildly when I eyed the screen and clicked to accept. "Joaquin!"

"You didn't answer my call," he snarled, the sound of a vehicle engine humming in the background.

I'd been so distracted, I didn't even know he had.

"You alright?" he demanded.

"No. It's Lucas. He's bad, Joaquin. I just gave him some Purge, but I don't know if I caught it in time. He's really pale." I shook my head and eyed my brother's chest. Still breathing, but it wasn't steady.

I loved my brother, and I wasn't about to leave him in that goddamn den for one more second. Lucas needed someone to shield him. Rip him from Isaac's clutches. There'd be a price to pay, but I'd cross that bridge, barter whatever I had to later.

"I'm getting him outta here," I told the Beta.

There was a brief pause. "Go." That engine revved higher. "We'll find you."

I threw Lucas's arm over my shoulder and used every ounce of strength I had to haul him to his feet, then aimed down the hall for the front door. I didn't know where the hells we'd go, but getting out of Victor's territory was the first step.

"Briar!" mom called, but her eyes screamed *Run!* Run until you can't run anymore and then keep running!

I kept going and barreled outside, struggling to hold my feet when I dragged Lucas down the steps.

My mother's cries broke behind me. "I *have* to call Isaac, Briar."

"I know." Rain pounded us, soaking our clothes and hair. "Let us get out of here first. Give us a head start. Once we're gone, then call. Can you do that?"

Her eyes pinched at the corners like she analyzed the problem in her head. She nodded, hands covering her mouth and muffling her voice when she said, "I'm so sorry."

I stumbled forward and threw open the passenger door on my car. Slumping Lucas onto the seat, I hefted his legs up and sealed him in. Reaching for mom, I took her hand in mine and squeezed. "Just buy us time, mom."

Water slithered through her hair, down her forehead and face. "This will be bad, Briar."

Oh, it'd be worse than bad seeing taking Lucas from Isaac had been what instigated his reign of terror against me in the first place. Doing it again was a shit ton of stupid. My stepfather's retaliation would come but abandoning my brother to die wasn't an option.

"I know." I released her, made for the driver's side.

"I love you."

My breath hitched. "You, too," I said, then climbed in. Slamming the door, I threw my phone down, turned the car over, popped it into reverse, and punched the gas. My head jerked as it careened back, tires shrieking when I hit the asphalt. Shifting into gear, I fled.

The rain fell in sheets, drowning the windshield and I set the wipers to full. They whipped back and forth, barely managing. Leaning onto the steering wheel, I squinted through the downpour.

I just needed to get out of Victor's territory. He was a power-hungry piece of trash, but I doubted he was the seven shades of stupid it would take to cross north and challenge Kane.

My gaze darted to Lucas. With the car's movement, I couldn't tell if he was breathing. I canted to the side and set a palm against his chest. He was warm, heart beating.

The Purge should've kicked in. Forced any V left in his stomach out. Unless it was too deep in his system. *Goddamnit, just fucking work!*

My hands shook violently as trees sailed by. "Hold on, Lucas. Please, just hold on." A few more minutes and we'd be outta there. Just a few more minutes and he'd be safe. Well, saf*er*. Safe wouldn't happen until he was free of the V and Isaac's body fed the ground.

I rounded the corner before the border, and an SUV came into view—Victor's SUV. Past him, a large, thick tree trunk sat broken on the road, blocking the boundary.

Close. We were so damn close.

I slammed on the brakes and the wheels locked up. The car fish-tailed, swinging left until we approached broadside. The wail of the tires pierced the world, and we skidded to a violent stop. My body snapped, hitting the door, then whipped to my right, digging the seatbelt into my flesh.

My brother crashed against me before he was jerked back against his window, then slumped in his seat. Limp.

"Lucas!" I reached for him. "LUCAS!"

Victor stood like some counterfeit gangster, hanging back behind the hood of his vehicle, as if he didn't want to intercede, while Amber loomed ten feet away, a poisonous smirk coating her lips. She exploded toward me.

My gaze flicked to the rear view. Nothing. I shoved the vehicle in reverse. Amber darted behind us and threw a fist into the bumper. A boom rang out, followed by the distinct sound of metal buckling as the car brought up short.

"Fuck you," I hissed, then punched the gas again. It hit with a thunk, knocking her back several feet. It didn't do any damage, but sure as shit pissed her off.

She loosed a bizarre screeching snarl as she aimed for my door. I clicked the locks in place as if that could stop her. Her fist went through the window, and I ducked when glass shrieked and shattered.

Oh, shit. Unlatching myself, I popped the door and swung to face her. I gripped my obsidian tight and dove deep into that connection with Kane. That power tore through the area and her eyes went wide a second before I thrust out with an upkick. It caught her chin, and a satisfying crack filled the world when her jaw snapped sideways.

A garbled growl ripped from her throat. The bones crunched and ground as they healed, sliding back into place. Her honeyed eyes blazed and lit the inside of the vehicle like a second sun.

She grabbed my leg and slurred, "How the fuck did you do that?"

I latched onto the wheel, so she jerked harder. Losing my grip, I went flying. My back hit the wet ground with a hollow thud. The air was knocked from my lungs. Rocks tore at my clothes and flesh. She kept dragging until we reached a pool of water gathered at a dip in the road.

"Just let us go!" I said through a gasp.

Victor rounded his hood and approached. "Lucas isn't yours to take, Briar. He belongs to Isaac. We all do."

My phone rang again from somewhere nearby. "We can help each other here, Victor."

"I make it a habit not to help anyone."

I glared at him through my brow. "You're protecting *something*." I shook my head. "Iron fires, you know what Isaac's trying to do. Working an in with the humans. Do you really think you'll be spared when that deal is done? *They'll* be his shields. He won't need any of us anymore. Including you!"

His body went rigid, nostrils flaring.

"Just let me protect Lucas. If I don't, Isaac'll kill him."

His eyes were hard, still, there was something there. Not regret, but something that looked like it.

Amber grinned, pure bitch with a side of menace. "Pretty sure the junky'll kill himself."

My blood turned to fire in my veins. Grabbing a clump of gravel, I whipped it toward her face.

She turned away but not in time. "You fucking witch," she snarled as she spit and rubbed at her eyes.

Her hold slipped, then clamped over my ankle. I thrashed against her and rolled to my stomach. The rain lashed down, streaming down my forehead and blurring my sight. I swiped my face to clear my vision and clawed at the ground, nails tearing over the asphalt.

"Briar?" Lucas called, voice groggy as he stumbled from the car. He jolted, then pitched forward and vomited.

Thank the Seven Iron Hells.

"Sorry, Briar," Victor said, aiming for Lucas. "This isn't up to me."

Wraith take me. "RUN, LUCAS! RUN!"

My brother retched again and Victor clamped onto his gangly, feeble arm as the roar of a fast-moving engine approached from the north.

"Just let him go, Victor! *Please!*" I cried, then tried to push up, but Amber planted a knee in my back, and I grunted as she latched onto my hair.

I glared at her from the corner of my sight. "Kill me and you kill Kane."

Ripping my head back at a painful angle, she offered me a smile that was entirely canines. "Who said anything about killing you? Kane likes power. That's what I am. Powerful. He needs to know what you are. Weak. And pathetic and unworthy. He'll see that eventually." Her voice deepened, darkened. "Then he'll come crawling back. He'll claim me too, and you won't be a problem anymore."

Claim her too? Was *that* her goddamn endgame? I didn't know if it was a thing, but either way, she'd straight up lost it if she thought Kane'd ever take that option.

She shoved my head underwater. I flailed like a feral cat and sucked in a mouthful. My chest tightened, burning for the lack of air. She ripped me back again. I coughed and hacked, spewing water before I sucked in heaving breaths to sate my starved lungs.

That engine roar grew louder when a familiar truck crested the hill and came into view. It sped toward us, no sign of slowing.

Kane. Heat flared through my chest. He'd come. Power of obsidian, he'd come.

Amber's eyes snapped up.

"Fuck!" Victor barked, going rigid when he shoved Lucas to the ground behind him. He adjusted his lapels, his cuffs, his collar, then did it again.

My head tipped up, my shake turning to a full-on tremble as the vehicle careened closer. Closer. Kane hit the brakes hard, painting the distant buildings in red. Rubber burned the road, shrieking as he drifted to the edge of the boundary, headlights tracking across the area, momentarily blinding me.

The driver's door flew open. Kane's broad, lithe, towering form maneuvered out, his eyes liquid metal. His power broke across the area and stole my breath. Water rolled over his gray hair, dripping from its ends, his mouth, his chin. That stare hunted the scene when he stalked to the edge of his territory and toed that line.

My blood thrashed in my ears. Joaquin exited the passenger side and edged forward until he flanked his Alpha.

Kane's arms hung loose by his sides, feet shoulder-width apart. "I heard there's a problem."

Victor's face fell slack. "Nothing I can't handle."

The arch of Kane's brow was sharp. "And what if I don't like how you're handling it?"

No direct threats. Questions weren't a challenge. Questions wouldn't start a war. They'd skirt the political minefield that was the wolves' existence, but it wasn't enough to prompt slaughter.

Whitney slid from the truck. I flinched, stomach imploding on itself. My eyes stung from the tears that tried to form, but none came. Not that I had any left. I'd run out—run dry.

Her eyes were wide as they fell on me.

My brother moaned.

"Lucas!" I cried, voice muffled against the white noise of the downpour. I tried to scramble his way, but Amber held me in place.

"Let them go, Victor," Kane growled, ratcheting the situation from tense to volatile.

"Can't do that, Kane." Victor tipped his fedora to shield his eyes. A barrier between them. "They're my problem now."

Was that a truth? He worked with Isaac so easily. Or maybe he was just better at hiding his hate. Either way, it didn't matter. The only thing that did was Lucas. My gaze slid my brother's way. I *needed* to get to him.

Amber shifted off me as her grip locked around the base of my neck. "Don't move, little bitch."

"Hand Luke over," Kane said, guttural.

Lucas. Only Lucas. Not that I'd complain. If he got my brother out, whatever Isaac had coming for me would be worth it. But really, could things get any worse?

"The boy doesn't belong to you, Slade," Victor said, all empty promises and false bravado.

Kane rolled his shoulders and bared his extending canines. Squaring himself to the other Alpha, he inclined his head. "I'll take that bet."

Victor's stare darted around. "They're in my territory. This doesn't concern you."

Kane advanced, the movement slow. Deliberate. And an unwavering declaration of power as he took a single step across the line. Those silver topaz eyes blazed voltaic. "Now it fucking does."

My pulse thrashed in my ears at the sight. Shadow and sage.

Amber ducked low, setting her mouth to my ear. When she spoke, her words were an acidic lilt. "You hear that, Briar? He doesn't give a shit about *you*. You're nothing to him. Just some dried up whore he used to fuck."

The words cut deep, but I'd bleed out before I'd *ever* tell her that. Instead, I did what I do best; Make. Shit. Worse. "Guess that makes both of us."

She flipped me onto my back, hand clamping over my throat as her fist came down, the speed impossible to block. It caught me hard across the cheek with a sickening crunch. Everything flashed white.

A roar split the night. At least, I thought one did. With the ringing in my ears, I couldn't be sure.

I groaned and crushed my eyes closed, then reopened them.

Kane's seething, electric glare speared Amber through. His legs shifted, readying, his next words forced through his tightly clenched jaw. "Do that again and see what happens."

But I couldn't let him take that on, not for me. Besides, it was my fight. My turn. Good thing I was petty as they came and twice as senseless. Amber shifted to a crouch. Rotating my obsidian, I gripped it hard and sought that Alpha power again. Kane tensed, stare flashing as I swung my leg out. The hit caught the center of her shin. The bone cracked, then buckled. She collapsed in on herself with a howl of pain.

It was music to my goddamn ears.

She screeched and scrambled away, breathing hard through her teeth while her leg crunched and cracked and reset itself.

"JOAQUIN!" Kane roared.

The Northern Beta crossed the border, hands loose by his sides when he aimed for me. "Nice shot, banshee."

Amber's hand swung down, grabbing hold before she jerked me back—a bone she didn't intend to share. "She's mine."

A low growl rumbled through Kane's chest.

Amber's? Oh, hard no! I opened my mouth to say as much but it didn't wanna work.

"Let her go," Joaquin said, then bent and took hold of her arm, "or I'll rip it off."

Her gaze flew wide. She speared me with a glare, hissed and sputtered and snarled, but released.

The Beta shoved her away, then eyed me. "You good?"

My sight went unfocused when I inclined my head.

"Stay still," he warned.

Still because movement could provoke. Because I sat at the precipice of a promised death. Because I was the catalyst.

More lights approached from both sides of the boundary. Tires screeched. Doors slammed. My vision split, then refocused. Theo. Naomi. Mason. I spit blood onto the pavement and the hair on the back of my neck rose. Isaac.

Isaac! No. *NO!*

Amber released a laugh so dark, it stole light from the world. "Oh, you're fucked now."

Naomi winced and Joaquin's brow dropped low.

"Hand Luke over, Victor, or get fucking ready," Kane said, calm. The kind of calm that came with confidence. Certainty. A certainty that he *would* destroy the other Alpha. "I won't ask again."

I chanced a glance. My mother sat in the passenger's seat of her car, Isaac behind the wheel. He flew out, whites of his eyes bared. A slip of his carefully crafted persona—one he snapped back into place as he threw his hands out in front of him in a placating gesture.

Kane eyed him with a 'The fuck did you get back?' disdain.

Victor's nostrils flared when his wolf kicked in. His power rolled through the area. "You don't want to do this, Slade."

Kane arced a lone brow and took his stance. "I already did."

Theo's forearms flexed. He met my gaze and gave an infinitesimal nod. He and Naomi crossed over, then flanked their

Alpha. My heart twisted because that loyalty had just thrust them directly into Isaac's crosshairs with me.

"I can take Lucas," Isaac cut in when he stepped forward. Tentative, like he wasn't sure what Kane would do. That made both of us.

"No," Kane said, the word torn from the distant chambers of his chest. "He comes with me."

Mason's eyes bulged while Victor's stare tracked to Isaac.

Kill him, Kane. Tear him apart and this'll all be over! Just kill him!

"He's my son," Isaac pleaded.

Kane rose to his full, dominating height when he prowled toward him and stopped less than a foot away. He glared down at Isaac, the shadow tracking over his expression dark. "Not anymore."

My breath hitched, heart lurching when it found its rhythm. Sage, I loved that man. With everything I was, everything I had, and to the depths of my soul, I loved him. Because he fought for the people he loved, and he loved my brother.

"Please, Kane," Isaac said. "I'm his father."

Whitney's stare snapped from person to person, wild like she tracked a storm.

"Best thing you ever did for him was leave." Kane stalked to the tree across the road, took it in one hand, and threw it aside like it weighed nothing. It crashed into the forest with the crack of splintering wood. "You should've stayed gone." He chucked his chin at Isaac's car. "Now fly the fuck outta here."

Isaac paled. That mask slipped again. It was only for a heartbeat, but it was there, and it was telling. Even with the preternaturals he controlled, against Kane, he found himself wanting. The muscles in his temple flicked as he worked his jaw. He found Victor. "Please," he said, the words even when he relented. "Just do as Kane says."

Victor inclined his head, raised his hands and edged back.

My stepfather turned on his heel and headed for his car. His face was downcast, chest curved inward, head stooped. His disguise. His goddamn lie. His glare met mine when he climbed inside—a promise of horrors to come.

He needed me for Zahara, but patience was my stepfather's weapon, and he knew how to wield it.

Even in the dark, my mother's expression was blanched. Our eyes met. There was a relief there. One I understood because there was no place safer for Lucas than with Kane. To him, my brother was family. A chosen responsibility. A loyalty. But to Isaac, he was property.

Turning the vehicle over, Isaac put it in gear and left, followed a second later by Amber and the Southern Alpha.

Kane half-faced to his cousins. "Get Luke in the truck." Pivoting, he closed the distance to me.

My body grew light, hands tingling.

Theo and Naomi gathered my brother and aimed for their Alpha's vehicle. Whitney shuffled around and opened the door for them. My brother moaned a pathetic sound, but he was alive, and free. My shoulders sagged with relief.

Joaquin gripped his wrist when his attention landed on me. "You've got a talent for finding trouble."

My laugh was hollow. Trouble didn't begin to describe it.

Kane crouched at my side, stare tracking my bloodied face before it locked with my own. Lines of strain ridged his eyes. He slid his dense arms under me and lifted me to his chest. His body was stiff, but warm, and safe, and the shield I desperately missed when he carried me away.

Mason approached, looking small among the weres. "You alright, Briar?"

Why was he even there? I could only assume Isaac'd ordered it, 'cause there was no way in the Seven Iron Hells Kane told him.

"Yeah," I slurred.

"Liar," Kane said, tone rough as he stalked towards my Coven Leader's vehicle. "Mason?"

Mason shrank in on himself, voice feeble when he replied, "Yeah?"

"Get her out of here."

No. Take me with you. Home. I'm yours. Don't let go. "I can manage."

Joaquin frowned. "Your goddamn eyes are crossing, banshee."

That connection with Kane was already kicking in, the healing slow while the pain in my head ebbed. "I'll be fine—"

"No," Kane cut in. He shifted my weight and opened the passenger door of Mason's car, then settled me into the seat. Power of obsidian, he was close. His scent, his heat, his mouth. Those eyes flashed, some other emotion I couldn't peg settling deep. "Naomi," he threw over his shoulder, "take Briar's car and follow them."

"On it," she said.

I found Theo and tipped my chin to Mason's vehicle. He offered me a salute and slipped into the backseat.

Kane eyed him before setting his canine against the pad of his thumb and bit down, puncturing it. Blood welled to the surface when he extended it my way. "Take it." My brows rose and he cleared his throat. "This'll make it go faster."

Heat pooled in my lower abdomen, and I was catapulted back to a different night and a painfully similar circumstance. Taking his blood was so . . . intimate. To taste him. Carry his scent again. I wanted it, but Isaac's command meant I couldn't touch him. Couldn't initiate.

"Kane, I—"

He set that calloused thumb to my mouth, voice gruff but oddly easy when he said, "Just fucking take it."

My lips parted. His stare ignited and he slid inside, pad pressing against my tongue. I sealed myself around him. He turned to stone while the metallic tang of his blood flooded me.

Warmth seared through my body, and the pulsing pain that pounded my skull ebbed more until it vanished altogether. The ache from the swelling around my cheek receded and my vision cleared. I loosed a soft, relieved sigh.

The taste of him. The touch. The feel. Everything. It was all I wanted. If we just stayed that way . . .

His knuckle brushed my cheek.

I froze.

That igneous gaze held. Never wavering.

See me, Kane.

The driver's side door creaked open. Mason climbed in.

Kane cleared his throat and withdrew. My soul shattered.

Next he spoke, his tone was flat. Impossible to read. "Luke'll stay with me."

I nodded, fighting to keep my voice steady when I uttered, "Okay."

"My blood'll be too abrupt on his system tonight. He'll need the Renew."

My throat ran dry.

His attention lingered for several broken heartbeats before it tracked to the windshield and landed on Whitney—looking for her.

A stabbing pain lanced my chest and cleaved it wide. Whitney. My replacement. Right. None of what'd happened was for me. He'd helped to avoid the fallout if I died. Noble, under the circumstances, but that was it, and it wasn't personal.

Tears stung the backs of my eyes.

Kane stretched his neck, loosed a rough exhale, then rose to his full height, and closed the door, taking everything I was with him when he stalked away.

"I'm sorry, Briar," Mason said as he turned the car over and aimed us north across that boundary.

I shook my head, 'cause not one ounce of this was his fault.

Theo's palm was heavy on my shoulder.

That twisting in my chest delved deeper. The silence in the car was a void I wanted to fall into. Let it swallow me whole. I had not one clue if my efforts were actually working. Yeah, the Beta'd noticed, but had it been the kind I'd wanted? Or did he just think I was weird?

My phone buzzed and I pulled it out. A text appeared.

Lisa: Can you swing by NML tomorrow?

My brow furrowed.

Sure. You alright?

Lisa: As fine as can be. Is noon good?

Lis was a right-between-the-eyes kinda straight shooter. If she wasn't filling the specifics in, it's 'cause she didn't want it in writing. Fair enough.

I'll be there.

Mason cleared his throat. "I don't know if this is a good time, but I, ugh, I've got something for you."

I peered his way. Reaching into his coat, he pulled a tattered book from its inside pocket and passed it my way.

Theo's face twisted. "What's that?"

It was brown leather—well, likely used to be, but age had weathered it to a yellowish tan. The pages were rippled at the ends, and the title on the cover read *Ancient Histories*.

My eyes widened. "Is this what I think it is?"

He shrugged. "It was the only thing I could find with a reference. I was gonna read it tonight, but I think you need the distraction more."

"So, cool!" Theo cut in, then deadpanned when he repeated, "What the iron fires is it?"

Chapter Seventeen

"No offence, chickie, but you're an idiot," Lisa said as she aggressively unpacked a load of steins from a tray she held. They softly clanked while she organized them behind the bar.

My brow furrowed as I shifted on my stool and flipped a page in the copy of *Ancient Histories* from Mason. "You know adding the 'no offence' actually *makes* it offensive, right?"

No Man's Land was surprisingly busy, considering it'd just opened. The day was overcast, the light dreary. It muted the colors inside and matched my somber mood. The ominous feeling that hovered over me since everything'd gone down the night before was a bomb waiting to be dropped.

I'd barely slept, scouring the book while I tried to make sense of it. The wording was . . . weird. Vague and open to interpretation. One passage in particular stuck with me.

Changelings are made of the Deep. Of the Dark. Fear is what they know. It is why and what they are. Broken things that seek the chaos. When the call to the wraith comes, they die in the light and return.

They die in the light and return? What the iron fires did that mean? Gnashing my teeth, I slammed it closed.

"That helpful, huh?" Lisa asked.

My answering glower was enough.

"Hey," a shadow walker down the bar called.

I pointed to the right. "Feeders and bleeders are over there." Twisting my obsidian, I closed my hand over it, drew on my power and cocooned our conversation from the ridiculously annoying and over-sensitive, preternatural ears around us.

Lis wiped sweat from her brow and stretched her neck. "Seriously. I can't believe you did that alone. You should've called me or something."

My stomach growled, so I reached into my purse, grabbed my sandwich and started scoffing it down. "It's fine. Joaquin knew." And told *everyone*.

She aimed one of those steins at me, then scratched her arm. "Lucky for you."

It *was* lucky. If the wolves hadn't shown up . . . I didn't wanna think about what could've happened next. "I'm just glad Lucas is outta there."

"And with Kane," she said, tracking a hand over her disheveled hair.

My gaze dropped and I stared down at my hands. "And with Kane."

She leaned across the bar and chucked my chin. "Speaking of Victor . . ."

Head snapping up, I angled forward. Interest piqued.

"He has a claimed mate."

A claimed goddamn mate!

No. Fucking. Way. My jaw dropped before I scooped it back up, because the bar of No Man's Land was not a good, nor recommended place for it to be. Who the iron fires would hitch their wagon to him?

"And," Lisa added, "she has a kid."

My eyes flew wide, and a memory twigged. One from ages ago when I'd tried to cross Victor's border as Kane's—a then newly minted Alpha—mate for the first time since we'd gotten together, as it were. The former Southern Alpha had rolled up in his SUV . . . a child in the back.

It fit. People Victor'd want to protect. Want out of Isaac's reach. Out of his awareness, because Victor'd watched my stepfather use everything that mattered against the ones he controlled. And on that front, I understood.

But still, there was something about Lisa's wording . . . "Is the kid his?"

"Don't think so. Either way, he's ordered the Pack to be quiet about them." She tipped her head toward a group of weres in the back corner. "His people found workarounds. Call her 'the bitch' and the boy 'the nephew who's not the nephew' before they grumble about having to dogsit."

The nicknames were crass as crass got, but still, I selfishly grinned wide. "Have I told you lately I love you?"

Standing, she shimmied her shoulders. "Not nearly enough."

I plunked my chin in my hand. "Speaking of interesting things, I met the Ithican Ambassador."

She rubbed her chin and started organizing some bottles, voice high when she replied, "Oh, yeah?"

"Yeah. He's, um, interesting."

"Interesting how?"

I lifted a shoulder in a half shrug and eyed her askance. "Seems to know a lot. Like, a lot, a lot."

"Funny that," she said, a little too easy.

I dropped my forearms onto the edge of the counter. "What'd you do?"

She glanced around, then back. "They came to me asking questions, so I pointed them at the best asset Cambria's got."

My heart swelled, smile small as my face heated. Even still, it didn't change what was coming. I took an unflattering bite of my sandwich. "I keep waiting. Between me calling for the Embassy and what happened yesterday, Isaac's *gonna* punish me." And likely Theo and Nay right along with me.

The bitterness in her scoff brushed my skin when she shoved her tray aside. "He's already punishing you."

There was that.

The same shadow walker from before smacked his palm against the counter like it was a bell to ding. "Hey!"

I released my obsidian and narrowed my eyes because that was an asking-for-a-throat-punch kinda move. "*What?*"

"If you two are done, I'd like a drink."

I tipped my head toward Lisa. "You wanna deal with Pissy Fangs here? Or should I?"

The vamp heavy-sighed. "I can fucking hear you."

"Oh, thank sage." I dragged the back of a hand across my forehead in mock concern. "I was afraid you'd missed it."

He loosed a low hiss.

The building shook, bottles and windows rattling. The train chuffed and clicked as it passed, then several long seconds later, faded into the distance.

A familiar figure crossed in, and my lungs seized at the sight of Isaac strolling toward us, my mother trailing behind.

Blood thrummed in my ears, breaths tearing from me in short, shallow bursts. I grabbed that copy of *Ancient Histories*, tucked it inside my purse and turned to Lisa. "Go." Because both of us didn't need to suffer him.

Her nod was tight before she beat feet toward her office.

My stepfather took one of the two open stools to my right, my mother the other as he settled in.

"Contain our conversation until we're done here, Briar," he instructed. "Just you, me and Lana."

I did.

He inclined his head like I was a good witch. "After your little," he flicked a dismissive hand my way, "show yesterday, I felt it imperative for us to talk."

The stutter of my heart was the "stop beating" kinda dangerous. My gaze darted to the exit, and my mother then back his way. "About what?"

"About exactly what I'm capable of."

The ominous pit in my stomach took root, burrowing deep. "I know what you're capable of, Isaac." Intimately. Painfully.

He tsked, the shake of his head slow. "No, Briar. You don't."

My mother's dull cobalt eyes crushed closed.

Isaac settled a hand on her shoulder. "Lana tells me you've never heard the *real* story of how we met."

I took a steadying breath, 'cause surer than the Seven Iron Hells, I needed to brace.

"She didn't know we were together at first, you see. It wasn't until our son was born that she figured it out."

What the hells? My brow knitted together. Until Lucas was *born*?

But I'd thought . . .

"You look confused," he taunted. "Let me clarify." He smoothed a hand down the front of his collared, short-sleeved shirt. "First, I took your father's face, then I took his house, and his family. I took everything he had before I fucked his wife until she gave me a child."

I leaned back, giving the bar my weight, 'cause obsidian knew I couldn't hold it. "What'd you do with him?"

"Oh. Don't worry. He's not far." He smiled, all sadism and teeth. "His pieces are scattered in the woods behind your home."

The world stopped, then rocked, knocking me off axis. My gaze grew unfocused. I couldn't think. Couldn't see. My father. He'd . . . he'd . . . I peered around like some alternative would present itself, but nothing showed.

Dead. By *Isaac's* hand. Or someone he knew. Someone he controlled.

What was truth? What was lies? What memories were real? Iron fires take me. Was there anything Isaac hadn't stolen from us?

Tears streamed down my mother's face, slithering from her cheeks. She reopened her eyes. "I didn't know, Briar. I didn't."

Of course not. And by the time she figured it out, it would've been too late. The tightness in my chest was a vice, crushing me. Guilt swept in and tinged my tongue with its bitter tang. It explained everything about her. About her choices with him. Because she'd seen just how far Isaac was willing to go.

Bile climbed my throat, and my hand shot to my stomach. How long had Isaac stolen behind my father's face while his body had been back there, rotting beneath the earth *the whole goddamn time*?

My mother hung her head.

"Why?" I demanded. "Why him? Why her?"

He cocked a brow, and my mother cringed as he ran his fingers through her hair. "Because she was easy." Lowering his arm to his side, he smiled and loosed a dry laugh. "You're playing games, Briar, trying to outsmart me. But you should know, I only keep things until they're no longer of use." He lifted a shoulder in a shrug. "Or until they become a problem."

Oh, and I *was* a problem. He needed me until the transfer with Zahara was locked, and then . . . That countdown on my life—Kane's life—started ticking.

He canted his head. "Do we understand one another?"

My hands flexed at my sides, itching to claw that smirk from his face. The nod I offered was so tight, it was a wonder I didn't creak.

"Good. Now," he dusted his hands, "I want my son."

No, he wanted his *possession*. I shook my head. "Kane's is the best place for him, and you know it. Just leave him be."

"The best place for any boy is with his father."

My mouth thinned into a hard line. "Kane is more of a father to him than you'll ever be."

His fingers dug into his palms while he vibrated from the strain. "Kane will never be a father, Briar. At least, not with you." His nostrils flared on a sharp inhale when he annunciated every word, "Again—I. Want. My. Son."

He was insane. Abso-fucking-lutely insane. "And how the Iron Hells am I supposed to get him?"

"I don't care *how* you do it, only that you do." He bared his tightly clenched teeth. "Go into that house and drag him out if you have to."

The command hit, and that imperious weight pressed in. No, no, no! I gripped my arm at the elbow. This couldn't happen! "You really think Kane's just gonna hand him over?"

"I don't," he said, the words level. Matter of fact, like he'd already calculated a solution. He checked his watch. "Naomi has informed me your wolf is currently indisposed." He reached into his pocket and discretely pulled out a bottle of wolfsbane. "Drink it. Douse yourself in it. He'll think Lucas left on his own."

Not even goddamn close. Wolfsbane or no, my Alpha'd know I was there. Feel it. Come hunting.

Isaac set a palm over his heart. "Don't forget, I do this because it's important for you to understand, Briar."

I swallowed around the razorblades in my throat. "Understand what?"

Beside him, my mother paled.

"What's coming." He flicked his wrist. "Now run along."

Chapter Eighteen

I veered down Kane's road, heart pounding like a kick drum and reverberating twice as loud. Shadow and sage, there wasn't any way to brace for what came. The chaos in my head picked up speed like a train rolling downhill without brakes.

The wolfsbane coated my skin and tongue. It tasted bitter, like secrets or lies.

What if Naomi was wrong? What if Kane *was* home? What if I was about to storm into an Alpha's den and a blood-soaked maw of certain savagery?

Cutting into the driveway, I found no sign of Kane's truck. My stomach sank and hardened, a ragged mix of disappointment and relief. I ached to see him, but seeing him like this . . . What I was about to do wasn't just criminal, it was so far past stupid it bordered on suicidal. Claiming mark or no, I wasn't welcome. Isaac'd made sure of that.

Scanning the area, I slipped from my car. The hydrangeas I'd planted were in full bloom, their white bouquets popping against the house's siding. A sad, beautiful detail.

My feet were heavy, as if they'd been coated in cement when I trudged onto the porch. I inhaled, the air knocking around my lungs with a death rattle. Withdrawing my key, I slid it into the lock and turned. There was an unmistakable click when the bolt slid out of place.

My gaze flew wide, and my brows tried to escape my forehead. Tears stung the backs of my eyes. He hadn't changed the lock. Those brows sank low. Why hadn't he changed the lock?

I shook my head. Probably didn't expect I'd be dumb enough to come back.

I bobbed my head side to side. *I sure showed him!*

My touch hovered over the handle for one breath. Two. Three. The compulsion kicked in and my fingers curled around the metal. I turned it and swung the door wide.

Stepping across the threshold, my heart climbed to my throat when I spotted a pair of Lucas's shoes in the entrance. Some of his balled-up socks sat scattered on the living room floor, while a half-eaten sandwich and mostly full glass of juice littered the coffee table. Definitely my brother's, 'cause the wolves didn't leave food behind.

"Lucas?" I called. *Don't be here. Don't be here!*

Silence answered me and hope bloomed in my chest.

I poked my head around the corner. "Lucas?"

Again, nothing.

My teeth worried my cheek as I took everything in, just wanting a minute to imagine—to feel—what life could've been with the two of them.

Picking up the dishes, I aimed for the kitchen, and set them in the sink. One of Kane's navy hooded sweatshirts was draped on the back of a chair. I trailed my fingers over it before I took it up and wrapped it around me. It swallowed me whole, just like him. I tied the arms across my shoulders and breathed in that wilderness scent. I'd worn the one at my condo so much, that smell had faded. It soothed my soul to have it back.

My gaze lifted to the window, and I froze. Lucas sat in one of those red Adirondack chairs on the dock, Hannah in the seat to his right, hands tucked into her sleeves. He grinned at her, and even from inside, the sound of his mule-laugh carried.

He looked so . . . happy. One day with Kane, that's all it took to turn him around. For his violet eyes to start clearing and that goofy grin to return. Warmth spread from my chest, and my palm pressed against it.

Lucas leaned toward Hannah. She met him halfway, setting her lips to his in a gentle kiss before he rose and aimed for the back door.

My hands flew to my mouth. I couldn't rip him from that—toss him back to a V-addled abyss. Back to Isaac.

But at the sight of my brother, the pull of that command didn't come. Why? Get Lucas. Isaac had been clear on that. Or had he? I rehashed the wording. *Go into that house and drag him out if you have to.* My mind twisted it around, testing the boundaries. Go into the house. Into the *house*!

Lucas closed in, steps away. Five feet. Four. Three. He reached out.

I bolted for the door, whipped it open and threw my palms up. "STOP!"

He jumped, and loosed a jagged breath as he stumbled back. His violet eyes narrowed like he had trouble understanding what the sage he saw. "B-Briar?"

"Don't come inside!" I said through a gasp.

His face twisted as he looked past me. "What's going on?"

Body sagging. I gave the frame my weight. "I'm circumventing Isaac's system."

His mouth dropped open, and I swore his brain cells all cocked their mini-teenage heads in unison.

"He sent me here to get you." He blanched and I shook my head. "It's fine. Don't cross this threshold and we don't have a problem."

"Okay."

"Just . . . wait out there until you're *sure* I'm gone, alright?"

"Alright." He glanced around, then back to me before he scrubbed a hand over his hair, making its errant strands stick off in a hundred directions. "I couldn't take it anymore," he blurted, then exhaled long and slow. "Being trapped." His eyes met mine, a regret there that was entirely too old for his sixteen years. "I'm sorry."

My ribs cinched around my lungs. "I hate that he did this to you, Lucas. But I'll never blame you for it. It's him. Only him."

His nod was small as he stared down at his feet and kicked a small rock there. "I wanna help, Briar. What can I do?"

Wraith take me. He deserved his vengeance just like the rest of us, but I already had too much on my plate to worry about. He was safe with Kane. That was enough. "Right now, the best thing you can do for me is to lay low." My attention flicked past him to Hannah. "And no hanky-panky!"

He rolled his eyes, some of that sadness ebbing. "Shut up!"

My grin was pure annoying-big-sister and all teeth. "You look good, you know."

His face flushed and he kicked another rock. "I feel good."

Hannah glanced our way, spotted me, a smile splitting her pretty face as she waved.

I waved back. "She's a special one, Lucas. Hold onto her."

"Yeah," he ducked his chin. "I will."

Chucking my thumb over my shoulder, I indicated the kitchen. "What'd you need?"

"Just some waters."

"Waters?" I waggled my brows and aimed for the fridge. "How respectable."

He snickered and shrugged. "Kane said he'd gut me if I got into any adult stuff."

Of course, he did. My heart smiled broad and deep when I pointed a nubby finger his way. "He's not the only one." I grabbed some ice and put two glasses together then aimed back his way. The condensation wicked against my skin before I handed them over. "Do me a favor and help Kane around here."

"I know, I know."

"I'm serious, Lucas. Don't make him pick up after you all the time because he loves you and he'll do it, but he shouldn't have to."

"I will," he said, the words sincere. He shifted his weight from one leg to the other. "How're you doin'?"

Tears stung my eyes and I looked away, because the crease of concern that worried his forehead was brotherly, and warm, and a total role reversal. "Managing," I said, the lie bitter on my tongue. But I wasn't about to dump more burden on his narrow shoulders. He'd carried enough already.

"I'm sorry," he said again.

I swiped the moisture from the corner of my gaze. "Don't ever apologize for *him*, Lucas. Never." I tipped my head toward the dock. "Go on, get back to your girl. I'll get this mess for now."

He took a swig of his drink, the ice clanking as it moved. "But you just said—"

My nose scrunched. "Oh, shut it."

His mule-laugh brought my shattered soul some much needed lightness. "Thanks, Briar." He peered down at the drinks. "For everything."

Lucas was safe. Happy. And if I had to give everything I was to keep it that way, I would. "Always." I flicked my hands and shooed him. "Now get outta here, pest."

He snickered, raised the drinks in salute, and bounced on the balls of his feet as he strode away.

I sealed myself inside and my stomach groaned. Sage, I was hungry. I supposed stress did that to a girl. I grabbed an apple from the fridge and chowed down while I loaded dishes into the dishwasher and turned it on. Heading upstairs, I grabbed the dirty clothes, piling them in the hall so I could lug them to the laundry in the unfinished basement.

My throat tightened. Sweet sage, I missed that house. Being under that roof with Kane, waking up to him. Touching him. Breathing him. Just . . . *him*.

But it wasn't *ours* anymore. My heart ached in my chest. Being there and hiding my scent just felt . . . wrong. Violating. An intrusion.

I peered down at myself as a thought ricocheted around my head. Again, I tested the boundaries of Isaac's order. He'd told me to wear the wolfsbane but said not a damn thing about leaving it on. Obsidian knew how Kane would react— well, that wasn't true. He'd be pissed as a predator and twice as savage, but it was a chance to make him question—likely my sanity. Still, any questions were better than none. If I was quick enough, I'd be out before it was a problem. An immediate one, anyway.

Kane was my everything, and he'd given everything for me. I could light another fire. An itty bitty one. Barely noticeable. And if I was lucky, he might see an ember.

I headed for the master bedroom. It looked exactly the same, yet entirely different. My attention flicked to the bed and the ruffled sheets. An image of Kane's powerful body holding Whitney's hips while he fucked her from behind flashed across my mind. My stomach torqued and I doubled over. My fingers dug into my knees, and I sucked in air like I breathed through a straw.

He'd moved on or was well on his way to it. And that truth hurt on a level so deep, it cut the strings of my heart—ones I couldn't afford to lose 'cause they were the only things holding it together.

I stripped, draping my clothes on the bathroom sink, then froze. My things still littered the space. Makeup, shampoo. Everything. I blinked, then blinked again. Why? Had he not gotten around to tossing it? Refused to go in there? Look at it? Had to be. It was the only thing that made sense.

I shook myself and climbed into the shower. Steam filled the room when I trailed my touch over the glass, tracing curlicue designs that led to the words "You're it for me". I stared at them for several long moments, then swiped them away.

Turning, I let the water soak my hair and the deep ache in my muscles. I gave the wall my weight, and sighed, staring down at that heart shaped tattoo.

The door exploded in, and I screamed. Wood and dust flew in every direction before it crashed to the floor. Kane loomed in the entrance, his broad, dominating form filling the frame. I covered myself with my hands, which didn't help considering there was entirely too much to cover.

His chest rose and fell on savage breaths that dragged through his teeth. Those molten eyes locked on me, wild with a territorial impulse. He prowled the few steps closer and ripped the shower door open.

My pulse pounded in my ears while I shook and fought against slinking into the corner. Retreating from the baddest of apex predators was a crap ass idea—and coupled with my break 'n enter—a sure fire way to end up mounted on his wall.

"The fuck are you doing here, Briar?" his deep voice rumbled.

I worked to hide a wince, because my name—that *formal* name—from his tongue, iron fires, would it ever not hurt?

Turning off the water, my gaze fell to his torso. "Let me out."

He didn't.

I pursed my lips. "Please hand me a towel."

He didn't.

Rolling his head on his neck, his hands flexed over the shower's metal edging. It groaned under the force. I made to leave but he shifted into my path, colliding with me. I sucked in a sharp inhale. Shadow and sage, I missed the feel of him. That chest. The way my delicate curves formed to his rigid lines.

Too bad he eyed me like a meal.

I homed in on the space under his arm and weaved toward it slowly, because keeping my limbs was preferable. His head rotated, stare following me as I went. I was too exposed. Emotionally—and literally. I inadvertently brushed his side as I ducked out, and that Briar-no-touchie-Kane command crushed in. I winced and grabbed a towel, sloppily drying before I threw on the closest thing to me, Kane's shirt. Taking the rest of my clothes in hand, I beelined into his room.

Giving him my back wasn't the bestest of options, so I spun toward him and yipped when I found him so tight on my heels, his heat seared my scarcely covered flesh.

I backpedaled, hitting the edge of the bed. He kept coming. His calloused hand hooked under my leg, and he knocked me back until I collapsed onto the mattress. He lunged. One knee landing by my hips, the other between my thighs while his forearms dropped to either side of my head.

He lowered his face within a hair's breadth of mine, stare blazing a liquid molten. "What are you doing here?"

I bit my lip, fighting the heat that flared in my core.

"Answer me."

Crap! What'd I say? What answer would work with the compulsion? Draw attention? Nothing came to me, so instead I just said, "Lucas."

A dark laugh as those eyes tracked between mine. "Why were you wearing wolfsbane?"

Oh, *snap*! My brows ticked up and my hand rose to my claiming mark. "Who said I was?"

His attention flicked there before it came back. "There's no goddamn scent trail through the house."

Sure, I'd *wanted* him to figure it out, but I hadn't assumed I'd be around when he did, which meant I was well and short on answers.

He edged closer until his chest crushed mine and his face pushed into my hair. I panted wildly as he set his mouth to my ear, his words thundering through me when he demanded, "Why'd you wash it off?"

Power of obsidian, that sound. His voice. *Him*.

His head angled, that unfathomable stare locking with mine. His tone lowered, less anger, more interest when he pushed, "*Why?*"

The compulsion's invisible grip stole my voice until the answer was suppressed. I turned my head away and pressed back into the bed.

His hand latched over my jaw and drew me back.

"Kane," a woman's voice cautioned from nearby. Whitney.

He tensed.

No! Don't take him away! He's mine. Don't take him!

My breath left me in a rush. It was one thing to imagine her there, in his home—his room—but another altogether to see it. A wave of pain struck while my heart rate kicked up, pulse thrashing in my ears. I couldn't be there. Couldn't watch them . . . together.

Kane's gaze bore into me.

Whitney's throat tracked up and down when she swallowed hard. "She's scared, Kane."

What? Scared of what they meant together, of him loving her, sure, but never scared of *him*.

His attention held mine as, slowly, he extended his arms and pushed back. Away. The bed rose when his weight lifted, my body cold and bereft at the loss of him.

Wait, had he . . . listened to her? His wolf had *listened* to her? He'd never done that for me. Not unless I'd thrown my body at him as a distraction. But she'd just said some soft-spoken words and he'd *listened*!

He hadn't just replaced me, he'd moved on. Past me. I was nothing. The woman he'd made the colossal mistake of hitching his life to. An undertow dragged me through that sea of despair, far below the surface. I drowned in that agony until it bathed my soul. Soaking me through.

Pain. Sage, so much pain! I winced when I slid from the bed onto my pathetically weak legs.

"Give her space," Whitney told him as she tipped her head toward the door, inviting him to her.

Again, he listened.

My stomach dropped, the burning in my chest so hot, it stole the air from my lungs. I recoiled. My nails bit into my palms and I sobbed into the prison of my mind. The noxious threat of my violence was so potent toward her, it was a wonder I didn't spit venom. Kane was mine. He was fucking *mine*!

But I couldn't say any of that.

My legs buckled. I grabbed the edge of the mattress to steady myself. I needed to leave. Get out. It was my only option. Seizing my clothes, I ducked my head and barreled out of the room, past Kane, and Whitney, then down the stairs. The rapid-fire thump of my feet was like a storm that boomed through the house.

"What the fuck's going on, Briar?" Kane roared.

"Nothing!" He was close. So damn close. I chanced a glance behind me. Like any predator would, he gave chase.

"*Liar!*"

I dipped down, took up my shoes, and bolted. The door whipped aside when I burst through and leapt from the porch. Rocks dug into my bare feet as I ran. I scrambled into my car, keys clanking when I fumbled to get them *out of my goddamn pants pocket*. Trembling violently, I shoved them into the ignition and turned it over. The engine boomed to life.

"BRY!"

My breath hitched and my head snapped up. My heart stopped—the *world* stopped. *Bry.* My lips parted.

Kane's hands landed on the hood, fingers arced down. His exhales exploded from his throat.

His expression was indecipherable. What went on behind those silver topaz eyes, I had no clue. He was a vault, one I couldn't crack. But even if I did, would I want what I found?

"Kane," Whitney said, gentle.

His chest heaved and he rolled his shoulders as if it took every ounce of power he had not to hunt me down. But he didn't need that power anymore. Not with her at his side.

His arms dropped and my heart shattered.

Jamming the vehicle in reverse, I punched it out of there and didn't look back.

Chapter Nineteen

I sat in Sierra's old office, behind her desk, side-eyeing that *Ancient Histories* book while I flipped through the list of Coven dues. Who'd paid, who hadn't. It was the definition of dull, but considering the chaos that was my life, dull was good.

The waning sun cut through the window, painting the opposite wall in a mix of coral and honey shades. It was warm, that incense scent still heavy on the air.

After what'd happened at Kane's the day before, I'd barely slept. An un-fun theme of late. When I'd called Isaac and said I hadn't gotten Lucas, he'd just told me we were meeting Zahara the next day, and hung up. I'd been watching every crack and crevice for his shadow since.

My eyes dropped, body slumping forward. Dropping my elbows down, I plunked my head in my hands to hold it up.

The door popped open and Mason sauntered in. "Hey," he said. "How's it going?"

"I've become one with the spreadsheets," I replied.

A small smile tugged his mouth. He tapped the book. "Any luck?"

My mouth thinned. "It's all a bunch of random stories. Encounters with changelings or suspicions of encounters. Stuff about locations frequented. I can't parse anything of use. The thing's a damn riddle."

He picked it up and thumbed through the pages, landing on the one I'd bookmarked with a pink foil gum wrapper. His face twisted. "They die in the light and return?"

Thank sage I wasn't the only one confused.

"I have no clue," I said.

His brow quirked, head canting to the side. "I didn't know it was a journal."

"A *journal?*"

He spun it my way and tapped the dates.

I frowned. "I thought those were just dates of entry."

"I don't think so." He scanned several sections. "The days and months are tracking. It looks more like continuations."

It didn't *read* like continuations. It read more like random observations or musings. My grabby hands reached for it, and he passed it back. How the hells had I missed that? Did it mean anything? I chucked my chin his way. "What about you? How's the research?"

He adjusted the arm of his glasses to sit more level over his ear. "I, um, brought you something."

My spine straightened, muscles aching as I sat taller. "Aren't you just a little gift giver lately."

His mouth tugged to the side. "Thought that might perk you up." Reaching into his pocket, he pulled out a glass vial. "I've tried a few serums now, but nothing's happened. I can't tell if it's me not knowing how to work them, or if they're just . . . not working."

The thing tinked when he placed it on the desk between us. "You don't need to do this, Briar."

But I *did* need to. Because sitting back while Isaac ran his game plan was *not* an option. I wanted to get us all out. Free Ivy. Get my goddamn life back. Wasn't sure what'd be left of it when the dust settled, but that was a later kinda problem.

Isaac couldn't close that deal with Zahara—hand over those vials. I couldn't let him come for Cambria and everyone else I loved.

Grabbing the serum, I waggled it Mason's way. "What's in this one?"

"Illusionist," he said.

Was that something I could use? Something useful? Wraith only knew. My heart thumped like a hummingbird's frenetic little wings. Yeah, testing it *had* been my idea, 'cause ideas were exciting. Full of promise. But reality was different seeing I didn't know what the hells else the mystery liquid before me was full of.

I exhaled an unsteady breath, then glared down at that shiny vial. "You better fix my entire life, you little son of a bitch." Before I could overthink the ten thousand ways this could go straight off the rails, I popped the top, then raised it in cheers. "Bottoms up!"

Setting it to my lips, I counted to three, then angled that bad boy up and chugged it down. A cool tingling coated my tongue and throat as it moved, permeating my mouth. It warmed my chest, and zinged through my arms, then my legs. My face pinched, eyes watering. I doubled over and hacked and gagged while I fought to hold it in, 'cause the stuff tasted like formaldehyde smelled.

Mason strode closer and slow-patted my back.

My fuzzy gaze sought him. "You could've warned me."

He shrugged. "I didn't think it would help." Propping a hip on the desk's corner, he asked, "How do you feel?"

My hand flattened over my stomach as I righted. "Like regret. I feel like regret." I waited while that zinging faded, then faded some more. "Am I supposed to feel . . . different?"

He downturned his mouth in a "*Hells if I know*" expression. "I didn't."

Seeing I wasn't an Illusionist, I had not one damn clue *how to use that*. Still, I drew on my obsidian, searching for something foreign, but nothing showed. I stuck my bottom lip out.

"Could just take time to set in," he said.

But we didn't have time. We needed the right-goddamn-now kinda solutions. My shoulders fell as I stared out the window into the waning day, completely deflated. I'd been counting on those serums to work. Counting on *something* to work. "Yeah," I breathed, "Maybe."

"Hey," he said, gaze narrowing on me. "You okay?"

Dejected, I rose. "Yeah. I'm just . . . exhausted." I needed bed. So much bed. "Think I'm gonna clock out."

He inclined his head. "We'll figure this out, Briar."

My answering smile was tight. "Thanks." Grabbing my purse, I adjusted my jeans and scarlet colored, scoop neck top, then left. My brown leather boots clicked as I wove through the magi wing toward the lobby. Rounding the corner, I nearly ran smack into Joaquin. He stood facing me as if he'd been waiting.

His head drew back as he sniffed the air. "What's wrong with your scent?"

"I showered." I fluffed my hair and offered him an exaggerated wink. "You're welcome."

"You smell like cat piss." He widened his stance. "The hells were you doing, banshee?"

My inner vixen steepled her fingers. "Assessing some magi stuff."

He glowered. "What *kind* of magi stuff?"

I tested the answer and got no push back. "Serums."

"What kind of *serums*?" the Beta said, lip curling as if talking to me was like pulling teeth.

Rude. I rolled my eyes. "I drank a cat-pissy one."

He stared at the roof like he might find some patience up there. "Shadowed fucking moon." He dragged a hand down his face. "*Why* did you drink the cat-pissy serum?"

My brows furrowed, 'cause I thought that answer was pretty obvious. "To see if it'd work."

His sigh was torn from the distant chambers of his torso. "And what is it you expected it to do?"

Face contorting in thought, I replied "I'm, um, not really sure yet."

"Iron fires, take me," he mumbled. "You also get that wolfsbane from here?"

Soooooo, he and Kane had apparently talked. Regardless, answering that one wasn't exactly on the table, which meant I shrugged instead.

His stare narrowed before he clasped his opposite wrist. "Where are you going?"

To wallow in my sorrows? Bathe in my sadness? Spend the night depressed and alone? "My place." I scratched my temple. "Been a long day." So damn long.

I was just about to ask if he wanted to join, but Ezra sauntered around the corner, hair pulled back at the base of his neck. He looked sharp in his black dress shirt and pants, overlaid by the RC standard issue lab coat. His attention roved the lobby like he looked for someone. When it landed on Joaquin, those eyes lit up.

Well, la, dee, dah. I pitched my voice low and turned to the Beta. "And here I thought you came for me."

That hazel stare met mine. "Something like that."

"Hey," Ezra said, sealing in.

The Beta gave a tight, nervous-as-shit nod.

My gaze narrowed on our newcomer. "I take it this means you totally got the job."

His grinned. "I *totally* got the job."

My answering smile was broad when I gestured around us. "I didn't know you worked here."

"So glad you read his résumé," Joaquin droned.

I batted away his sass.

Ezra inclined his head. "I've been trying to get out. This place pays good but I'm not a fan of the 'we only help the rich' thing. Just not built for it."

Ooh. A man of passion and principle. Wasn't he just checking all my approval boxes. Still, he wasn't wrong. It was pretty damn awful.

The Beta chucked his chin Ezra's way. "You finished?"

Stripping his lab coat off, he said, "Yep. I'm all yours."

Red crept up Joaquin's neck, staining his cheeks.

"So," I rubbed my palms together, "what are you kids up to?"

Joaquin cleared his throat and found me. "I'm taking him by the shop again. Let him get acquainted with the equipment."

Only way he'd do that was by using it. "Someone getting a tattoo?"

Ezra opened his mouth to reply but the Beta beat him to it. "We've got a volunteer."

I lifted a shoulder. "Better than snatching people off the street, I suppose."

Ezra smirked. "Would be a quick way to get our names out there, though."

Joaquin shook his head. "Shadowed moon, don't encourage her."

"Ignore him, Ezra. I *love* being encouraged." I nudged the Beta with my elbow and waggled my brows his way.

He pivoted and aimed for the door. Ezra and I followed behind. My lips pursed when a thought hit me. If the Beta hadn't known him before, then he couldn't be Pack. Not Northern, anyway.

"Hey," I said, side-eyeing Ezra as we crossed outside, "can I ask you something rude?"

Joaquin groaned in that "wraith take me" kinda way.

Ezra's brow quirked, curious. "Sure."

I flicked my hair over a shoulder and offered him my demurest smile. "How much does it suck having a piece of shit like Victor for an Alpha?"

***

I spent the night in bed in my pity-party PJs, reading while I ate my feelings. The thick blanket smothering me was warm, the room dark, save my bronze bedside lamp. I'd kept testing my power to see if anything had changed, but nada.

Theo and Naomi were out . . . somewhere. Which was fine, seeing I wasn't exactly the bestest company.

I restarted the book I attempted to read for the twentieth time. A thousand thoughts swirled through my mind. I couldn't concentrate. Kane, and Lucas. Zahara, Bower, Victor his mate and her boy. Ivy, and gutting Isaac.

Eventually, I turned out that light, rolled over and closed my eyes. I tossed and turned a while more, but eventually, the world faded, and sleep took me.

I stood surrounded by blackness. I was nothing and nowhere. But there was something about it that felt . . . familiar. I was alone,

I thought. No, wait. There was someone else. Someone powerful and close. So damn close.

"Bry," a voice said, its low rumble coming from everywhere. All around me.

Warmth rolled in, wrapping me up. I knew that warmth. Knew it better than I knew myself.

"Kane?" *I breathed.*

"I'm here, Bry." *That warmth cinched tighter.* "I'm here."

I spun, looking for him. "Why can't I see you?"

"Because I'm somewhere else."

"If you're somewhere else, then how are you here?" *My brow furrowed.* "What is this?"

He cleared his throat. "It's a dream." *That warmth grazed my temple and down to my jaw.* "You're safe. You'll always be safe with me."

I relaxed into that dream, feeling whole and shielded and all things Kane for the first time since I'd sent him away. I breathed deep, letting my lungs expand. It was just us, alone. Together. I loved his unyielding hold. Being cloaked in that Kane warmth, where the fire between us burned so hot, it left me malleable. Changed the shape of who I was.

"I miss you, Bry," *he said, the words full of agony and gravel.* "So fucking much."

Wraith take me, I missed him too. Missed being loved by him. I tried desperately to say it back but my tongue locked around that truth. Weird.

His pain rolled over me. Through me. Like we were separate but one. It pressed in, all-consuming. "Tell me you still love me." *That warmth brushed my lips.* "Tell me you're still mine." *It tracked lower to my claiming mark.* "Tell me to take you home," *he begged, voice breaking on the words.*

Kane Slade begging? I couldn't understand. It wasn't real. Why weren't we happy here?

My mouth parted but the words froze in my throat. I tried for an answer, but the walls closed in. I exhaled a harsh, frustrated breath. "I can't."

That warmth seemed to ... tense somehow. "Then tell me you're okay."

Iron fires, why was my tongue tied? It was a dream, for sage's sake. Isaac's compulsion shouldn't reach me there. Again, I replied, "I can't."

A rough exhale, less frustration, more anguish. "What's going on, Bry? Shadowed moon, just tell me something. Anything. Please. Fucking hells. Please!"

What was wrong with this stupid dream? Seven Iron Hells, I couldn't find peace, even in sleep. Why did it hurt so goddamn much? My hands plunged into my hair, and I gripped it hard as I shook my head again and again and again. "I can't." *My head whipped around, trying to shake the pain that crushed me.* "I can't. I can't! I ca—"

A knock came at my door. I sucked in a gasp and shot up in bed like a bullet. My bleary gaze snapped to the side, and I blinked hard.

I was still in bed, alone. So damn alone. My heart plummeted and tears seared my vision. I curled in on myself, tucking my knees to my chest to stem the flow.

The dream must've escaped from some deep cavern of my subconscious. Shadow and sage, dream or no, it'd been so real. I could've sworn I was there, that it was *him*. And I wanted it back.

That knock came again.

I flicked on that bedside lamp. "Yeah?"

"Hey," Theo said, slipping into the room. "You were making some weird noises."

Naomi poked her head in next. "You alright?"

I blinked hard to clear my sight. It didn't work. "Just a dream." One I wanted to cling to. I needed out. Needed air. I needed someone to gut Isaac where he stood because I didn't know how much more I could take. Every step forward had felt like progress, but I was still there, exactly where I'd started. And so was everyone else.

My shoulders shook when I heaved a sob so loud, it stole my breath and I grew dizzy.

Theo's eyes flew wide. "Oh, shit."

Nay crossed the room and took a seat on the edge of the bed beside me. She rested her palm in the center of my back, and rubbed in slow, soft circles. "Deep breaths."

I gripped the back of my neck and hung my head between my knees.

"What's going on?" Theo asked, closing in.

I side-eyed him through the scraggly curtain of my hair with an "*Are you shitting me?*" expression.

He shrugged in a "*What the hells else am I supposed to say?*" kinda way.

"I'm worried about you, Briar," Nay said, squeezing my arm.

"Yeah," Theo chimed in, flicking a hand in the general vicinity of my face. "The bags under your eyes have bags and you're losing weight fast. You look like shit."

I frowned.

"Helpful, brother," Nay deadpanned. "Very helpful."

"What?" He dropped down at my other side, mattress bouncing under his weight. "Subtlety ain't her language."

Not wrong, but still . . .

I thunked back down and curled onto my side.

"You look like you need some company," Nay said.

My nod was feeble and sad and as miserable as I felt. She lay beside me and tucked into my back. Theo settled against my front, sandwiching me between them.

It wasn't Kane, but it was Pack. Family. Some of it, anyway. I wanted the rest back. Needed it, because if that boring ache in my chest delved any deeper, I didn't think I'd survive.

Chapter Twenty

A blinding ray of light broke through the windows, stinging my sleep-addled eyes, and I groaned. Raising an arm to shield myself, I blinked hard to clear my sight. That sun was up . . . high. I glanced at my watch.

Three o'clock!

I'd known I was tired, but sweet sage, waking up in the middle of the afternoon was next level.

I sat up, my stomach twisting as an ominous feeling settled in so deep and cold and nestled into my bones. I was set to meet Isaac soon, and that should've been enough to explain it, but for some reason, it just . . . didn't.

That heavy dread pressed in and constricted my lungs, making it hard to breathe. I slid from the bed, dressed, and left my room. The scent of grilled meat hit me, and my starving mouth watered.

"Hey," Theo said from the couch, one leg dangling over the back while he scarfed down a burger. "I made more, if you want."

Nodding, I grabbed one from the plate, then moved on autopilot as I stuffed my feet in my shoes.

"Where's Naomi?" I asked.

"Don't know." He took a bite, a swath of ketchup and barbecue sauce rolling down his chin. "She was gone when I got up."

That ominous feeling pressed tighter.

Wiping his face, he sat up. "What's wrong?"

"I'm heading to meet Isaac," I said, grabbing my keycard and purse from the counter.

"Fuck." He set his burger aside, then stood and aimed my way. "I'm coming."

"No." I shook my head and pressed the call button. "It's for Zahara. He's not about to let you come anyway. Last thing we need is to piss him off more." Besides, if Theo wasn't within range of Isaac's mouth, he couldn't be ordered by him.

He cursed again, hands clenching by his sides like he didn't agree.

"I'll be alright," I said, praying it was true.

Those doors dinged open. I stepped inside. His chest heaved while they sealed as if he felt it too. That unease.

A short while later, I pulled through Mason's gated property and up to his house. I was early, and there was no sign of my stepfather yet.

My gaze flicked to that basement. I worried my lip. Throwing my door open, I darted inside. From the kitchen, Mason's eyes flew wide as I passed.

"Hi!" I said, then threw open the door and thumped down those squeaking metal stairs.

Ivy sat in the back corner, head rocking side-to-side, hypnotic, like a cobra. She scampered closer, gnawing her arm until she broke skin. Worse. She looked so much worse, like the thread tethering her to sanity had frayed to a single strand.

She offered me an incisored smile, those pointy biters coated in pink. "Magi girl," she said, voice hoarse and entirely inhuman.

"Ivy," I said.

Mason padded down behind me, like backup. Backup I appreciated because I suddenly wasn't confident those iron bars were enough.

I cleared my throat. "How are you?"

"Lost."

That definitely tracked.

Her head cocked so sharp, her eyes sat vertical. "You're not like his other toys."

That was a trip, coming from her. I frowned and scuffed my foot over the floor. "Pretty sure I'm exactly the same."

"No." She scuttled closer so fast, she kicked up dust. "They're weak."

Mason frowned with an "*I can hear you*" expression.

I huffed a rough and sardonic laugh. "I wouldn't be here if I was strong, Ivy. I'd have gotten Lucas out. I'd be free. I'd be with Kane."

"Alphas don't fall for prey, magi girl." She sucked her teeth, then darted her tongue out, the movement lizard-like.

I snorted, wholly uncool and one thousand percent bitter. She'd been locked up *way* too long. Didn't know the forest from a tree. I'd literally been preyed on. Caught in Isaac's trap. Madness in-goddamn-deed. I shook my head.

"The others offer the changeling something, but you are an obstacle."

"I'm an obstacle because of Kane."

A feral snarl built in the back of Ivy's throat, and I fought not to flinch before she spat, "They are not predators like you." The crimson in her stare ignited. "You are an obstacle because you are their best chance for ending him."

Their, not *our*. As if she couldn't see a future for herself past those bars.

Mason edged forward. "She's right, Briar." He lifted a shoulder. "You don't quit, ever. Especially on the things you love."

Reaching back, I gave his hand a squeeze, 'cause disagree or not, I appreciated the support. Appreciated him. Swallowing hard, I squared my shoulders to Ivy, because if I was short on anything, it was time. "Is there something different about changelings?"

"You must ask my Lady."

"Your Lady?" My expression twisted. "You mean Cassandra?"

Her head dipped low, then lifted high. Dip. Lift. Dip. Lift. "Yesssssss."

My gut hardened. Asking Cassandra meant fielding questions. Questions I unequivocally couldn't answer, and not just for Isaac. "Even if I could I tell her the truth, she'd come for my brother, Ivy."

She scratched her leg, gouging her skin. "It is possible."

"And she'd hate me." Hate me for hiding that truth when I knew her own. Knew what she'd been through in losing her father. Knew about Ivy, knew Cassandra and I were friends and still held back. Guilt stung my heart.

She scooped a clump of dirt up, then twisted her hand. It slipped through her fingers and hit the concrete floor. "It is possible." The crunch of tires sounded as they closed in on the house. Her glare snapped that way before she shrieked.

The sound was so loud and cutting, my palms shot to my ears, and I doubled over.

"My walls close in. They take me from the night. It will happen soon."

Sweet sage. "Is there anything I can do? Anything I can bring you to help?"

"Yes," she hissed before she angled forward and bared her wicked incisors in a summoner's smile. "A swift death."

***

Isaac and I trudged down that path to those same creepy coordinates. Well, the Mason-faced Isaac, anyway. My arms strained against the weight of the two large boxes I carried, both filled to the brim with serums. They tinked and clanked as I trudged up the hilly path toward that illicit Ithican border crossing, trying to keep my feet.

The sun fell on the horizon, still hot on my skin. Sweat slicked my spine and trickled down, down, down. The warm breeze cut through the farm field before blowing my hair across my face. It caught in my mouth, and I spat it out again and again.

My phone buzzed with a call. Repositioning my load, I pulled it out, heart stuttering its beat at the sight of the name there. Kane. My bizarre dream from the night before flashed across my mind.

It rang again. But there was no chance I could answer . . . not with Isaac so close. Chest constricting, I tucked it away.

"You can't just hand these to her, Isaac," I barked, trying to make him see reason. He was a selfish creature. Maybe he'd understand selfish means. "Iron fires, your weaponizing her against yourself. What're you gonna do when you realize you *handed her all the power*?"

He tsked. "Did you forget, Briar?" He eyed me over his shoulder. "I *always* have a plan."

I arched a lone brow. "What the hells does that mean?"

He flicked a wrist in a *"you'll see"* kinda way.

Wraith take me.

"You've been a bad girl, Briar," he said, maneuvering around a rock. "Much worse than I knew."

I swallowed hard, then waited for him to elaborate, but no explanation came. And somehow, his silence was worse than any threat. That ominous pit from earlier returned, because with the way he'd said it . . . it set my teeth on edge.

We crested that hill and froze.

Zahara stood there, hands delicately linked before her. Her black pantsuit a stark contrast to that gray, pixie wig hair. Six men surrounded her, faces covered in balaclavas, their guns drawn and aimed our way. She smiled.

Wonderful. My stare tracked to Isaac when I gritted out, "Got a plan for this, asshole?"

"Briar, Mason," Zahara greeted, like we didn't have *iron weapons pointed at our heads*. "I'm so glad you could make it."

To a scheduled meeting? Sure.

Her attention lit on the boxes I held, and she smiled, arms spreading wide. "Are these my serums?"

Mason-Isaac inclined his head. "They are."

One of the gun-toters advanced, voice a thick baritone when he jabbed him with the end of his gun. "Move!"

My stepfather flinched, eyes wide when he stepped aside, clearing a path.

Baritone guy glared at me, his two-toned yellow-brown eyes hard when he looped his weapon over his chest and took those boxes from me. Pivoting, he marched away, gait even. Almost militant. He set them down before her, and she crouched, popping them wide.

Row upon row of vials sat there, glistening in the evening sunlight. Her gaze narrowed, eyes tracking between the supplies.

The rustle of the grass was loud as the breeze kicked up.

Mason-Isaac pointed. "The blue are magi, and the red, shadow walker."

She straightened, head snapping up. "Where are the wolf serums?"

He linked his hands before him. "They're next on my list."

Inhaling good and slow, she rose and dusted herself off. "They're not ready?"

"No. But I've acquired what I need, the serum is just setting now."

Acquired what he needed?

Zahara's expression darkened like he was the first name on her kill list. "You tricked me," she said through her perfectly lined teeth as her men closed in around us.

My body locked up. Shittiest of shits!

He shook his head. "No." His stare slid across her goons. "I've given you the product."

"But not *all* of it."

"You'll get the rest," he stammered. "It'll be done tonight."

She adjusted the lapel of her suit coat, then gestured to the boxes and instructed her men, "Take them."

Brows dipping low, I frowned.

Clearing his throat, Mason-faced Isaac nudged the glasses up his nose and took a half-step back. "I should inform you, the serums have a limit."

Her hand twitched like she was ready to slap him before she dragged it down her face. "What kind of limit?"

"In most cases, they began working immediately with the effects wearing off after several hours."

"Wearing *off*?" Her nostrils flared wide. "Your message indicated your tests were successful."

"And they were. You get the desired results. Magi and shadow walker powers."

"For a limited time."

"For now," he agreed. "I'm seeking a more permanent mixture, but until our relationship is cemented, I felt it . . . prudent to ensure my expertise was required going forward."

Oh, snap! I hated Isaac with the fiery passion of a thousand suns, but at least he'd had that much sense. It wasn't optimal, but it was something.

He smiled. "I had hoped this to be a long-term, mutually beneficial relationship."

"Mutually beneficial?" she snarled.

My lungs seized at the sheer, triumphant smile in Mason-Isaac's eyes, 'cause he was finally about to open that door. "There are some—"

She raised a hand, silencing him. "We'll discuss what you need the second I get the rest of what's mine." Her glare speared mine like I was part of the problem.

The scowl I offered was deep. "Don't look at me. I never wanted this deal in the first place."

Tipping her head, she stepped back. "You *will* call me the instant the rest is ready."

"I will." He tugged the collar of his shirt. "Is it necessary any longer for Briar to attend in the future? Or can her time be better suited elsewhere?"

I froze, body turning to ice.

"She's served her purpose. I have no use for her anymore," Zahara said, voice lowering to a menacing threat. "And, Mason—don't fuck with me next time." With that, she and her henchmen turned and left.

Isaac swallowed hard. He waited until they slipped between trees on their side, vanishing from sight, then made to leave. I fell in behind him, the thrash of my pulse and crunch of my feet the only sounds as I moved.

When we crested the path by the car, I stopped dead.

Amber stood there, hip leaned against a red sedan while she checked her nails. Those eyes lifted to mine, and the saccharine smile she offered was the definition of dark.

Isaac strode to her side. "Amber's informed me your scent has faded."

My spine locked up, chest seizing around my lungs. The hairs on the back of my neck stood so straight it hurt. *That fucking bitch!*

She pulled out a blood-filled syringe, putting it on perfect display as she handed it to him.

He raised it high and toddled it side to side. "Be still until I'm done here, Briar."

My shoulders rose and fell in violent pants and my arms collapsed to my sides like an anvil dragged them down. Tugging the sleeve of his shirt, he advanced one step. Two. Three. He stopped less than a foot away, then drew back his arm. Swinging forward, his palm collided with the side of my face in a painfully loud slap.

I wavered, cheek stinging.

His nostrils flared and he shook out his shoulders like he calmed himself. "I can't help but wonder, stepdaughter, what other secrets are you keeping?"

It wasn't a directive, but it was entirely too damn close. Sweat slicked my palms, and my gaze darted to my car. If I could just get to it—

"I have one final job for you."

Final job? My heart stopped, blood running cold.

Amber's head snapped his way. Not for me. But it was clear reality'd finally struck at the idea of losing my Alpha. "Isaac—"

"Silence," he ordered her.

She tensed, then clutched her throat.

My voice quavered, words barely above a whisper. "What fucking job?"

"To die, of course." His lip angled up at the corner and he angled closer. "Your world is about to implode."

Iron fucking fires. My breaths exploded from me, chest heaving.

"Kane will need you tonight, and you'll be there, just not for him. He'll never touch you again."

No! His touch was all I had, no matter how ragey or fleeting it was. The order set in, cinching around mind and binding across my soul.

He crossed his arms over his chest, surveying me from his imaginary throne. "When the Conclave comes tonight, when they ask you about the body, you're not going to answer their questions."

The body? That iron dread moved in, because not answering the Conclave was tantamount to—

"After I'm done, I anticipate they'll handle you themselves." He lifted that needle, then set its tip to my arm and depressed the plunger.

Heat spread through my body. Mason's blood. Mason's scent. *No.*

A tear slithered down my cheek.

"I'm done with threats, Briar. It's time for action." He softly stroked a hand over my hair. "You have no idea what you've unleashed." His fingers latched on, and he snapped my head back. "But you're about to find out."

Chapter Twenty-One

My car was hot. Too hot. Not the temperature, but I burned alive because I couldn't get Isaac's words outta my head. I needed to do something . . . find a way to stop whatever was coming, because wraith take me, I couldn't let Kane die. I *couldn't*!

My phone rang through the Bluetooth system. The Beta's name appeared.

A knot torqued in my chest, a spiral of fear twisting my stomach, and making me nauseous. I answered.

"Joaquin?"

"Hey, banshee," he said, but the words were off. Broken. As if he had trouble speaking them.

Dread, all-consuming moved in. "What's wrong?"

"There's been another murder. I need you to meet me at No Man's Land."

My tremors were so intense, my hair shook in the periphery of my vision. "Is Lisa—"

"She's alright." He cleared his throat. "I sent her off."

Fear locked around my throat as I hyperventilated, voice hoarse when I uttered, "Who is it, Joaquin?"

"Just meet me—"

I crushed the wheel in my grasp while the world narrowed to a singular focus. "WHO IS IT?"

His silence stretched to eternity. It was empty and hollow and an agony only matched by the name he spoke as he said, "It's Naomi."

My heart stopped, my sight tunneled. The world faded out, then in. Jerking to the side of the road, a violent sobbing cry broke from me.

Joaquin said something but it was drowned out in the sea of my pain. I rocked in the driver's seat, clutching myself like a lifeline. Naomi. Dead. It was all my fault. It was all my goddamn fault. My punishment for the Ithican Embassy. For taking Lucas and not bringing him back. For *everything*.

Oh, sage. My palm clamped over my chest like it could hold back the tidal wave of agony that crested me.

Theo. No, *Theo*. It'd cost us both, but it'd cost him so, so much more.

I needed to get there. Pray the wraith hadn't come. Talk to Naomi. Tell her I loved her and I was so fucking sorry.

The city flew by as I whipped back onto the road. One building blended into the next while the broken white lines ticked by. My attention flicked from one to another, something to focus on until I drew up to the tavern.

The night was dark, swallowing the light that escaped from inside. The place was empty. Chairs knocked over, spilled or unfinished drinks on the tables like the place had been abandoned in a hurry.

A soft mist dusted my windshield, the thick scent of ether clouding the air.

Joaquin was there, several members of the Pack hovering nearby, faces gaunt, stares distant. Forlorn. I climbed from the vehicle, hands shaking while I held the door for support. Eyes flashed. Heads tipped back, and nostrils flared, scenting me. Scenting Mason. Joaquin's brow furrowed. He cursed.

My throat grew thick, and my knees weak when a shame I hadn't earned seared my skin. My pulse thrashed in my ears. I stayed where I was.

The Beta's jaw worked. He took a rigid step, then closed the distance between us. My gaze was narrowed in a wince when he took my elbow, flanking tight to my side as I stagger-stepped my way to Naomi—at least, what was left of her.

Her mangled, ghostly pale body hung from the dumpster. Discarded. As if she were nothing. Her leg was gone, precision cut like everything else. Her once sable eyes were dull. Vacant and void. No blood soaked the ground, telling me she'd been killed somewhere else, dead, and dealt with before she'd been dumped—thrown out like trash.

A sob burst from my chest as I looked away and swiped the tears that blurred my vision. "Does Theo know?"

"Kane's with him now."

Kane.

A sharp prick stung my body and I winced. It spread like wildfire, burning my veins as it moved. My teeth clenched, and I sucked in short, shallow breaths before I doubled over.

"Hey." The Beta's grip flexed against me. "You alright?"

The weight of his touch was too much. I flinched and twisted away. Sweat slicked my forehead, temples, the skin above my lip. I crushed my eyes closed and forced myself to breathe. In. Out. In. Out. Several seconds passed before that pain ebbed, several more again before it subsided altogether. I reopened my eyes and blinked hard.

He peered at me from the corner of his gaze. "What was that?"

My foot bounced and I shook my head. "I don't know." And the riot of agonizing emotions coursing through me meant I wasn't about to parse it out. Rubbing the backs of my arms, I righted. "We should get her outta there."

Joaquin nodded. Moving off, he gathered her pieces, cradling what he could to his chest before he settled her onto the ground. When he stepped back, his breathing hitched.

I reached for his hand, wrapped mine over it, and squeezed.

That ether grew thick. Cloying. It coated my tongue and seared my senses.

His Adam's apple dipped. He stared straight ahead as a ragged, choked sound escaped him.

My heart slammed to a halt when realization struck. "Autumn!" Naomi's lover. Her mate. The claiming mark. They were tethered just like Kane and me—

He shook his head.

My head fell. I needed to talk to Naomi. Sage, I needed it like air. My hand trembled so hard, it took three tries before I could grip my obsidian. Drawing on it, I let my eyes go unfocused. I hesitated, inhaled long and slow, and sought her aura. It was there. Faint particles like dust, drifting loose on the wind.

I hovered over those sunset markers, waiting. Grazing by, those images began flashing. Isaac and Amber, scents followed by a cascade of Naomi's emotions.

"*Naomi. Are you there?*" I said my mind, 'cause it'd worked for Frances.

"*I love you, Briar,*" *she said, the words rushed.* "*You and Theo and Kane. I wanna say more. Say everything, but we don't have time. Isaac got what he needed.*"

Her wolfy genetic makeup. Yeah, he had.

"*You need to go,*" *she said.*

"*What?*" That ether was so heavy, it stung my eyes. "*Go where, Nay?*"

"*Just leave!*" *she cried, voice breaking as it faded.* "*Just … fucking—*" *She cut out.*

The air snapped when the ephemeral wraith descended.

My heart stopped, reaching out like I could grab those translucent wings. Stop it. "No!" I cried. "Don't take her. Please, don't fucking take her!"

The night fell still. Naomi's aura vanished.

I dropped to my knees and collapsed forward onto my palms, hyperventilating wild and frenetic. "She's gone." I slammed a fist down. "She's gone. *She's fucking gone!*" The scream that broke from me tore from the recessed chambers of my soul. It clawed at my throat until it strangled and faded. I tell her I love her. Would never get to again. I screamed again.

Joaquin's heavy hand found my shoulder.

Naomi and Autumn, both dead. All for Isaac's revenge, because that's exactly what it was. Payback for my disobedience. I raked my hands up my face and into my hair, pulling so hard it stung my scalp.

"We've gotta get this guy, banshee."

A shuddering exhale left me.

The low rumble of a heavy exhaust brought my head up as a vehicle drew closer and closer. The truck closed in, silhouetted by the streetlights. A broad, shadowed form occupied the driver's seat, silvered stare flashing in the dim. He slowed while he veered into the lot, then stopped.

My stomach torqued when Theo exploded out of the passenger seat and stumbled our way. His red-rimmed gaze slid over his sister before he fell to his knees beside me and roared. The sound was soul-rending, and it ravaged the barely-there pieces of my heart.

Kane climbed out next, movements slow and stiff. He scented the air. That stare snapped to me. And with that one action, any questions he might've had, any suspicions about me and my red-flag behavior, were gone. I couldn't breathe. *I couldn't fucking breathe!*

He set his hip against his hood as if he needed the support. Those silver topaz eyes were hard as granite, the creases that lined their corners deep. He crossed his arms over his chest like he held himself together.

My hand twitched, itching to reach for him. I wanted to say something, anything to make it better. To wrap myself around him and take some of that burden instead of sitting there like the cold, callous husk he thought me to be. Problem was, I *was* that burden.

Whitney drifted out of the truck next. There to comfort Kane. And as much as it hurt that it wasn't me, I was glad he wasn't alone.

The Beta stepped away.

I turned to Theo and held my breath, praying to sage he didn't hate me for bringing this on him, that I hadn't lost him too. There was so much I wanted to say, but the only thing that came out was a muted, muffled, "I'm sorry."

His pieces were broken. Warped. Scattered. He was lost in his agony. His shoulders heaved with his breaths, and he was silent so long, my heart tremored. There was a question in those eyes.

Time slowed. Shadow and sage. My pulse thrashed so hard, a tight band formed around my chest and my ribs hurt. I just shook my head and repeated, "I'm sorry."

The gentle murmur of Whitney's voice carried as she spoke to Kane. What she said, I had no clue. Not that I listened, I wanted him to have someone, but listening to another woman care for my Alpha, the man who held the pieces of my soul . . . it was too much.

Theo crawled closer. I fell deathly still. He was cut deep—a wounded predator. Beyond dangerous. And I was the reason for that wound.

He slumped to the side, his shoulder thumping into mine. My spine locked. He gave me his weight as if he expected I could hold it—as if I was strong enough. But I was weak in every way that mattered.

I rocked toward him, and I slipped an arm around his shoulders, holding tight. The last thing I wanted was to hurt him more, but he was my friend. My chosen family. He deserved to know. I threw a cocoon around our conversation. "Isaac did this because of me."

The laugh that ripped from his throat was as dismal as him. "No." His head lifted, those sable eyes—the match of his sisters'—swollen and bloodshot when they found mine. His lips drew back from his canines when he snarled, "Isaac did this because of who *he* is."

Heavy footsteps pounded against the ground when someone stalked closer. Fast. My head swiveled to the side as Kane advanced our way, attention voltaic when it landed on me.

Whitney glided in, stopping just behind him. She stared at me. *Watched* me.

My tongue locked down, stomach clenching as I turned back to Theo, words rushed when I told him, "Isaac's ordered me not to answer the Conclave's questions."

His stare snapped my way, flying wide. "Shit!"

Kane edged closer. "The fuck is going on?" I couldn't gauge if it was a pissed off question or an accusation.

Joaquin's attention fixed on me and Theo, brows furrowed into crevices.

"She didn't die for nothing, Briar." Theo jerked me into a hug. "I won't let her die for nothing."

"We don't stop," I told him. Even until my dying breath, I wouldn't stop.

"Release the conversation," Kane snarled.

"We don't stop, Briar," Theo repeated, his hold crushing me, making it impossible to breathe. He shook his head, teeth clenched so tight, they ground like stone. "We never fucking stop."

My Alpha moved in beside me, eyes a silver writhing fire. His chest pistoned with the force of his breaths. "RELEASE THE FUCKING CONVERSATION!"

I swallowed hard. It wasn't a command, but his power rolled off him, dusting my flesh, so doubtless, one was on its way. "We don't fucking stop," I promised Theo, then dropped that shield.

Kane's gaze landed on me, tracked to his cousin, then back. He loomed there, the weight of his stare a demand. Frustration ridged his forehead and corded the thick lines of his neck. He flexed his square-knuckled fists at his sides. "What the shadowed moon was that?"

My focus fixed on a tree in the distance.

Rolling his shoulders, he tugged the legs of his pants and took a knee beside me. "Look at me."

The tremble of my body was violent when my eyes met his—steel on water.

He braced a hand against the asphalt before him. "What was that, Briar?"

I bit the inside of my cheek holding back the pain until it bled. Wraith help me, because no one else would. "Nothing."

Joaquin's expression torqued into a "*What the Iron fucking Hells, banshee?*" expression.

Kane's stare flashed, brows drawing in, his suspicion so thick on the air, it was palpable. Not suspicion of the lie, he'd already scented that, but suspicion of *me*. I knew because I could . . .

feel it. It touched me, pushed, shoved. He canted forward until his heat brushed my flesh. He pitched his voice low, and even with the supernatural hearing around us, it was only for my ears when he rumbled, "Liar."

I held my breath and dug my fingers into the ground.

Whitney twisted the fabric of her airy dress shirt tight around her hand, gaze softening when it fell on Theo.

A low huff rent from the recesses of Kane's chest. "Something ain't fucking right here."

I gripped that ground harder.

Another sob tore from Theo when he angled forward, slid his arms under his sister's stiff body, and scooped her up, cradling her to his chest as he rose. "I wanna get her outta here, Kane. Find Autumn."

The crease at the corner of Kane's eyes cleaved me in two. His focus stayed locked on me for two agonizingly long heartbeats. Three. Four. He turned away. He exhaled a broken sound and rose to his full height. And there was something in that sound—a finality that broke me. "Yeah." He found his Beta. "Stay with—" He cleared his throat, then cleared it again. "Come find me when this is done."

Joaquin nodded.

Kane hesitated several agonizing moments, then stalked away, Whitney flitting behind him before she vanished into his passenger seat. Theo maneuvered himself into the bed of the truck with Naomi. Kane squeezed his cousin's shoulder before heading for the driver's side. The truck dipped under his weight, then rumbled when he turned it over. Putting it into gear, he drove away and didn't look back.

The crack of my heart was so violent, I was surprised the world didn't hear it.

Joaquin's hand appeared in my periphery when he extended it my way. I took it, thankful for that help as he drew me to my feet, because I needed the support.

But that grim grip on my spine didn't loosen because Isaac'd mentioned the Conclave. Why mention them if he didn't want them there? Plan for it. I'd missed something. I scanned inside the vine covered tavern, the cars, the lot, the Spanish moss covered trees.

The Beta squared himself to me. "I don't know what the fuck's been going on, but you *need* to start talking!"

My head snapped back.

"We gave you time. Wanted to make sure we were right, but this has gone too far now."

We?

That Spanish moss swayed just steps away. Beyond it, something moved deep inside the tree line. My eyes narrowed, trying to see through the dim. I sidestepped the Beta and strode closer.

"What the shit, banshee?"

I kept going until I broke into the woods and took one step. Two. Three. I jolted to a stop. A strangled sound burst from my lips.

Joaquin stormed up behind me looking ready to do murdering until he followed my line of sight. His hand locked around his hair. "Shadowed moon."

Bodies. So many bodies piled over the deadfall. Their mouths were slack, dresses and hair drifting in the breeze.

Humans. *Isaac's* tester humans. Zahara had said they were his to deal with. And he had.

Lifeless eyes stared at me, fixed and milky. Judging. Bile chased up my throat. I pitched to the side and vomited.

The Conclave would come. Sweat slicked my spine. They'd want answers—answers I couldn't give. Oblivion had come knocking, and I was about to answer.

Chapter Twenty-Two

I sat on the hood of Joaquin's G-Class while the weres organized the bodies.

There were ten in total. Unsurprisingly drenched in wolfsbane. Nothing was missing. Simply killed for the sake of killing. For the sake of Isaac's plans.

It hadn't taken long for the Conclave to show. One by one, they drew up, moving slow as they took in the carnage. Alistair was ashen, hovering near Victor and Amber who lingered several feet away. Danika stood deathly-still at the periphery, her crimson eyes a fire readying to ignite. Her restrained violence tinged the air with a sharp tang. It coated my tongue and set my teeth on edge.

Mason was the last to arrive. He climbed from his car, and I pushed my sight to sharpen it. No, not Mason. The infinitesimal smirk that tugged the corner of those lips was entirely too aware for Mason. My gaze dropped to his right hand. To that scar.

Isaac.

His expression fell, that practiced façade sliding into place as he closed in. His words were so thick with bullshit, it was a wonder they slipped from his tongue when he uttered, "Who could do this?"

Cassandra glided to my side with that eerie, balletic grace. "This is bad, Briar Stone."

"Yes," I murmured. Bad didn't begin to describe it. I settled my hand over hers, the contrast between my warmth and her cold marked.

Her long, translucent-skinned fingers held tight, like she welcomed the support for several long heartbeats before she released. "Where is Kane Slade?"

Joaquin shifted beside me. "On his way back."

Mason-Isaac adjusted his lapels and cocked his head. "What do you mean, *back*?"

My hand twitched to punch him right in his exposed throat.

"He took his cousin's body away," the Northern Beta offered. Not an excuse. An explanation. A difference with a distinction.

"But he left," Mason-Isaac accused.

Son of a bitch! "It was his *cousin*," I snapped, but the groundwork he laid took hold as Danika's ever-darkening attention volleyed between us.

The uptick of Isaac's lip was almost imperceptible when he gestured toward the massacre. Almost. "And he missed *this*?"

A shot fired. One aimed straight at Kane's competency. One Joaquin wasn't about to abide when he squared himself to Isaac. "They're soaked in wolfsbane."

My stepfather dropped his gaze.

"Whoever this is, they're taunting us," Alistair said, voice level.

Isaac pushed Mason's glasses up his nose. "He's sending a message."

"Yes." Danika's rage creased her crimson glare as it tracked the carnage. "This is personal."

Victor nodded. "He means to incite."

I straightened, heart fluttering when an idea hit. "We should call Bower," I said, 'cause Isaac might've ordered me not share with the Conclave, but he hadn't said I couldn't talk at all.

"You mean to start a war?" Danika snarled.

My head cut to the side. "I mean to prevent one." My gaze flicked to the bodies, then away. "Loop him in now, it looks honest. Wait too long and it looks like a cover-up. Then we're right back where we started with Ithica."

Isaac glared at me over the rim of Mason's glasses.

"If we do, they're going to have questions," Alistair said, rubbing his palms over the legs of his pants. "I'd suggest we collect as many answers as we can first. Have you read any of them yet, Briar?"

I shook my head. My stomach tensed, trying to brace against what came next. But no amount of bracing would ever be enough. "And I won't."

Joaquin went rigid.

Danika's nostrils flared, head angled down. "You refuse to read for us?"

"She is not our slave, Danika Trevino," Cassandra cut in.

Isaac folded his Mason-shaped arms over his chest. "I know you're scared, Briar, but this is important."

Oh, fuck him and fuck his games! It wasn't like I could answer anything they asked anyway. He'd need *his* voice to compel me to read them, and there was no chance in the Seven Iron Hells of that.

My eyes locked with his, hard and unyielding. "I said no."

The Beta's stare tracked between us then went unfocused as he took a step closer.

Eyes flashed around the lot, and I fought to keep myself rooted, because running from predators was a good way to end up the permanent kind of dead.

Amber's nostrils flared, spine straightening with a righteous indignation that wasn't hers to claim. "She's sabotaging the investigation!"

"That is a dangerous accusation," Cassandra said, the softening of her delicate lilt somehow all the more terrifying. The hairs on the back of my neck stood on end.

Victor flicked the brim of his fedora up and found me.

Sage, I needed him to do something. Anything! But he wouldn't . . . not unless he had something to gain. I inhaled good and slow, 'cause it was worth a shot. "*I know about your mate*," I mouthed. "*I can help you.*" And I could. Isaac was in the dark about Victor's situation. We could get her and the boy out. Take them north to Kane. My Alpha wouldn't turn her or the child away, even if he had not one damn clue why they were there.

Victor turned to stone. And there was something in those eyes. Something that looked a lot like . . . regret. He shook his head, the panic in his face clear. "*No one can help me.*"

Wraith take me.

The snare Isaac'd looped around my neck drew taut, choking me. My stepfather always had a purpose. A plan. That deal with Zahara was secured. He didn't need me anymore. He'd draw the preternatural attention my way to make it easier to destroy me. Make me look guilty. Complicit. Keep his hands clean while he watched me die.

A searing pain, the same as before, blazed through me, and I cried out. *Iron fires, not again!* I crumpled to the gravel as it cut through my nerves like razor blades. There was a crunch of approaching feet. Bodies loomed in the periphery of my vision.

Voices. They spoke. Angry.

Joaquin hovered over me, face filling my sight. "Talk to me, banshee" he said, but his voice was distant. Muffled. Lost in the pain.

My head lolled back and forth. I opened my mouth to speak, but another burst of torment struck and I loosed a blood curdling scream that ripped from the recesses of my chest. Even to my own ears, the sound wasn't right. Inhuman. I curled in on myself. Sweat streaked my forehead and rolled down my temples.

"Hot." I tore at the collar of my shirt. "Too hot."

Cassandra drifted closer, her dress billowing around her like falling petals as she took a knee beside Isaac. Her crimson eyes sought mine before she laid a cold, delicate palm against my forehead. "Your flesh is fire, Briar Stone."

My breaths spewed from me in frantic bursts. I nodded. Her icy touch felt good. Soothing. It pushed the flames back until I could find air, then pushed them back further. That pain retreated, then retreated more and more and more until it subsided altogether.

Sweet sage, that'd been so, so much worse. I rubbed the backs of my arms. What the Seven Iron Hells was wrong with me?

Joaquin leaned back, but barely. His forearms flexed, the sinewed fibers flicking like guitar strings.

Danika barked a derisive laugh. "Just another distraction." The shake of her head was violent when she sliced a hand through the air. "Two sisters I've lost to this city's madness." Her gaze landed on Cassandra. "To its incompetence. I'm done playing these games."

Cassandra bared her teeth.

Amber gave a tight nod. "If I didn't know better, I'd say Briar's protecting someone."

"Please, everyone." Mason-Isaac stepped forward, hands raised in placation. "Let me try speaking with her. See if I can bring her to reason."

Bring me to reason? As if everything that happened wasn't his *entire fault*!

Victor's head bowed. He took a step back.

Leaning close, Isaac used his own voice when he whispered so low in my ear, I scarce heard it. "Shield the conversation to just you and I."

Joaquin's stare narrowed on the Mason-faced Isaac before it tracked to me.

I gripped my ring, cutting us off from the others, then hissed. "What?"

He cupped my cheek, gentle like he gave a shit. That touch was acid on my skin. "You've outlived your usefulness. I'm done with you now, Briar." He leaned closer until his mouth was a breath from my own. "Time for you to die."

My heart slammed to a stop, world tilting on its axis. I opened my mouth to speak. Beg. Something. *Anything*.

"You will find a way to end yourself now." He drew back and the smile he offered was sheer malevolence.

My stomach dropped when the order pressed in, sealing around my consciousness. Bile kissed the back of my throat, burning, burning, burning. A choked sound tore from me. I released my ring and rose.

No! Stop! I silently screamed at my traitorously compliant body. Shadow and sage! *No!*

Kane! He didn't deserve to die. *He didn't deserve this!*

My gaze darted around like a solution would reveal itself, but it wouldn't. Couldn't. The compulsion was too strong. Tears pricked the backs of my eyes, stinging like needles.

Joaquin edged to my side. "You alright?"

"No," I breathed.

If I was gonna die, I needed it to cost Isaac. Needed it to draw attention. To raise questions. Needed it to be something that didn't make sense. At least, something that didn't make sense to those who mattered. Kane and I would be gone, but maybe Joaquin and Cassandra could figure it out. Stop him.

Kane. Iron Hells. This couldn't be it. Couldn't be our end!

I peered around, gaze landing on my solution. Victor. If he wasn't there to help, then he was only in the way. My end would be ugly and painful, but it'd likely mean Victor's death, and while his death would also mean his mate's, he'd made his choice. And I was willing to accept the boring guilt of that responsibility if it meant one more weapon out of Isaac's hands.

Taking a shallow, shuddering breath, I closed in. My body was tense, muscles so taut they tugged painfully on the bones. His stare met mine. I angled my head, pulse thrashing like the cornered animal I was when I glared at him through my brows. I kept advancing until I stopped all but a few feet back. I didn't look away.

His eyes flashed, ringed in a lethal mix of cunning, fury and violence. "What the fuck are you doing?"

Just enough time to skirt one more line. "What I have to."

"The hells, banshee?" Joaquin said, voice thick with strain.

Victor stormed closer, chest heaving when he exhaled like a bull through his flared nose. His chest slammed into mine and rocked me back. "Look away!"

My stare held.

"Briar Stone," Cassandra cautioned.

"Briar," Mason-Isaac called, seeing my game. "Stop!"

Fuck. That! I'd rip Victor and his entire Pack from my stepfather's hands. One less weapon. "Make me!" *Use your voice, Isaac. Use it!*

"LOOK THE FUCK AWAY!" Victor roared.

"Shadowed fucking moon, *stop*!" Joaquin threw me back.

But still, my stare held while I gave a slow shake of my head. "I can't."

The clack of the train started in the distance, drawing nearer.

My brow rose, and I fought back a bitter laugh. Victor didn't *want* the fight, because he understood, Kane or no, the entire Northern Pack would come for him if he took it. But regardless, his wolf couldn't back down. The level smile I offered was a promise. "You're a coward."

"You stupid bitch!" He exploded forward, hand latching around my throat. It crushed painfully until it cut off my airway. The pressure built through my head and chest. Burning.

Chaos erupted.

Joaquin's fist connected with Victor's face as he dove between us and broke us apart.

Amber's foot slammed into my side, sending me flying. Away from the carnage. She wouldn't kill me, not with Kane at risk, but that didn't mean she wouldn't maim. I crashed against a car hood, buckling the metal. I groaned as I slid to the asphalt, sucking in air when I landed on the jagged ground.

Cassandra hissed as she stepped between us, body torquing before she backhanded Amber. The Southern Beta's head snapped to the side with a force so violent, it would've killed me.

Joaquin's snarl followed by his wave of power cut through the night. Not as consuming as Kane's, but terrifying, nonetheless. His eyes were a riot of fire when he charged for Victor. The two collided with a crack and the Beta caught him across the jaw with an elbow. Victor staggered back and lost his footing. He collapsed onto his back.

Mason-Isaac scurried my way. He crouched, and took my hand, helping me to my feet. Pitching his voice low, he used the anarchy of the fight to hide his words when he seethed, "You just can't help yourself, can you?" He stabbed his arm to the side. "Go stand on the fucking tracks, Briar. Now!"

The train grew louder. Closer. *Closer*. I whimpered and winced when I staggered on unsteady feet. Tears blurred my vision, and I stumbled. I wanted to drop, to stay down, to live for me, for Lucas, for *Kane*. But my body belonged to Isaac as I pushed on. My legs were heavy, arms weak. Sobs broke from my chest as I closed in.

Iron fires take me.

I stepped onto the rails. The train rounded the corner, the deafening noise drowning out the world. My lungs seized as I stared straight ahead. The beam from its headlight blinded me. The blare of the horn blew. The screech of the brakes engaging cut through the world, but it moved too fast. It wasn't enough.

The ground shook. It vibrated through my legs, and torso, up my arms, and head. Stones trembled at my feet. My teeth clenched tight as I braced.

A roar boomed out, overpowering the train. A familiar power rocked the area. One I'd give anything to save.

Kane.

He was there. Close, but still entirely too far.

I couldn't bring myself to look. To see the betrayal that painted his eyes.

"BRY!"

Sparks flew from the train's wheels, their shrieking sliced through my ears. Twenty feet.

My arms fell slack by my sides.

"Briar Stone!" Cassandra shrieked.

Ten feet.

I closed my eyes.

"BRY, NO!"

My chest heaved on its final breath.

The hit was hard. It stole my thoughts and the air from my lungs. Bones cracked before it stole the light from my eyes, and everything went black.

Chapter Twenty-Three

My eyes opened with a snap. I blinked hard trying to orient myself. I was in a bed, warm. Safe. And agonizingly familiar.

How?

The train. I'd been hit. I went rigid as everything rushed back in. The bodies. Kane. Me challenging Victor. Isaac's order. I was supposed to be dead.

I was dead . . . wasn't I?

The pulsing of my heart beat like a drum in my head. Everything hurt. My arms, legs, my side.

I was in Kane's room. *Our* room. Well, not anymore. The agony that took me twisted my soul. I didn't belong there. Wasn't wanted. It was wrong. So, so wrong.

There were voices somewhere nearby. Low. Familiar. Heavy.

I sat up and set my feet to the floor. The world spun and a deep ache lanced through my side. My body hummed, its song rattling through my bones—specifically my ribs. I hissed and slid to the floor, then hissed again.

"*Easy*, Bry. You're still healing," Kane said from a chair by the door. One that blocked the entrance, like he was a guard. Or a shield. He leaned forward, elbows on his knees, that silver topaz gaze bloodshot and red-rimmed, his expression haunted.

Cassandra and Joaquin stood across the room, attention on me. What in the ever-growing sage?

My breaths rasped from my throat. I scampered gingerly to the side until I gave the wall my weight, skin clammy.

Kane rose, chest heaving. His body was rigid, arms taut by his sides when he approached. He dropped down before me, hands crashing against the wall on either side of my body.

Isaac's compulsion had me drawing back.

"Why, Bry?" His voice was broken and guttural when he set his forehead to the wall above me. His body was a cage that engulfed mine, swallowed me whole. "Shadowed moon, *why*?" There was a strain there, like he was being shredded inside. Clawed and ripped and torn to pieces.

No. That didn't make sense. Wasn't possible. His pieces were in another woman's hands. Yeah, he was tethered to me forever, but his heart—

"You don't ever fucking hurt yourself!" A lone tear tracked down his cheek and I followed it with my gaze.

Whitney stepped around that chair and crossed into the bedroom, attention tracking over me. "She's confused."

Kane's head angled to the side. Toward *her*. He gave a sharp nod.

The glare I threw her way was so piercing, it was a wonder it didn't cut. Fire ignited in my veins, searing. Charring. It left the blackened husks of my soul in its wake before it blazed toward my heart.

"You alright, banshee?" the Beta asked.

"I'm breathing," I croaked, then froze, panic setting in. "Where's Lucas?"

"He's downstairs," he answered. "Safe."

My nod was feeble. Safe. He was safe. My gaze tracked around the room and narrowed. "What's going on?"

"Cassandra tackled your ass before the train could," Theo said from the door, shoulder leaned against it, giving the frame his weight.

Tears pricked my eyes when they met the Dowager's.

Kane angled in, so damn close, his heat grazed my flesh. "You're mine, Bry. *Mine*." He shifted and the floor creaked under his weight. "And I come for what's mine."

The words were thick and heavy, which meant they took a second to absorb. To comprehend. I rolled them around my awareness again and again seeking holes, alternate meanings, some other explanation because he was with Whitney, so he couldn't have said what I'd thought.

I come for what's mine. The way he looked at me, it was like he used to. Protective, and fierce, and craving. He'd . . . come for me? No. That couldn't be right. Not after what he'd been put through. What he'd been made to believe. It didn't matter if it wasn't my choice, the result was the same; I'd shattered him.

"None of it made sense, Bry." Those molten eyes slid to my claiming mark. "I know you need help. And I'm right fucking here."

He knew. My arms and head grew light. It worked. *It goddamn worked!*

I come for what's mine.

Like he'd read my thoughts, he gave a single, slow, un-fucking-yielding incline of his head.

"Relief. Hope. Frustration," Whitney cut in. "Uncertainty."

My head whipped her way. If I was his, then why the iron fires was she always there? Around. With him. Lurking. Power of obsidian, he was *mine*. My heart. My soul. My mate.

She took a half-step back. "Jealousy." She blinked hard and shook her head like she tried to clear it. "Sage, so much jealousy."

Kane's stare blazed. Liquid metal and heat. Some of the tension in his shoulders and the sinewed fibers of his arms eased. A low, hungry rumble vibrated from his throat. "She's an Empath, Bry."

"An . . . Empath?" What did that have to do with—

"More confusion," Whitney said.

He shifted, chest a hair's breadth away. "I used my Binding Vow with the Coven's, called Alistair and brought her in."

The Binding Vow! I crushed my eyes closed when a shimmer of something akin to hope fluttered in my chest.

Reopening them, I trailed a finger over my heart tattoo and murmured, "Why?"

"'Cause nothing was fucking right. It wasn't you. I messed up before, and for a minute I thought you'd meant it. That you'd changed your mind, and actually wanted—" He cleared his throat. "That I'd hurt you too goddamn much and you didn't want me. That you wanted Mason instead. But the more I looked, the pieces just didn't fucking fit. I needed to know. Be sure. So, I brought Whitney in to read you. Gauge if your emotions matched. If you meant what you'd said." He shook his head. "Shit's been off since you left. Mason's scent faded, you spoke different, your clothes changed, you got thinner. Nothing tracked."

An Empath. She was an *Empath*! That truth hit hard. Power of obsidian, he'd seen my flares. *All* of them! I wanted to throw my arms around him. Kiss him. Touch him. Thank him. Love him.

"Relief," Whitney added. "Gratitude."

He exhaled a steady breath, like whatever piece of him he'd lost had been found. "I didn't spend four years fighting my way back to lose you all over." His hands curled into fists. "That'll *never* fucking happen." That stare hooded. "You're it for me."

More tears seared the backs of my eyes but refused to fall. Trapped by Isaac's stupid control. Some of the weight crushing me lifted, eased by Kane's shoulders. A whimper tore from my throat and even to my own ears, it was a tattered, broken sound. I wanted to tell him it wasn't just me. To help Theo and Lucas and everyone else, but I'd made it that far. I'd do whatever I needed to figure out the rest.

His mouth hovered over my ear. "I get you can't say it back. I don't know why, but I promise, I'll figure it out." He edged away to better see me. "I was scared tonight, Bry. So goddamn scared."

I nodded. "I know." The desolation in his tone when he'd called to me—tried to stop me—it'd echo in the halls of my mind for eternity.

He bit into his thumb and blood welled to the surface. "Here." He angled it toward me.

I thrashed back. Away. "I can't!" I said, then whimpered when that ache lanced through my side again.

Kane turned to stone, then withdrew. "Shit, Bry."

Pain stung the back of my throat, and I sank in on myself.

Whitney winced. "Guilt."

"No." Kane shook his head. "No fucking guilt. Whatever this is, it isn't your goddamn fault." He thumped his chest with his fist. "*I'm* sorry. I hid shit. I should've said something." The shake of his head was violent. "I tried to help, but I screwed up. This is on me."

My fingers flexed, itching to touch him. To smooth the pain that creased his face. "No, Kane."

"*Yes*. It is. And I'll never hurt you like that again."

My body relaxed, knees dropping to the side. I winced. He reached for me, and I jerked away, then winced again.

He cursed, shoulders falling when he drew back his hand.

"Are you unable to let Kane Slade touch you, Briar Stone?" Cassandra asked.

I met her crimson gaze, and my arms grew heavy.

"Resignation. Sadness," Whitney said.

Kane cursed again, voice flat. Hollow. He cleared his throat. "Why do you carry Mason's scent, Bry?" The question was low and easy. Not an accusation. There was no anger. It was a probe to get answers, figure it out.

I clenched my jaw, struggling to think of a reply. Something to offer, but nothing came. So I pulled on my new favorite words. "I can't say."

He gave a slow incline of his head like he took that in. His voice thickened. "Before you said Mason didn't force you." It wasn't a challenge, more a confirmation.

A truth I could offer. "No, he didn't."

The furrow of his brow was deep while he worked the problem.

My stomach hardened and I bit my lip.

"Frustrated," Whitney cut in.

Kane's palms made a *tsh* as they glided down the wall, stopping beside my shoulders. "Why are you frustrated, Bry?"

Cassandra glided closer. "Because, Kane Slade, we are not asking the right questions."

I wanted to jump to my feet and point a stabby finger her way.

Whitney's nod was vigorous. "Eager."

Smoothing her dress, Cassandra asked, "Did you and Mason have sex, Briar Stone?"

The difference in the question was barely perceptible, but it was there. The sea of agony that'd crested my shore receded a bit. Another truth. A pivotal one. I shook my head. "We didn't."

Kane's brow furrowed deeper.

"Are there other ways to share scent?" Cassandra asked, head canting in that owl-like way.

Theo edged deeper into the room, coming to Whitney's side when he pushed Cassandra harder. "What are you thinking?"

"Can one be *given* a scent?"

The space fell silent.

"Iron fucking Hells." Kane's spine unfurled one segment at a time until it locked straight. The muscles along his neck corded. "Blood."

My emotions must've lit up like a meteor shower because Whitney's head bobbed enthusiastically as she pointed my way. "Bingo!"

Kane's eyes flashed, voltaic and lethal when he roared, "*Fuck!*" His stare locked on mine. "Shadowed moon, Bry. I'm so fucking sorry."

I shuddered, body sagging against the wall. He knew. Thank the wraith and the Seven Iron Hells. He finally *knew*!

My phone rang from nearby, the tone shrill. My head snapped toward it.

Joaquin pulled it from his pocket and held it up, cracked screen facing Kane. "It's Isaac again. He's called non-stop." He tossed it Kane's way. "He's all over her call history since this started."

My voice rose when I asked the Beta, "You checked my phone?"

"I ordered him to," Kane said without a hint of remorse while he scanned the device, jaw working.

My gaze flicked to Theo's. His wide-eyed stare mirrored my own.

Heat burned my chest. Happy. So damn happy. Until that compulsion to answer rolled in. I reached for the device.

Kane pulled it back. "No. Not until we figure out what's up."

"I don't get it," Whitney asked. "He's her stepfather, right? He could just be worried."

The rage that quickened my pulse was a dangerous thing.

Her gaze met mine, brows rising. "Or not."

Cassandra's finger tapped her thigh, rhythmic and mechanical, like a poorly oiled robot. "What is it Isaac wants, Briar Stone?"

There was a flutter in my chest like a fledgling butterfly flopped around. I pressed my lips together, trying with all my might to make myself glow the right emotion.

Whitney squinted. "I don't . . ." She gestured in my general direction. "I don't know what this is."

Gah! I huffed a frustrated breath.

The phone rang again. Kane's head angled his Beta's way. "Isaac."

My gaze lifted to my Alpha's, that compulsion thrumming again as an idea bloomed. One that—if I was lucky—just might save us all. "I *have* to answer that," I blurted. Isaac would give me another order, I had no doubt about that. But Kane was there, knew something wasn't right. And my Alpha wasn't about to let me go again. Not without a fight.

"Bry—"

I softened my voice. "Please, Kane."

A low rumble climbed his throat. I, without touching, plucked the phone from his grasp and rose, slipping from the cocoon of his safety before I scurry-hobbled to the washroom. He followed, nipping tight at my heels. I crossed inside and put my hand up to stop him before he could pass that threshold. Because if my plan was gonna work, that line between us was imperative.

His stare was melted ore, honed on me.

I shook my head, gaze imploring, *Trust me* before I cleared my throat and answered, "Hello."

"Where are you?" Isaac demanded.

I tried to calm the frenetic beat of my heart. "I was taken to Kane's."

"Are you alone?"

Red flag number one.

Kane's head canted.

My attention flicked to that threshold. "Yeah. I'm alone in a different room."

"Good. Now shield the conversation," Isaac demanded.

Red flag number two.

My Alpha's lip drew up, baring a canine.

The order sank in, and I smiled, 'cause I'd finally gotten good at Isaac's game, and he'd finally slipped. Shield the conversation, yes. But shield it from who? He was always specific on who to include, but my misdirection worked, and his overconfidence won out, because his wording was loose. Maneuverable. It left a clear work around. Specific, yet not nearly specific enough.

So sloppy, Isaac.

The vise that'd been clamped over my lungs loosened and I took my first deep breath in ages. I gripped my ring and expanded my cocoon until it encompassed my Alpha, Joaquin, Cassandra, Theo, and Whitney.

"Done," I said, keeping my voice dismal because like sage I needed him figuring me out.

Kane rolled his shoulders, then his neck. His power pulsed around him, brushing my skin in waves. Obsidian, it felt good. Like a salve that healed my fractured pieces.

Mine. He was still *mine*.

"You've drawn too much attention, Briar," Isaac snarled.

Kane gripped the doorframe, and the wood groaned as he filled the entrance.

Again, just so sloppy. Sure, *I* couldn't say anything to expose my stepfather, but he'd said not a damn thing about protecting him from himself.

"Why did the wolves take you?" he asked.

I needed a reason—a good one, otherwise he'd start putting pieces together on his own. "I stepped in front of a train, Isaac. I'm Kane's claimed. They can't *let* me kill myself."

His laugh was a caustic vow when he said, "You just keep fucking up, Briar." There was a shuffling on the other end. "That's going to cost you."

My Alpha's stare blazed as it dropped to the phone, glaring at it like it was Isaac himself. Like he'd rip it apart. Beyond him, Theo leaned forward while the Dowager's stillness lingered between eerie and menacing.

My shoulders fell.

Isaac exhaled a savage breath. "How much do they know?"

Shit. What'd I say? Was there a workaround? I needed a truth, and my next one came easily. "I'm not sure." I had to cut him off at the pass before he pushed for the wrong thing. "They're just asking a lot of questions I can't answer."

He laughed, derisive. "Excellent. Keep it that way." Another shuffling. "Hold tight, dear stepdaughter. I'll see you soon." The call ended.

Damnit! I'd thought he'd order me to come to him. Tell me where he was. Make it easier for Kane to rip him into itty bitty Isaac shreds. I lowered the phone.

"Isaac," Kane said, resonant. Guttural.

Whitney's chin rose. "Relief."

The expression my Alpha wore was unfathomable. And I understood the thoughts that echoed in his mind. His jaw clenched like he concentrated. A second later, his voice probed my mind. "*Isaac's a changeling, Bry.*"

A fact. One he already knew, which meant Isaac's compulsion didn't engage to block me when I said, "Yes." Pump the brakes. I rapid blinked and stiffened, his presence inside me so palpable, it was almost like we touched. Almost. Shifting, I gave the wall my weight while I used his broad back as a barrier to block me from sight and hide the widening of my eyes. "*We're not touching . . . How're you doing this?*"

His lip arced. "*You found me.*"

I'd found him? I sucked in a soft breath. My training. Sage, I'd touched his power. I'd *found* him. Realization struck like lightning. "*My dream. It wasn't . . .*" My fingers settled over my claiming mark. "*That was you.*"

He inclined his head slow, easy.

"Has Isaac been controlling you, Briar Stone?" Cassandra asked.

I rocked into her line of sight, gaze drifting her way, then on to the Empath.

"Eager," Whitney added.

"*Can changelings compel?*" Kane silently questioned.

I rocked back to him and tested his words. Poked and prodded them. They were general, about Isaac's kind, not Isaac himself. "*No, they can't.*"

He leaned closer and growled. "*They can't. But he can.*" His rough fingers flexed while the senseless puzzle pieces I'd dumped at his feet clicked together in his mind. "*Shadowed fucking moon. He's been Mason.*"

My heart twisted.

"But Isaac's human," Joaquin cut in.

"Human?" Cassandra seethed. "How does a *human* hold such power?"

Theo's expression creased while guilt twisted my chest, sending a bitter tang to coat my tongue. Cassandra and Joaquin had fought for me. Stood by my side. They deserved to know the truth about Isaac, what he was. And sage, I wanted to tell it, scream it to the goddamn world, then spike a "kill on sight" target to his back. But that meant endangering Lucas, a fact my stepfather knew well.

Whitney's mouth pursed as if she rode my emotions with me. "Desperation."

Joaquin's eyes narrowed, considering. "Has Isaac *acquired* that power?"

I could've kissed the Beta.

A single *clap* cut through the room when Whitney said, "Satisfaction!"

Cassandra hissed and the primal sound of it made the hairs on the back of my neck stand on end.

"What makes you say that?" Theo asked the Beta. Pushing. Guiding. Forcing him to vocalize what we couldn't.

While the question had been for Joaquin, it was the Dowager who answered. "Because he issued the commands."

Joaquin rubbed his jaw like he tried to understand. "Is that even possible?"

Kane's hands tracked higher on the doorframe, his shoulders broadening with the move while the sinewed muscles of his arms tensed like they held it up. "It has to be."

"But what's he using to do it?" Joaquin said. "And how the shit did he get it?"

"He stole it." My Alpha forced a sharp exhale through his powerfully clenched jaw. "He motherfucking *stole* it!" His spine straightened when he came to his full, towering height. "He was the goddamn Phantom."

My body heated, knees growing weak. I loved Kane. Always had, always would. But I'd never loved him more than that moment.

Joaquin dragged a hand through his hair. "Son of a bitch! It fits. All of it. The deaths, the missing body parts, Briar leaving you, her cagey-ass behavior, challenging Victor, then picking a fight with the train."

Kane's head angled low, eyeing me through his brows. "You went to the border."

Blood thrashed in my ears.

Whitney nodded. "Excitement."

Joaquin's brow arched. "That have anything to do with that cat-pissy serum you were testing?"

That blood thrashed wilder. It might've been a different solution, but it revolved around the same problem.

Whitney nodded again. "More excitement."

The Beta's voice levelled, even. "There's only one reason for that."

Kane's lips drew back from his teeth. "He's up to shit with Ithica."

Cassandra's incisors lengthened. "If he is controlling Briar Stone, we must assume there are others."

Theo's Adam's apple dipped when he swallowed hard.

Kane's unwavering stare met mine. "How do we stop it?"

My gaze pinched at the corners.

Joaquin folded his arms over his chest. "You could try a command."

Yes. A command. *Do that!*

Kane tipped his head my way. "Only if she's good with it."

"She is," Whitney said.

He stretched his neck and rolled his hands into fists. His eyes sparked, and his power broke through the room. "YOU'RE RELEASED FROM ISAAC'S HOLD!" he said with that thick, dominating tone.

The pressure in my skull built, closing in on my mind with a preternatural force. I grabbed the sides of my head and screamed. My legs buckled and I fell, crying out again when my ribs shifted. "Make it stop! Take it back! MAKE IT STOP!"

"Fuck!" Kane dropped to my side. "You're released, Bry. You're *released*!"

That pressure vanished and I sagged, collapsing forward onto my hands. I gasped for breath to ease the frenetic thump of my heart. My lungs seared. Ached. I'd wanted it to work so badly. For the solution to be simple. To be goddamn free.

Curses rang from across the room. Theo's body coiled.

The growl that ripped from Kane's throat was a promise of a bloody death. "It's fucking *compulsion*."

Cassandra snarled, eyes darkening to a savage shade of massacre and carnage. "The thief steals from *my* kind."

Whitney's gaze jumped between them. "How do you know?"

"Commands can be overridden if they're issued by a more powerful were," Joaquin said. "Kane's the strongest in Cambria. But commands and compulsion hold equal footing in the mind. If the order that's given conflicts," he gestured to my crumpled form, "they war for power."

Holy shit on a stick! I sat straighter and groaned at the pain.

The flesh along Kane's throat drew taut. "Easy, Bry."

My gaze searched him. I was bone weary and tired. But for the first time since everything started, I was safe. Because of him. Always him. He was there. Every hot, sinewed fiber of his arms, and torso. Iron fires, what I wouldn't give to touch him. Taste him. To wrap myself around him and—

Whitney tugged the collar of her dress shirt. "Excited." She scratched her cheek. "And, uh . . . some *other* feelings."

"What other feelings?" Kane said.

Her gaze darted around the room to the curious onlookers. "Desperate ones."

My face heated while a flush crept across my cheeks. My toes curled. I fidgeted with my pant leg.

Kane's head canted down, slowly. His stare raked my body, dipping low, then back up. He watched me through his brows. Those eyes flashed. When he spoke, his words were for Whitney, "You can't know that."

She raised her arms, palms out. "I promise, it's very, *very* clear."

Damn right, because the depth of my need for Kane was immeasurable. The need for his touch. His unyielding hold. Just . . . *him*. I'd been without him so long, too long. If I needed to be bound and gagged to feel him for even a moment, I'd take it.

His stare pinched at the corners, mouth thinning into a hard line. "That's not an option. We get to Isaac, and finish this. Then, I promise."

My heart sank.

"Defeated," Whitney said.

Kane's neck corded; his head fell.

"I suspect Briar Stone . . . needs a moment, Kane Slade," Cassandra said. "One of freedom. With you."

And I did. Desperately. I wanted Isaac too, but I needed to breathe. To feel safe. To take a moment for my barely fixed pieces to settle. Just for a while.

My Alpha cursed then cursed again. "I touch her and she fucking recoils. I won't hold her down. I can't do that. Not to *her*."

The way he said her, as if I was everything. *His* everything. All it did was make me want him more.

My expression must've told him something, 'cause he cursed under his breath. "I *can't*, Bry. Not without you telling me. If I ever did something you don't want . . . I couldn't fucking handle it. I won't chance being wrong."

No! It was like a carrot dangled in front of my face that'd been jerked away. I wanted that damn carrot. Needed it. Sage on a stick, why couldn't I have the goddamn *carrot*?

Joaquin advanced a step. "There might be a way."

Every eye in the room ticked to him.

He lifted a lone shoulder. "Blindfold her."

Kane's glare pinned his Beta. "She's scared enough."

Joaquin raised his hands. "Isaac ordered her not to let you touch her. If that's the case, coming at her head on won't work, so play with the blind spots in the command. Literally. If she can't *see*, she can't *know* it's you. She'll suspect, but the compulsion needs confirmation. It doesn't have to be certainty. A thread of doubt's enough."

Cassandra inclined her head. "I believe your wolf is correct, Kane Slade."

My heart tumbled inside my chest. It was such a simple suggestion, but so, so pivotal. The difference between assumption and certainty was finite, a sliver. But if the circumstance was right, that sliver could split to a chasm.

The war inside my Alpha's gaze was clear, and it ripped him to shreds because he wanted this too. Badly. He found his Beta. "Will she be able to talk freely?"

Joaquin's stare narrowed. "Possibly."

"But she should not speak your name," Cassandra noted. "If she did, and you were to acknowledge her after, it could fail."

Thoughts twisted in those silver topaz eyes. Kane's jaw pulsed as he clenched it. "Both of you better be fucking right." He grabbed his shirt at the shoulder and snapped it off. "Leave us."

Power of obsidian. The rigid lines across his broad chest and abdomen tensed as he moved, putting that V of muscle at the edge of his low-slung jeans on full display. It pointed down. Down. *Down.*

I raked my tongue along the back of my teeth.

The others left, their footsteps padding away before the soft *fick* of the door closing sounded out.

My gaze lit on something covering the cap of his shoulder. A tattoo. New, yet wholly familiar, because I'd seen it before, when my brother had drawn it for my Alpha.

Heart stutter-stepping, I took in the spectacularly silver wolf stood at the center of a briar patch that held wild, pink roses. One with an open flower to represent Lucas. And an unopened bud to represent our child. Our family.

The lines looked familiar too. Ezra . . . when he'd practiced with the equipment. It had to be.

My chest filled to the brim with every emotion. Too many. I loved Kane Slade. I fucking loved him.

He folded his shirt into a thinner line before his fists clenched around its ends. His exhale was gruff when he stared at it.

He reached behind me, careful not to touch, then dropped that material over my eyes and tied it off. His wilderness scent wrapped around me. The cloth stole the light. Hid him. Hid *everything*. And I prayed to the wraith below that it hid the truth.

Chapter Twenty-Four

A warm, calloused hand wrapped around mine. Familiar. But Isaac's command didn't press in. Kane lifted it, settling my palm against his rough cheek.

It was him. Every thread of my poorly woven soul knew it, but without my senses, without *seeing* his face, my brain had no means to confirm it. A work around. Shadow and sage, a work around! A whimper broke from me.

His hold was ginger when it enveloped me and pressed me to his chest. My still healing ribs hummed when my arms came up and looped around his neck. Gripping him tight, I crushed my face into his throat, breathing in his musk and wilderness scent. I didn't need to see what I touched because I knew every ridge, and angle . . . every part of him.

His mouth brushed my ear when he rumbled, "I've got you, Bry."

The tears that'd been forced back broke free. It worked. Power of obsidian, it worked.

His calloused hands found my face, engulfing it before he angled me up. He set his forehead to mine, shoulders rising and falling in a deep rhythm while our ragged breaths mingled.

My nails grazed his flesh, fingers splaying wide as my palms flattened against the broad form of his chest. My body sagged. I knew that chest—every hill and valley. Every scar. Every*thing*. He shuddered under my touch.

I pulled him close until every soft line of my body formed to the hard planes of his. His mouth brushed mine, the stubble along the curve of his jaw skimming my flesh. His lips slanted over mine. His tongue dove deep, tracing my every curve when it twisted against my own.

The kiss was warm, and slow, and so full of desperate and simmering desire, it nearly burned me to ash right there. That heat melted the broken shards of my heart, binding them together. And if his reaction was any indication, it'd fused his shattered moonlight too. Not completely, there was still an edge there—a violence to be sated. One I had no doubt Isaac would taste. But first, there was us. This. We both needed mending because facing what was to come would require every ounce of strength we could muster.

I drew back, gasping for air and his thumb traced a steady line beneath my eye, stealing my tears. The anticipation of each touch sent a warm shiver rolling down my spine. My muscles weakened, mouth running dry.

But then I quivered as the anger set in. Anger at myself. I touched my fingers to the blindfold. "I'm sorry I didn't figure this out sooner."

"No. Not your fault. Full fucking stop. Joaquin's a wolf. The guy was under Ronin. He's been circumventing commands a long time."

Ronin, who'd killed his brother. Ronin, who'd watched Joaquin coming. And Joaquin, who'd outsmarted the former Alpha at his own game.

Kane loosed a ragged exhale. I kissed him again, lifting my leg and hooking it over his hip. He gripped it, holding it in place, the hard length of him growing harder by the second when it pressed into my abdomen. I moaned.

He gripped my waist, locking me still. "No, Bry."

I clutched at him. "Please." My cheek dropped to his chest. "I need you, Kane. If you're afraid it's 'cause I'll scent like you—"

The laugh he let loose was dark. "That's not an issue. Isaac won't be getting fucking near you again."

Another tear slipped free. "Then why?"

"Don't cry, Bry. You'll rip the heart from my chest." His hold flexed against me. "I don't wanna hurt you."

"You couldn't." My fingers pressed deep into his shoulders when I begged, "*Please*."

His exhale was a wild mix of eager, ragged and resigned. Bending, he took my other leg, wrapping me around him as he carried me away, then settled me onto something soft. The bed. *Our* bed.

Home. I was fucking *home*.

He ranged over me, his weight barely there. I dragged him down, or at least, tried to. But he held his position.

I stuck my bottom lip out in a pout.

He nipped that lip before a huff of laughter broke from him. Still tense. Not free. I doubted the storm on his horizon would break until he'd broken Isaac.

"How's the pain?" he asked.

Right. That. I'd been so caught up in him, my injury'd fallen into the background. Concentrating, I tested my ribs. "It's gone."

Sage, I'd missed him. I'd known it, felt it. But he'd ingrained himself so deep into the makeup of who I was, being separated had ripped my soul out, stolen a piece of me. My heart hadn't worked the same. I hadn't realized just how much I'd crumbled without him. But the straightening of my spine, resetting of my shoulders, and lift of my chin were like pieces being maneuvered back into place. Integral ones. I was, myself, enough, but with him, I was so much more. Substantial. Whole.

I wanted him. Needed more. Close. I needed to be closer. I tugged his pants and ordered, "Off."

He lifted. There was a clank of a belt. A zipper drawn down. It was intense, being lost to my senses like that. Each sound more poignant, every nerve more sensitized, every touch more intimate.

"Take it all off," I amended, then blurted, "Just strip!"

Another laugh. Rich and hungry.

When the noise disappeared, I uttered, "Now take mine."

Those warm hands grasped the hem of my shirt first and drew it free torturously slow. I crushed my eyes closed as he pulled it from my body. The tie shifted. I slid it back into place. My clothing *wisped* when it landed somewhere nearby.

Silence fell, absolute. Kane's breaths grew rapid and heavy. His fingers skimmed my ribs. "I'm gonna kill him, Bry."

He was. And when he did, it would be spectacular.

"I know."

His touch skimmed that blindfold. "Does this change anything else? Make it easier to talk about him?"

I tasted Isaac's secrets, tried to spit them out. They refused to leave. I rehashed his command.

"You will share nothing of my plans unless it is to me, or someone you know to be one of my people."

My lips pursed. I shook my head.

"It's alright," he vowed, and flexed his hand over my side. "You got this far. I'll get us the rest."

And he would, because when it came to me, Kane Slade had no quit. My palm flattened over his touch, then guided it back, leading him to my bra. "Make me better."

He took over, and a gruff, grating sound ripped from his chest when he unlatched it, then, with a gradual torture, nudged the straps from my shoulders. They slithered down, freeing my breasts.

He unfastened my pants, knuckles grazing the tops of my thighs when he skimmed them and my thong free. Gooseflesh rose, following his touch while cool air brushed my skin.

He kissed me again, but there was a hesitance there—a concern. An unease over what'd happened, and how much I'd endured. Like he feared pushing past my limits. But with him, there was no limit. I had no fear, because if Kane had proven anything, it's that he'd *never* hurt me.

Anything he wanted, everything I had, was his to take. But in that moment, he needed me to steer our ship. And I knew exactly where I'd lead him.

My palms trailed his back, caressing his scars, up and up and up until my hands knotted in his hair. "I want everything we've missed."

His mouth found my throat, those canines raking over my claiming mark. He tracked lower, tongue flicking along my collarbone, and sternum. He palmed my breast, laving my nipple before he took it between his teeth.

I hissed as my spine arched, head driving back into the pillow.

He prowled down my body until he dropped to the apex of my thighs and nudged them apart. "I've missed you, Bry." He pressed that tongue to my clit, and I gasped. "So fucking much." He flicked and tasted, working me while his palm settled against my stomach.

My hands gripped his shoulders, digging deep into his flesh. He fell into a rhythm. Suck, stroke, lick. Suck, stroke, lick. I panted, the sounds feverish when they broke from me because there was being touched, and then there was being touched by Kane Slade.

"Right there. Oh, sage. Don't stop."

I'd been so long without him, the pleasure rose fast, reaching that crescendo and bursting over. I cried out and rocked my hips, grinding against his tongue. He groaned, savoring me until my trembling slowed, then slowed more and stopped altogether.

His breath grazed my thigh when he asked, "You okay?"

Was I *okay*? I wanted to tease, to push him further but that edge was still there. He needed the reassurance. Needed not to break me more than I'd already been broken. I took his face between my hands. "Come here."

He followed as I guided him, climbing up my body. I spread my thighs wide, opening to him. The thick tip of his cock pressed against my slit. I moaned. Patient as ever, he lingered. I squirmed against him, trying to entice.

A thick huff rent from his chest.

"You waiting for an invitation?" I breathed, voice so sultry, I barely recognized it as my own.

He pressed forward, the head of his shaft breaking that threshold. My mouth opened on a silent scream as he sank deep. He ranged over me, arm sliding under my shoulder before he latched on. He withdrew achingly slow, then filled me again.

I sighed, sheer ecstasy.

Power of obsidian, he felt so good. He fit every corner, touched every wanton nerve. He was made for me.

What I wouldn't have given to see those silver topaz eyes. To see their fire. To watch it burn.

He took both of my hands in his, fingers threading with mine, then eased my arms above my head. I bit my lip and smiled.

Iron Hells, I'd missed this. The pleasure. The want. The *need*. My body screamed for it—screamed for him. And he answered that call. He was warm. Careful. Thorough.

I rolled my hips, arcing up to meet him, angling to take him further. Take him all. He glided in and out, his pace easy. Unhurried. Like he had all the time in the world because he did. He'd never let go again, and neither would I.

His inhales were harsh. Sharp. Barely controlled. A gruff sound grated from his chest. It drove me wild, and my already sensitized body soared to that crest again. His shoulders tensed like it took every ounce of control he had not to lose himself.

My core tightened, orgasm exploding through me when I begged, "Come with me."

He cursed, then growled, shuddering as he spilled himself inside of me.

That heat spread, tracking out as a wave of dizziness moved in, heady and overpowering. I set my palm against the bed and blinked hard into the darkness of my blindfold to steady myself.

"I forgot how powerful that is." I smiled, all languid and desperate for more. The "ready for everything" kind. The "I'm not done with you" kind. And the "I'm about to get a taste of my own" kind.

I rolled, shoving him onto his back, then scaled down his body until I took his slick cock in hand.

"Fuck," he snarled, and the sound of it had a new heat pooling between my thighs.

Wrapping my lips around him, I took him deep, tasting myself there.

He groaned and my inner minx purred. His fingers grazed the back of my neck and gathered my hair. He drew me up, then guided me down as I slid him to the back of my throat. Right where my Alpha liked it.

I took him, sucking harder, deeper. I worked the base of his shaft with my hand, edging him, bringing him to that brink before I pulled back. Again and again, I offered that sweet torture.

"Shadowed fucking moon. Just like that, Bry."

I loved it when he talked that way. Feral and reckless with need.

His breaths grew harsher and his hips bucked. That hand on my hair locked tight when he growled a savage and untamed sound. I didn't pull back.

The hint of a salty tang invaded my mouth, then flooded it a second later as he came. I worked him up and down, over, and over, guttural grunts escaping him as I took every last drop.

I trailed my tongue along his entire length, teasing the tip before I drew back. "Now," I said, stalking my way north. I straddled him, then mounted, taking every pulsing inch until I was filled to the hilt. "Fuck me like you mean it."

It was a role reversal. My Alpha was always in charge. Not that I didn't push, or he didn't give, but being on the commanding side, having him—his *wolf*—yielding to me, was a heady kind of power.

His grip found my ass, and he thrust into me from below. My fingers dug into his pecs, and I gasped, spine arching back as I took him. He thrust again and I rolled my hips.

"You're so goddamn beautiful, Bry."

I grinned, then taunted, "That's because half my face is covered."

He growled but didn't take my bait.

He thrust again, seating himself inside of me. But I needed that tempestuous touch. Needed that explosive passion. Needed everything he had.

The laugh that slipped from me was pure, insatiable vixen. "Come on, now." I clenched around him, and his breath hitched. "I want it rough."

He filled me once. Twice. He drove deep and his palm came down on my ass. Hard. *Smack*.

The sting was a sweet torment. He knew my body, knew the threshold—that edge between pain and pleasure. Knew exactly how to straddle it.

"Again," I pleaded.

He drove deeper, then found the other side. *Smack*.

I cried out and he massaged my flesh before he launched forward and flipped me onto my back, taking control as he speared me again.

One hand held my hip while the other knotted in the hair at the base of my skull. He snapped my head back, arcing my spine. I curved my leg around him, driving my heels into his ass.

He reared back, then slammed forward. The force sent the bed scraping across the floor obnoxiously loud. A riot of sensation chased out from my core. It licked like flame over my body, burning. Searing. Leaving an irreparable brand.

"More," I urged. Begged. *Pleaded*.

He didn't disappoint.

His hips crashed against me, more edged and frantic. His mouth descended on mine. His grip on me tightened as he pinned me to him, kissing me with his whole damn body. His tongue consumed mine, and his serrated breaths rasped across my lips.

Iron fires, take me. What that wolf did to me. The noises that escaped me were sheer animalistic need and matched only by his own. The angle he worked hit every overly keen nerve of my clitoris and my climax ratcheted to the forefront. It bore down on me like a tidal wave, drowning me in him. My favorite way to die.

I gripped him with my core, arms cinching around his neck. His orgasm hit next, and he growled when he bore into me again and again and again. He came and that familiar heat pooled between my thighs. His heat.

We rode the rest of our need together and before long, the bed dipped under his weight when he collapsed beside me.

He dragged me to him, hand sealing over my back. I nuzzled my face into the crook of his neck, and draped myself across him, completely, totally, and utterly sated. Dragging the blanket over us, he traced a slow line along my spine.

He cleared his throat. "I love you, Bry. More than anything in this world, I love you."

"I love you too."

He breathed deep. "Fuck me, you smell so goddamn good."

My lip ticked up before I grinned like an idiot. "I smell like vanilla."

A laugh. "That what you saw when you were poking around my aura?" The words were light, impish, but still, my guilt rushed in.

It wasn't about Isaac, so I wasn't blocked when I said, "I'm sorry. I know it's intrusive and I shouldn't—"

"No," he said. "Anything that's mine is yours. That includes my aura, my memories. Everything."

That weight lifted. My body grew light.

His chest rose on a breath. "What *were* you looking at in there?"

Twisting, I brushed my lips over his throat. "Just us."

The resonant rumble he loosed rolled through me.

I wiggled closer. "Why didn't you try and command me that day?" The day I'd left him. The day our worlds were torn apart.

"'Cause I hurt you, and if you didn't actually want me, I wasn't gonna make you stay. I'd never do that. I love you too damn much. I wanted you happy with me, but more than that, I just wanted you happy."

My smile was soul deep. How did a man with his power, and looks, and unmatched ability to give, and love, and fuck, ever have any doubt?

I sighed, a wholly contented sound. Knowing I carried his scent, that I was his again, that I was *home* . . . the truth of it nestled into my heart and I couldn't stop when the tears flowed.

His arms wrapped around me, burying me in his hold as he crushed me to his chest. "I'm here, Bry. You're safe."

I nodded against him.

He was there. I was his. Shielded.

I come for what's mine.

"I'm not going anywhere for now." There was a distinction in the words, one that had the pit in my stomach dropping to an abyss unknown before his voice darkened, a malevolent promise when he finished, "But tonight I'm going hunting, and I'm not coming home until Isaac's dead."

Chapter Twenty-Five

An hour later, the mood in the kitchen was heavy—the readying for violence kind. Myself, Kane, Cassandra, Joaquin, Theo, and Whitney gathered around our kitchen—a war council presiding.

I sat—sans blindfold—safely positioned between my Alpha and his Beta, while the Dowager lingered before the window, staring out into the moonlit night.

The place was warm, the heady scent of rage thick on the air. I'd paused, taking every damn second I could to feel Kane. Touch him. Bite, taste and lick him. Convincing myself it was real. That everything would be okay. That *he'd* be okay. I wanted Isaac dead, to see the cage he'd trapped me and the others in obliterated, but the closer it came, the more my stomach tensed and the panic set in.

I crammed a bite of pasta in my mouth—my second helping. I was the only one who ate. A lot. The sex must've zapped me because my appetite wouldn't quit.

"Do you know where Isaac is?" Joaquin asked me.

Twirling my fork around my plate, I frowned. "No."

"Where *could* he be?"

Theo's stare held on Whitney as he rang his hands.

I tested the walls of the compulsion. They pushed back. My mouth thinned into a hard line when I tried to say something. It didn't work.

"Frustrated," Whitney said.

Kane's arms folded over his chest. "He ordered you not to say?"

My jaw clenched but I was tapped out, so solutions were less than possible.

"No." Cassandra's chin dipped. "He ordered her to protect him."

I jump-clapped. *BINGO!*

Whitney nodded.

My Alpha's chair scraped across the floor when he shifted it to face me, his words rough when he vowed, "I'll find him."

And he would, or he'd die trying. But what if Isaac knew he'd been had? What if he'd taken someone else's face? Or worse, jumped ship and crossed to Ithica?

I was so damn happy to have Kane back. Have a way to touch him and love him. Be with him. But I'd never be free. Never see his face as we kissed. Never look him in those voltaic eyes when I told him I loved him. I'd always be checking the shadows, watching over my shoulder. Never able to breathe deep.

And while I'd gotten lucky, the others under Isaac's thumb, not so much.

My stomach turned. I set my fork down with a clank and pushed my plate away.

Kane checked the time, stare fixed on the map of Cambria spread across our table. His eyes were narrowed as he canvassed it for possible locations. "We start at Lana's house." He found Cassandra. "Victor's not about to invite us over, so once we cross the boundary, it'll be war."

Her silver dress wisped as she drifted closer. "If Victor Davis stands in our way, Kane Slade, we will simply remove him."

My ribs locked down, cinching around my lungs, 'cause I had not one clue where Victor landed—on our side, Isaac's, or his own. Regardless, my stepfather controlling him weaponized the Southern Pack. So, if Victor wasn't out of our way, he was in it.

Whitney's gaze narrowed. "How can you know that's where Isaac even is?"

The shake of Kane's head was sharp. "We don't. But we start somewhere."

Theo ran a hand over the back of his neck.

Kane inclined his head then checked his watch again. "My strongest wolves are en route. Once they get here, we move." My Alpha leaned back, giving his chair his weight while he owned it like the king he was. Those square knuckled hands linked over his abdomen as he watched me, the mix of emotions playing across his expression impossible to peg.

My attention slid to Lucas where he played some video game in the living room. Well, *pretended* to, anyway. His gaze kept flicking our way. Eavesdropping. Not that I blamed him. He had just as much invested in what was to come as anyone else seated at that table. Probably more. But there was a fury for his father there. One that darkened his violet eyes and made my heart shudder.

This needed to end. And there was only one way Kane would actually find Isaac. If I learned where he was, then I could—

"No," Kane said. The veins along his neck strained against his throat. "I know that look, Bry." He shook his head. "Not fucking happening."

Cassandra's stare glided between us.

I bit my lip and offered my wolf an apologetic wince. The last thing I wanted was to leave his side and throw myself back into Isaac's line of fire, but if we intended to finish this—finish *Isaac*—then the options were slim. And if Isaac couldn't be found . . . "I should go, Kane."

His eyes blazed, pinning me to the spot. "Like the fucking hells. I'll chain you to the goddamn bed if I have to."

Cassandra inclined her head. "And I will assist him, Briar Stone."

My chest tightened. I really didn't deserve either of them.

Joaquin drummed his finger over the table, attention lifting to Kane. "We just need to find him." He chucked his chin my way. "If she talks to Isaac, she can lead us there. We stay close, track her to where he is. Then we end him."

Kane angled forward and rolled his shoulders, his guttural words pushed through his aggressively clenched teeth. "She's not getting anywhere near that piece of shit again." His chest heaved, breaths harsh, something akin to panic flaring when he shoved to his feet. "He wanted her dead. Tried to kill her. Don't ask me to hand her back. I won't. Fucking. Do it."

The raw pain in those words almost gutted me. I inhaled slow and easy, then tested my next thought before I spoke. "What if Theo took me?"

Whitney peered back and forth between us, eyes narrowed. Concentrating. Her hands flew to her mouth.

Kane's brow slammed down. "Why can Theo take you—" He went rigid, eyes fixed. Wide. His cogs slipped their gears, then synced. The moment the realization hit was clear in his hollow expression. "Shadowed fucking moon."

Joaquin cursed.

Every preternatural eye in the room snapped Theo's way.

Theo sagged, chest caving as he sank in on himself. His elbows hit the table, and his head dropped. A sob broke from his chest. His gaze turned red-rimmed and shiny. A tear caught on his lashes before it fell to his shirt.

Reaching across the table, I took his hand and squeezed hard.

The Beta's fists clenched, his focus fixed on the far wall. "Who else could drive you, Briar?"

I blinked hard when the question hit, bounding around my brain until it slowed, then sank in. Joaquin was a goddamn *genius*! Shadow and sage. I'd wanted to scream those answers for so long. They'd sat like an iron weight on my chest. Crushing. Killing. My mouth ran dry, and my throat grew thick, words shaking wildly when I said, "Victor, Amber," my voice broke, "Mason, Lisa, my mother, Naomi." I found Kane. "Lucas."

My Alpha stumbled back a half-step. His gaze grew distant as if he was lost, caught in a thick fog. Nothing was clear because nothing made sense—or everything did. He pivoted, setting a hip against the counter like he needed to brace.

Naomi and Theo's challenges. The disruption in the Pack. Their bizarre camping trip to the Immortal Inc lot. My conflict with Victor. The deaths. All of it.

I drifted my gaze Cassandra's way. "And Ivy."

She paled—if that was even possible. Her crimson eyes hardened. Petrified blood. She peered at me, then away, then back again. "Ivy Trevino lives?"

My heart broke for her, but wraith take me, having her, having them *all* know the truth . . .

"Relief," Whitney breathed.

I wanted to scream where Ivy was. Lead Cassandra to her. Iron fires, I wanted to *help*.

The edge of the counter groaned under Kane's grip. His thoughts didn't take much to read, 'cause they were the same ones poisoning my mind. What was real; what wasn't; how long had it been happening; what else had he missed.

He rose, coming to his full, dominating height. His power ripped through the room. It grated over my flesh, every muscle of his torso torquing when he threw his head back and roared. It was graveled and thick and coated in regret. It was agony, and it was agonizing to hear.

Lucas appeared at the kitchen's threshold. His eyes were pinched at the corners. And suddenly he was a boy again. One who needed help. One who needed *someone*. And that someone was there. Kane exploded toward him and engulfed him in his hold. The two collided with a *thump*. Reaching to the side, my Alpha grabbed Theo by the arm and jerked him from his chair, bringing him in too.

Cassandra's skirts flitted as she floated across the room while she, once again, stared into that distant night. The menace that rolled off her had the hairs on the back of my neck standing on end. When she spoke, her voice was light. Soft. Terrifying in its own right. "If Anthony Bruno were alive, could he have driven you, Briar Stone?"

The image of Anthony's lifeless body flashed across my mind. I pushed deeper into my seat, and it creaked. "Yes."

Her eyes closed like she sought to steady herself, but the steadiness when she reopened them set my teeth on edge. "It is Ivy Trevino's venom Isaac has used?" A suspicion and a confirmation.

My mouth was glued shut on that one, so I turned to Whitney. "Sadness. Resignation," the Empath added.

Cassandra's nod was steady. Gradual. Like the weight of that information settled on her shoulders.

Kane drew back from Theo and Lucas. "I failed you. All of you. *Again*."

I shook my head because he could never.

"No, Kane," Lucas said.

"You didn't know," his Beta cut in. "None of us did."

He slammed his fist against his chest. "IT'S MY FUCKING JOB TO KNOW!"

My heart broke for him. Isaac's web was so intricately woven, it was impossible to sort the layers—tell truth from lies. Or faces. He couldn't have figured it out. No one could. "Kane—"

He shook his head. "I don't get a pass, Bry."

Pulling the blindfold from my pocket, I slipped it into place because my Alpha needed me. I reached for him. He was there, grasp locking around my wrist as he pulled me to his chest. My palms glided along his too-tense shoulders and up to his jaw, tracking over the stubble there.

His arms snapped out before he crushed me to him. "I'm so fucking sorry."

I shook my head against him. "You figured it out."

He gripped my waist and rested his chin on my hair. "Not fast enough."

"You got Lucas out, and brought Whitney in." I nuzzled my face into his neck and buried myself deeper, breathing him deep. "You came for me. You knew something wasn't right and you came."

That hold locked tight, chaining me to him. "I'll always come for you. *Always*."

And sage, I wanted to stay there forever, but that forever was tainted if I couldn't have him—*all* of him. If I couldn't look in those tempestuous, silver topaz eyes and tell him I loved him. See their fire when he hungered for me. To tell him that final truth—the one about our child.

My touch raked back into his hair. "I should go."

"I should go too," Lucas added.

Stepping back, I ripped my blindfold down while Kane and I barked in unison. "NO!"

My brother scuffed his feet. "It's me he's after."

"You'd be leverage, Luke. Against me, against Bry. If he's got you, he's got everything. One of my Pack will guard you here."

My heart beat again, the slow build of a drum reaching its crescendo when the reality of what was to come hit. What if Isaac got *Kane*? Sure, my stepfather feared him . . . but what *if*? I'd just gotten him back. I couldn't lose him again.

"You should use me," I said. "Make me a distraction. Draw Isaac's eye my way."

Joaquin gave a tight nod. "If we don't let Briar go," he said, tone level—full Beta, "she could be stuck under Isaac's control forever. They all could."

"It's not up for debate," Kane snarled. "The Pack's coming. When they get here, we hunt Isaac and cut him off at the fucking knees. That's it."

The Beta was smart, and his mind worked different. Find a fix. A workaround. He was strong, but Kane had *always* been raw and brutal power. He didn't go around the rules; he went through them.

"Fine," I said, folding my arms over my chest. "Then take me with you."

Kane tore his hands roughly through his hair. He rolled his neck and stalked the perimeter of the room like a barely leashed predator. His stare found mine. The sinewed muscles of his forearms torqued. He prowled toward me. I flinched. He stopped dead. Less than a foot stood between us, but with what was about to come, it could've been the world.

He shook his head, voice gruff when he said, "I. Can't."

Cassandra turned to face us, her lengthened incisors pressing against her bottom lip. "This is going to be ugly, Briar Stone."

I opened my mouth to reply but a knock thumped at the door.

Kane scented the air, then grunted.

Cassandra's crimson stare flared. "It is the right thing, Kane Slade, but the Conclave will not be pleased."

My gaze bounced between them, then to the door. Who the Iron Hells was out there?

Kane's chin dipped in a sharp nod. "I'll take their heat."

She rose to her full, delicate height. "You will not take that heat alone. Though, I fear I should warn you, my first meeting with him did not go . . . well."

My Alpha's lip drew high, exposing the bitey-est of canines. His stare flicked to me. "Neither did mine." Whoever it was didn't set his wolf on edge, but the way he stretched his neck and stalked for the door made it clear he wasn't a fan.

The Dowager followed and I padded along behind them, nipping at their heels.

My Alpha's grip latched over the handle, jaw flexing when he jerked the entrance wide.

The blond haired, blue-eyed, Ithican Ambassador stood on the other side. He was dressed in a head-to-toe black suit, that same confident, spine straight, chin up air from the first time we'd met on full display.

My eyes flew wide. Ho-ly-shit! My Alpha'd called him. *He'd called him!*

Reaching between Cassandra and Kane, I extended a hand, and greeted, "Bower."

He took it and held. "It's good to see you again, Miss Stone."

Attention dropping to his right hand, I confirmed. No scar. Not Isaac.

"Excitement," Whitney said from somewhere behind me.

My Alpha's brow slung low when he glared down at me, totally misinterpreting what the hells that meant.

I released Bower and rolled my eyes. "Not like that, Big Bad."

Whitney scampered away.

He huffed, then turned the full weight of his domineering attention on the Ambassador. "Her name is Slade."

My heart tripped and stumbled in my chest, because while we'd never had the name conversation, hearing it from his lips . . .

"Ah," Bower replied, tone even. "I'll keep that in mind."

Kane's fists worked as he shifted his weight. "We have a problem."

The Ambassador straightened to his full height, attention piqued. "What kind of problem?"

My Alpha's hooded stare met mine like he needed to see me, make sure I was really there, before it tracked back to the Ambassador. "Isaac's orchestrated the killings here."

Bower clasped his hands before him, stare assessing. "Isaac Jenkins? Briar's stepfather?"

My brows ticked up. Sweet sage. Someone had clearly gone down my family tree for their homework.

A low growl rumbled through Kane's chest when he acknowledged, "Him."

I had to give Bower credit, 'cause he didn't balk, or flinch, or run screaming into the night.

"Ithica had been informed Jared was responsible," Bower replied.

"A misdirection on Isaac Jenkins's part," Cassandra said, voice soft.

"So he's been behind the chaos?"

My Alpha's words were low and guttural—full apex predator, when he said, "He *is* the fucking chaos."

"And he is a problem we seek to rectify," Cassandra added.

The Ambassador's head bowed. "Why tell me now?"

"Because he already gutted ten of your people." He set a broad shoulder against the doorframe like he held it up . . . or maybe the house. "We don't want more." The "or Ithica's retaliation" was silent. Deathly so.

"Fucking hells." Bower's throat dipped and he dragged a hand through his hair. "The bodies—"

"I'll get you the bodies."

The Ambassador rubbed his jaw. "This isn't exactly an official channel." His attention slid past us into the house. "Is the rest of the Conclave aware we're talking?"

Cassandra shook her head. "Several of the Conclave are under his thrall. We felt it prudent to circumvent them."

He folded his arms over his chest. "Thrall?"

"They are compelled."

Bower's gaze churned his thoughts as he processed that. "So, what is it you're suggesting Ithica do?"

Kane straightened, arms loose by his sides. "Get the humans the fuck out of Cambria. If Isaac gets wind of what's going down, he might go to ground. So, we all move at once. Rally your people fast and move them quiet. After they're across, lock the border. No one crosses."

Panic flared in my chest, and I blurted the only thing my Isaac-held-leash would allow. "Lisa!" She needed to go. Get the hells away . . . from Isaac.

Kane inclined his head.

Bower's expression hardened, brow slamming down. "Is she involved in this?"

"Not by choice," my Alpha said. "She's in danger too. Take her with you. Confiscate her phone. Strap her the fuck down if you need to, but she can't be in Cambria."

The fewer tools in Isaac's arsenal, the better. Especially ones that connected to Ithica. And the ones I loved.

"What about the patients at the RC?" The human ones, some too sick to move.

Kane's stare went unfocused in that talking-to-the-Pack kinda way. "I'll have it guarded." He reached into his low-slung jeans and pulled a piece of paper from his pocket. A series of coordinates sat there—the same coordinates to Zahara's super secretive villain crossing. "Check it. I'm guessing you've got a breach in your border."

Bower took it and cursed.

My gaze fixed on Kane's.

He reached for me, caught himself, then drew back before he told me, "We pulled it from your car's GPS."

Big Bad was smart.

"Is there anything else I should know?" Bower said, all business readying for action.

Yes. So much fucking yes. About Zahara, the serums, Isaac being a changeling and his identifying scar. But it was all locked inside the stupid vault in my mind.

A horde of vehicles drew up to the yard, one after the other. Wolves filed out. Big. Strong. Ready.

The Pack.

Kane shook his head. "We'll keep you posted."

"You have my number." Bower extended a hand Kane's way. "Thank you," he said, voice sincere before he offered the same to Cassandra. Pulling his phone free, he punched a number, stuck it to his ear, and left.

The pound of feet sounded out as the weres climbed our porch and Kane led their crush to the kitchen.

Theo edged back, giving the wall his weight. He rang his hands, attention flicking my way. There was something there. Something more. Something I recognized all too well. Something Isaac.

I worried my cheek between my teeth. Kane returned to the map and started plotting routes. An idea formed in my mind. An awful one my Alpha would surely murder me for later, but it was the only way I could see forward, because Isaac hid. It's what he did best. Behind places and people and faces. Was literally built for it. It'd taken Cassandra an age to hunt her changeling down—time we didn't have. Kane would *never* find Isaac.

Not unless I showed him the way.

"Cassian guards Luke," my Alpha commanded. "Not a fucking soul gets in here, not even me until I order you otherwise."

'Cause no chance in hells could we risk Isaac taking Kane's face. Stealing my brother away.

Cassian's brow furrowed, but he inclined his head.

"Come on, Lucas," I said, steering him toward the living room.

Kane's head snapped my way.

"I shouldn't listen to this," I breathed. A truth because I couldn't. Not if I wanted to keep his plans from my stepfather... or if I wanted my next, horrible, and high-risk move to work.

"The living room," he said, voice tight like he understood but even *that* distance was too far.

My gaze met Theo's, and I put as much 'Get your ass over here!' into it as I could muster.

He gave a single nod. "I, ugh, should probably go too," he said, then edged outta the room with me.

Lucas aimed for the couch and picked up his controller but just stared at it.

I set a hand on his back. "It's gonna be alright."

He shrugged. "This all started because of me and I just... wanna help."

The weight Isaac had asked him to carry was so goddamn much. Too much. More than anyone should, least of all his son. I got where Lucas came from, the need for action. I felt it too—was literally planning something dumb as we sat there. But Kane was right, if Isaac got his fingers on my brother again...

"The best thing you can do for everyone now is lay low."

He flicked the controller's toggle and inclined his head.

Theo took a seat at the far end of the couch, and it creaked when he gave it his weight. I whipped a cocoon over the two of us and squared myself to him. "What is it?"

His jaw worked as he ground his teeth. "Isaac called when you were alone with Kane. He ordered me to bring you to him."

Bring me to him. The reality of my plan smacked me in the face. The twisting of my lungs was violent, and I stuttered my next breath, 'cause the fact that Theo wasn't snatching me up and barreling outta the house could only mean one thing. "He told you to be discreet."

His hand flexed over the arm of the sofa. "Yes."

"Can you say where we're going?"

The pinch around his eyes creased deep. "No."

"How about where we're *not* going?"

His chin dipped in a nod. "Yes."

My gaze flicked to Kane and back. "Are we going to my mother's?"

He shook his head.

Which meant Kane would be headed the wrong way. The second he crossed the Southern boundary, Victor'd know something was up. And so would Isaac. He'd have time to hide. To flee.

Not if I could help it. But the more prepared I could be, the better, and I *needed* to know what I was walking into. "Does he suspect something's up?"

"Not sure, but he knows Kane. I think he's just hedging his bets."

The clamp around my chest loosened. Barely. "What *does* he know, Theo?"

The shake of his head was tight. "I've got no fucking clue."

I worried the hem of my shirt because that was the farthest thing from helpful. My gaze tracked to my Alpha. My stepfather was many things, but stupid wasn't one of them. There was no easy way around this. There was only through. Through the Iron Hells Isaac had dragged us into. And if we were lucky, through Isaac's skull when we killed him.

"Take Kane's keys and go start the truck," I told Theo before I could think better of it.

He went rigid. "What?" His hands balled into fists. "No, Briar. Don't let me take you."

"You have to, Theo. This is the only way we stop him."

Grabbing his hair, he angled forward.

I got it. I did. And I hated seeing his anguish, but it needed to be done. "Kane knows a command will hurt me now, so he won't give one. But he might for you, so I'll need to be the one to drive." It was a chance, however low, that I had to take because I was only gonna get one kick at the stupid can. But if I knew anything, it was that my Alpha *would* give chase, violently.

Theo's knee bounced rapid-fire. "Isaac's expecting me to take you."

"We just need some distance from Kane. We'll switch once we're outta here."

His spine was rigid. "Kane'll hear the truck."

"No." I tapped my obsidian, then extended my cocoon outside the house and covered the vehicle. "He won't."

"Shadowed moon." Theo crushed his eyes closed.

I loathed the idea as much as him. My body trembled, hair shaking in my periphery. Handing myself back to Isaac was a deadly sort of problem, but it didn't change the facts ... I settled a hand over Theo's forearm and gave a squeeze. "It's the only way."

His grip clenched and unclenched over the couch. "Fuck." He reopened his eyes and scrubbed the back of his neck. "*Fuck!*" He peered around, voice hitching when he said, "I can't lose you too, Briar." He shook his head. "Kane'll never forgive me for this."

"Yes," I promised, "he will." And Kane would because he was decent. Because after the rage quieted, he'd get that Theo had no choice. And because I'd never forgive him if he didn't.

I inhaled deep and low, filling my lungs to the brim. Brave as my sentiments were, it didn't stop the quaver of my voice. "The keys are on the entrance table." I tipped my head that way.

Theo's wide stare met mine.

"Go." Before my brain cells linked up and I talked myself out of it.

He forced a jagged breath through his teeth and rose. Grabbing those keys, he headed for the door. I followed his journey through the front window as he climbed into the truck, turned it over and slid to the passenger side.

"What's going on?" Lucas asked.

I leaned over and gave him a hug. "Stuff's about to get ugly, but you'll be alright."

His expression hardened. "Will you?"

Sage, he'd grown. It warmed and broke my heart in tandem. "Here's hoping." I pressed a kiss to his hair. "I love you, Lucas."

"I love you too." His stare fell, then rose again, more resolute. "Kill him, Briar."

My smile was tight when I repeated, "Here's hoping."

Kane stood at the head of his gathered Pack, giving orders. I threw a silent apology his way before I stood, moving on unsteady legs as I slipped on my shoes and exited the house. The second I crossed the threshold onto the porch, I bolted.

Sweat slicked my forehead, kissing my spine as I ran. Theo was pale, his expression the picture of regret as I clambered into the open driver's side door. Sealing myself in, I jammed the truck in reverse and punched it. Rocks kicked up when I flew backwards down the driveway.

Kane's roar filled the night when he exploded outside and bellowed, "BRY!"

I hit the road and the tires squealed as I came to a stop, then chanced a glance back.

My Alpha's stare was a molten blaze that rivaled the moon for intensity.

Cassandra's dress billowed around her as she flew out beside him.

"We're so fucking dead," Theo said.

Probably. But if I was going down, I was taking my piece of shit stepfather with me. Popping the vehicle into drive, I sped off into the night.

Chapter Twenty-Six

The silence in the truck as Theo and I approached the Northern magi border meant the beat of my heart filled the void when it pounded like a bass drum. We wove through the skyscrapers that edged the neutral grounds as that politically bullshit—but ridiculously real—red line of Coven territory came into view.

Theo downshifted, those wolf's eyes pinched at the corners while he scanned the area.

Understanding dawned and my mouth ran dry, fingers tingling as they gripped my shirt tighter. "He's at Mason's."

His stare met mine, skin creaking when he rolled it around the wheel. It was all the confirmation I needed before his attention tracked forward again. "You did it, Briar. You got us out."

My stomach tightened, because there we were, two geniuses, headed right back in. "*We* did it, Theo. You, me, Lisa, Mason." My voice hitched. "Naomi."

Bullrushes lined the ditches, overgrown rose bushes curving up the sides of buildings and houses as we ventured deeper and deeper.

Theo loosed a heavy breath. "I owe you."

"Like sage you do."

"You saved our asses."

I raised a finger. "First, our asses aren't even close to saved yet. Second, it was the others who figured it out. We lobbed a grain of sand into the ocean and crossed our fingers someone would find it." I clutched his hand. "And they did."

His eyes misted and he shifted in his seat.

My blood thrashed in my ears as we passed that gate and Mason's massive, three-story, all too terrifyingly familiar home came into view. "Isaac's game finally caught up to him. What he made me do, leaving Kane, trying to kill me . . . he picked the wrong fight."

"Yeah," Theo inclined his head, "he did."

I set my shoulders, feigning a confidence I definitely did not feel. "I should get out first."

He laughed. Dry. Like, the bone kinda dry. "Like the shadowed moon *that's* happening." I opened my mouth to offer a witty retort, but he snapped a palm out. "First, I already abducted your ass. Second, you did your part, now it's time I do mine. So, *hells* fucking no."

I scowled.

His shrug was a dish of "*I said what I said*" with a side of "*Deal with it.*"

The truck tires crunched over the ground as Theo cut into the driveway. A warning pricked the back of my neck as I eyed the house's one-way glass, as if I could *feel* someone looking back.

My mother's car was parked off to the side, Victor's SUV beside it. And the sight of the latter slammed my heart to a halt.

"What the fuck's Victor doing here?" Theo said, stealing the question from my tongue. It was less the shock of his presence and more the dangerous inconvenience of it.

Shit. Shit! *Shit!* A giant ass wrench had just been shoved between the spokes of my itty-bitty wheel, sending things from perilous to catastrophic. A rookie fucking mistake. One I prayed didn't cost me.

Oh, sage. What had I done? I gulped down heaving breaths to sate my starving lungs. It didn't work.

"Victor'll scent me, Theo."

Isaac and the Southern Alpha loaded Victor's vehicle while my mother, a wide-eyed Mason, and Ivy stood, off to the side, the shadow walker hissing as the iron cuffs clamped around her wrists seared her flesh. Her eyes dark pits, with all but a trace of crimson. That madness had burrowed deep.

Mason held Ivy's upper arm, fingers delving deep where they latched over her semi translucent flesh. His glasses slipped forward, those copper eyes creased with an apology he unequivocally didn't owe.

My stepfather placed a box of lab supplies into my mother's car before he advanced our way, stride measured. Meticulous. Victor stepped out next, body coiled tight.

"Fuck," Theo said.

"Get out of the vehicle," Isaac instructed.

The shake of my hand was so fierce, I could barely find the handle. My breaths left me in staccato pants while my chest rose and fell in rapid-fire bursts. The salty smell of Ivy's cooking flesh filled the air. Bile seared my tongue, and I gagged.

Victor's stare slid over me as he scented the air, and his stare flashed, but he kept his maw shut.

"Briar," Isaac crooned. "How lovely to see you again."

"Shove it, asshole."

The smile that crested his lips was a promise of things to come. Super bad ones. Linking his hands before him, he turned to Victor. "Does she smell like Kane?"

Iron fires, no!

The Southern Alpha's stare narrowed. "Yes."

Theo advanced a step. "He gave her his blood."

Hope sparked in my chest. A technicality, not a lie. More like an escape clause. Sure, I'd taken Kane's blood, but when? Thank obsidian, after my injuries, it had the benefit of being plausible.

Please, buy it. Please, buy it. Pleeease!

Isaac glared through his brows. "Is this true?"

Victor lifted a shoulder. "I can't tell."

A spark of hope flared in my chest. Victor wasn't working with us, but as long as he wasn't against us, I'd take it.

"Fine." Isaac's tongue prodded the inside of his cheek while he tilted his head. "Then tell me yourself, Briar. Did Kane fuck you?"

The world dropped out from under me. My gaze darted around. Bad. Very bad. My throat hurt, jaw fighting the answer, which meant it was forced through my teeth when I hissed, "Yes."

He dragged his thumb and forefinger over his brows. "I'm impressed. I didn't think you were smart enough to find a workaround."

"Get fucked, Isaac," Theo cut in. "You're not the genius you think you are."

My stepfather released a derisive laugh that hummed through his closed mouth. "I don't need to be the smartest person in the room. Just the best planner."

Planner? The word was innocuous. Simple. But Isaac didn't plan. He laid plots so thick they were denser than a graveyard.

"What does Kane know, Theo?" he asked, folding his hands together.

"No one told him where you are," Theo replied.

My gaze flicked to Victor. His hands were balled into fists. A bead of sweat held on his temple. His glare was on Isaac, looking hungry for his own vengeance.

"Perhaps I wasn't specific enough. Tell me what Kane knows about *me*," Isaac demanded, 'cause he needed to know just how fucked he was. Whether he should flee then, or whether he could take his time.

I peered back toward the laneway as I prodded that connection between my Alpha and I, finding the roll of power and warmth that was decidedly his when I silently called, '*Where are you, Kane?*'

Theo's Adam's apple dipped, muscles straining like he fought to keep his mouth shut. "*Fuck!*" he gritted out. "Everything. He knows everything."

Isaac's face paled to a deathly shade of 'scared shitless'. "Your wolf just couldn't let you go. And now, you're both going to pay for it." He flicked a finger. "Mason. Take Ivy to the car. Lana. Go with them."

Mason dragged the shadow walker, thrashing and spitting. Less defiance, more agony and madness. My mother followed hot on their heels.

I widened my stance. "What're you doing, Isaac?"

He aimed for my mother's vehicle. "Exactly what it looks like, Briar dear."

No. He couldn't leave. Kane needed to kill him. End the compulsion. Get us the Iron Hells outta this! *Where the shadow and sage was he?*

The laugh that broke from me was one hundred percent witch and stall tactic when I taunted, "You're a spineless piece of shit."

His nostrils flared, mouth cinching into a hard line. The glare he threw my way made my blood run cold. "I intend to leave a mess in my wake. And I have no intention of cleaning it up."

"Where are you going?"

He cocked a brow. "Where do you think?"

To Zahara. To Ithica.

The rotation of his head was slow, like he thrived on the tension before he said, "Finish her, Victor. And don't fuck it up this time."

My eyes flew wide.

The Southern Alpha's jaw clenched as he advanced, steps rigid like he fought each one. I scrambled away and Theo dodged into my path, arms out as he faced off with him.

"Come now, Theo. Whose side are you on?" Isaac's smile touched his eyes and his goddamn blackened soul. "Help Victor."

"*KANE! WHERE ARE YOU?*"

Theo stiffened, his movements broken and mechanical, controlled by someone else when he pivoted to face me. His brows were down, eyes pinched at the corner, the definition of tortured. A sheen of sweat slicked his forehead as he fell in step beside Victor. The muscles of his neck strained, and those sable eyes turned glassy. "I'm sorry, Briar."

My lungs refused to work as I backpedaled more, scuffing my feet across the gravel when I sealed my grip around my obsidian and reached for Kane's power.

Ivy's wild gaze jerked toward the forest. The woods were ghostly still. Like a graveyard. Moonlight slashed through the canopy, highlighting the brush beneath it in strips.

Victor's head snapped that way. He cursed. "They're here."

The whites of Isaac's eyes gleamed across the night. Fear. It looked good on him. I wanted to see more.

"Call them, Victor. Now!" he ordered.

The Southern Alpha's hands shook, arm jerking as he raised it and set his fingers to his mouth, then let loose a piercing whistle.

The front door flew wide, and wolves streamed from the house—*Victor's* wolves. Sage, there had to be at least fifty, maybe more. Amber led, that well-honed-bitch stare trained on me. Ezra burst out, expression afflicted as he closed in. My head snapped side to side while I looked for something, *anything* to help.

Two lights blazed in the distance. Voltaic. Familiar. They vanished, then reappeared.

Eyes.

More emerged, scattered through the forest, every shade of fire and metal, and crimson blood. They lit the distant dark and rimmed the trees. A low, rasping growl tore free from the recesses of a very powerful and broad chest before it echoed across the night.

A relieved breath exploded from my lungs. *Kane.*

My pulse quickened when my Alpha stalked from the tree line. The scarce moonlight sharpened the hard planes of his face, casting the rest in shadow. That stare fixed on me.

I winced and poured as much apology into my expression as I could. *It was the only way.*

A barely perceptible nod before his sights trained on Isaac. "You picked the wrong fucking fight."

More wolves followed. Thirty. Forty. Less than Victor's numbers, but not perilously so.

Even in the dim, my stepfather's face fell slack. He swallowed, throat tightening. He took a step back—a coward ready to flee because he'd finally faced off against someone he couldn't control. "Victor, Theo, come to me!"

They stopped, then backpedaled.

Joaquin and Cassandra advanced, flanking Kane's sides. Isaac's attention flicked around. He retreated another step. My heart thrashed against my ribs, eager to see him squirm. To feel that fear. To see him fucking pay.

Cassandra's face angled down, glare boring through her brows. "You took what you should not have taken, Isaac." That predatory lilt was there, but it was different somehow. Darker. Less luring, more ominous. A warning, and a vow. Her incisors lengthened. The whites of her eyes and the hollows beneath blackened. Lines from shadowed veins tracked over her forehead, through her temples, down her cheeks and jaw to her neck.

Iron fires, take me.

This was the Cassandra the hairs on the back of my neck had sensed. The Cassandra everyone revered. She was a carnivore, starved, wild, and ravenous for her next meal. And she hungered for Isaac.

It took everything I had to hold my position while I thanked sage and obsidian and even the shadowed goddamn moon itself that she was on our side, because there were shadow walkers, and then there was *her*.

Joaquin scanned the South Cambrian wolves before he found me.

"Release them and I'll kill you quick, Isaac," Kane ordered.

Isaac's hands trembled. "I'm afraid I can't do that."

Kane rolled his shoulders, then stretched his neck. There was an edge there, different than I'd ever seen. Last time he'd squared off with Victor, there'd been restraint. But whatever self-imposed leash had held him back was torn free and lay mangled at his feet.

Bridging our connection, I said softly into my Alpha's mind, "*I don't think Victor wants this, Kane.*"

"*He's a barrier, Bry. Take Victor out, and Isaac's alone. He's got nothing. No shields. No power. Just him.*"

The Southern Alpha must've come to the same conclusion, 'cause the frantic pants that exploded from him steamed the night air. "You shouldn't be here, Slade."

My Alpha edged forward a sinister step, then another. He stopped, arms loose by his sides. Open. Ready. His power ripped through the area, rocking me back. "I won't be for long."

Victor swallowed hard, head angling down like he tried to shelter his eyes.

The night fell quiet. Not the calm before the storm kind. More like a predator going silent before it struck—and eviscerated.

Sweat glistened along Theo's temple when Victor's wolves spread out in an arc behind him. The Northern Pack moved into position, mirroring them. My shoulders were tight. I held my breath. Sage, there were so many.

Cassandra glided my way, her underworldly attention fixed on Ivy where she stood by my mother's car. "This is no place for you, Briar Stone." The softness in her tone was a stark contrast to her demonic demeanor.

Every one of my survival instincts nodded in unison. But even *if* I could've run, I wouldn't. My claiming mark wasn't just a symbol, it was a tether. Kane and I lived together. We died together. And we brought Isaac's world to its motherfucking knees together.

"You're not the only one who can work a system, Isaac," Kane said, foot torquing into the gravel.

My stepfather's glare landed on me, his skin mottled, fisted hands shaking. I'd fucked up his game, broken his toys. Stolen his power. "You *really* should've listened, Briar."

Kane advanced another step, brash, eager, and a hundred shades of brutal vengeance. "You don't look at her. You don't talk to her. You don't breathe her fucking air." He set his stance, legs bent, feet shoulder-width apart. "You deal with me now."

Isaac edged back, panic flaring in his gaze, followed swiftly by an idea. He ticked his chin up. "Did she figure out how to tell you about *it*, Kane?"

My knees weakened.

Kane's jaw was clenched so hard, he forced his next words through his teeth. "Tell me about what?"

The prickle along my scalp hurt.

Isaac tipped his head toward my stomach. "About what *really* happened to your little mutt?"

Seven Iron Hells. No!

My Alpha froze. *Time* froze. Everyone stilled. The only noise the soft whistle of the wind, the rustle of the trees and the frenetic beat of my heart when it tried to escape my chest. It was like the world held its breath—or *couldn't* breathe. No. Kane wasn't supposed to learn like this. It was supposed to be me; those gut-wrenching words coming from *my* lips. Just the two of us, alone, where we could grieve together. *No!*

"You took my child," Isaac said, antagonism and malevolence warring for dominance in the smile that spread across his lips. He cocked his head. "So, I took yours."

The words dropped like a hammer, shattering that wall of secrets. Kane's eyes crushed closed for a fraction of a second before they reopened. His stare was unfocused, doubtless lost in the barrage of memories and questions that beat down on his mind. He pivoted my way.

My world dropped out from beneath me at the question in those eyes: *Is it true?* Is it true he tortured you? Is it true you went through that alone? Is it true he took our *fucking child*?

"Tell him, Briar," Isaac swept an arm my way. "Let it all out."

The order cleared a path, shifting some of his barriers. Tears pricked my eyes and blurred my vision. I swiped them away and offered my Alpha a single, solemn, heart-wrenching nod.

Kane's shoulders sank, and his stare hollowed, a desolate torment taking root in those silver topaz eyes. His chest heaved, collapsing on every exhale. He was lost in a storm of agony for one heartbeat. Two. Three. Four. Those breaths slowed, then steadied. That stare lifted, homing in as he gathered his storm and rose to his full, sinister height. His neck and torso grew taut, his jaw locked down, glare sharpening like a knife—one he aimed Isaac's way.

The skin ripped from Kane's hands. His boned claws extended. He bared his canines. His voice was Alpha, and guttural and sheer apex predator as he spoke. "Your death will be slow. It will be bloody. And it *will* be fucking painful."

My chest tightened. Please, sage.

"Victor," Isaac scurried quickly away. "Kill Kane."

Chapter Twenty-Seven

Victor stripped his dress coat, chucking it aside, head low, shoulders rounded and eyes wild when he advanced.

A rasped growl tore from Kane's throat. Isaac might've been his target, but like it or not, Victor stood in the way. Kane faced off with the Southern Alpha. "Consider this a challenge, Victor. Winner takes all."

"You don't wanna do this, Slade," Victor told him.

"Yeah. I do," Kane said, hard and sure and a goddamn vow. "I come for what's mine, Victor. If going through you is how I get to him, then so fucking be it." He chucked his chin to Joaquin. "Handle Theo."

The Beta's stare held on a trembling Ezra. He nodded, then aimed Theo's way.

The air was so thick with tension, it made it hard to breathe. Power grazed my flesh. The Northern Pack set their positions. The Southern Pack readied.

Victor's claws tore free and extended. He exploded forward. Kane stood stock still, anticipating. Victor lunged, swinging wide for Kane's throat. My Alpha dropped low and ducked under it, then rose with a snap. Arcing his arm back, he caught Victor with a backfist across the face. There was a sickening crunch of bone before Kane's claws ripped the flesh over Victor's cheek and nose wide.

Victor stumbled aside and snarled, but Kane was on him again before he could reset. My Alpha stabbed forward. Fast. So damn fast I could hardly track it. Victor shifted and the strike punctured his shoulder. He howled and spit. Blood poured from the wound, staining his suit.

The wolves were restless. Waiting.

Isaac crept back.

My gaze darted around. My mother, Ivy and Mason stood by the car, frozen with Isaac's order. I needed to get to them. Get them out of there—out of Isaac's clutches. I took a step to the side, then forward.

"No," Cassandra warned me.

Kane gripped Victor and ripped him from the ground as he advanced, driving him into the passenger side of my mother's car. The metal buckled, leaving a body-sized imprint. Victor's grunt morphed into a fluid-filled snarl. He thrust a kick down and forward, catching Kane in the knee. Kane's stare narrowed, but he didn't retreat. Victor kicked again, trying to force my Alpha back. Kane rolled his fist closed one finger at a time, then aimed his claws straight at Victor's chest.

The whites of Victor's eyes reflected the moon—and his panic. A sharp breath rasped from my throat, dread wrapping its talons around my spine.

"KILL SLADE!" he roared, the command careening through the air.

Amber screamed, the sound agony. Loath her to the depths of my marrow though I might, on wanting Kane alive, we could both agree.

Wraith take me. Kane was strong, but not take-on-fifty-fucking-weres-alone strong. "KANE!" For the briefest of moments, our gazes met through the anarchy. My heart seized when I said inside his mind, "*Don't you die on me. Don't you fucking die!*"

He looked away.

Ezra and every other South Cambrian wolf burst forward, but their claws and canines didn't extend when they descended on my Alpha.

Kane was there for me, for Theo, and Lucas. For Naomi and everyone else. Anthony'd sacrificed himself for Olive. And I had not one shred of doubt, if our lives weren't tethered, Kane *would* do the same for me. Victor's death cleared a path to Isaac, one that made the world safer for his son. For a minute, I'd thought I'd seen something in him. That he cared for anything more than himself. But when push came to shove, Victor just cared about Victor.

Joaquin grabbed Ezra and Theo, taking them to ground and pinning them both while the Northern Pack launched into the fray. Claws and bodies collided. The Southern wolves scrambled for Kane. Ours intercepted. Fists flew. Blood misted the air. Victor and two other wolves charged at my Alpha.

Isaac slithered away like the spineless snake he was as he made for my mother's car, ordering her, Mason and Ivy, "Get in!"

The fire in my veins ignited. I wanted to watch, make sure my Alpha was alright, to enjoy every blow he landed, but the endgame was Isaac. Stopping him meant stopping the carnage. I hoped.

I bolted, giving chase. "ISAAC!"

Cassandra flew past and my hair snapped in her wind, that preternatural speed impossible to track. Isaac and the other's reached for their doors. The Dowager grabbed the car by the trunk. It groaned, metal crunching when she lifted, then whipped it toward the house. Stone snapped and shattered before the vehicle crashed to the ground, clearing her path.

Shadow and sage.

Isaac's expression grew slack.

Three of the Southern wolves veered our way, beelining straight for me. They must've counted ending me as ending Kane, because their canines were bared, bodies poised for a killing blow. Bile scorched my tongue, coating it with a putrid taste.

"GET TO BRY!" Kane roared. "GET TO FUCKING BRY!"

Cassandra lunged fangs first as she tore into the lead were's throat. Blood spurted in waves from the gaping, jagged hole she'd made. His eyes flew wide and he gripped his neck. She spat a clump of meat to the ground at her feet. It landed with a thwack, a sinewed strand of ... something hanging from her bottom lip.

That bile climbed higher.

The other two weres went wide, coming at me from both sides.

I reached for that wolf—that power. "This is a bad idea," I told them, hands out like it could ward them off.

"We don't have a choice," the female to my left said.

No, they didn't. And they'd pay the price for their Alpha's cowardice.

They pounced.

Cassandra hissed when her foot punctured the abdomen of the one to my right. Kane's strength tore through me when I sidestepped. My arm shot out, clotheslining the female so hard, a loud crack filled the night. The wolf fell to her back. She stared skyward, eyes rolling in and out of focus. Cassandra moved in and drove her heel down, puncturing the female's skull. Bone and ligament and muscle snapped and popped when she broke through.

Flicking her foot to clear the carnage, Cassandra offered me a delicate nod. "Good work, Briar Stone." Taking my arm, she dragged me away. "Come, now. I failed Anthony Bruno at his end. I will not do the same again. We must get to Ivy Trevino and finish this."

My face twisted. "Ivy?" I shook my head and corrected, "We need to kill *Isaac*."

"No, Briar Stone."

No? *No?* He was the whole goddamn point.

Her blackened eyes turned dull. "He is not your master."

I froze. Master. She'd used the word before. I tripped over the word until I got so tangled in it, I couldn't focus on anything else. There were two things that word could mean; the one who'd executed the compulsion, or . . .

Power of obsidian. How had I missed it? Compulsion was tethered to venom, and venom was tethered to the shadow walker. Isaac might've stripped Ivy's genetic marker, made it so *she* couldn't command, but its *power* was still hers. Tethered to *her* life. Just like Anthony's compulsion failed when he'd died, so would Ivy's.

Isaac wasn't my master.

Holy shit! Holyshitholyshitholyshit! Realization hit and my heart plummeted. Ivy needed to die for our freedom. Because of *Isaac*.

Rage seared my veins, rolling through me like fire.

"Stay with me, Briar Stone," Cassandra said as we closed in on my stepfather.

His stare danced between the Dowager and I when he pulled something from his pocket. A key. It sizzled against his flesh when he unlatched Ivy's cuffs and ordered her, "Finish Cassandra."

Mason and mom stood like pillars amidst the carnage, my mother's chest heaved, breaths breaking from her in short, shallow pants.

"Run!" I told them.

She shook her head, lip trembling when she breathed, "We can't."

Ivy scraped a hand over her face as she spat and snarled and shook her head like a feral dog. The cuffs clanked where they hung from her right wrist. A flicker of crimson sputtered in the recesses of her eyes, like a flame readying to die.

Cassandra faced off with her. "Free them, my child."

Ivy dropped to all fours and scuttled to the side. She stretched her jaw, stare on her Dowager. "Can't."

The black around Cassandra's eyes deepened, stealing all the light it touched. "Then you know what I must do."

Ivy's neck rotated at an awkward angle.

Kane roared and my head snapped his way. One of Victor's weres clung to my Alpha, canines sinking into his shoulder. Kane grabbed the back of the wolf's neck, ripped him forward, then launched a blow straight for his chest. His fist punched through the ribs with a snap, hand plunging deep before he tore it free. I sucked a sharp gasp at the sight of the beating heart in his brutal grasp. Kane crushed it and that soft muscle eked between his fingers.

Ivy inhaled a shriek and made for Cassandra. She swiped at her Dowager's stomach. Cassandra dodged, lips pulling back from her teeth, all pretenses of humanity gone. Her knee came up, catching Ivy in the chin.

Movement to my right brought my head around.

Isaac lurked behind my mother, stroking her hair like she was some well-trained pet. He drew an iron knife from behind his back and set the blade across her neck. It sizzled, burning her skin. Steam rose while an acrid scent drifted on the air. His head canted down when he glared at me through his brows. "Where's my son, Briar?"

I shook my head. "Not here."

Mason's shoulders were tight as he watched on.

Isaac's stare tinged a vicious shade of retribution. "You should know, she has them, Briar."

My eyes narrowed in question.

"The were serums." His tone turned mocking. "The ones your poor Naomi's severed pieces helped make."

Sweet fucking sage. He really hadn't needed me anymore.

Mom whimpered when Isaac dragged her around Victor's SUV, out of sight of the others, and pressed that knife deeper.

I swallowed hard and edged forward, following. "Let her go, Isaac."

Another growl from Kane. Savage. Weaker. My gaze shot his way, then back to Isaac.

My stepfather's laugh was darkness and vengeance. It was a promise of pain. And it was the most terrifying sound I'd ever heard.

"Don't move, now." He chucked his chin my way. "It's imperative you watch."

My body locked, adrenaline kicking into overdrive. "What are you—"

He jerked my mother's hair, wrenching her neck back. His skin rippled, eyes morphing from violet to cobalt.

I hyperventilated when my world tipped its axis. "ISAAC, NO!"

Ivy's body went airborne, crashing against Victor's hood before she rolled to the ground. Cassandra rounded the vehicle, dress torn, incisors bared. Her stare snapped from Isaac's rippling form to me.

It didn't take a genius to connect the dots, a fact that was obvious in those creased, crimson eyes when they speared me. Isaac was a changeling and Lucas his son. I'd known her painful truth, and I'd kept that secret. Isaac lied—no surprise there. But more than that, *I'd* lied. To her. My friend.

My gaze pinched at the corners, guilt stinging my chest when I breathed, "I'm sorry."

Isaac cursed. Too late. He was caught as his hair slithered from his scalp like thousands of mahogany-colored snakes. His body curved and his clothes distorted. Shadow and fucking sage. My mother's face. *He'd taken my mother's face.*

Ivy snarled and dove for Cassandra. The Dowager's fangs extended as she swung, catching Ivy across the jaw with a blow that would've cleaved me in two.

A sob broke from my mother while tears streaked her face. She shook so violently, her teeth clicked. "I'm sorry, Briar. I love you."

"No, mom." No apologies. Apologies were for ends, and that wasn't going to happen. "LET HER FUCKING GO, ISAAC!"

"You never learn, do you?" His stare flicked past us. "Tit for tat, Briar. You take from me, I take from you. It's what we do." He smiled. "Say goodbye, now." Isaac's empty stare was so cutting, it speared me through when he swung wide and plunged the knife into her temple.

I screamed, air leaving my lungs as I reached for her, but his order locked me in place.

My mother's body jerked, eyes flying wide. Her arms snapped straight and rigid. Blood spurted everywhere. It painted my face, hers, it dusted the air and poured from the wound, pulsing in time with her waning heart.

Victor's voice was broken and a grated exhaustion when he bellowed, "Get Briar! Kill her, we kill him! Kill her, we kill *him*!"

Iron fires take me.

Another roar from Kane, followed by a screech from Ivy.

My stepfather's gaze met mine, a dark smile in those eyes at that revelation, like Victor'd no doubt intended. He shoved my mother's limp body aside, then threw open the SUV's door. "I'll see you around, Briar." Climbing in, he turned it over. The clunk when he shifted it into gear sounded out before he fled.

"Mom! MOM!" I cried.

She collapsed to her side. No! She couldn't die. I needed her. She couldn't fucking die!

Dropping to my knees, I reached for her. Our fingers brushed. "Mom. Don't go, mom. Stay with me." My tears fell free, streaking my face. "*Stay with me!*"

Wolves closed in. Kane's. Victor's. They circled me, biting and tearing and snarling. The South fighting forward, the North fighting back.

Ivy crouched, setting her position, and leapt. Cassandra's hand snapped up, then sealed around her throat. Ivy thrashed and whipped her iron cuffs into Cassandra's face.

The Dowager's head sagged. "I am sorry it took me so long, child. Rest in the shadows." She shrieked a shattered death cry that rang through the night and echoed across my soul. Gripping tight, she pulled, cleaving Ivy's head from her body.

A whoosh of rescinded power ripped through me, tearing Isaac's walls apart brick by brick. I sagged as it crumbled, then collapsed, imploding to dust. My head swam, I grew dizzy and buckled forward. The world spun, body trembling hard. The compulsion vanished. My body was light. My breaths deep.

Free. I was free.

I scrambled to my mother's side and ran a hand over her hair. "It's okay. It's okay. It's okay." I chanted it like a mantra. Or a wish. It had to be true. We needed more time. We needed to grieve and live and love. I couldn't lose her. I'd just gotten her back. Lucas needed her. *I* needed her. *We couldn't fucking lose her!*

She coughed. Blood sprayed from her mouth, fanning over the ground. Even under the faint moonlight, the paling of her skin was clear. Iron Hells, so pale. Unsurvivably pale. Her stare grew distant.

Mason's expression was creased as he crouched across from me, focus on my mother when he uttered, "Shadow and sage."

"No, mom! No, no, *no*!" I threw my arms over her chest and my voice shattered when I cried, "I love you. I love you! Don't leave, mom. *Please*!"

Her hand fell to the ground and her face grew slack.

My eyes blurred, the tears so thick, I could only see shapes. The hint of movement. I scrubbed them until my mother's lifeless body came clear. A keening sound tore from me, and even to my own ears, it was blood curdling.

Dead. She was dead. Gone. Forever. All that time, that opportunity, lost. Because of *him*.

Kane grunted. I chanced a glance. Fifteen feet away, he staggered to the side, soaked in blood. Long gashes cleaved his torso, and back. Whether Isaac's control was gone didn't matter, because Kane's challenge had been made . . . a challenge that required an end. And seeing Victor still stood, so did his command.

My Alpha squared off to Victor and two of his wolves. One sliced a wide gouge across Kane's back. The second, his chest. Kane dodged and struck, catching the latter in the side, but it was weaker.

Iron fucking fires. My Alpha couldn't take that onslaught. Panic swelled, and my heart rate quickened. I needed to do something. Stop them. Help!

The wolf to Kane's left thrust a kick at his knee. It cracked, then bent at an impossible angle. Kane grunted and dropped.

My breath pushed through my teeth as my glare landed on Victor. I couldn't lose anything else. Wouldn't. Reaching for the knife, I pulled it from my mother's skull.

Mason froze. "Briar, what are you—"

Shoving to my feet, I ran, driving my legs as hard as they could go. I weaved through the fray, feinting left and right as I dodged elbows and claws and snapping maws.

A Southern female pivoted my way.

Gripping my obsidian tight, I drew on that power and kicked out, planting my foot in the center of her chest. It knocked her back, and she collapsed onto her ass. I kept going. Her hand snapped out, latching over my ankle. I stumbled and fell.

"Secure Slade!" Victor ordered his wolves.

Six of his weres dogpiled Kane, three per arm. My Alpha's stare met mine over Victor's shoulder.

"Get the hells outta here, banshee!" Joaquin bellowed, gripping Ezra in one hand as he slammed another were to the ground.

The female wolf crawled toward me. I snapped my elbow back using that power, colliding with her jaw. It cracked, sitting off-angle as she howled and ambled back.

Theo fought against the onslaught, but whether he aimed for me or his cousin, I couldn't say.

Amber's wails pierced the night.

My pulse thrashed in my ears, breaths short and shallow. My gaze locked with the Beta's. "DO IT!" I said, then made to throw the knife his way.

Something powerful rolled deep in his eyes. He shook his head.

Victor set his stance, and drew back his arm, the clawed death blow aimed straight for Kane's throat.

Joaquin ran, his own boned claws extending. "VICTOR!" he boomed, the savagery in his voice more Alpha than Victor'd ever be.

Victor wheeled to face him.

The Beta bared his teeth, shoved Ezra away from the carnage, and lunged, closing that final distance between them. My heart stopped as Joaquin swung, ramming his claws into the hollow under Victor's chin where they lodged in his brain. Victor's eyes bulged, his mouth nailed shut. Blood seeped from the corner of his lips, slithering down.

Joaquin torqued his arm, twisting those claws before he ripped them free. Victor convulsed as his limbs kicked and jolted, the front of his dress pants soaking through when he pissed himself.

His jaw hung loose while he stutter-stepped to the side as his knees bent and buckled. He collapsed face first onto the ground, body making a sickening thump when it landed. His eyes grew distant, then dark. He jerked, and twitched, before he fell still.

I dropped the knife.

Power snapped through the air and Joaquin's spine arched back when it flooded him. His eyes sparked and blazed as he roared.

Every South Cambrian were left standing stumbled back. The six holding Kane released and threw their hands up, disengaging. A surrender. An apology. Bodies littered the ground, so mangled they were barely recognizable.

My Alpha's chest heaved, breaths exploding in shallow bursts. Blood poured from his face and torso, soaking his hair. His clothes. I crawled to him but stopped short. He was mangled and broken. I didn't know where to touch. Where I wouldn't make it worse.

His mangled leg righted, those wounds pulling at the ends, slowly stitching together, and every thread of those scars was like a patch over my heart.

Kane was alive. We were okay.

He rose, then stumbled as he limped forward, sealing the distance between us. His eyes blazed, him or the wolf, I didn't know. His jaw clenched, muscles there pulsing when he looked me up and down then ground out, "You're alright?"

My voice was hoarse and low when I said, "I'm alright."

A nod. Stiff. Unsure. "Tell me he's fucking dead."

My chest tightened. I shook my head.

He winced. "You're still—"

"No." I edged closer. "We're free."

His shoulders sagged. "Then get the fuck over here and touch me, Bry."

Touch him. Sage, it was a simple request, but I held that tempestuous stare as, slowly, I settled my palms against his stomach and let my fingers sink into him.

Free. I was free.

A sob broke from me. His arm shot out and he jerked me to him. Setting his chin on my hair, he snarled. "You're in so much goddamn trouble."

I angled up while my tears rained down, streaming over my cheeks as I set my lips to his. That calloused thumb came up and tracked them aside. Our tongues met, and I tasted him. His blood.

His head drew back, taking me in again as he scented. His eyes narrowed, his next words level when he asked, "Why are you covered in Lana's blood, Bry?"

My gaze drifted to where she lay, Mason still crouched and shell-shocked by her side. Kane followed my line of sight. His hold cinched tighter.

"Please, Joaquin," Amber begged. "It was Isaac. Please!"

"It wasn't all Isaac." He rolled his shoulders, eyes blazing when he boomed, "You're fucking out."

Another wave of power tore through the night. Amber's mouth opened, a shrill shriek tearing from her throat. She sucked in a gasping breath. Her neck strained, eyes ablaze. It was different somehow. Less a gathering of strength and more a release of it.

What the Iron Hells?

Kane threw me behind him.

I gripped his side. "What's going on?"

"Joaquin's throwing her from the Pack."

My head drew back. A lone wolf.

Amber gasped and stumbled, then collapsed to her back. She writhed, heels scuffing the ground as she kicked. Those kicks slowed. She fell still, staring skyward as she sucked in air and steadied herself.

The new Southern Alpha turned his back on her, guiding a shaken Ezra with him as he closed in on us. His body was strained, eyes creased like that he concentrated, adjusting to that new power when he said, "She's on her own."

Theo hobbled our way. He was battered and beaten, but still alive when he found me and grinned. "You did it."

I swallowed around the lump in my throat. "It wasn't me."
A new fear took root as my head whipped around finding Cassandra gone. And after the truth I'd kept, I couldn't blame her. But Lucas—

Yeah, Kane had ordered Cassian not to let anyone in which might've thwarted Isaac, but the Dowager was strong. Too strong. I gripped my obsidian to shield our conversation. "Cassandra knows, Kane. She knows about Isaac. About Lucas."

He cursed and his hand locked over mine. We ran, and his legs pumped fast, dragging me as we aimed us for the truck.

Whipping the driver's door open, he practically threw me inside.

"Isaac has a scar on his right hand," I blurted. "It doesn't matter what shape he takes, it follows him."

He inclined the head, turned the vehicle over, and it rumbled loudly. Jamming it into gear, he punched the gas. The tires chirped as we fled. He dragged me to him and held tight, that touch saying what neither of us could voice. *Please, Sage, let Lucas be alright.*

My heart refused to beat. There was only my brother. I'd already lost mom, I couldn't lose him too. I fucking couldn't.

Time dragged as we careened through Cambria, crossing the neutral grounds to the north before we veered onto our road. The driveway came into view. Then the house.

My throat tightened.

Kane flew into the driveway. We screeched to a halt and burst out.

Cassian was there, body coiling.

"You're released from the command," Kane roared as we barreled up the stairs. Cassian moved aside as my Alpha reached the door first and surged inside.

I held my breath as I crossed over next.

Cassian followed, hands raised. "He's safe."

My head snapped to the left. Lucas sat on the couch, tears streaking his face. A relieved whimper escaped me as I careened across the room and threw myself around him. My Alpha closed in, engulfing us with that unyielding hold.

Safe. Lucas was safe. Alive. Not out of danger, not even close. But alive.

"Are you guys alright?" he asked, the words high and tight.

I nodded against him, voice shuddering from me when I breathed, "We are now."

His breath hitched. "It's gone," he said. "The compulsion—"

I hiccupped a sob. "I know." I squeezed him hard. Together. We were together. No longer prisoners. Unrestrained.

Fucking free.

Epilogue

My scarlet, strapless dress clung to my body, cutting just above the knees as I strode down the condo hall. My date with Kane had finally come, but with the threats looming over us, we weren't exactly ready for public consumption.

Isaac had vanished. Seeing Bower'd locked the borders tight, I could only assume he was still in Cambria. Doubtless, he'd taken another face, hence the horde of Kane's Pack surrounding the house while Lucas and Hannah had a date of their own. Supervised, of course . . . by Theo. And I wasn't overly confident that was better.

Joaquin had spent the time cleaning up the mess Isaac and Victor had made with his Pack before settling Victor's stepson into a new home. He'd taken to his Alpha seat well. And it suited him.

My hair wisped, its soft waves falling back over my shoulder as I moved. Easy music played from the living room as my heels clicked and I sashayed that way.

The table and room were filled with candles. My Alpha's musk and wilderness scent filled my senses and soothed my soul.

Kane stood, wearing head-to-toe black in his dress pants and shirt. They hugged his body, showing off those rigid lines of muscle. His hungry stare took me in, those hooded, molten eyes holding mine like he made sure I was real. Every night, every morning. It was always the same. He refused to be separated or let me out of his sight. He wasn't willing to lose me. Not again. And I thanked the Iron Hells for it every damn second of every damn day.

"Hi," I breathed.

It'd been just over two weeks since everything with Isaac went down. Between the unfinished business with my stepfather, Zahara, and the unknowns of Cassandra, it wore on him. Wore on us both. Especially after we'd sent some *vaguely* worded letters to the Conclave about what'd gone down, leaving out the potentially problematic bits about what Isaac was and Ivy, Danika's now gone sister, being the source of that venom.

Extending a calloused hand, Kane skimmed it over my waist, then pulled me close.

His wounds had healed, adding a macabre collage of new scars to his tally. Sage, so many scars. But he was alive. And he was mine.

I pursed my lips when that guilt ridden, bitter tang pervaded my mouth because I was lucky, but Cassandra . . . She hadn't answered any of my or Kane's calls, not when I'd told her I was sorry. When I'd explained about Isaac's scar. When I'd invited her to the small goodbye we'd planned to hold. Still, no angry shadow walker horde had arrived on our step calling for Lucas's head, so I could only assume she hadn't said anything. Yet.

That goodbye that'd been three days before—one that'd been simple, and beyond beautiful. We'd laid flowers in our lake, speaking for each person. My mother and father, Naomi, Anthony, Ivy, Frances . . . our child. Tears fell. Hearts broke and mended. And I'd wished Cassandra was there.

Of course I'd had to protect Lucas, but Cassandra was a friend. She'd fought for me and killed one of her own to free us all from Isaac's prison. I couldn't just let that go. I needed to find a way to thank her, to mend things. But under the circumstances, I had not one clue how to do it.

I tucked tighter against Kane and trailed a finger over his chest.

He loosed a deep, shuddering exhale.

I'd filled him in on Zahara and the serums, but the name returned nothing on his search. Ithica'd played their cards tight to their chests, so what their next move was, I had no damn clue.

Kane must've read my thoughts from my expression because he hooked a squared knuckle under my chin and angled me up to better see him. "We'll figure it out, Bry. But not tonight." He grazed my cheek with the rough stubble of his jaw. "Tonight is for us."

My nod was soft as my arms looped around his neck. "Thank you for coming for me."

His hand tracked back, twisting around my hair. "I'd raze the fucking world for you."

I bit my lip, worrying it between my teeth. "I'm sorry."

That brow dropped in a "*What the hells for?*" expression.

"For putting you through . . . all of it. If it weren't for Isaac in my life, he'd never have been in yours."

His grip flexed against me. Less anger, more control. "If you ever apologize for that again," he tipped his head to the side, "I'll heave you out the window."

The ghost of a smile haunted my lips. I'd told him everything my stepfather had done, all the horrid bits and details I'd been forced to hold back. The truth about Ronin, Jared, Anthony, my brother, mother and father, our baby. Everything. He'd held me, then held Lucas. Started mending those wounds, but there were others I was sure would never heal.

I took his face between my hands. "You're all I want, Kane. You're all I've ever wanted." I poked his chest with the tip of my finger. "And if you ever doubt that again, I'll heave *you* out the window!"

A huff of laughter. The arch of his playful brow. "You'll do what?"

I rolled my eyes. "Fine. I'll feebly and unsuccessfully push you towards it!"

"You'll try." His mouth descended on mine, tongue tracing a languid line over my own as he kissed me deep. Kissed me with his whole damn body. Pulling back, he set me at arm's length, then cleared his throat.

"I want you, Bry. Every goddamn piece. You and Luke, you're all I need." Reaching into his pocket, he lowered himself down and took a knee.

I sucked in a sharp gasp, hands flying to my mouth.

His breaths were rough and ragged when he raised the three-carat princess-cut diamond ring high. "Marry me, Bry. Shadowed fucking moon, just marry me. Please."

My breath hitched. Tears pricked my eyes, then trickled down my cheeks. How long had I waited for those words? Dreamed of them? Too long. I wouldn't wait another second. "I love you, Kane. Only you." My arms lowered, touch grazing his mouth. "I want your name. I want your body. I want every piece of you. Always have. Always will. You're it for me."

The tension in the lines of his chest eased as he took my hands, kissed the heart tattoo over the inside of my right wrist, then slipped that ring into place over the left finger—a perfect fit. It felt right. It felt good.

My heart fluttered like a hummingbird's wings as I squealed and threw myself at him. He huffed a rough laugh when he crushed me to him. My tongue flicked out, tasting his jaw, then his throat.

I moaned and smiled against him, but that smile faltered when an ache in my lower abdomen made me pull away and flinch.

Kane tucked several loose strands of hair back from my face. "What's wrong?"

"I'm fine." I said, but his grip cinched tighter. Softening my expression, I gave him a reassuring smile. "I just need a minute, Big Bad. I won't be long."

His eyes were narrowed, his nod tight.

Withdrawing from his grasp, I aimed for the washroom, then closed myself in. Popping open the medicine cabinet, I reached for my monthly lady products. My eyes lit on the series of boxes next to them and I froze. That ache took my stomach again.

Wait.

Staring at my reflection, I ticked off the days on my fingers. Then ticked them off again. The weight loss, my insatiable appetite. I'd chalked them up to my circumstance . . . Kane's power.

My pulse thrashed in my ears while I gazed into nothing. There'd been so much happening, I'd completely lost track. Hadn't even considered.

It *was* possible. It was. And I prayed to the wraith and the Seven Iron Hells I was right. Grabbing one of the pregnancy tests from the shelf, I fumbled like a fool as I tore open the package, used it, then waited. And waited.

And waited.

Please, sage. Let it be real. I needed this. A light in the dark. A gift. A life. *Please!*

The result came clear. My heart stopped.

I glanced around, forcing my brain to kick in. It didn't work. "Kane!" I uttered, trying to find my voice. I had to tell him. Needed to. I spun, unlocking the door. "KANE!"

"BRY?" he roared, voice strained as he exploded into the washroom. His grip latched over the doorframe, eyes molten, body taut, and ready for slaughter. He took me in. "What's wrong?"

My throat seized around the words and my hands flew to my mouth. Tears stung my eyes. I looked down, back up, then down.

He took my shoulders. "I need you to talk to me, Bry." The tension and sheer terror in those words snapped my mind back into gear.

Last time things had been perilous. Last time he'd learned in the worst way. Last time we'd lost everything. But this was different. I wanted it to be special. To be right. But how in the bloody sage did I tell him? I hadn't thought it through. Simple. Simple was always best. And if I couldn't find the words, then I guessed there was only one option left.

A lone tear skimmed down my cheek. I smiled, weepy but broad, then set my hand against my lower abdomen—my womb—and cradled it.

His stare dropped there and held while the clues clicked together. His voltaic eyes flew wide. His head snapped up. Those warm hands took my face between them, wrapping into my hair. "You're sure?"

I grabbed the test off the counter and showed him. He stared at it like he needed that confirmation. Something tangible. Real. Shadow and sage, like his life depended on it.

His chest rattled on a ragged exhale. "You're fucking sure?"

My soul breathed easy. "I'm sure."

A choked sound escaped him before his mouth collided with mine.

It was our second chance. Our time to make a family of our own—us, Lucas, and our child. *His* child. Rebuild what'd been taken. Together.

Bending, he gripped the back of my thighs and lifted. I quiet-squeaked as he hooked my legs around him. His hand skimmed my spine when he aimed us for the bedroom, then lowered me to the mattress, giving it our weight. His stare misted, going glassy and bloodshot.

The feelings that barreled through me were so wild, I could scarce control them. I loved him. I loved him with everything I was and everything I'd ever be. And this moment was ours.

He broke from my lips and pressed his face into the curve of my neck. "Fucking hells, thank you." His voice was hoarse when it grazed my flesh, and the raw emotion there had me curling tighter around him.

Thank you, as if it was a gift. As if it was the world. As if *I'd* given it to him.

The curve of my mouth reached my eyes and tickled my soul. "You helped, you know."

His laugh was rich, and thick, and rumbled over me. Through me. "This is all I've ever wanted, Bry. You. Luke." His hands plunged into my hair, and he tipped his chin toward my abdomen. "A family."

A family. His family. *Our* family.

My heart filled to the edge, shifting, growing, making room because it wasn't big enough. It'd *never* be big enough.

His mouth found mine again, the kiss gentle. Our tongues met, gliding in an easy dance. I sighed into him. My body heated, warmth pooling between my thighs. Power of obsidian. Would I ever get enough of that man?

My hands raked down his back. Want, need, desperation. "Take me, Kane. Now."

A grin took him, one that morphed from warm, to hungry, to eager and roguish. He ranged over me, torso pressing against my breasts. A low growl echoed through his chest. Fumbling, I unfastened his pants, then drew down his boxers. He locked his arms around my waist and shifted to his knees. Taking the hem of my dress, he tore it up my body, then shredded my thong.

Those eyes flashed as they raked from my slit to my stomach, up to my breasts, then my claiming mark. "Hold onto me, Bry."

I held that wild gaze as my touch looped over his shoulders and around his neck.

"Tighter than that," he ordered.

I squirmed in the happiest of dances and latched on.

He nudged my legs apart. I opened for him, straddling his body while he placed his rock-hard shaft against my clit and arced his hips, sliding over it. A riot of pleasure chased through me. I hissed.

"You like that?" he taunted when he arced his hips again, and again, and again.

Iron Hells, he was so damn good. He knew my body. Knew every corner, every nerve. Knew what I wanted. What I needed. I trailed my tongue along his throat and purred in answer.

He positioned his cock at my apex. "Ready?"

My smile was sweet, and seductive and all for him when I uttered, "What are you waiting for?"

He thrust in, hard and deep, then set a ruthless pace. I gasped when he filled me to completion. Our eyes met, that voltaic stare bordering feral.

The sounds of our bodies colliding, of our savage breaths, and ravenous sounds filled the world. My orgasm rose, building like a fire in my core.

"Fuck!" he snarled.

His hips arced with a snap, and I cried out. His jaw clenched, teeth bared as he grunted and slammed into me again, and again, and again.

My climax erupted through me, chasing along every nerve as my core locked around him. He growled, body bucking wildly before he jerked, and groaned. His cock jolted as he came, his seed flooding me, filling me with that heat.

He kept moving until he slowed, and our sated bodies collapsed back onto the bed.

Looming over me, he edged his way down, lowering his face to my stomach before he brushed his mouth over it. I smiled, fingers threading into his hair.

"Our baby," he said.

"Our baby," I breathed.

He nuzzled that soft flesh above my womb, and my heart shuddered a happy beat when he said so low, I could scare hear, "I fucking love you."

★★★

Immortal Inc was warm. Heat from the midday sun kissed my skin as it beat through the window. The neon yellow of the "Open" sign glowed bright. The day of the grand opening had finally come with everything in its place. Those hardwood floors were finished, the tattoo chairs uncovered and in position. Business cards were set up on the counters. Several pieces of Lucas's artwork sat framed on the wall, along with a photo of the original shop. The new Persian rug I'd picked out that tied in all the blacks, and teals, scarlets and bronzes sat just inside the entrance. The place looked so damn good, it tickled my heart.

Small tables lined the perimeter where I stood readying the food for our soon-to-be-customers. My knife made a wet, tearing sound followed by a thud as it hit the cutting board when I chopped the cabbage into thin lines. Tear. Thud. Tear. Thud. Finished, I scooped those choppings into the mixing bowl for the coleslaw.

Kane stood less than three feet away, organizing things for the barbecue. A barbecue strategically placed directly outside the main entrance for my Alpha to keep watch . . . and check every hand that passed for Isaac's scar—discreetly, of course. But Isaac wouldn't show, not without his preternatural shields, seeing he was on his goddamn own. Finally.

That gnawing pit in my stomach just kept growing because Lucas's secret was no longer safe. Because I had no clue how many people actually knew it. And because Isaac had fled with his lab. Chances of him getting his hands on another shadow walker were slim. And even *if* he managed, Cambria knew his game. Knew what to look for. His jig was up.

Still, he had Zahara in his back pocket—or whatever the hells her name was. With his supplies, slipping her that subsequent were serum he'd promised wasn't off the table. And if that happened, sage help us, 'cause the wraith herself only knew what'd come next. But everything in me said we'd be finding out.

My Alpha's stare tracked to me, down over my teal, strapless cocktail dress that fit like a glove where it hugged my curves before it landed on my still-flat tummy, then back. My heart thudded a happy beat. It was hard to keep my mouth shut and not share that news, but we'd agreed. With Isaac gone to ground, we needed to be ready for whatever trouble could come our way. The last thing we wanted was something he could use against us. Or worse, try and take.

"Are you sure I can't help with anything?" Hannah asked, hands linked before her while she pressed up onto her toes.

Lucas brushed back his carefully coiffed hair, adjusting a piece that'd fallen out of place before he stepped in behind her and set a hand over her low back.

I bit my cheek to fight my grin. "No, no." My engagement ring reflected the black crystal chandelier above me when I flicked my wrist, waving her off. "The wolves and I have got this."

Feet aching, I shifted my weight. Turned out my wolfy lover'd been right when he'd thought carrying his baby would be a job of its own.

A thump, thump, thump pounded the entrance as someone beat on it. My eyes snapped that way, spine locking up while my hands started to tremble.

Kane stalked to me, those calloused palms gripping my hips when he spun me to face him. Loose fist hooking under my chin, he angled my gaze to his. "I've got you, Bry."

I nodded. I wanted to pretend what'd happened hadn't left its mark. That I wasn't terrified of every-goddamn-thing, but I was. And Kane being my shadow, refusing to leave my side, was the balm I needed.

He took my hand and tucked me flush behind him as he stalked to the door. His shoulders were relaxed, posture easy when he gripped the handle and swung the entrance wide.

Theo discreetly flashed his hand for I.D. then sauntered in, several packs of hotdogs in hand. "The party's here," he said, pushing past as he headed deeper inside.

I shook off my momentary fear when I mumbled, "Please, come in. Make yourself at home."

His stride was quick, like he was on a mission. He waved me off and stopped several feet away, then frowned. He scratched his head and peered back toward us. "So, uh, is Whitney coming?"

Kane and I joined the others again and set about organizing things. I smirked, my Whitney-tinged jealousy long since gone . . . well, maybe not *long*. "Possibly."

He stalked to Kane's tray of supplies, ripped the bag of hotdogs open and plunked them onto a plate there. "She single?"

My brows danced a waggly jig on my forehead. "Theo, you dog."

He laughed and shoved my shoulder. I stumbled to the side. Kane huffed.

Theo raised his hands in surrender. "Sorry, cuz," he said before he turned a mock scowl my way.

I flipped my hair and granted him a grin that was all pride and teeth.

His cheeks flushed. "But, like, can you introduce me to her?"

Lucas snickered. "Didn't you already meet her?"

Theo stabbed a hotdog my brother's way. "Listen, Boss. Just because you've got your girl doesn't mean the rest of us are so smooth."

Hannah and my brother blushed the same shade of embarrassment and the warmth that squiggled through my chest was so strong, it made my limbs tingle.

I patted Theo's back. "Calm down and put your flimsy weapon away, pup."

His expression fell and he dusted his palms over his pants. "I know after Naomi . . ." He cleared his throat. "It might look like I'm moving fast—"

Taking his wrist, I gave it a squeeze, softening my gaze when I told him, "I'll give an official introduction later."

He took a jagged inhale, then shook himself out, that jovial demeanor slipping back into place. Cocking his head my brother's way, he winked. "See, sometimes it's about working the system."

My brow lowered. "I'm a system?"

"More like a portal." He flourished a hand. "Or a door."

"A *door*?"

He smirked, then chomped down on that hotdog. "How's Lisa holding up?"

Seeing Bower'd done exactly like my Alpha said, and confiscated her phone, we hadn't talked for a stretch, so she'd called me from her girlfriend Rosa's instead. "Missing No Man's Land, but glad to be free."

His nod was tight, because if anyone understood, it was him.

"How're you?" I asked. He might've worn his pain better than the rest of us. Hidden it behind his taunting or a coy expression, but there was something there, an agony he'd tucked away . . . for now. One that showed in the lines of deep-seated exhaustion that dulled his eyes.

"I'm doing." His Adam's apple dipped when he finished, "I'll get there."

My Alpha and I exchanged a glance.

"Can I carry anything out front for you?" Hannah asked me.

"I can get it all," Lucas said like it was his *totally normal behavior*.

Kane handed off a plate stacked with obnoxiously large, thick steaks. "Take these. Pick the ones you two want before Theo gets into them."

"I can hear you," his cousin grumbled.

Kane smirked. "Stay on the steps, Luke." The "*where I can fucking see you*" was silent.

Lucas grinned. "Can do." Nudging the entrance open with his shoulder, he held it wide, and Hannah passed through. Peering back at Theo, my brother taunted, "Lemme know if you need a wingman, *Boss*."

My Alpha barked a laugh and clapped my brother on the back. "Get the hells outta here before he starts biting."

Theo smirked, shoving my brother's shoulder as he followed him out like the loveable pest he was.

"Hannah's sweet," I said.

My Alpha watched them through that window. "She's good for Luke."

I inclined my head. "He needs good right now." He'd been quiet about mom after I'd told him, like he either hadn't fully accepted it yet or refused to think about it. But if he'd talk to anyone, it'd be Kane. And my Alpha was ready.

I finished with the coleslaw, headed to the washroom to rinse my hands, and glanced at that mirror, taking myself in as I straightened my sleeves.

Kane stepped in behind me. He groaned, eyeing my ass like a meal before he cupped it. Those dense hands kneaded hard. "This dress is fucking killing me, Bry." He tugged the hem up inch by core-tightening inch.

"Kane," I scolded through a laugh. "Everyone'll be here soon."

He growled. "They can wait."

Sweet sage, the things that voice did to me. I arched back to wrap my arms around his neck.

He pressed his hard cock against the small of my back and canted down to rake his teeth over my claiming mark. His laugh was thick and carnal when he said, "I haven't fucked you here yet." He dragged that hem higher still before he stopped, then jerked it back down.

The sound of the front door opening carried. We stepped out as Joaquin sauntered in. There was an air about him, a power that hummed. Still not as strong as Kane's but, obsidian, it *was* strong. Not something Isaac could fake. Not Isaac.

He chucked a thumb in the general direction of outside. "You might wanna get out there."

A chorus of yells had our attention darting out the window. Theo and Lucas jumped back as a flame shot from the barbecue—one of a wildly concerning size while Hannah sat several feet away, wide-eyed.

"What in the Iron Hells are they doing? It's a barbecue, not a bonfire!" I pinched the bridge of my nose between my thumb and forefinger when I found Kane. "Can you please save the idiots from themselves before they burn the food . . . or the whole damn shop."

My Alpha rolled his shoulders and swallowed hard. "Not leaving you alone, Bry."

"I need to finish here," I told him. Besides, Joaquin and I needed to talk, because if I'd learned anything from losing Cassandra, it was that the origin of some truths—some *secrets*—mattered. I set my palm to Kane's chest and my next words were as much for myself as they were for him. "Isaac's not here."

His hands flexed by his sides.

"I've got her, Kane," Joaquin said.

I flicked my wrist toward Theo and Lucas's ensuing chaos. "Go. I'll be out in a minute."

The muscles along his neck corded, shoulders tense. He growled, inclined his head, then stabbed a finger at the barbecue. "I'll be right fucking there."

I nipped the corner of his mouth.

He headed for the door and grumbled a string of epithets when he pushed outside.

Joaquin strode to the counter and rested a hip against it.

My heart did a stutter step, throat tightening as I stared straight ahead. I'd held the secret so long, getting my tongue to work, to say the words proved so damn hard. But Joaquin had come for me too. Had been there to pull me up when the tides had rolled in. I trusted him with my life. And I trusted him with my brother's.

I faced him, offering him the full weight of my gaze while I tried to keep my voice even. "Isaac was a changeling."

He crossed his arms over his chest. "And so is Lucas."

Swallowing hard, I uttered, "You know?"

A singular nod. "Saw Isaac turn during the fight."

I bit my lip trying to decipher his thoughts, but in that moment he was a goddamn vault. My chest heaved, breaths coming in panicked waves.

He raised his arms, palms out. "Easy, banshee. Lucas is good. He's not his father."

I winced. "I'm sorry I didn't tell you."

"I get it. Some secrets are too dangerous to share."

I couldn't tell if he meant his own but either way . . . "Do you think anyone else saw?"

"I don't know. The Pack's quiet about everything that went down. I haven't pushed about it yet. I need them to figure out they can trust me first. That I'm not Victor. But if they know and they haven't said anything . . . "

His subtext hung heavy in the air, because the wolves *loved* to talk, so them potentially knowing and keeping their maws shut meant one of two things; they were either afraid of Joaquin's retaliation, or they were okay with what they knew. Selfish as it was, I'd take either. We'd need to figure things out sooner than later. Decide what course to take . . . but not yet.

Striding his way, I wrapped my arms around him and held tight. "Thank you, Joaquin. For saving Kane and me. For everything. You're a good man." Better than I deserved. "And the Southern Pack's lucky to have you."

He gave a hard squeeze, holding tight before he patted my back, then waved me back, shooing me away. "You better get out there before they start eating each other."

A grin took me before I tugged his sleeve, ordering him with me before I pivoted, grabbed those salads and headed outside. Taking up a bottle of wine and two glasses, he followed behind.

Setting the food aside, Kane stalked my way, hooked an arm under my ass and lifted, carrying me with him toward the barbecue.

Whitney climbed from her car, then ascended the steps, a deep smile splitting her face when she found us. "Greetings." She displayed the tray of baked goods she held. "I come bearing gifts."

My Alpha lowered me to the ground as I faced Whitney and loud-whispered, "There's a Theo-shaped wolf here who's *very* eager for your arrival."

Theo face-palmed himself and groaned.

Whitney arched a brow my way. "Is that a nudge? Or a warning?"

I plucked one of those delectable looking treaties from her plate. "That's wholly dependent on whether he's your type or not."

He groaned louder.

"Tall, hot, funny." Her lips twitched and she covered her mouth with her hand. "Definitely my type."

His ears pricked.

"Excellent!" I shoved that cookie into my mouth and said around it, "Now do us both a favor and don't tell him that."

Her laugh was high and light when she peered his way.

I waved a hand, then not-so-subtly threw a wink his way before I guided her toward him. "Just do me a favor and make the pest earn it."

Ezra rolled up next, and the second he crested the steps, Joaquin handed him one of those glasses of wine. My chest warmed.

Customers started arriving, checking the place out. Lucas and Hannah took the honors of showing them around and taking appointments.

Kane scanned every guest as he passed food out then set more on the barbecue and closed the lid. The rich scent of grilling meat filled the air and made my mouth water.

Mason appeared, sliding his glasses up his face, his posture timid. Like he was unsure.

My Alpha cleared his throat, tugged up his sleeves and stretched his neck, then approached. When he stopped before Mason, he inclined his head. "Bry told me everything. Said you tried to protect her from Isaac."

He lifted a shoulder. "It didn't work."

Kane shook his head. "You tried. And you need to know I'm fucking grateful."

Wow. A day I'd never thought would come. And with the way Mason's gaze kept flicking to Kane's square knuckled hands, neither did he.

My Alpha stretched his neck again. "I probably shouldn't have punched you."

Probably. I fought back my snort.

Mason's mouth quirked when he rubbed his fingers over that scar on his nose. "I'm getting pretty good at taking them though."

If by pretty good, he meant "*he'd barely survived*" then he was *totally* good at it.

Kane huffed a low laugh. Offering Mason a beer, my Alpha sat himself down in the chair to his right and pulled me into his lap. I wiggled back, snuggling deep against him. His arm banded around my waist, palm settling over my lower abdomen like he felt for the baby. Wanting to touch, or shield.

The warmth that wriggled into my chest settled deep inside my heart.

Ezra and Joaquin talked, their gaze intent on one another. I met the Beta's eye, waggled my brows and gave an obnoxious grin. The glare he lobbed back at me was of the "*keep your banshee mouth shut*" variety.

I laughed and set my head back on Kane's shoulder. His fingers flexed against me. Protective. Always protective.

At that, my thoughts shifted to my mother. I missed her. Wished we'd had more time.

Something inside me clicked. A piece moving into place. Something powerful and possessive, vigilant, silent and strong. I was bringing a life into this world. And that child would know safety. They'd know family and friends and happiness. And if it took everything I was, they'd know a world without Isaac. My heart rate quickened. I would not fail. There was no room for fear.

That same agonizing pain from the night Kane had come for me shot through, spreading like wildfire. I cried out. The pressure of my Alpha's touch was too much. I scrambled from his hold. Hot. I was so damn hot. I needed to cool.

Bursting into the shop, I beelined for the sink inside that office washroom.

Kane followed, Joaquin, Mason and Theo hot on his heels. Crossing that threshold, my legs gave and I collapsed beside the desk, hitting the ground hard.

My Alpha dropped down beside me, stare hard. "What's wrong, Bry?"

It hurt so much, it stole my breath and my thoughts. I couldn't speak. Couldn't anything. Iron fires, what the hells was it?

That office door clicked shut.

"Bry?" he demanded.

I wanted to answer, but the words were lost in my agony. My body heated, then burned. It faded back to normal, then heated again. Something inside me surged. A power. Different from before. *What the sage is happening to me?*

Kane's eyes were creased like he had not one damn clue what to do.

Gasps and curses sounded around us, but I couldn't take them in. Kane was my anchor. My level.

An orange glow lit the world when fire sparked from my hand, licking up my skin before it careened over my body and engulfed me. But it didn't burn. Why the hells didn't it burn?

Joaquin edged in. "Shadowed fucking moon."

Kane advanced, grabbing hold, ready to help. Do something.

My eyes flew wide, gaze snapping to his. That pain receded, but the flame held. I raised a palm to stay my Alpha. "It's . . . I think it's alright." I rolled my wrist, eyeing that flame. "It's not real," I breathed, then louder, "It's not real."

Mason's jaw dropped. "Wraith take me."

An illusion. It was a fucking illusion!

Iron fires. The serum I'd drank . . . Sierra's concoction for magi.

It worked.

The End.

Acknowledgments

As always, thanks to my husband for being my rock and sounding board and for always supporting my dreams.

To my mother for her heart, and my father for his strength.

To Keri, May, Tara and Justena for your eyes. You're the best writing group and friends a girl could ever dream of.

To my agent, Helen Lane, whose talent, tenacity and humour are incomparable. Without you, none of this would be possible.

And, finally, to Molly, Tara, Jo, Sophie, Marina, Dominique and the entirety of my UK and North American team at Hodderscape for your kindness and talent.

About the author

K.C. Harper grew up on Canada's east coast and spends her time plotting to destroy the happiness of her characters. She's an avid reader, developmental editor and a full-time human servant to a 4.5 lb teacup chihuahua.

WANT MORE?

If you enjoyed this and would like to find out about similar books we publish, we'd love you to join our online Sci-Fi, Fantasy and Horror community, Hodderscape.

Visit hodderscape.co.uk for exclusive content from our authors, news, competitions and general musings, and feel free to comment, contribute or just keep an eye on what we are up to.

See you there!

HODDERSCAPE
NEVER AFRAID TO BE OUT OF THIS WORLD

@HODDERSCAPE   HODDERSCAPE.CO.UK